CW01545614

DEAD TO ME

Dubbed 'Queen of the Underworld', Jessie Keane is of Romany gypsy stock. She was born in the back of her gran's barrel top wagon and fled to London as a teenager, finding there a lifelong fascination with the criminal underworld and the teeming life of the city.

Twice divorced and living in a freezing council flat, she decided to pursue her childhood aim of becoming a writer. She sold her wedding dress to buy a typewriter and penned her first book, *Dirty Game*. This was followed by further acclaimed crime novels, all *Sunday Times* bestsellers. Jessie lives in Hampshire with her partner.

Also by Jessie Keane

ANNIE CARTER NOVELS
Dirty Game
Black Widow
Scarlet Women
Playing Dead
Ruthless
Stay Dead
Never Go Back

RUBY DARKE NOVELS
Nameless
Lawless
The Edge
Gangland

OTHER NOVELS
Jail Bird
The Make
Dangerous
Fearless
The Knock
The Manor
Diamond
Dead Heat

JESSIE KEANE
DEAD TO ME

HODDER &
STOUGHTON

First published in Great Britain in 2026 by Hodder & Stoughton Limited
An Hachette UK company

The authorised representative in the EEA is Hachette Ireland,
8 Castlecourt Centre, Dublin 15, D15 XTP3, Ireland (email: info@hbgi.ie)

1

Copyright © 2026 Jessie Keane

The right of Jessie Keane to be identified as the Author of the Work has been asserted by her in accordance with the Copyright, Designs and Patents Act 1988.

All rights reserved. No part of this publication may be reproduced, stored in a retrieval system, or transmitted, in any form or by any means without the prior written permission of the publisher, nor be otherwise circulated in any form of binding or cover other than that in which it is published and without a similar condition being imposed on the subsequent purchaser.

All characters in this publication are fictitious and any resemblance to real persons, living or dead, is purely coincidental.

A CIP catalogue record for this title is available from the British Library

Hardback ISBN 978 1 399 72104 2
Trade Paperback ISBN 978 1 399 72105 9
ebook ISBN 978 1 399 72107 3

Typeset in Plantin Light by Manipal Technologies Limited

Printed and bound in Great Britain by Clays Ltd, Elcograf S.p.A.

Hodder & Stoughton policy is to use papers that are natural, renewable and recyclable products and made from wood grown in sustainable forests. The logging and manufacturing processes are expected to conform to the environmental regulations of the country of origin.

Hodder & Stoughton Limited
Carmelite House
50 Victoria Embankment
London EC4Y 0DZ

www.hodder.co.uk

To Cliff – the man who really did say: 'Isn't it time you got a proper job?' when I stood in the post office queue with the package containing the completed draft of my first book, Dirty Game, *in my hand.*

Cliff – I hate to say 'I told you so', but I did.

And thanks for the title.

AUTHOR'S NOTE

This Annie Carter book, *Dead To Me*, is set in the 1960s between the events of the very first Annie Carter book, *Dirty Game*, and the second, *Black Widow*.

Recently I got to wondering, *what about the sister*? Annie was always the star, but what about her long-suffering older sister Ruthie? As I thought about it – over weeks, months, maybe even years – Ruthie began to emerge and to shine in her own right.

So picture this: it's London in the Swinging Sixties, the land of the Krays, the Beatles, Carnaby Street, Christine Keeler, Profumo, Mary Quant. Everything feels fresh and new and exciting: anything is possible.

Just take my hand and I'll lead you into it.

Here we go . . .

CAST OF CHARACTERS

THE CARTER CLAN
Max Carter – East End gangster
Queenie Carter – Max Carter's mother
Jonjo Carter – Max's middle brother
Eddie Carter – Max's youngest brother
Ruthie Bailey – Max Carter's fiancée
Annie Bailey – Max Carter's mistress

THE DELANEY CLAN
Molly and Davey Delaney – matriarch and patriarch of the clan
Tory Delaney – their eldest son, gangland boss
Pat Delaney – their second son
Orla and Redmond Delaney – twins
Kieron Delaney – their youngest son

THE LIMEHOUSE TARTS
Celia Bailey – the madam of the house and Connie's sister-in-law
Dolly Farrell
Aretha Brown
Ellie
Darren

PROLOGUE

She could hear her attacker yelling obscenities as, bouncing wildly, the car careered off the road.

Then the car hit the grassy verge at frightening speed and shuddered, tilted. In panic, she threw all her weight onto the steering wheel, ignoring his punches and shoves and yelling as he tried to get her off it.

The car bumped and thumped along and then suddenly, shockingly, tilted hard down and was nose-down in the ditch, wheels spinning, engine still roaring.

Then the motor cut out and there was just him, shouting insults at her, saying, *I'll kill you, I'll kill you.*

Thank God for little miracles, she had time to think, because his side of the car was in the ditch and hers was up in the air.

She scrabbled for the door handle and shoved the door open with a massive effort, gravity working against her, him battering at her with his fists, the wind snatching at her clothes and her hair and lashing at her face as she hauled herself out and fell onto the grass, kicking herself free of his grasping, hurtful hands. Suddenly she could hear the birds, singing up in the thrashing trees – imperfectly, because she heard everything imperfectly these days. She was still alive – but for how long? Once she had wanted to end it all. But now?

Now she wanted to *live*.

But she couldn't run back to the house. *He* would catch her first, stop her.

Instead she scrambled upright and ran away from her husband's Surrey mansion, away from the certainty of help and into the unknown. Her legs trembling with every step, she ran, stumbling, falling, righting herself then running again.

She could hear him back at the car, swearing, shouting, but no matter about that, he was struggling to get out of the car and for a moment she might be able to get away.

She *had* to get away.

Was he coming? Was he going to get her? He wasn't shouting anymore. God, that was a bad sign.

This was a quiet country road and all she could hear above the pounding of her own heartbeat and the shuddering, struggling intake of every breath was the wind, the birds.

She ran.

Focused on that and that alone now.

One foot in front of the other, she focused on *escape*.

RUTHIE

I

1963

Her name after the wedding, *that* wedding, was Ruthie Carter: she was the wife of Max. Before *that*, she was plain old Ruthie Bailey: daughter of Connie; cousin of Kath; niece of Maureen or 'Mo', Connie's sister. Oh, and older sister of Annie.

Ruthie may have seemed like the dull one, the one who wanted to blend into the woodwork, while Annie was the bright shining star who was impossible to ignore; Annie, the immovable object to Max Carter's unstoppable force. Ruthie was pretty enough but too polite, a touch too nice. That was probably because she caught the tail-end of the fights and the drunken rages between her parents Frank and Connie, and she learned early on that it was best to keep a low profile.

Her younger sister Annie had a different take on things. Any attention, good or bad – and mostly it was bad – fed her need to be *noticed*. And anyway, most of their parents' marital battles passed over her head. All Annie knew was that Dad left and that broke her heart because she loved Dad and *hated* Mum – and then things got a lot quieter.

Ruthie saw the lot and it scarred her. The drinking. The swearing. The shrieks. The blows. She learned to keep her head down, to offend no one, and growing up in a war zone was pretty much normal to her. And finally, there was Dad – leaving, going out through the front door, closing it with a bang behind him. Years later, Ruthie could still picture him, his cheap old leather suitcase in hand, his back to the lot of them, going.

Annie was devastated. She'd loved Dad so much, and she was even like him to look at. Dark-haired, green-eyed; striking. Ruthie? She was relieved. No more fights, thank God. That was her take on it all. There was no doubt about it – Dad had *abandoned* them, left them to struggle. Not to put too fine a point on it, the uncaring bastard had left his family in the shit.

Connie drank more after Frank went, so she couldn't work at her cleaning jobs. For days she'd lie on the sofa and swig whatever she could get her hands on. There was precious little food in the larder, maybe sometimes a bit of stale cheese, bread so solid you'd kill someone if you hit them over the head with it, rancid butter. Maybe a tomato, blue-whiskered with mould. But there was always, always booze.

Neither Annie nor Ruthie ever bothered much with school. If an inspector called round, they and their mother hid (and usually the inspectors didn't call at all, because the Baileys lived in a tatty and aggressive little enclave where even the toughest coppers tended to patrol the streets two by two). Any warning letters were chucked in the fireplace. Finally, of course, the inspectors didn't bother to call at all and the letters stopped coming.

After the girls' sparse education was done – neither could even remember receiving a final report – they got jobs. Sweeping up in salons. Working on deli counters.

Then Ruthie managed to get a place at the Blue Parrot nightclub dodging filthy propositions from greasy tycoons, while Annie got a job at the local corner shop, dodging gropes from Ted the owner. One way or another, they managed.

It was at the Blue Parrot that Ruthie first came into Max Carter's orbit. He owned the Parrot, and the Shalimar, and the Palermo Lounge; all top-end clubs with famous acts performing live.

Max was at that stage of his life where he could accept the need to settle down. His mother Queenie was getting older and she was prodding him hard in that direction.

So – the stars conjoined. Ruthie and Max met. They talked. He seemed – and remember here that Ruthie had heard all sorts about him, about protection rackets and the endless fights he had with the Delaney lot, all that scary turf-war East End stuff – but he seemed, very much to her surprise, *nice*. She was charmed by him. At first scared, a bit overwhelmed, actually. But soon he put her at ease. Before very long he moved her on from a junior position at the Blue Parrot to a more senior one at the Palermo Lounge. That sounds good, impressive, but it was just a title. She was still taking people's coats and smiling, still keeping the punters happy.

Then – and this was crazy, an unbelievable shock to Ruthie at the time – Max asked her out. Took her to a swanky French place to have a meal. No prices on the menu beside the dishes. She sat there feeling a right fool, all these haw-haw types around her, all the furs and the jewels on the women, and the dresses! Ruthie had never seen anything like it. The satins and silks and the colours – vivid emerald, shocking pink, purple, canary yellow. And there was she, wearing a plain little grey Crimplene shift dress, feeling as out of place as it was possible to be.

'We'll have to run you up something better,' said Mum when Ruthie told her how awkward she'd felt. At this point Connie actually hauled herself off the sofa and took a bit of interest. Connie was getting a strong sniff of money in the air and that would call for effort and maybe even some modest investment, if she could scrape together a little cash for ground bait. 'I'll get Mo to do it for a couple of quid, she won't mind,' said Connie.

Auntie Maureen – or 'Mo' as she was more often called – lived next door with her daughter – Cousin Kath – and she had a Singer sewing machine that had fallen off the back of a lorry somewhere. Not wishing to crush Mum's hopes, Ruthie obligingly went along with Connie to Woollies and they purchased a bolt of cheap but silky-feeling midnight-blue fabric for Mo to run up into an evening dress.

Ruthie didn't have the heart to tell Mum not to bother – that the dinner date had been a one-off, that she had shown herself up to be woefully ignorant (half of Max's conversation went straight over her head) and that he wouldn't bother with her again. Which was probably just as well, because she'd started having girlish fantasies of a life with him. Him holding a chubby little dark-haired baby and smiling adoringly down at her as she lay, exhausted but delighted, in a hospital bed.

Ruthie had always wanted that. A settled life, a secure married family life. But then – could she see that happening, really, with this man? He was scary. All those gangland tales she heard about him. Nasty, frightening stuff. People left bleeding in alleys. Him on the phone, issuing orders, contacting a mob of men who – whenever she saw them – chilled her to the marrow.

Anyway, it didn't matter. Soon, he wouldn't bother with her anymore. He'd dump her and all her dreams would be over.

Still, though – it had been sort of nice.

While it lasted.

2

Much to Ruthie's surprise, Max *did* bother with her again. This time, he took her dancing down the Palais. Dancing, she could do. Ruthie and Annie had often practised the Jive up in their bedroom, having a great laugh, twirling each other around. Annie was – of course – the better dancer out of the two. She could even do the Twist.

Annie could do *anything*.

So the midnight blue satin became a lovely dress with a huge swirly skirt and Max and Ruthie danced the night away, and she thought: *Well, I'd better make the most of it, because pretty soon he's going to be bored as fuck with all this.* Ruthie knew her own faults, all too well. She was so shy she had little conversation, nothing to keep a man like him interested. He'd find other attractions soon and then she'd be back behind the coat counter.

But no.

Instead, there were more dinners, more dances.

'Gawd, you're going to need more dresses,' said Connie, panicking but loving it. This was *amazing*.

So Connie and Ruthie bought more fabric. Dearer fabric too. Connie got a loan off one of the local sharks and bought black lace. Red satin. Fabulous, the silken feel of these lovely things, things Ruthie had never experienced before.

And now Connie was talking *strategy*.

'Don't let him feel you up,' Mum advised as she hoisted Ruthie into one of her own dire knicker-pink corsets and yanked it tight at the back.

'Fuck, I can't breathe,' Ruthie complained.

'Yes you can. Just breathe shallow, that's how it's done,' Mum said, and slid the newest of Auntie Mo's creations over Ruthie's head and down. She zipped it up. It was beautiful, the red edged with the black. *Fabulous*. Ruthie wondered how she'd ever summon up the nerve to wear such a thing. You couldn't fail to be noticed in a dress like this.

'Did you hear what I just said, Ruthie?'

'Don't let him feel me up,' Ruthie repeated dutifully. 'I heard. But he won't do that. He's not like that.'

'They are *all* like that,' Mum said sniffily. 'Show them a bit of skirt on a plate and what do they do? They reach for a knife and fork.'

'That's what Annie says,' Ruthie smiled.

'Oh, her.' Connie sniffed derisively. 'Always out on the town, ain't she, hooking her pearly. Look, she don't know nothing about this, about you and Mr Carter, Ruthie, and make sure you don't tell her anything about it either, because she'll only do her best to put the boot in.'

Ruthie didn't think Annie would put the boot in. She'd always been nice to her. Not only a younger sister but a dear friend. It was only around Mum and her constant jibing that Annie became hostile.

'What about if she sees all these new frocks?' Ruthie asked, while Mum started wrenching a brush through her regrettably fine mousy hair.

'I've sorted that. Mo's keeping them hid round at hers in the spare room. You can get dressed there before you go out. Just keep quiet about everything; okay, Ruthie? A man like Mr Carter wouldn't appreciate his business being talked about by every Tom, Dick or Harry. Got me?'

'Got you,' Ruthie said, but she knew that Mum's excitement was all going to go to waste, that one of these days Max would kick her straight to the kerb.

This blissful situation could not *possibly* go on.

And if it didn't? Well, Mum would be gutted, which was a shame. And her? How would *she* feel? Sort of relieved?

Yeah, maybe.

Because even though Max Carter seemed like the perfect gent, there was that other side to him, wasn't there? Sometimes she glimpsed it in him – a glance, a movement, that sudden threatening lift of the scorpion's tail. There was no doubt in her mind that Max was a very dangerous man. If he was on your side, you were utterly safe, completely secure.

If not . . .?

She wasn't sure. Didn't even want to *think* about it.

Best not.

3

The next outing was a dinner dance at the Shalimar, then there was more dancing, then the theatre to see *The Mousetrap*. Ruthie had never, ever been to the theatre before then. She'd hardly known anything like that even existed. They were in the best seats – a box, high up, very posh – and Max bought her an orchid corsage to wear on her dress.

And all the while she was almost – *almost* – falling for him and trying not to because this all had to come to an end soon, simply *had* to, plain little Ruthie Bailey and this handsome powerful and rather frightening man with his flashy clothes; he wore a gold ring on his index finger, engraved with what he told her were Egyptian cartouches on either side of a square slab of lapis lazuli. She'd never even heard of lapis lazuli, but it was a rather nice royal blue.

The longer all this went on, the more convinced Ruthie became that it was doomed to be over someday soon. She had a stern word with herself about it whenever she wavered and started to fall under the almost hypnotic spell he cast. Yes, it was all lovely. But it couldn't last. She had never been lucky; life in the thick of poverty had ground her down, polished off any hopes she might once have possessed. So she braced herself for the inevitable falling-out, the point at which he would say sorry Ruthie, it's been fun, but . . .

Well, she would take it on the chin. She would smile and say, it had been wonderful. Well, it *had* been wonderful. No lie there. All the way through it she had been longing to tell Annie, to confide in her just as she always had in the past. But Ruthie went on with the subterfuge, humouring Mum, saying nothing to her sister.

Then one day she got the most unbelievable shock.

They were sitting at Max's table in the Shalimar – funny that, one of his clubs and the lovely perfume he'd bought her that she now always wore, both having the same name – and they were listening to Millicent Martin singing, accompanied by a jazzy piano player. The place was packed out, everyone was enjoying the show. Millicent and the pianist were up on the little semi-circular stage with the huge, red, gold-trimmed tasselled curtains hanging down behind them and the gold MC at the top where the curtains joined. As Miss Martin's set finished, and the applause died down, Max turned to Ruthie and said: 'I've got something I want to say.'

'Oh?' Her stomach clenched. This was *it*. The end to all Mum's elaborate plans. *You're dumped.*

'I want you to come to tea one night. Meet my mother.'

4

Queenie Carter lived in a plain two-up-two-down in Bow, nothing outwardly fancy; but an invitation to tea with the mother of one of London's leading crime bosses was a very big deal indeed. The notorious Kray brothers had Violet: the equally fearsome Max Carter had Queenie.

'Christ, what the hell should you wear?' Connie fluttered around, turning Ruthie this way and that. In the East End, this invitation to tea at Queenie's was what amounted to a royal summons.

Her fag in one hand and a glass of voddy in the other, Connie gawped at her daughter's unimpressive figure. She stood thinking, pondering, *agonising*. She mustn't get this wrong. 'Nothing tarty,' she pronounced. 'Something *wholesome*. Make you look like a lady. Yes?'

'Like what, then?' Ruthie was at a loss. She'd been wracked with nerves ever since she'd received Max's invitation, and now Mum's twittering around was only making her feel worse. Making her see that this was a big, big thing. Huge. Maybe life-changing. Who knew? She thought again of her dreams of a family life with Max. The beautiful dark-haired baby in his arms. God, who was she kidding? It *couldn't* happen – could it?

Finally they settled on an appropriate outfit. A simple knee-length black skirt and a high-necked white blouse. When Ruthie first put the blouse on, Connie shrieked in alarm.

'What's the matter?' asked Ruthie, startled.

'The bloody thing's almost see-through. That's your bra out on display, right there. Go and put on a full-length petticoat.'

'I don't have one.'

'Take one of mine. Bottom drawer upstairs.'

Ruthie put on a petticoat.

'Better,' said Connie, then Annie came in.

'Going somewhere special?' she asked, smiling at Ruthie.

Don't tell her, Mum's eyes told Ruthie.

'Dancing class,' said Ruthie.

'Gawd, what a drag,' said Annie, and went off upstairs.

'We'll have to tell her sooner or later,' said Ruthie, hating keeping things from Annie. All their lives they'd shared a bedroom, whispered secrets in the dark. Keeping this massive news from her just felt *wrong*. But then – she didn't want to set off one of Mum's spectacular drunken rages; she *had* to keep quiet.

'Later, maybe. We'll see how it goes,' said Connie. She grabbed Ruthie's shoulders. 'Ruthie, do you realise how important this could be? You don't do you. Well I'll tell you. You could end up *Mrs Max Carter*. What do you think of that?'

The idea was terrifying. But Ruthie nodded. She'd never seen her mother so enthusiastic about *anything*, ever. And she didn't want to piss on Connie's parade and destroy her mood, not when she seemed so happy.

'We'll see,' she said, thinking that Connie was kidding herself. Max Carter, married to *her*?

Yes, she might have dreamed of it – but for that dream to become a reality?

No.

No way could she see that ever happening.

5

When Ruthie entered the Carter family home, she was even more convinced that Connie was deluded. The little house was immaculately kept, a fitting little palace for one of the ruling queens of gangland.

And the queen herself?

Queenie Carter was warm as an icicle. A neatly dressed matron, she sat there and watched Ruthie enter her lounge with cold assessing eyes.

'One of the Baileys, ain't that right?' she snapped out.

'Yes.'

'Seen another one about. Darker than you. That your sister?'

'Yes. That'd be Annie.'

Queenie turned her head and said in a loud whisper to Max, who was sitting right there: 'Tarty piece, yeah? You seen her?'

Max only smiled.

It was as if Ruthie wasn't even *there*.

Straight away Ruthie decided that she hated the older woman and that Queenie would probably hate her right back.

Tea was a miserable long-drawn-out affair, with Ruthie half-choking on inedible meringue cakes and tea as weak as gnat's piss. Finally, she and Max were able to say goodbye and she made her escape, only drawing breath when she was outside.

Oh thank God.

Well, she wouldn't be having to go through *that* again, would she.

The meeting had been a disaster.

Ruthie was a little sad, but only for Mum's sake really. She'd had such high hopes for this.

Max saw her into the back of his Jaguar Mark X. There was a big bald man sitting silent behind the wheel.

'Just a minute, Tone,' Max said to him, and closed the door after Ruthie and went back into the house.

Tone and Ruthie sat there in silence.

What the hell was Max doing?

Ruthie just wanted to get home, kick off the new shoes which were pinching like mad, and somehow – with some relief – break the news to Connie that it was all off.

Minutes passed. Long, silent minutes.

Finally, Max came back out of the house and got into the back of the car beside Ruthie.

'Take a walk, will you, Tone?' Max said to their driver.

Tone obligingly got out of the car and strolled off, up the road.

'Ruthie,' said Max.

Here it comes. The kiss-off. Sorry but fuck off, will you? It's all done, all over.

'Yes?' Ruthie asked.

'Will you marry me?'

6

Of course Ruthie said yes. She still could not believe her luck. Here was this fabulous man, asking her – of all bloody people – to marry him. So she said yes, what the hell else was she going to say? And suddenly they were engaged, and if it all seemed too quick and too overwhelming – too bloody terrifying really – then she just ignored that. It would be fine. For once, she was going to be lucky, to live the dream. She was dazzled by Max's attention. And he loved her. She knew that. Well, he'd never actually said so, but he did. He *must*.

He treated her very respectfully, maybe *too* respectfully she sometimes thought. The odd peck on the cheek, a squeeze of her hand. But . . . shouldn't there have been more, if he truly loved her? Hot, hungry kissing, the sort she dreamed of but never seemed to get?

No. It was okay. He was restraining himself, saving all that for the wedding night. He must be. And she had passed inspection by Queenie, his terrifying mother. Max Carter was going to marry her.

So they were engaged. Connie was ecstatic! She couldn't get over it. The thought of their small struggling household having access to all Max Carter's money was as intoxicating as gin to her. When Ruthie told her about the proposal she danced Ruthie all around their dingy, mouldy, threadbare little front room, croakily laughing and singing and praising her, telling her what a clever girl she was.

'A ring!' Connie shrieked. 'You've got to choose a ring, yes?'

Ruthie thought: *Yes.* It was exciting. Crazy. A ring to say that she was engaged to Max Carter! Still, it was like a dream. They would trawl the shops, and she would – yes – choose a ring. A modest one, of course. She wouldn't be bloody cheeky and ask for the earth, not when she had already gained so much.

But it didn't work out that way.

Max, Ruthie soon discovered, did not – ever – trawl shops.

A discreet and smiling young man appeared one day at the Palermo with a large suitcase. He was accompanied by a bulky minder. With a theatrical flourish, the young man opened the case.

Ruthie gasped at the sight that was presented to her. The suitcase was packed with twenty padded purple velvet display beds, each one of them glittering with dozens of rings. Diamonds, opals, rubies, emeralds, sapphires; it was stunning. Like nothing she had ever seen before.

'Choose whichever one you like,' Max told her.

It was *unbelievable*.

Like the menus at the restaurant dinners they'd attended, there were no prices on display. She went to choose a modest diamond – quite small – but Max said no.

'What about that one,' he said.

'Excellent choice sir,' said the young man.

Ruthie tried it on. The diamond was big; the ring felt heavy.

She never found out the price.

Truthfully, she was scared to even ask.

When she got home, she insisted to Mum that it was time: they were going to have to tell Annie what was going on. It was only fair.

'Oh, we can wait a bit longer,' said Connie.

'No,' said Ruthie, putting her foot down for once. 'Now. Today. It don't feel right, keeping this from her.'

'What's going on then?' asked Annie, coming in looking – as always – weary and fed up after another day avoiding Ted's wandering hands at the corner shop. 'What's up with you two?'

Connie's face was wreathed in a gloatingly triumphant smile as she stepped behind Ruthie. She caught hold of her daughter's shoulders and made her face Annie. 'Right! Shall we tell her?' she asked, hissing the words against Ruthie's ear. 'Shall we, Ruthie? Hm?'

'Oh come on,' said Annie tiredly, slumping down in a chair and kicking off her shoes. 'What is it?'

'Your sister's getting married,' said Mum.

'Good God!' Annie stiffened in surprise. Then she gave Ruthie a delighted smile. 'You kept that quiet.'

Ruthie felt bad about that. Of course she did.

'I know,' Ruthie said. But—'

'She had to. Didn't want to say too much in case it all fell through,' jumped in Connie. 'Didn't want you putting the kybosh on it, did she.'

'I wouldn't do that,' said Annie, her face hardening. Ruthie wished Mum would shut the fuck up. 'Why the hell would I do that?'

'Dunno.' Ruthie felt Mum shrug. 'You don't like her having anything you don't have, I know that.'

'That's bollocks,' said Annie, standing up, snatching up her shoes. She looked at her sister. 'Well – congratulations, Ruthie.' Ignoring Mum, she came to Ruthie and, smiling, hugged her tight. 'You never said anything was going on.'

'It's all been so sudden,' Ruthie said, blushing at the lie.

'Well it's wonderful news. Well done. Who's the lucky man?'

'You're never going to believe it,' said Mum by Ruthie's ear.

'Go on then,' said Annie. 'Who is it? Is it Arthur from down the docks? He always had a soft spot for you. Why didn't you say?'

'It's not Arthur,' scoffed Mum. 'The very idea! Look! Look at the ring, do you think that waster could afford something like that?'

Shyly Ruthie flourished her left hand. On her finger was perched the ring Max had bought her: a diamond solitaire. And not a small one, either. It twinkled like fairyland at a summer circus.

'That's *fabulous*,' said Annie, admiring it. 'So who . . . ?'

Suddenly Ruthie wished that she and Annie were on their own. Ruthie had a feeling – maybe a premonition – that Annie wasn't going to like this news. That it would be her, Goody-Two-Shoes Ruthie, once again getting the good stuff while Annie – except for a few tired hand-me-downs and a clip around the ear – got fuck-all. And that Mum was just about to enjoy rubbing Annie's nose in it.

'Ruthie's caught herself a much bigger fish than poor bloody Arthur,' said Mum.

'Oh? Who then?' asked Annie.

'It's *Max Carter*,' said Mum.

There was something in Annie's eyes. Shock, maybe? Disbelief? It was there for the merest second, then it was gone and she was smiling again, her bright, hard-eyed smile.

'Fuck me,' she said faintly. Then she patted Ruthie's arm. 'Good for you, Ruthie. Well done.'

And then she left the room. After that, Annie didn't say much at all about her sister's engagement. She had seemed startled by it, for sure. But when Ruthie spoke to her the next day, Annie just hugged her and said she deserved every happiness.

'Don't worry,' Ruthie told her. 'Next it'll be your turn. You wait and see.'

'Yeah,' said Annie, and kissed Ruthie's cheek.

7

Ruthie remembered – oh so vividly – the first time she ever saw Max and her sister together. By that time she'd got used to the big flashy diamond on her finger, although she'd initially been frightened to wear it.

'It's expensive isn't it?' she'd said to Max. 'I'll only lose it.'

Actually she was more afraid that some chancer would knock her over the head, sending her flying into the gutter, and nick it off her while she lay there spark out.

'Wear it,' he said. 'If you lose it, we'll get another,' he said.

So she wore it. Now she was Max Carter's fiancée, and overnight people's attitude to her changed. Suddenly they were respectful, stepping around her, taking care over what they said and did whenever she was about. And slowly the truth dawned on her: there was absolutely no danger of her engagement ring getting robbed off her in the streets, for the simple reason that nobody would dare in a million years to rob off Max Carter's fiancée.

Max didn't want her working in the cloakroom at the club anymore, but she just filled in now and then when other staff were off and he didn't mind that. Ruthie was still sometimes handing out tickets to punters while they gave her their coats. But even the club clientele treated her differently, because of him. Everything was just *fine*.

Well – until *it* happened.

Ruthie was there taking coats, standing in for one of the girls who was off with the flu. The club was packed, the women in glittering jewels and furs, the men in dinner jackets smoking cigars and drinking whisky out of crystal glasses. 'Mona Lisa' the Nat King Cole song was being played by the band. Ruthie would never forget that.

That was the night Annie dropped in to see her. Annie looked lovely. Years later, Ruthie could still remember Annie on that night, in her white PVC boots, her white frilled blouse, her black miniskirt, her dark hair all bouffed up in a tangled exuberant mass. It was the outfit she wore when she was trying to make an impression, her 'killer' outfit. Ruthie knew that. They'd joked about it together, getting changed for evenings out on the town.

'No man could resist you in that get-up,' Ruthie told her more than once. It was utterly true. They couldn't.

Even then, Ruthie didn't have a single clue where all this was going. Maybe she was blindsided by love; although, shy virgin that she was, she hadn't really much idea of what 'love' really was. Max had kissed her a few times but had otherwise been a perfect gentleman. She was blindsided by *something*, anyway. By the aura Max created around himself, maybe. By all that money, all that dangerous power. And – of course – she didn't think her sister would ever hurt her.

Maybe it was that big sparkling engagement ring that fooled Ruthie, dazzled her, made her unable to see what was truly going on, but she was right there on the spot when Annie and Max met. They shook hands, they said hello. Ruthie was *right there*, watching it.

She saw them dancing together that night and reflected that Max was a superb dancer, guiding his partner faultlessly; that he was talking to Annie as they danced, and that she was smiling at him.

Even then, Ruthie didn't see it.

Fool, or what?

8

Max's two brothers Jonjo and Eddie were there on the night of the engagement party – and Queenie of course, lording it over the rest of the commoners. Jonjo had with him a voluptuous blonde in a dress that was a tight-fitting low-cut shimmering swathe of bright pink satin. She had the biggest tits Ruthie had ever seen in her entire life.

'Marilyn Monroe was Jonjo's idol,' Eddie told her. 'When she died last August he went proper into mourning the great big sap. Now every woman he gets, it's because she looks a bit like her. It's always blondes with Jonjo. And – darling – don't get offended, but up until now I always thought it was brunettes for Max. I'm delighted to say you've broken the mould!'

'She's beautiful,' Ruthie said, eyeing up the glamorous blonde with envy.

'If you like that sort of thing,' said Eddie. His eyes sparkled. 'We haven't really met yet, have we. Bit of a crush in here.'

'You're Eddie,' she said. 'Max's little brother.'

He smiled. 'It's easy to tell us all apart, no? Max is hard, Jonjo's thick – and I'm a fruit. Oh, and Mum's a tyrant, but having endured the tea and cakes with her I'm sure you've already gathered that. Good Christ, girl, what *are* you marrying into?'

They shook hands and both felt so absurd at this that they burst out laughing. When Max had very casually pointed Eddie out to Ruthie earlier in the evening, the one thing uppermost in her mind had been that this *couldn't* be Max's brother. Max was so physical, so muscular, so much a man. Jonjo, she could believe, although Jonjo was bigger than Max, bulkier. He'd run to fat in his middle years, you could see it. He was, as Annie would put it, a bit of a mouth-breather. Not terribly intelligent, but probably very handy with his fists.

Eddie, on the other hand, was slender, delicate, almost feminine. And he dressed very strangely. At the party, Max was suited and booted just like his big beefy brother Jonjo, but this odd little person, Eddie, was different: he was dressed in tan corduroy flares and a lilac floral shirt, with a purple bandana around his throat and stack-heeled black cowboy boots on his feet. A pearl earring dangled, glinting, from one ear. And was that – could that possibly be? – a trace of pink lipstick on his mouth?

'So darling, tell me all about yourself,' he said, sitting down beside Ruthie while the band played 'Stranger on the Shore'. Ruthie could see Connie out there on the dance floor, drunkenly waltzing with Uncle Tom. Eddie handed Ruthie a glass brimming with champagne and clinked his own glass against hers.

'There's not much to tell,' she said.

'Oh I'm sure there is. Cheers, honey,' he said, smiling, and drank deeply. 'Well, this is nice. Now, come on. I want all the details. What about you? You're very quiet. Of course I understand that. Maxy boy can be a bit overwhelming, I know. All my friends *adore* him, they absolutely charge past me to shake his hand and be mates with him, you know. I get quite overlooked whenever Max is about the place.'

'I find that hard to believe,' Ruthie told him, sipping the champagne. It was lovely. She had been literally sick with nerves before this party, thinking of all the strangers she would have to meet, that they would judge her, see her as that weedy little tart Ruthie Bailey who'd somehow, by some miracle, struck gold. But the champagne steadied her a bit.

She was wearing a silver lamé dress that Auntie Mo had run up for her. It made her look, for possibly the first time in her life, curvy; even elegant enough to become Mrs Max Carter. But there was one person missing tonight, who she really wished could be here – Annie. Annie's brimming self-confidence was like a shield to Ruthie; she always found that, while Annie carried any conversation with effortless poise, she could relax, let her take the load.

But not tonight; Annie was missing. She'd said she was busy. Stock-taking or something at the corner shop. Ruthie didn't believe that. There was no way Annie would loiter in the store after hours and run the risk of Ted cornering her in the stock room. She was up to something different, something more interesting, no doubt; maybe a new boyfriend. Ruthie was deeply hurt by her absence, truth be told. This was a big occasion and she could have done with her support, but what could Ruthie say? Annie had a mind of her own.

9

Chatting with Eddie, Ruthie knew she'd found a friend. Maybe someone to stand by her, now that Annie didn't seem interested any more – heartbreaking though that might be.

'I love the way you look,' she told him. 'Like a pirate. *So* attractive.'

'Do you think so?' He was pleased. 'This old thing?' he tapped the lilac fabric on his chest, 'got it up Carnaby Street market, I've had it yonks. You like it? Darling, it's yours, but only if I can have that *divine* dress in return.'

'You couldn't wear this,' she said, laughing.

'Says who?'

'Says me. But that outfit's gorgeous. Suits you so well.'

He was looking at her sideways. 'You know, I think you and me are going to get along just fine.'

'I'm sure of it,' she said, and they clinked glasses again.

'You two okay?' said Max, coming over. He'd taken off his jacket and tie. His white shirt was open at the neck and his shirt sleeves were rolled up, revealing strong, tanned arms. She felt a jolt of something. Love? She wasn't sure. How the hell would she know? She had never been in love before. Not even once.

'We've been getting acquainted,' said Eddie to him. To her he added: 'Haven't we, darling?'

'We have,' she said, watching as Jonjo and his big-chested blonde twirled around the dance floor.

'She'll have someone's eye out with those in a minute,' said Eddie, following Ruthie's gaze. 'Get you a drink, brother?' he asked Max.

'Go on then,' said Max, and Eddie left her there.

Max sat down in Eddie's vacated chair. 'You okay with Eddie?' Max asked.

'What do you mean?'

'He's . . . ' Max made a rocking motion with his hand.

'He's what?'

'It's men for him. Not women.'

'Should that bother me?'

'It bothers some.'

'Well not me. He's nice.'

The music came to an end. Connie staggered back to her table, Tom supporting her with a hand on her elbow. Jonjo walked the blonde back to her seat and some other men joined him – men Ruthie vaguely knew now, through Max. Steve Taylor, wide as he was high, dark-eyed, dark-haired. Rat-faced Gary Tooley, blond and hard-eyed, tall and thin as a stork. That ugly leather-jacketed little person Jackie Tulliver, who hadn't even bothered to put a suit on for this occasion. And Jimmy Bond, who she knew was Max's right hand man and who was now engaged to her cousin, Kath. No lavish parties like this one for Kath, though: Jimmy was notoriously tight with cash.

The group of men came over to where Max and Ruthie were sitting. Eddie returned, handed Max a tumbler with an inch of amber liquid in it. Max took it, thanked him, drank it down, placed the empty glass squarely on the table.

'Time to go,' said Jonjo. He looked at Eddie, who'd sat back down by her. Then he lashed out a foot, kicking Eddie's chair. It was so sudden and so hard a blow that it nearly unseated the smaller man; made him shake and lose his balance. Then Eddie righted himself and stared up at Jonjo with loathing.

'You comin' out with us then, pansy?' asked Jonjo, grinning, glad to have unsettled and embarrassed his younger brother.

Ruthie made up her mind then and there that she hated Jonjo. She felt terrible for Eddie, shown up like this in front of her – and by his own brother too. It was horrible the way Eddie visibly shrank as Jonjo loomed over him, gleefully humiliating him in front of all his tough-guy mates, a couple of whom were suppressing grins.

Eddie flicked a look at her, full of embarrassment and unease. She was reminded of a whipped dog she had once seen cringing on the street; she had never forgotten its expression.

Max wasn't grinning though. He was straight-faced as he spoke up. 'No, he's not coming. He's going to stay here and look after Ruthie – aren't you, mate,' he said to Eddie, patting him on the shoulder.

'Glad to,' said Eddie, visibly recovering his poise.

'I appreciate it,' said Max to Eddie, and Ruthie was gratified to see the smile get wiped off Jonjo's face as Max turned to him with a flare of anger in his eyes.

Jonjo had pushed Eddie down – but Max had raised him up again. She wondered how often this scene had played out between the three of them. Many, many times, she guessed, right back into childhood.

'Eddie will look after me,' she said to Max. 'We're getting along famously.'

'Yeah, darlin',' piped up Jonjo. 'Gawd knows you're safe enough with him.'

Max dropped a kiss onto Ruthie's cheek. He took his jacket from Jonjo and shrugged it on, then turned and gave Jonjo a hard shove in the chest.

'Oi!' Jonjo complained, startled, staggering back.

'When will you ever learn to shut your fat mouth?' said Max sharply. 'I swear to God . . . '

'Just havin' a laugh,' said Jonjo, shrugging.

'Well *don't* fucking have a laugh,' Max advised, and he led them all away and out of the hall.

The band started up again. Connie lurched back onto the dancefloor, grabbing Auntie Mo by the arm and taking her along, leaving Uncle Tom at his table smoking one of Max's Cohiba cigars.

Ruthie sat there, quietly considering what she had just witnessed. The one thing she had never expected her fiancé to be was *kind*. Scary, yes. Charismatic, certainly. But never, ever kind.

Next day, the streets were abuzz. A rival up-and-coming gang leader's house had been destroyed. The man and his family had fled the area. That was the sort of thing that could sometimes happen, around Max. Ruthie was beginning to get used to it.

But then there came worse news: horrific. Max's mother Queenie had died down in Guildford, at Max's posh country place.

Suddenly, things were very tense on the Carter manor.

It was said that Queenie's death involved violence, a botched robbery – and the Delaney gang.

10

Ruthie said to Max that they should postpone the wedding, push the date back after hearing the awful news about Queenie, but everything was already in hand and he said no. It had been his mum's dearest wish to see him settled, and he was going to go ahead, respect her wishes. Anyway – all the arrangements had been made, it would be a hell of a job to alter things now.

'Well,' said Ruthie. 'If you're sure?'

'I am,' he said, and dropped the subject.

Max seemed to be dealing with his mother's death with whisky and solitude. He didn't want company, he didn't want sympathy. He was sheltering, Ruthie thought, behind a hard shell, keeping his grief inside.

'Only we could—' Ruthie went on gently.

'No,' he snapped. 'It's done. Leave it.'

And so she did.

The wedding was, of course, lavish. There were hundreds of guests invited. Everyone wanted to be in Max Carter's orbit, everyone wanted to give presents and good wishes to him and his new bride.

The reception was planned like a military operation. There were mounds of peach-toned flowers everywhere, extravagant gifts for the bridesmaids and the best man and the ushers. Brand new outfits for the whole bridal party. Ruthie's mum was in seventh heaven; her daughter, her little Ruthie, marrying such a prize!

After the misery of Queenie's funeral, the wedding was a blessing; it seemed to lift the whole of the East End in a great communal wave of wellbeing. And there Ruthie was on the morning of the big day – primped and powdered and made up to the nines. Her unremarkable mousy hair was swept up on top of her head, a pearl-studded coronet pinned in place, her make-up all done, faultless. And the dress! It was fabulous, like something out of a fairy tale. The train was a full twenty feet long, with real crystals sewn into it. Despite flatly refusing to attend at first – why, Ruthie neither knew nor understood at the time – Annie had finally agreed that she would join Cousin Kath and the two of them would be Ruthie's bridesmaids, all done out in peach to match the bouquets.

'I look rotten in peach,' Annie complained at every fitting.

'Yeah, but it suits Kath,' Ruthie told her, wondering what the hell could have put Annie in such a mood. Annie was always snappish, these days. Always finding fault. 'You're so pretty you don't need to worry about the colour, but spare a thought for Kath, Annie. She's built like a ruddy tank and the peach really suits her, so have a heart, please.'

It was going to be the happiest day of Ruthie's life, right?

They arrived at the church, Ruthie and Uncle Tom stepping out of a pure-white Rolls-Royce motor car draped with peach ribbons, to be met by the photographer, busy snapping away. Ruthie was feeling sick with nerves. She wasn't like Annie. She wasn't used to being the centre of attention, and the thought of all those people, all those guests inside the church, turning and staring at her as she walked up the aisle . . . her knees were literally shaking.

Uncle Tom was giving her away because of course Dad had cleared off years ago, never to be seen or heard from again. She had a dream sometimes that Dad would show up at the last minute, snatch her away from Uncle Tom and proudly escort her up the aisle, but it was just that: a dream. Dad wasn't coming. Dad was *never* coming.

Then there was a lull in proceedings before they had to go inside the church, the bells were clanging deafeningly above their heads. Annie and Ruthie were standing together while Uncle Tom drew aside, took a nip of his hip flask. Kath giggled and took a sip too when he offered it to her.

And then Annie turned to Ruthie and said it. Maybe she even *deserved* it, for being a smug cow of an older sister, for being happy and excited enough to say once again, trying to make Annie smile when she looked so grim: 'It'll be your turn before you know it.'

Ruthie thought that she would never forget the hard, furious look in Annie's dark green eyes.

'I've had your hand-me-downs all my life,' she said sharply. 'But today, guess what? You're getting one of mine.'

At first Ruthie hadn't a clue what Annie was talking about. Then all at once *she knew*. Everything was explained. Ruthie understood Annie's bad moods, her absences, her sudden rages. And all Max's wealth and power, his hard-fought ownership of his East End manor, the posh house he'd acquired down in the country, it was all ashes, all dust, all a great big pile of *nothing*. Because – at last – she knew. And she couldn't ever un-know it. Her sister had *been* with her fiancé. Had *sex* with him. She'd heard it out of Annie's own mouth. And she could never rediscover the happiness she had felt before. It just wasn't possible.

It was all finished, right there.

The dream was *done*.

11

Ruthie didn't know how she got through the rest of it. All those measured strides up the aisle with Uncle Tom, each step accompanied by 'Here Comes the Bride' booming out of the church organ. She faltered a couple of times, felt Uncle's hand tighten on hers, saw his swift glance of concern.

Behind her? Annie.

Annie, matching her step by step, and thinking what? *It should have been me?* Yes. Of course that. And there up ahead, the vicar in his sparkling white surplice, smiling at Ruthie as she approached.

And there was Max.

Max, gazing back at her. Handsome as the devil, and thinking what?

Yes.

Of course.

If only it was Annie and not her.

It was Annie who took Ruthie's bouquet, her eyes not meeting her sister's. It was Max who lifted Ruthie's veil, preparing her for this like a lamb for sacrifice.

Somehow, she got through it, the hymns, the lessons, everything, and then she was saying the words that would bind her to him, make her *Mrs Max Carter*, and then the register was signed and they walked back down the aisle together, a married couple.

The sunlight dazzled her in the doorway of the church. The photographer fussed around. The guests grinned and threw confetti. The flash fired.

Jesus!

She was married.

Married to Max Carter.

They got into the white Rolls-Royce and the driver popped open a bottle of champagne. Everyone clapped and cheered and Ruthie caught a glimpse of Annie there, standing beside Kath. Annie wasn't smiling: her face was set in cold lines. Ruthie quickly looked away. What the hell was happening to her? She found herself waving at the crowds and all the while she was thinking: *I'll run away. That would be best. I'll just* bolt.

But . . . how would that leave Mum? Mum, who was so thrilled with it all, who didn't know what Ruthie knew about Max and Annie. What would happen to her? Would Max turn on her, chase her off the Carter manor in revenge for the humiliation of his new wife doing a bunk?

He would, wouldn't he. Ruthie didn't know him well – she hardly knew him at all – but she thought he would do that. And she had a picture in her head, of Connie Bailey, her mum, dead in a ditch somewhere, penniless, driven out. She couldn't do that to her.

She was *trapped*.

At the reception there were speeches, telegrams. Endless, pointless words of congratulation. A few fairly smutty jokes, dutifully laughed at. The best man's speech. Then Max's, followed by applause. And all through it, the food, the laughter, the drink, Ruthie sat there with her sister just a few feet away.

'You all right then, honey bunch?' asked Eddie, leaning over her seat, startling her out of her dark thoughts.

'Fine,' she said, smiling.

'Anything I can get you? Just say the word.'

'No, I'm fine. Really.'

With her new husband sitting silent beside her and her sister just a few seats away, not eating, not drinking.

Eddie departed.

When she could at last escape to the ladies' loos, Ruthie hurried from the packed airless room and – oh thank God – all the stalls were empty, there was no one in there. She shut herself in a cubicle, sat down on the loo seat, stared at the floor.

Then movement. And then some bastard was rapping at the door.

'Ruthie! You in there?'

Annie's voice.

'Go away,' said Ruthie.

'Are you all right?'

A gasp escaped Ruthie. The sheer audacity, the fucking *cheek* of Annie Bailey, to ask her that, after what she'd said to her.

'How long?' said Ruthie.

'*What?*'

'How long's it been going on?'

'Look, let's not get into that. I just want to know you're okay.'

'I'm fabulous. Really fine. My husband's a cheat and so's my sister.'

'We never intended it to happen.'

'Oh you just fell into bed together by mistake, is that it?'

'I shouldn't have said anything,' said Annie.

Ruthie stared at the closed cubicle door. Then she stood up, flung it open. Annie stood there in her peach bridesmaid's dress. She stepped back a pace when she saw the rage on Ruthie's face.

'No – you shouldn't have *done* anything,' she rapped out. 'You slept with my fiancé. You're my *sister*, for God's sake. How *could* you?'

'There were two of us,' Annie pointed out.

The outer door to the loos opened. A woman stepped in.

'*Get out!*' shrieked Annie.

The woman retreated, quickly.

'You ought to be *ashamed*,' said Ruthie. 'You *tart*.'

'Listen,' started Annie.

'No! I've listened enough to you. Now fuck off and leave me alone.'

'Ruthie—'

'No.' Ruthie thrust a finger into Annie's face and she flinched back. 'Annie bloody Bailey, you listen for a change and take notice of what I'm telling you, all right?'

'Ruthie—'

'No! You are dead to me, you got that? *Dead!*'

12

Maybe Ruthie ought to have kept quiet. Just soaked it up. All her life she'd been good at doing that; at swallowing pain, suppressing it. But somehow hearing about her own sister and her own fiancé was just too big a shock to be fought down, bundled away, rubbished. She just *couldn't do it.*

The truth was, from day one, Ruthie had felt that this was all too good to be true. She had been unable to believe her luck when Max turned his attention on her. And this just proved that she'd been right to have doubts. It *was* too good to be true; it was far too much of a miracle.

After the reception, Max drove her, his new bride, down to his big Surrey place and he actually carried her over the threshold. Ruthie was wearing an expensive cream wool suit – Max had paid for it, Max paid for everything. While wishing it was *her*, maybe? Annie? Ruthie guessed so.

Brunettes for Max, she remembered Eddie saying. And Annie was a brunette.

Then Max set Ruthie on her feet in the hallway and there was this skinny sour-faced woman in black standing there, ready to welcome them.

'This is Miss Arnott who looks after the place,' said Max.

Miss Arnott shook Ruthie's hand. Miss Arnott's grip was light, damp.

'Let me show you around,' she said, and although Ruthie was drooping with exhaustion after this huge and awful day she dutifully trailed around this massive wood-panelled Victorian barn of a place behind Miss Arnott, her pointing out this and that – the grand piano in the hall, the costly rugs, the exquisite furnishings – while Ruthie nodded, a captive, her mind whirling, nothing in it except Annie's devastating words.

I've had your cast-offs all my life . . .

And there was something more that was running through Ruthie's head all through the dinner Miss Arnott cooked and served to them. Not only Annie's vicious words but also this single, crushing thought: they'd slept together, Max and her sister, and that was bad enough. But worse – oh God, so much worse, was the thought that now came right on its heels.

Was their affair going to carry on now that Max was married to her? She knew Annie, knew her right to the bone. Once she fastened on a thing, then it was hers. No arguments. No turning back.

She couldn't speak to Max about it, couldn't stand up to him about it, no way could she do that. The very idea made her shudder. Talk to Max, of all people, about divorce, which he would see as a disgrace, a reflection on his manhood? She couldn't. Didn't dare.

Run, she thought. *I could run.*

But she couldn't drop Mum in the shit like that. Couldn't leave Connie to face the consequences of her actions. Every way she looked at it, there was no way out. She was locked into this. Yes – trapped.

It *was* going to carry on, him and her. Of course it was. Ruthie knew Annie too well. She was irresistible. Ruthie's brain kept presenting her with tormenting little cinema-like snatches. Annie, dancing with him. Annie, turning to see him at the cloakroom entrance, something in her eyes that Ruthie should have known, should have seen, and now . . . oh Christ, now it was too late. She was tied to this, tied to him. She was Mrs Max Carter but it meant nothing, nothing at all. Because all she could hear in her head were Annie's terrible words:

Guess what? Today, you're getting one of mine . . .

13

Miss Arnott's lavish wedding-night meal almost choked Ruthie.

'You're not eating very much,' Max noticed.

'Big day,' she managed to blurt out. 'I got a bit nervous, it's ruined my appetite.'

After dinner they sat in the drawing room for a while, Mozart on the radiogram.

'I didn't know you liked classical music,' said Ruthie.

'Well, I do.' He smiled.

Ruthie hated it. She liked Manfred Mann. And that new lot, The Beatles. 'Please Please Me' – she loved that.

I know absolutely nothing about this man, she thought.

And then – oh God – then it was time for bed.

Now came the moment when they had to get on that huge bed upstairs and cement their relationship. She didn't know how the hell she was going to manage this. She'd never slept with a man, ever.

Well, it was too late now to cry off, back out. She got changed into her nightdress in the bathroom and when she came back into the bedroom he was there wearing pyjama bottoms, softly lit by the bedside lamps. He was standing beside the bed, taking off his watch.

If any man could be described as beautiful, she thought, then that man was Max Carter. He was all tanned skin and taut muscles, dark hair dusting over his arms and his chest, arrowing down on his stomach, pointing the way to his manhood.

She stood frozen to the spot, awestruck, as he undid the tie on the pyjama trousers and let them slip to the floor. He stepped out of them and suddenly he was naked.

Ruthie had never seen a fully aroused man before, and it was shocking. His cock jutted hard out from between his thighs, full and long: ready for her.

'Come on, come here,' said Max.

As if in a dream – or maybe, more accurately, a nightmare – Ruthie walked over to the bed, stood in front of him. He reached out, smiling slightly, and loosened the tie at the neck of her nightie. He paused, then pushed the thing down, off her shoulders, down onto the floor so that she was naked too.

Ruthie felt the urge – stupid, she knew – to cover her breasts, to hide herself. But this was her husband, standing here in front of her. He touched a hand lightly to her waist, drew her in closer. The tip of his penis touched her thigh and she felt moisture there, felt the life-giving throbbing power of it.

Could she have a beautiful dark-haired baby from him tonight?

Would that make up for the pain he and Annie had caused her?

All her life, she had dreamed of a family, a happy home, a loving husband, adorable kids. Could any of that still come true?

No. Of course not.

'Touch it,' he said gently against her throat, kissing her there, his hand on her breast, teasing the nipple into a rigid response.

God, could she?

But he expected her to do this.

She clasped his cock in her hands and almost recoiled in surprise. It was hot: hard, but silky to the touch. You had to marvel at something so impressive, so vibrantly *male*. It was magnificent.

It . . . had been *inside her sister*.

Her hands fell to her sides.

Her husband had fucked Annie.

'Come on,' said Max. 'Lie down.'

They got into bed and very soon Max was kissing her, pulling up her nightdress, he was going to do it, and she couldn't, she just couldn't . . .

Ruthie was sweating, feeling suffocated beneath him. She was panicking. Trying, finally, unable to stop herself, to desperately beat him off. She had never felt such anger, such stress, such an unbearable burden, and it had to come out, somehow she had to say the words that were bubbling in her throat, crying out for release.

'I know about you!' she burst out, wrenching her lips free of his.

'What? We'll talk afterwards,' he said, touching her . . .

'I know about you and Annie!'

Ruthie could feel his nakedness, could feel that hard unforgiving male body pushing against hers. Then he shoved even harder and suddenly, shockingly, he was inside her and she was no longer a virgin bride.

He thrust quickly, ten, twenty times, and all she could do was cry as he poured into her, claimed her, made her his for keeps.

He said nothing else that night. After a while he got up and left her there.

Her dream of happy-ever-after was over. Over, before it had even begun.

She was Mrs Max Carter.

She was in a cage, and she couldn't get out.

14

Next morning, knowing that she couldn't keep this to herself, she went downstairs. The housekeeper Miss Arnott told her Mr Carter had gone out but that she had set out breakfast for her in the dining room. Ruthie couldn't even think about eating; she left the bacon and eggs and the sausages and the coffee where it all was and instead went to the phone in the hallway. She had to tell someone about this, and she couldn't call Kath because Auntie Mo didn't have a phone. Annie? The one person she would have confided in over anything else? But what could she have said to her?

You bitch! You bloody treacherous bitch . . .

Ruthie phoned Mum. Max had got Connie a phone installed, a great luxury, but Ruthie wondered if Mum was even up yet, after the festivities of yesterday. Connie'd been very drunk at the reception, maybe she would still be sleeping it off?

But miraculously Connie did pick up.

'H'lo?' she muttered. 'Who's this?'

'It's me, Mum. Ruthie.'

'Gawd, it's early. Ruthie, what's up?' she asked. Ruthie could hear Connie scrabbling about for her fag packet; she heard a match strike.

'Something . . . it's something awful, Mum,' Ruthie said.

'What?' Ruthie heard her inhale deeply. 'What's up then? You all right?'

'No, I . . . I don't know what to do.'

'Bit of a shock, was it? The wedding night? Don't worry my duck. You'll get used to it.'

'No, it's not that.' The wedding night had been brief. She supposed she should be thankful for that.

God, he could have already made her pregnant . . .

That thought chilled her.

'Then what?'

Ruthie took a deep breath. Could hardly bear to even think it, much less say it. But finally she did.

'Annie said something to me yesterday outside the church. Before the wedding.'

'Oh yeah? What then?'

'She said I was getting one of her cast-offs.'

'You what?'

'She meant that she'd been there first. That she's slept with him. With Max.'

There was a silence. Then Connie exploded. 'You fucking *what*?' she roared out. 'Say that again. Say it slowly. She said *what*?'

Ruthie told her. She missed out nothing.

'She won't spend another single night in this house,' Connie yelled. 'That conniving *bitch*!'

With a shaking hand, Ruthie put the phone down. She should have felt vindicated, triumphant that she'd caused Annie grief when Annie had certainly caused her much the same. But stupidly, she couldn't quite feel that way. She was too soft-hearted to enjoy the fact that she had set in motion events that would wound Annie right back.

Annie would be in big trouble, for sure. She would be made to suffer. Left to fend for herself on the streets that Max Carter and the other gangs ran. Because Connie would speak to Max about it. And he would be enraged at Annie, to have caused his new marriage to run so quickly into trouble.

Yes. Of course he would.

You didn't cross Max. Not over anything, and certainly not over this. So yes – he would make Annie suffer. He was good at making people suffer, Ruthie knew that. Over the past months she'd heard a lot about him. Too much, maybe. He could be civilised but he could also be frighteningly physical – and he had people at his disposal who could inflict a lot of damage at his say-so. He ran the streets with a rod of iron, claiming money from all the businesses on his manor – protection money. And she supposed he did protect people, in a way. If anyone in his area had trouble with rowdy customers or bad payers, Max's boys were in there straight away, sorting it out.

Max was so good at sorting things out.

Maybe *too* good.

He would sort this out too. She knew it.

15

There was news of more trouble: a gangland killing. All the papers were full of it and the police were 'investigating'. On the streets and even from Mum Ruthie heard rumours that Max had 'sorted' Tory Delaney on the night before their wedding. That sometime in the hours before he'd married her, his shattered and unloved bride, he'd gone out to the Tudor Club in Stoke Newington and shot rival gang leader Tory Delaney three times in the chest and once in the head, killing him.

The rumours circulated all around Ruthie. That it was a revenge killing, that ever since Queenie, Max's mother, had died in the spring, Max had sworn he'd get even with those responsible. Rumour, speculation – Ruthie didn't much care. She had her own problems, but thankfully they did not include a baby. She bled as normal; Max hadn't given her a child and she was glad. He hadn't touched her – or even been near her – since the wedding night. She was glad about that, too.

She felt so cut off: so alone. She was married to a man who didn't love her. She was estranged from her sister, who had once been her companion, her friend; and she heard that, as expected, Max had made Annie very sorry indeed for telling Ruthie about their liaison. And Connie had kicked Annie out of the house, just as she'd promised.

'I'll not have that little whore in the place,' Connie told Ruthie, raging for weeks over the whole matter.

But then, Ruthie wondered, where would Annie go? What would she do? Fool that she was, once the red rage had subsided and numbness crept in, Ruthie worried about Annie and how she would fare on the streets. She mentioned it – carefully – to Mum, on the phone.

'Don't waste your pity on her,' Connie advised Ruthie tartly. 'I reckon she'll have gone over to your father's sister in Limehouse. You remember her?'

'What, Aunt Celia?'

They never saw Aunt Celia, their father's dodgy sister, these days. She was rarely even talked about. If Dad had been a black sheep, then so, for sure, was Celia. Ruthie could vaguely remember her from family occasions years back, when she had still been acceptable, still part of the Bailey family fold. She remembered Celia's lively dark eyes and her warm laughing smile. She remembered that she'd always been beautifully made up, neatly dressed. That she'd sported an ivory cigarette holder and carried a selection of flashy covetable handbags.

'Yeah, and that's fitting, don't you think?' demanded Connie. 'That little whore Annie going to a whorehouse. Because that's what Celia runs over there, did you know that?'

Ruthie hadn't known that. She was pretty shocked by it.

'You what?' she gaped.

'You heard. It's a knocking shop. So your ruddy sister should fit right in.'

16

Ruthie wished that Mum hadn't told her that. Now she was even more worried about Annie. She didn't belong in a place like that, no matter what sins she'd committed. But then – didn't she *deserve* such a punishment? Such a fate?

Still, Ruthie couldn't help wondering what would become of Annie there. Would Annie truly become a whore?

'Who cares?' Mum snapped on the day Ruthie put this worrying notion forward during a visit to Connie's place in Bow. 'She belongs in a place like that. May she rot in hell.' Connie took an angry draw on her cigarette and exhaled twin plumes of smoke. She stared at her daughter in disbelief. 'Gawd blimey Ruthie, you serious? Look what she done to you! And you're soft enough to feel sorry for the tart? Well, don't!'

On the one hand, Ruthie could see Mum's point. And in her meaner more vengeful moments she did sort of hope that Annie was in for a rough time. But on the other hand . . . this was her sister. So how could that really please her?

She couldn't bring herself to actually *hate* Annie.

She *should*. But she couldn't.

More rumours piled in. That the Limehouse place where Annie was hiding out in the depths of her shame, having gone against Max's wishes and reaped her just reward, was run by the Delaney mob from Ireland, the head of which, Tory, had been gunned down. Apparently, by Max himself.

'Mad red-haired tinkers,' Mum said in satisfaction. 'A whole tribe of them. Well, there was a whole tribe, until Tory went and got himself wiped out. They reckon that it was Max who did for him.'

Ruthie felt herself go pale. 'You mean *killed* him?'

'What the hell else would I mean?'

Ruthie thought of her husband, shooting a man dead. Her husband, who was a total stranger to her, who came and went as he pleased, who ruled the streets.

'So . . . who's taking over from Tory then?' Ruthie asked.

'Everyone thought Pat. But I hear it's to be Redmond. Now,' Mum said, putting the troublesome question of not only the Delaney mob but her own daughter Annie to one side. 'When you going to take me down to the country then, show me this nice big house of yours?'

As if nothing had happened! As if Ruthie was now a properly respectable and married lady and everything was perfectly fine. That her sister's treachery and her fiancé's betrayal had been nothing at all, quickly swept under the carpet, and now forgotten. As if her world hadn't already crumpled and fallen apart.

All right, she might have expected Max to have the odd affair later on. A lot of men did. But they'd only just gone up the aisle – and this was *her sister* he'd shafted. She couldn't get over that.

Mum, seeing Ruthie's face, leaned forward and patted her hand with her long yellowish fingers.

'I know it's been bad. Terrible shock, wasn't it. I know that. But look! You're the winner here, Ruthie. You have the husband, the house, all that goes with it. And you have respect! You won't have to wait to be served anywhere, not anymore. You are Mrs Max Carter. That counts for a lot.'

Ruthie looked her mother dead in the eye. 'But you're telling me that word on the street is Max shot Tory Delaney. Which means he could get banged up for life, couldn't he?'

Connie sat back, puffing out her cheeks. She stubbed out the remains of her cigarette and shrugged. 'So? Not proven, is it? And it won't be, either. The police will look the other way. They always do, around here. He's got them in his back pocket.'

Max – Ruthie's husband – had the police in his pay. He had the streets under his control. He was a powerful, fearful man. And her? What was she, now? The unloved wife, the 'her indoors' who was free to spend his money and reflect his status. Yawning before her were years and years of this. She was stuck, terrified.

'What's he like then, in bed? Nice, is he?' her mother asked her.

'What?'

'Some of 'em are like animals,' said Mum. 'Bastards.'

'He's . . . all right. I suppose.'

She couldn't tell Mum that Max hadn't touched her since the wedding night. There'd been no hugs. No kisses. Certainly no sex.

'Sounds like the honeymoon's over already,' Connie laughed.

Honeymoon?

It had never even started.

But . . . maybe there was something she could do about that.

17

Perhaps Mum was right. Ruthie *was* Mrs Max Carter now. She did have the Guildford house to live in, even though she didn't much care for it. She did have respect. People were nicer to her now than they had ever bothered to be, before.

And Max?

Well . . . she'd rejected him, hadn't she. And he'd responded – she thought about it – like a gentleman. Giving her space, distance. He hadn't persisted as many other men would have done. She'd pushed him away and he'd respected that, and now he was probably thinking that she wanted it that way. A marriage in name only. But . . . did she? Really? Hadn't she always dreamed of a happy family life, children, an adoring husband?

Well, he might not adore her, but maybe the situation was not yet completely beyond rescuing.

So over dinner one night – dinner was usually conducted in silence – Ruthie asked Max if he'd had a good day.

Max looked at her in surprise. 'What?'

Oh God.

'Just making conversation,' she said.

'Right. Yes. Okay I suppose. Busy.'

Silence fell again.

'Max – maybe we could do something together?' she asked, a tinge of desperation in her voice.

He looked at her. Shrugged. 'I don't know. You suggest something.'

'Right. I'll think about it.'

He put his knife and fork together on his empty plate and stood up. Every night when he was here at the house – which was rare – he left her alone, went into the drawing room, played that horrible classical music then retired to one of the other bedrooms or the dressing room.

This night was going to be different. She was determined on that. One of them was going to have to make the effort, get past the disaster their union had so far turned out to be.

Instead of staying there, she stood up too. Blushing, she looked him dead in the eye.

'Max?'

'Hm? What?'

'I want us to sleep together again.' Ruthie felt the hectic blush on her cheeks deepen. She mustered all her courage and went on: 'I want you to . . . to fuck me. Like you did on that first night. I *need* you to do that.'

'Ruthie—'

'All my life I've wanted a proper family,' she said, quickly rushing on, hotly embarrassed. 'And I'll never get that if you don't do it. I was shocked, you see. About you. And Annie. But I'm over that now,' she lied. 'We can make this work. I know we can.'

But Max was shaking his head.

Ruthie dashed toward him and planted her lips on his. She felt him recoil. His hands caught her shoulders, pushed her back, away from him. She snatched at his hand and placed it on her breast. 'I . . . I'll please you,' she said. 'Anything you want me to do, I'll do it. I swear.'

Max took his hand away. 'Ruthie.'

Ruthie's cheeks were bright red with humiliation. 'You . . . you want me to s-suck you? Down there? I'll do it. If that's what you want. I don't mind.'

Now he looked angry. 'But I do,' he said, and pushed her back, away from him. 'Ruthie. Stop it. Go up to bed for God's sake.'

'Max . . . ' She was starting to cry. This was awful.

'No! Go on.'

And he left the room, left her standing there, numb with hurt, tears slipping unheeding down her face.

18

Days later, Connie came down to Guildford to visit, driven by Dave, who was supposed to be Ruthie's minder. Ruthie wasn't exactly delighted by this new addition to her household, but Max insisted. Dave was one of his workers, a blond, blockish and charmless youngster who she found faintly intimidating.

Connie spent all her time at the Guildford house oohing and ahhing over it. Well, it was – admittedly – impressive; it was fabulously furnished with thick velvet drapes, massive pot plants, expensive flock wallpaper, carpets so thick you sank into them almost ankle-deep. There were seven massive bedrooms upstairs in total, big cellars and an attic suite which had once been servants' quarters when there had been ten housemaids in service here, back in Victorian times. You walked down the grand curving staircase to a hall you could hold a dance in it was so big, and then into the drawing room . . .

'A bloody drawing room!' Connie enthused, admiring the roaring fire, the big Knoll couches on either side of it, the huge gilt mirror above the massive Portland stone mantlepiece. 'How you getting on then, you and him?' Connie asked.

'Okay,' said Ruthie, trying not to think of the other night and Max's flat rejection of her hopeful advances.

She shouldn't have even tried it: she could see that now. The look on Max's face haunted her, made her cringe at the memory. She'd been trying to be the perfect wife – and she'd failed, dismally.

'We're fine,' she said, smiling brightly. 'Everything's fine.'

A week later, Cousin Kath came down too, marvelling at the place and settling down for a cosy girly chat, asking Ruthie – much to her horror – what it was like, you know, doing it?

'It?' Ruthie queried, sipping a schooner of sweet sherry. She felt frozen all the time, numb, and the sherry, which she had never even tried before *that* day, the wedding day when her world had ended, always seemed to warm her a little.

'You know!' Kath's eyes were avid with interest. 'Is it good? The sex stuff, I mean. Oh, you know. I haven't done it yet of course. Jimmy keeps pushing for it but I'm holding out for the wedding ring. Do you just melt when he does it? He's very handsome, ain't he? Are you trying for a baby yet?'

The very thought made Ruthie feel sick – and brought back unpleasant memories not only of the wedding night but also of offering herself up to her husband – only to have him turn her down.

'It's like being poked with a stick,' she told Kath.

'Come on! It's not. Sometimes I really wish Jimmy would just do it to me. You know, just force me. I really do.' Kath coloured up. 'When he's – you know – touching me – I get this feeling come over me and once or twice I've nearly gone the whole hog. That sounds awful, I know.'

'Kath – be careful,' Ruthie told her. A bastard child and the struggling life of a single and despised mother would be a nightmare. People sneered at such women, called them loose, said they were no better than they should be, spat at them in the street. All very fine for Jimmy to take his reckless pleasure, but what about Kath, the poor cow who'd be left with the result?

'Yeah, Mum says that. She says the whole sex thing is overrated. But sometimes, I tell you, I really just want to – well – do it.'

And Kath went away, back to the Smoke, leaving Ruthie alone but for the silently disapproving glances of Miss Arnott and the unwelcome background presence of her 'minder', Dave, who rarely spoke a single word.

'You've got to have a minder,' Max had told her. 'Particularly now when there's trouble.'

'What trouble?'

Was he about to confide in her? Max never did that. He hardly even talked to her, really.

Sometimes he'd ask what was for dinner. Or say there were people coming over, scary-looking men and their wives or girlfriends, could she get Miss Arnott to organise a meal? Of course she could. She deployed the formidable Miss Arnott, who hired in catering staff.

Ruthie was getting used to being the sort of woman who directed her housekeeper to 'hire in'. No more washing, housework or ironing for her. She'd done it all, often enough, when Mum had been on the drink. But no more. The laundry here was collected on Fridays and delivered back, crisply ironed and spotlessly clean on the following Monday. Miss Arnott had charge of a pair of female cleaners who did the whole place, top to bottom, every other day, and the unused annexe – which had once been Queenie's domain – was cleaned once a week. And a dinner party? Miss Arnott had that nailed, straight away. Didn't even consult Ruthie on the menu and, to be honest, Ruthie didn't much care.

'What trouble?' Ruthie asked Max again.

'Just trouble,' he said.

No. He wasn't going to confide in her. Of course not. Mostly, he wasn't in the country with her at all, he was up in London – staying at his late mum Queenie's town place, Kath said – so Ruthie was left pretty much in isolation.

Dave wasn't all that as a bodyguard. She didn't go out much, but she was free to roam about the Guildford place unhindered. She took to wandering around the house, examining every nook and cranny of the old place. Then she looked around the grounds. And there was the annexe. Curious, she wondered what it would be like inside. She found the key to it on its hook by the back kitchen door of the main house and wandered over there. She unlocked the door, went inside. The annexe was small, cosy. It actually would have suited Ruthie herself far better than Max's vast, chilly but impressive Victorian mansion. Ruthie couldn't for the life of her think of that huge imposing place as *her home.*

She strolled into the annexe's lounge – and then stopped dead. There, over the small tiled fireplace, was a portrait of Max's late mother, Queenie, all white hair and hostile eyes. She seemed to stare at Ruthie and – as always – find her wanting. And of course Queenie would have a portrait of herself hung up in here. She'd no doubt commissioned it herself, before her death, imprinting her huge bossy personality on the place, stamping her authority on it.

Queenie had died in this place. It gave Ruthie a shudder, thinking of that, so when the voice came from behind her she spun round, startled.

'What's going on?'

But it wasn't Queenie, back from the dead to ask her why she was such a useless wife to Max. And it wasn't Dave. It was the gardener.

'Oh!' he said. 'It's you, Mrs Carter. I saw the door open and thought I'd better check. Don't usually see anyone in here. Not since Mrs Carter died. I mean, the *old* Mrs Carter.'

'I know who you mean,' she said. And she could see it now. This wasn't so much an annexe as a shrine. A shrine to Queenie Carter. And she wasn't welcome in here. 'She died. I didn't.' Then Ruthie added: 'I'm still alive.'

But as she wandered back to the main house, she wondered: was that really true?

19

Of course, she grew bored and she was horribly lonely. Before very long she was asking Dave to drive her into London. Sometimes, much to her delight, Eddie wanted to accompany her. She loved Eddie. They had massive wedges of cash in their pockets whenever they hit the town. Max was far from tight, you could say that for him. His idea of 'weekly housekeeping money' went far beyond what the average man could earn in a year. The instant they'd married, he'd set up a bank account for her and he topped it up lavishly every month, without fail.

'Get some decent clothes,' said Max, casting a disparaging eye over her old handmade efforts, things she had once thought were perfectly fine but clearly were not quite up to scratch for him – or for those glamour-pusses who came and took dinner with them at the country house.

At those dinner parties, Max was different. Quite warm and attentive. But when the guests were gone, he was cold again. 'Lara'll take you up Bond Street, see you kitted up,' he said.

'Don't let that cow Lara intimidate you,' Eddie told Ruthie when they were up in his room one evening, Ruthie trying on his big collection of hats – boaters, caps, Stetsons, he had everything.

'What do you think?' she asked, posing and pouting in front of his dressing-table mirror.

'Exquisite. The boater's best on you. I could just see you swanning around Cap d'Antibes in that. We could fly out.' Eddie grinned. 'You could sit at the back by the rear gunner.'

'Yeah? And where would you be?'

'In the cockpit, of course. Why don't we do it honey? Come on! Max wouldn't mind.'

'Max wouldn't *care*,' said Ruthie. Instantly she was embarrassed at the slip. She hadn't meant to say that.

'Why? What's wrong?'

'Oh, ignore me,' she shrugged, flushing brick-red.

'You got trouble with Big Bro?' Eddie asked.

'Oh, you know him,' she said.

'I do. Is he not treating you well then?'

'Of course he is. We just don't . . . don't see much of each other. That's all.'

'Well, he's busy.'

'I know.'

'Try the bowler. Or the cloche, what about that? Very twenties. What was I saying? Yes. Lara. Thinks she's a bit of posh, don't she? But I tell you, don't fall for it. Before she snagged Ernie Beaconsfield she was trading cash for blowjobs out behind the Palais.'

Lara was the wife of one of the dodgy-looking men who frequently came to dinner. She was tall and black-haired and stunning; a mature woman in her thirties, very assured, very knowledgeable.

Ruthie sometimes used some of Max's 'housekeeping' money to check in to a hotel. A good one, five star. She didn't want to stay with Mum, she'd feel like an intruder in Queenie's old house in Bow – and she certainly didn't want to have to stick days of Lara's company, however well-meaning she might be. What, and endure the third degree? The inevitable questions? Was everything right between Max and her, were they sound? Wasn't the Surrey house fabulous? Wasn't Ruthie a lucky, lucky girl? No. Ruthie was not. And she didn't want to have to smile and lie about it, so the hotel was good. Anonymous.

'I'll have to tell him where you are, though,' said Dave, frowning.

Pure self-interest, much like her mother's. Dave was scared Max would fire him – or worse. And Mum? She didn't want the steady flow of money from Max to ever stop. She – like Ruthie – was quickly getting used to a better standard of living and she didn't want that to ever change.

'Fine,' Ruthie told Dave. 'Tell him I'm staying in a hotel. Not with Lara. Not at Queenie's. Not with Mum. That suit?'

So, she stayed in a hotel – a good one – and she even quite enjoyed shopping in Bond Street and all around St James's with Lara, who laughed outright when Ruthie saw the price label on a cashmere cardigan and yelped: 'How much? Gawd, they should be wearing masks, these people.'

'Get used to it,' Lara advised Ruthie. 'Max will want to show you off in nice things. And darling, while I'm thinking of it – don't lose any more weight. Thin is good. Didn't the Duchess of Windsor say that? That a woman could never be too rich or too thin? But there's a limit, you know. You're looking drained.' Then she laughed her bright chiming laugh, nodded understandingly and added: 'Oh, he's wearing you out I suppose? These men when they're first married! Tell him to let you rest sometimes, darling. Really, you must.'

Ruthie hadn't been eating much at all and it was beginning to show. Misery always made food repulsive to her, and she had been miserable ever since her wedding day, picking at meals, enjoying nothing very much at all, although Miss Arnott saw to it that her and Max always had the very best – wild smoked salmon, turbot, Aberdeen Angus fillet steaks, foie gras, Dover sole, omelettes sprinkled with shavings of costly black truffle; everything the very best of the best.

Lara took her to places she had never been before, never been able to even look at, much less afford. Ruthie was measured, primped, petted, served champagne and sent on her way kitted out in silk bras and knickers that flattered and didn't have the scratchy nylon feel of her old, tired grey over-washed undergarments.

'Max will love those,' Lara assured her.

Ruthie didn't comment. Max would likely never even see them and thank God for that. She was still angry at him. She'd been quiet and accepting all her life, and was this why he had felt it was okay to betray her with her own sister? And *her*. If Ruthie was still fuming at Max, what about her, what about Annie? That cowing *bitch*. What had she ever done to her, to deserve such treatment – except love her and support her and protect her when she was a kid?

Ruthie told herself often that she was *glad* Annie had been forced out of home, made to find lodgings with their dirty Aunt Celia. She thought of Annie when she lay in bed alone at night, thought of what she might be going through at the Limehouse place, among women like that. *Prostitutes*. And yes, Ruthie told herself she was *pleased*. Yes, delighted, to think of Annie being forced to join in with all the depravity that must surely be going on all around her. Good. That was all she deserved.

20

Lara sorted Ruthie out with stylish two-piece suits, gorgeous evening dresses, Italian shoes, and she began to see the remarkable difference there was – a yawning chasm, in fact – between cheap clothes and expensive ones. There was no warmth in cheap clothing, but in fine wool, in pure cashmere, in the best silks and the most exquisite laces, there was both cosiness and comfort.

'If I can be of any more help, you know where I am,' said Lara, and kissed her cheek and left her in the gilded reception area of the hotel in which she was currently staying. Watching her go, Ruthie wondered vaguely if Max might be knocking off the very obliging Lara. Maybe his fling with Annie was over? But surely he wouldn't be so foolish as to start anything with yet another woman who was too close to home? Lara was the wife of one of Max's closest business associates, surely he'd learned his lesson when he'd bedded Annie?

Or . . . had he?

Once the doubts got into Ruthie's mind, they were hard to shift. Was there a chance, any chance at all, that it was still going on, this thing with Max and Annie? Ruthie thought of Max's friends sitting around the dinner table at the Surrey place, laughing and joking, and all the wives, smiling, whispering between themselves and now she wondered – were they laughing at her behind her back, were they thinking 'oh poor Ruthie, it's still going on isn't it, Max and that sister, the wild one, the beauty. Well, so long as he's discreet about it, I don't suppose his wife will worry too much . . .'

Once the notion was there, the agonising feeling that it might still be happening with him and her tormented Ruthie. Annie was living in a whorehouse, she was a whore, all he had to do was *go* there . . .

But then – Aunt Celia's place was on Delaney territory.

No. Max wouldn't go there, would he.

Would he?

Ruthie began to feel feverish as she thought of it all.

It wasn't likely that Max would visit Annie in a Delaney stronghold – although with Max you could never be too sure – but he could see Annie elsewhere, couldn't he. In Bow at Queenie's old place, or in other parts of Limehouse or even up West. In the clubs, what about that? The Blue Parrot, the Shalimar, the Palermo Lounge . . .

There were flats over those clubs. Places for clandestine meetings among Max's gang, places where Max could meet up with women. Or with one woman in particular. With Annie.

The idea was troubling. Sometimes Ruthie had Eddie for company, but at others – far too many – he was out on the town with his boyfriends and on those occasions she would lie sleepless in bed alone at night, the wind whistling around the eaves of the big Surrey house, and her mind would churn. At those times she could almost *see* them in bed, coiling together like snakes, Max bronzed, black-haired, so muscular; Annie so pale. It would be so beautiful a contrast, between her skin and his.

She didn't want to be taken for a fool. She couldn't bear that. She hadn't known about them until the wedding day when Annie had told her about it, but how long had it been going on *before* that day? And was it still going on, was that possible?

Yes. She knew the answer to that.

Yes.

It was.

21

'Let's go to the Shalimar,' she said to Eddie one evening. 'Heinz is on.'

Eddie's eyes widened. *Is* he by God. Then darling I am *there*. Such a beautiful boy.'

So they set off together for the evening and were treated like visiting royalty inside the club, ushered past the waiting crowds outside, shown to the very best table by the stage. Champagne was opened for them and poured by one of the smiling hostesses.

When Heinz came onstage and started on his big number 'Just Like Eddie', Ruthie crept off to the cloakroom and embraced her old pals there, the hat-check girls she'd once worked with. One of them, Brenda, she had always been especially friendly with. Brenda hugged her with obvious delight.

'Ruthie! What you back here for then? You slumming it, girl?'

Ruthie giggled. What she had been hoping – and fearing – was that tonight Max would be in, and not alone. He would have Annie with him, she suspected. That was the whole purpose of this excursion, to catch them together . . .

And do what?

She didn't know. But she hugged Brenda back and said lightly: 'You seen Max this evening?'

Brenda shook her head. 'He was in yesterday.'

'What, with Jonjo?'

'Nah, on his own, I think. But I didn't take his coat, that would have been Sally.'

'Does he come in here much these days?'

'No. Not really.' Brenda's expression had changed to one of wariness. 'Why? No problem is there? I'd have thought you'd know exactly where he is most of the time – *Mrs Carter*.' And then she said: 'Look, he's a very busy man, Ruthie. Is he neglecting you, that it?'

'No, I just . . . I'm down in Guildford a lot of the time, I thought I'd catch up with him in here tonight, surprise him, you know.'

'Hey!' It was Eddie, appearing at her elbow. 'What's happening, angel?' He hugged her. 'Hiya Bren. You all right there darling?'

'I'm fine Eddie. They've been playing your song!'

'I know! Come on Ruthie, Heinz is *ace*.'

He dragged Ruthie back into the main body of the club. They sat down, drank champagne, watched the rest of the show. Eddie loved it.

Ruthie really couldn't concentrate on any of it.

22

One day, Ruthie had another talk with Eddie, discreetly of course, skirting around the fact that she was probing for information about her own sister. And she checked back in with Sally at the Shalimar, since it was her who'd taken Max's coat on the night before she'd visited with Eddie to see Heinz.

'He was with a woman, I think,' said Sally.

'Did you know her?' Ruthie queried.

'No. 'Course not. We get hundreds of people going through here of a night, I don't take much notice. They're punters, or guests. That's all.'

So, no help there.

'Do you think Max has affairs?' she asked Eddie.

'What a question!' Eddie looked at her in astonishment. 'Why would he do that, darling?'

'I don't know. Maybe that type of man always does. Always will. What do you think?'

'I think you're crazy,' said Eddie with a grin. 'Come on, let's get you out of this silly mood. Let's go raid the shops.'

But for her it was far from okay. Once, she felt she had almost loved Max – whatever love was – but now all she felt was anger. She was Ruthie the good girl, the tolerant, quiet one. She sat at his dinner table when he 'entertained', she smiled, she played the serene hostess.

She endured every anguished day but she knew she had been duped, deceived, made a fool of.

And she thanked God – the God that she no longer believed in because she was not the good little Sunday schoolgirl anymore, she had been betrayed and she knew better – she thanked God that Max never even tried to touch her now.

Still – if he wasn't getting sex from her, then who? Someone, surely. She had discounted Lara – she just didn't seem like Max's 'type' – but she found herself watching him with the other women who came to the house. He was polite and attentive to them. That was all. But . . . what about when he came across Annie? *Did* he come across Annie? Did he at any time seek her out? Did she go to his clubs? If Ruthie had still had her job checking in customers' coats, she would know, she would see. But of course all that was the past. She was a married lady now; and married women didn't work.

So maybe it *was* still going on.

Maybe everyone was laughing at her.

Max and Annie, meeting in secret, falling into bed, laughing, crowing with delight because they'd fooled her. They'd got away with it. Pulled the wool over her docile, stupid eyes.

She spent many evenings alone in the Surrey drawing room, sipping on pale sweet sherry and when finally she felt numb enough, tired enough, she would stagger up the stairs and try to sleep. But usually instead she lay there churning and sweating into the small hours of the night. She wanted to see Annie brought low; she wanted to see that she was suffering, that she was a fallen woman, a whore just like all those whores she was surrounded by at Aunt Celia's place.

And Ruthie knew that she was going to have to follow this mad, tormenting thread until it broke – or she did.

Somehow, she was going to have to spy on them. On Annie. And Max.

23

Ruthie was walking through Harrods when she saw her sister for the first time since the wedding. There she was, suddenly. Annie. The unmissable, the gorgeous one. For a moment it was as if Ruthie had been punched in the gut. She stopped dead in the middle of the perfumery department and stared. People passed her, girls sprayed her with sweet smells, smiled, gave her the sales pitch, but she heard nothing. She just *looked*.

She had wanted Annie brought low.

She had wanted to see her suffering.

Hadn't she?

But that didn't seem to be the case. Annie looked better than ever. Still beautiful, dark-haired, pale skinned, arresting to look at. Annie, Ruthie's little sister. But somehow more polished, more elegant, than she had been before.

Ruthie recognised the woman with her as their Aunt Celia. Celia had aged well; she hadn't changed that much. Of course Mum had always hated Celia because she was Dad's sister, and by association Celia was the devil incarnate. Just as Mum had despised Annie because she had the same darkly handsome well-sculpted looks as Dad, so she had also stored up a particular river of poison for Celia.

'She's a tart,' Connie had often declared, if Celia's name got mentioned.

But Ruthie had never disliked Aunt Celia with her bright brown button eyes and the bright slick of lipstick on her smiling mouth. She'd always slipped her little nieces a sixpence if she could – which was generous in the extreme – but her visits had been rare because Mum made it clear she wasn't welcome, and soon they'd stopped altogether.

Annie was in a black coat, Celia in a white one. They looked fabulous and they were with a handsome couple, all of them talking and smiling.

Ruthie's attention was so taken with this new grown-up Annie that at first she barely registered the couple that her and Aunt Celia were so engaged with, but they were arresting too; red-haired, green-eyed, white-skinned; the woman dazzling, the man film-star handsome and holding a tiny, scruffy-looking dog barely concealed beneath his jacket. Some paces behind the group stood a burly man, his eyes scanning the crowds. His eyes stopped moving and fastened on Ruthie when he saw her staring, transfixed. Ruthie quickly moved on, walking fast, seeing nothing.

Annie and Aunt Celia were chatting to the Delaneys. The watchful minder confirmed it. These two stunners were part of the Irish clan who ran the Battersea area. The red-haired woman would be Orla. And the Robert Redford lookalike was . . . well, who? He wasn't Patrick. She'd seen Patrick around town. Patrick was a bruiser of a man, built like a bull not an athlete. This wasn't Redmond, either, Orla's twin. She'd seen Redmond about town too. He was tall, thin, elegant. This wasn't him.

Who, then? Who was this man?

When Ruthie was a good distance away she paused, looked back; but they were gone. She glanced down at her hands and found they were shaking. Annie hadn't looked like someone under duress, she didn't look to be suffering at all. She looked like she was thriving and that handsome man with the reddish blond hair had clearly been taking a very keen interest in her.

Damn it!

Ruthie should have known that Annie would flourish wherever she was set down. She was the survivor and Ruthie was the fool, the poor patsy she'd deceived. But . . . Celia's whorehouse was on the Delaneys' manor. So was Celia offering her niece, her own niece, up for the delectation of that striking unknown Delaney man?

It could be. Ruthie felt a pang of something almost like sorrow but she squashed it quickly.

No! She would not, could not, feel sorry for her.

If Annie was being used, then she deserved it.

Ruthie walked on.

Somewhere, she was going to get a drink, and then she would think what her next move should be.

24

Much to Ruthie's delight, Eddie sometimes stayed longer at the Guildford house.

'I love you, Eddie,' she told him. He was so nice, such great fun.

'That's Max you're supposed to say that to,' he grinned at her.

Ruthie was sad that Eddie was so often away in London, keeping busy in dodgy bars. Eddie was of course always welcome at Guildford – but her cousin Kath was making a nuisance of herself, often showing up uninvited, basking in Ruthie's reflected glory as Mrs Max Carter. Basking too in the fact that her and Jimmy had now set a date for the wedding. Jimmy Bond was one of Max's most trusted lieutenants and clearly Kath felt buoyed up and ready to 'mix with the nobs' – Ruthie and Max – given her newly elevated status as his fiancée. Ruthie sat and chatted to Kath whenever she came down, glad of the company even though she'd never really liked her very much.

It was during one of these visits from Kath that, running out of small talk, Ruthie said: 'I saw Annie a while back. In Harrods.'

'Ah, did you?' A pause, then Kath said: ''Course, she always did fancy him – Max, I mean. She must have been pretty cut up when you got him up the aisle.'

Ruthie sat there for a moment in total silence: frozen. Amazed.

'What do you mean, fancied . . .?'

Kath, her smile fixed on her face in surprise, stared at Ruthie and then said: 'You must have known. Didn't you? She's been eyeing him up for years. We used to stand in the shop doorway at Ted's place and watch him go past in that big car of his, sitting in the back like he was royalty. Annie would go berserk every time we saw him. Surely you must have known . . .?'

Ruthie hadn't known. Hadn't had a bloody clue, not until Annie had stood there in her peach bridesmaid's dress on Ruthie's wedding day – and callously broken her heart.

'When you say . . .?' The words almost choked Ruthie. She took a drink and went on: 'You mean, she'd been after him for years? That's what you're saying?'

Kath sat back, her smile fading as she saw the expression on Ruthie's face. 'I thought you must have known about it. You were close, weren't you, the two of you? And it's been puzzling me and Mum too, the way Aunt Connie kicked Annie out of the house with no explanation. Auntie usually tells my mum everything, but she wouldn't speak about it. Was that something about Max then? Is that why she was booted out the door?'

'Kath, I've got a headache, would you mind . . .?' Ruthie got shakily to her feet, indicating the door. She wanted Kath gone. She wanted to think about this. To try to make sense of it. So it was possible that her sister had been having a full-on affair with Max for a long time. Annie had never mentioned the fact that she wanted Max Carter. Ruthie thought they'd discussed everything, but Annie had kept that from her while Ruthie had planned the wedding, announced the engagement to Max, ordered invitations, done dress fittings, organised the wedding cake and the reception. All throughout, Annie had said *nothing*. Not a bloody word. Not until that cruel moment outside the church when she told Ruthie she was getting a cast-off of hers. Which was plain enough. Even an idiot like Ruthie could see what *that* meant.

They'd been at it before the wedding. Were they still at it now?

She felt fury boil through her like a molten river.

Ruthie saw Kath out of the door and then she went back into the drawing room of this grand awful echoing empty bloody house, and she picked up the bottle of sherry with trembling hands and caught her reflection in the mirror over the fireplace.

She stood there, staring at this thin mouse-blonde woman, her face beautifully made up. But she was skinny, the flesh almost shrunken onto her bones. She stared at the woman's immaculate expensive clothes and saw they were hanging on her ribs like tent poles draped on canvas. This was her, Ruthie Carter. Mrs Max Carter. She looked miserable and she was standing there holding a bottle, about to pour it.

And why not?

What did she have, really? What *was* she, really?

With a roar of utter despair she raised her arm and threw the bottle at the mirror. It shattered instantly, sending shards of mirror and bottle and trickles of booze raining down, staining the rug.

Presently, Miss Arnott, alerted by the noise, knocked at the drawing-room door and opened it, looked tentatively inside. She saw the damage Ruthie had inflicted. Her eyes went wide as she looked at the destroyed remnants of the mirror, then at her employer's wife.

'Mrs Carter? Everything all right?'

Clearly it wasn't. But Ruthie fixed a bright brittle smile on her face and said: 'Yes! Just had a little accident.'

Miss Arnott stood there in silence for a moment. Then she said: 'I'll clear that up, shall I?'

'Thank you,' said Ruthie, and moving quickly she swept past her, across the hall and up the stairs to the master bedroom Max never shared with his own wife.

Of course not.

Because – after all – he'd rather be sharing it with *Annie*.

25

Life as a married woman went on. Life was dinner parties, drink, lunches in town with Mum, more drink, shopping – endless bloody shopping for stuff she neither needed nor wanted. But all throughout there was a steady thread of torment. Ruthie kept seeing Annie's face, glowing with health and self-confidence, on that day in Harrods.

She dreamed of Annie's face as it had been at other times, too, throughout their shared lives; Ruthie picking her up when she'd fallen over as a tiny girl, wiping her tears away. Big sis, that was Ruthie. Looking after the little one, shielding her from Connie's rages, comforting her when she was ill. They'd even attended Sunday School together, once upon a time.

Now, Annie had done this to her. Robbed her of any chance of happiness. Robbed her of any purpose in life. Another dinner party, then. It almost looked respectable, like a board of directors and their sleek, well-groomed wives. But these people were criminals, law breakers. She was sitting at the base of the table, Max at its head. Miss Arnott and serving staff were fussing around, pouring wine.

People were chatting, laughing, saying how good the food was, these people who worked with and for Max. Kath and her nasty-eyed hoodlum fiancé Jimmy Bond were there. Eddie was there with a new boyfriend, a tall streak of piss with big glasses like Michael Caine wore, which gave him the air of a bruiser and an intellectual, all at the same time. And Jonjo was there too, with another of those interchangeable blondes. The blonde wore a dress that was cut low to show off the goods, everything out in the shop window, with her hair swept up in fashionable bouffant and plenty of jewellery on display to complete the picture.

And Max?

He didn't have a woman here at the dining table with him – only Ruthie, and she didn't count. Tonight, he would say goodnight to her like she was his maiden aunt and he would go into his dressing room and sleep there. She would sleep alone in the master bedroom. This was the pattern their marriage had fallen into, ever since the wedding night. Separate bedrooms. Icy politeness. A veneer of respectability. A pretence that all was well.

Well, what about Max? she wondered, watching him.

Eddie had his Michael Caine lookalike, Jonjo his blondes. But what about Max? There was no woman seated here tonight who would really appeal to him, Ruthie could see that. She knew that his true sexual leanings were toward dark-eyed brunettes – like Annie.

Max was not demanding sex from Ruthie, he was not even suggesting it, and he had every right to expect that she would do her wifely duty by him. So he *had* to be getting his jollies from someone else. Max had an aura of intense sexuality about him. He prowled through the streets of London like the predator he truly was. He wouldn't be going without. So . . . who?

Maybe he visited upmarket prostitutes? There were plenty of them to be had around Mayfair, servicing MPs and the like. Ruthie knew that. She wasn't a complete innocent.

When dinner was over, Ruthie called Kath to one side. She felt light-headed from all the wine, one to suit every course. And no rubbish. Of course not. Max had a cellar stocked to the rafters with the finest, the best.

Kath put out a hand, held Ruthie's arm. Steadied her when she knocked against a chair. Ruthie felt more than saw Max shoot her a look from across the room.

'You all right?' Kath asked.

Ruthie ignored that. All right? No, she wasn't. She'd heard a whisper at the table, caught a laughing glance in her direction.

Goody-Two-Shoes . . .

'Kath, do you really not know why Mum kicked Annie out of the house?'

Kath looked at her uneasily. 'No. I don't.'

'You don't?' Ruthie smiled at her ignorance. 'Well I'll tell you. She kicked Annie out because she'd been to bed with Max.'

Kath said nothing. Her eyes were like saucers, astonished, fixed to Ruthie's face.

'Well?' asked Ruthie.

'Shit! I don't know what to say.' Kath looked shocked and embarrassed. Like she didn't want to hear this. That Ruthie shouldn't be inflicting this knowledge on her.

'It's the truth,' Ruthie said. 'Annie told me at the wedding, just before we went into the church.'

'Gawd.' Kath was looking at the floor, the walls – everywhere but at Ruthie's face. 'I didn't know that. Didn't hear it. Bloody bells were clanging away. She *said* that?'

'She did. What do you think of that?' Ruthie demanded. She was a little drunk.

'I . . . I knew she liked him. That's all. But I didn't—'

'Here's what I want you to do, Kath,' Ruthie cut across her.

'What?' Kath's eyes flew to Ruthie's face.

'I want to know if it's still going on,' Ruthie said, leaning in close, clutching at Kath's arm. 'I want you to find out for me. All right?'

'No, I . . .' Kath tugged at her arm, but Ruthie held on. 'You're hurting me,' she whined.

'I'll do worse than that if you don't do this for me,' Ruthie hissed at her. She was Miss Goody-Two-Shoes, was she? She'd show them what she was really made of. She'd show the whole fucking world.

'Do what?' Kath was pale, her eyes afraid.

'You find out what's going on between the pair of them. And if you don't, I'll tell Max that Jimmy is screwing him over – fiddling the milk run or undercutting him on payouts, the tight git, which wouldn't surprise me anyway so I bet it wouldn't surprise Max either – and then where will you be, eh, Kath? Up shit creek without a fucking paddle, that's where. That's all his prospects, gone. Max might not want me, he might want Annie instead, but nobody gets to mess with Max Carter's property. Money or women, what's his is his.'

26

So it began. Kath was to be her insider, her spy. It tormented Ruthie to know what was going on at Aunt Celia's whorehouse, how Annie was thriving there, actually doing well in the most unlikely of places – but torment or not, she still had to know every detail.

'One of the tarts there, I got her onside,' Kath told Ruthie.

Kath was behaving differently toward Ruthie these days. She wasn't her giggling 'mate' anymore. She was diffident, almost nervous. Ruthie was Max Carter's wife, after all. Eight months into married life, and her and Max were like polite strangers. But married was married. If Ruthie turned on Kath, turned on her precious Jimmy, there would be trouble and Kath knew it.

'Oh? Who is this tart?' Ruthie asked.

An insider would be useful. More useful than Kath, who could only ever give her the outside track on the happenings there.

'Her name's Ellie.' Kath's face crumpled in disgust. 'She's horrible. A real turncoat. When I approached her, asked her if she'd keep an eye on things and report back to me, she nearly bit my arm off. She was straight on the money.'

'I'll pay you a tenner every time you give me new information from her,' said Ruthie.

'A tenner?' It was a fortune to Kath, but she thought she could do better.

Ruthie was like a cat on a hot tin roof: edgy, needing information, *desperate* for it. So why not cash in? 'I have to pay Ellie a fiver, that don't leave me much. Oh come on Ruthie – you *know* Jimmy's tight as a duck's arse. Help me out. We're cousins after all.'

'Fifteen then – but that's it.'

'Great,' said Kath, beaming.

'Good,' Ruthie said, and sent Kath on her way.

'I don't like your cousin,' said Eddie as Ruthie waved her off at the door.

'Oh? Why not?'

'I dunno. She seems sly. Don't you think she's sly?'

Ruthie had to agree to that. 'Yeah. But she's family, you know how it is.'

Eddie was pulling on a tan suede Stetson hat, getting it at just the right rakish angle, straightening his floral tie.

'Going out then?' Ruthie asked, and he kissed her cheek, blew a raspberry on her neck.

Eddie always made her laugh, and laughter in this house was in very short supply. She loved their times together, particularly when they went up West and splurged on nonsense stuff or high-end designer gear. They had fun together. She had almost forgotten what fun was like, until Eddie. He was the little brother she had never had.

'I certainly am,' he said, and was off to the waiting taxi. He didn't have a minder, not like Ruthie, not like Max and Jonjo. Max had insisted, of course, but gay-friendly little Eddie could dig his heels in with the best of them. He refused to have one.

'What would he do, this "minder"?' he'd demanded of Max when the subject was broached, not for the first time. 'I'll tell you. He'd sneer at my tastes, call me a poofter behind my back. He would, Max. You know it. And I don't want that in my life. I get grief enough, God knows.'

So Max let it go.

Ruthie spent a lot of days and nights alone at the Guildford house. Eddie was busy with boyfriends, Miss Arnott was stone-cold, Dave was no company at all. Max didn't come home very much, and when he did he would closet himself away from her. If Ruthie said she was bored, he said: 'Redecorate the place then. Do what you like with it.'

She had scant interest in the house, but maybe a project would cheer her up. So she called in interior designers, sorted through swatches of bright silks and floral damasks, and wondered when Eddie would be coming home to give her advice on all this. He had more of an eye for colour and fabric than she would ever have. Did purple really go with orange?

'It does,' the female decorator told her with a superior air. 'It's across the spectrum wheel, you see.'

What would Ruthie know about spectrum wheels?

She sent the woman away and decided against further action until Eddie returned and could advise. She drank a little too much and awoke on the sofa in the early hours of the morning, having passed out there the night before. Miss Arnott was disinterested, having gone out to her little bungalow out in the grounds. Ruthie was so, so alone. God knew where Max was or what he was doing. Her sister, probably.

Then one day Kath phoned her.

'What is it? Something happening?' she asked. What Ruthie was waiting to hear – dreading it but expecting it – was that the thing with Max and Annie was still going on. Ruthie didn't love him – how could she? – but it would be painful to hear, anyway. Kath was silent at the other end of the phone. 'Kath? What's going on?'

'I thought I'd better call. Connie told Mum and she's just told me . . .'

'What? Told you what?' This was it. What Ruthie had suspected. Annie and Max were back on.

'About Eddie.'

'What?' Ruthie was blindsided. Eddie? It was *Annie* she wanted to hear about. 'What do you mean, Eddie?'

'Oh God, it's awful . . .'

'What?'

'I had to phone you before Max got back down there . . .'

'Kath, you're not making any sense. What's all this got to do with Eddie?'

'There was an . . . . well, an incident. In your Aunt Celia's knocking shop. Eddie was there. He shouldn't have been there, but he was.'

Ruthie stared at the phone. 'But that's a Delaney place. What was Eddie doing?'

'I phoned Ellie to get some dirt on Annie and she was bloody nigh hysterical. She said someone had attacked Eddie Carter; Deaf Derek had taken him there to see one of Celia's male tarts, Darren, just for a lark if you can believe it, and then some big masked bastard burst in and she said there was blood all over the place.' Kath paused, drew in a trembling breath. 'She said it's all gone tits up. Madam Celia's left, run for the hills, Christ knows where she's gone.'

Ruthie was shocked. And Max was coming down here why? He rarely did, these days, and if Eddie had been injured in London as Kath claimed . . .

She felt shaky all of a sudden. She reached for a chair and quickly sat down, thinking of Eddie and his flamboyant charm, his big rakish grin.

'Is Eddie in hospital then?'

'He has been. But Max has moved him out of there and he's bringing him down to your place. He's been shouting and bellowing at the doctors, he's like a man possessed, Jimmy says. I'm just letting you know that he's coming. I thought I should warn you.'

'It's bad then?'

Kath's voice was tearful.

'It's bad,' she told her. 'Oh Ruthie, it's really bad.'

27

Max arrived late that same day with both his brothers, in the dark and with a private ambulance. Three nurses came too, and a plain-suited doctor in a fancy car. The doctor looked pale and terrified. Several bulky male orderlies bustled inside the house and Miss Arnott supervised them as they stretchered Eddie up the stairs and into his bedroom. The doctor and the nurses followed.

Ruthie stood aside and watched all this happen around her. Jonjo went into the kitchen, Max disappeared into the drawing room. She stood there in the hall, in the aftermath of this invasion, with the cold air blowing in. Gently, she closed the front door, her whole brain focused with disbelief and horror on what she'd just seen – Eddie, but not as she'd ever known him. Eddie sheet-white and skinny, sweating, bruised, his eyes closed; looking more like a corpse than a living man.

Ruthie wondered if she was about to be sick.

Couldn't Max have phoned ahead, let her at least know what to expect? She wasn't supposed to know about Eddie's 'accident' at the Delaney whorehouse. She walked into the drawing room and closed the door behind her and leaned against it and said: 'What's going on? What's happened to Eddie?'

Max was standing in front of the dying embers of the fire, still in his coat. For a moment Ruthie thought he hadn't heard, then he slowly turned and she saw – to her utter shock – that there were tears, actual tears, in his eyes. Her bad, fearful husband could feel pain too, she realised. She hadn't really known that, until now.

'Max! What the hell's happened?' she gasped out, hurrying toward him.

'There's nothing the doctors can do, not anymore,' said Max. 'And I didn't want him in that bloody hospital. So I brought him home.'

And then he told Ruthie all about it. About the attack at the Delaney whorehouse. Someone – probably one of the Delaneys – had 'slit' Eddie so badly that he couldn't recover.

'God, I'm sorry,' she told Max. Eddie was like her own little brother, too. She could understand Max's pain. She felt it, shared it instinctively. After a moment's hesitation she put her arms around him and hugged him, and she cried for Eddie, the Eddie she had come to know so well and to love, with his manic smile, his mad arm-waving, his head-tossing exuberance.

Presently, Max pushed her back, away from him. His eyes were dry and they were fastened on her face.

'You poor cow,' he said. 'You didn't sign up for any of this shit, did you.'

Ruthie realised that this was as close to an apology as she was ever likely to get from him. And suddenly she could see herself, humiliatingly, through his eyes. She was a mess. Her hip bones stuck out and her tits were gone so that no designer gear, however costly, looked good on her. She had never been a looker but now, with the stress and misery of the past months, what few looks she'd had were quickly vanishing.

I must be repulsive to him.

And she supposed that was good, really. Because even if he'd tried to make love to her, she knew that she would only have flinched away from him, reacted like he was a filthy, disgusting rapist. No man would want a wife like that. All her efforts to turn the tide in their relationship had failed. He wasn't interested. Didn't want her.

Ruthie took a breath, composed herself and asked the question. 'What happened?'

'That stupid fucker Derek took him into one of the Delaney places. The one where your aunt's the madam. In Limehouse. Said there was a boy there he'd fancy.'

'And this boy hurt him?'

'No. Not him. It was Pat Delaney, I reckon. Burst in on the pair of them and . . . Max paused, swallowed. 'He stabbed Eddie. Did him a lot of damage. He won't recover. The doctors, they tried everything, but then they said the kindest thing would be to bring him home, let him die in peace.'

Now Ruthie really did feel sick. Bile surged up into her throat.

Please no. Not Eddie.

'There's no hope at all?' she asked.

'None,' he said.

'What can I do to help?' she asked him.

28

As it happened, her contribution to the whole rotten, horrifying situation was small. The nurses sneered at all Ruthie's efforts, said it was 'best to leave it to the professionals'. And slowly she came to know what had been done to Eddie, how bad it was, how awful. One of the Delaneys had cut him up the rear end, sliced him open. And in so doing, they had poisoned his system, condemned him to a slow painful death.

For hours she sat by Eddie's bed and when he was awake and lucid – which wasn't often – she chatted to him about the life he loved. He lay on his side and they talked about Carnaby Street and all his friends and she saw to it that he had anything he wanted, anything that might serve to distract him from the fact that he was doomed.

'It wasn't Derek's fault,' he told her once, weakly. 'Don't let Max do him over. It was my own fault. I ought to have had more sense than to go there.'

Ruthie wondered if Eddie had seen Annie while he'd been at Aunt Celia's place, but she couldn't ask, much as she wanted to. The words choked her. As for Deaf Derek, if he hadn't already got a pasting off Max or – worse – Jonjo, Ruthie would be very much surprised. Derek had led Eddie into harm's way, and she couldn't see Max forgiving that.

'They reckon the madam's disappeared,' Eddie told her.

'If she knows what's good for her, she'll stay that way,' Ruthie told him.

'Your auntie, isn't she? Maybe she didn't disappear on her own accord.'

'What, you think Max . . .?'

'Who knows? Who knows what he's capable of, eh?' Eddie's eyes were closing. She dabbed at his sweating brow with a cool damp cloth. His colour was awful; yellowish. She'd got used to the stench in here, the smell of sickness, of the infection that was now rampaging, unstoppable, through his wasting body. 'That's nice. Thanks, Ruthie. What a lovely girl you are. You keep the hats, darling, they're yours.'

'No. They're yours. When you're better—'

'Oh shut up, Ruthie, there's a good girl. I'm not going to get better.'

'Oh Eddie . . .' She mustn't cry in front of him. She *mustn't*.

But then he was gone again, vanishing into merciful sleep. They were giving him morphine for the pain, a lot of it, and it made him drift off like this, time and again. She stood up, moved away from the bed and hoped that he would die soon. This was no life at all. This was torture.

The nurse bustled in then. 'I'll change the dressings. If you can . . .?' She indicated that Ruthie should leave the room, and she was glad to go.

She didn't want to see any more.

She couldn't bear to.

29

That was the last time Eddie spoke to Ruthie. That same day she had a stupid row with Max over his mum Queenie's little annexe. Rootless and tormented by what was happening to Eddie, she suggested maybe letting Mum come down to keep her company, do the annexe up so that Connie could move in there. Max hit the roof. Said to leave the damned place alone. And something in Ruthie just snapped and they stood there, for the first time in their dull useless marriage getting enraged, flinging insults at each other, actually *feeling* something, until one of the nurses interrupted them, telling them they should summon the doctor, quickly.

Ruthie didn't go upstairs. She wanted to – she knew this was goodbye. But she wasn't brave like Max. When it came to it, she couldn't face it and so she skulked downstairs. She did phone for the doctor – and the bastard said he was in the middle of a dinner party. At that point, she snapped again – twice in one day, a record for her! – and told him to get his scrawny arse here, pronto, or Max would come and drag him out of his house by the neck and then he would be damned sorry.

Ruthie could have gone upstairs after she'd made the call, but she was afraid. She could hear Max shouting at the nurses and she just knew that this was it; the thing they had been dreading, the coming of death with his skull features, his black cloak, his scythe. Death was up there right now, stalking around Eddie's bedroom, ready to deal the final blow – and she just couldn't face it.

A quarter of an hour later, the doctor arrived and Max came into the drawing room where she was sitting, tense as an overstrung bow. He stood there, staring at the fire.

'Is he . . .?' she asked, praying that Eddie was gone, released at last.

'Yeah,' said Max. 'He's dead.'

30

The funeral was hellish. Ruthie would never forget standing, Saul's 'Dead March' thrumming deafeningly out of the organ, in the church. It was the same East End church where Queenie had been buried and it was packed with mourners, all eager to show their respect for the Carter family.

Ruthie feared that Annie would be there. She kidded herself of course that Annie wouldn't have the sheer effrontery to show up, but then, this was Annie.

If Ruthie actually had to *see* her, she didn't know what she would do.

No. Annie wouldn't show up.

She ought to be hiding her face in shame. The tart.

All the same, Ruthie found herself looking for her sister in the church. She looked all around, but she couldn't see her. Then Ruthie stared blindly at Eddie's casket, mounded with flowers in warm tones of pink and orange and peach, while the vicar droned on about eternal life. By the time the ceremony was over, Ruthie was convinced – and also mightily relieved – that Annie wasn't in attendance.

Then the mourners proceeded outside to cluster around the freshly dug grave.

And – at last – shockingly – *there she was*.

Ruthie stared at Annie and could hardly breathe, so great was the sheer amazement at her sister's audacity, showing up here when she ought to have been somewhere, *anywhere* else, hidden, disgraced.

And oh God – Annie looked so grown up. No more wild dark bouffant hair, no more silk shirts and daring miniskirts high enough to show your rent book. Today Annie's hair was tucked up in a neat chignon and she was wearing a black pillbox hat, a neat black skirt suit – it was a Chanel rip-off; Ruthie was married to a wealthy man, she could spot a knock-off at a thousand paces – with cream piping and gold buttons, black court shoes, black stockings. She carried a square black handbag. She looked elegant, composed – serene.

And Ruthie? She knew that, by contrast, she looked a mess. And as Annie's eyes flicked over to Ruthie she could see herself, just as Annie was seeing her: the expensive and genuine designer suit Ruthie wore, hanging off her skinny frame, her undernourished body transforming the thing from a costly work of art to a worthless rag. Ruthie was too thin, her face too miserable.

Christ, did Max see Annie there?

Ruthie knew he did. Of *course* he did.

Ruthie looked sideways, at his face. And there it was. The proof. He was staring at Annie. Ruthie saw Annie return his gaze for a long, long moment; and then she looked away.

Ruthie felt her guts convulse with pain. Whatever had been between them, it was still there. She could feel it. And then all at once Annie was gone, climbing into a car out in the road and making her getaway.

All through the wake, through all the useless platitudes that were uttered, all through the drinks and the sandwiches and everything else, it stayed in Ruthie's mind.

That *look*. Max's eyes meeting Annie's.

It mocked her. Tormented her.

Then Kath came up and said: 'It's awful this. I'm sorry for your loss, Ruthie.'

Ruthie caught hold of Kath's arm. 'Never mind that. This "Ellie" you say you've got in that rotten house of whores . . .'

'Yeah, what?' Kath looked alarmed at her sudden intensity.

That look. *Oh Christ in heaven – that look!* It was as if Max and Annie had been in their own world for that moment. It was as if the small patch of earth between them had burst into flames and burned and scorched and blackened a fiery trail between them, such was the heat of it. Ruthie felt she would never forget that. Max had married the wrong woman – the safe one, the dull domestic that she so clearly was. Not the one he should have wed, Annie the leader, the firebrand, the one he wanted in bed. His mistake had been to stick to his – or maybe Queenie's? – original plan and marry Ruthie – not Annie.

'Do you think I should pay Ellie more?' Kath was asking, her eyes anxious as they rested on Ruthie's face. 'I can do that, if you want.'

'No. I don't. You just keep her looking out, reporting back. Okay?'

And Kath left Ruthie alone there, drinking and thinking dark thoughts. Trapped thoughts. Thoughts that were slowly turning toward revenge for all that Max and Annie had put her through.

31

Through Kath, Ruthie knew that everyone in London was talking about what had happened to Eddie Carter at the Delaney knocking shop, and everyone was wondering why his brother Max hadn't yet seen the place burned to the ground.

Everyone knew that Madam Celia had vanished.

'Gone on the run I expect,' Kath told Ruthie on one of her visits to the Guildford house. 'Getting out of Mr Carter's way while she still has legs to carry her. He's going to want someone to pay for this, and pay dear.'

'And what's to happen to the place without Celia there?'

'I told you. Max will flatten it.' Kath's eyes sparkled with excitement. 'And you'll never guess,' Kath went on.

'No. I won't. So hurry up and tell me.'

'She's sitting on a fucking time bomb the silly cow, but can you believe it? Annie's taken over. Astonishing, yeah? But it's true I swear. Ellie told me. Annie's put herself in charge, saying she won't have Celia coming back to a wash-out of a business – that's if she ever does come back, which I doubt. She'll stay away if she's got the tiniest bit of sense. As for Annie? Everyone knows she's on borrowed time, but there she is, playing madam in Celia's place, sprucing the place up, making changes.'

Ruthie was stunned. 'Like what? What changes?'

'Ellie says she's opening up the front room and putting on Friday "parties".' Kath's lip curled. 'You can imagine the stuff they get up to at them, can't you.'

But all Ruthie could think of was that she – along with everyone else – had expected Max to have already *destroyed* the knocking shop, which was right on Delaney turf. She had anticipated that, almost feared it, but he hadn't done it. And now she was reaching a conclusion that caused her pain. He hadn't flattened the place *because Annie was there.*

Ruthie remembered once again the look that had passed between Max and Annie in the churchyard, and she shivered.

'Annie's got the Delaney mob behind her, Ellie told me,' said Kath. 'Redmond's the new boss of the firm since Tory Delaney got done, and he's backing her with the finances.'

'Is he, by God?' Ruthie muttered.

'And she's pulling in a ton of money, by all accounts. And—'

'Christ, there can't be more,' Ruthie objected.

'But there is. She's getting pally with the other Delaney boy. Not Pat, he's a thug. And not Redmond, he's like a block of ice that one. No, the other one, the younger one who got all these high-toned ideas and went to study art in Paris. Kieron.'

The one that Ruthie had seen in Harrods, talking to Annie? Handsome as a Greek god with strawberry-blond hair and a face to launch way more than a thousand ships. Tall. Broad-shouldered. Gorgeous.

'Are you telling me she's going out with Kieron Delaney?' Ruthie snapped at Kath.

'Nah, not as such, no.'

'Kath!'

Kath laughed. 'Sorry. But your face.'

'Shut up, Kath. Tell me what's going on.'

'She's sitting for him. You know. Posing.'

'She's what?'

'As an artist's model.' Kath's eyes were dancing with delight. 'Nude, Ellie told me.'

For God's sake! Was there nothing her sister wouldn't sink to? Was there no depravity too low for her to get involved in? It killed Ruthie, all this. Annie was happy and thriving and – it was obvious – she was also somehow remaining under Max's protection while she stayed at the place where Eddie had met his death.

That jammy deceitful *bitch*!

Annie could fall in a ton of shit and emerge smelling of roses. That was her. Ruthie's sister, the rebel, the lucky one, the beautiful one, the one who life never spat at, never destroyed. Not like Ruthie, her dull as ditchwater Goody-Two-Shoes sister.

'Fuck off, Kath,' Ruthie told her cousin. 'Go on. Clear off!'

The smile dropped from Kath's face. 'I'm only telling you what's been going on. Which you asked me to do,' she protested. 'Which you're *paying* me to do. And I wanted to talk to you about that. Ellie's demanding more money and you can see she's got a point. It could be dangerous, all this. So if you can make it twenty . . .?'

Ruthie grabbed a cushion from the settee and lobbed it straight at Kath's head. It bounced harmlessly off but it was heavy and she staggered back a step.

'Well really—' Kath started.

'You'll get your bloody money. Now get out!' Ruthie screamed.

32

With Kath gone, Ruthie went straight upstairs and packed a bag. She couldn't stand this a moment longer. Sitting here isolated from life, miles from anywhere in the depths of the country while all of this shit was kicking off in London. Max had refused to let Mum come down and stay in Queenie's annexe, so Ruthie decided she would move back to the Smoke and stay up there with Mum instead. Get her own ear closer to the ground. Why not?

After all, what the fuck was keeping her *here*?

Might as well be in a nunnery, as here. Out of sight, out of mind. That was Ruthie. The forgotten bride. And now she was crippled by an intense sensation of jealousy, because she should have been the winner, the triumphant one – and it was pretty bloody clear that she was anything but. It was Annie who had triumphed. Annie had built a life for herself in – of all places – a house of whores. She had Redmond Delaney on her side, and Kieron Delaney panting over her, painting her in the nude of all damned things, and worst of all – this really, really stung but she knew it was true – Annie had Max who was *Ruthie's* husband, not hers, under her spell.

Well – no more.

Ruthie phoned through to Dave in his flat over the garage block and told him her plans.

'Does Mr Carter know about this?' he asked.

'No. Do I need his permission?' she snapped.

'No. Of course not. I'll have to tell him what we're doing, though.'

'Fine. Do that,' she said, and slapped the phone down. Much Max would care, anyway.

Ruthie phoned through to Miss Arnott in her bungalow in the grounds, telling her the news. Then she looked around the grand hallway of this place she hated, this huge wood-panelled prison, and opened the front door. Dave had brought the car round. He grabbed her bags, put them in the boot, and Ruthie was away. Free.

33

Mum was glad to have her back, of course. But the home where she'd grown up looked so tiny now. She saw it as it truly was – a pitiful little hovel in a long row of them, all identical, all scruffy and in need of a good scrub-up.

Ruthie had got used to living the high life but the inside of Connie's house was as shabby as the outside. Connie didn't have housemaids, laundry maids, housekeepers, cooks. Too feeble to work at her cleaning jobs anymore, she relied – like Ruthie – on Max's generosity to keep body and soul together. And her drinking hadn't improved. She had a bloated look, her eyes were red, her skin was a patchwork of angry-looking thread veins, her hair was dry as dust. Her clothes were un-ironed and food stains marked the front of her cardigan.

Ruthie went up to the room she had once shared with Annie to unpack. A spasm of panic gripped her then. What the hell was she doing, coming back here? But she couldn't have stayed in that damned place in the country, she just couldn't have done it.

Ruthie took a breath, tried to calm herself. Connie was downstairs, making tea. Up here, there were so many memories. She remembered it all so vividly. Her, quivering and giggling on a stack of Bibles at Sunday School. The little palm crucifix was still up there on the shelf, alongside the little notebooks into which they'd pasted images of Jesus, Mary, Joseph. So many memories here of her and Annie together, talking about Johnny Ray and Buddy Holly as they lay in their twin beds at night. Chattering happily until Connie yelled for them to get the Christ to sleep or she'd be in and knife the pair of them, them collapsing in giggles, reluctantly – at last – turning out the light, going to sleep.

Ruthie unpacked her belongings and went back downstairs.

Connie was at the table in the kitchen, waiting, the tea set out, biscuits and everything. She was pleased to see Ruthie. Possibly she had been lonely here with only Auntie Mo next door. She poured the tea and asked if Ruthie was all right, if Max was okay. Probing, testing. Was everything good in the marriage still? Was this going to impact her way of life? Or – worse – her vodka consumption?

'We're both fine,' said Ruthie.

'You've heard about that whore, your sister?' asked Mum.

'Kath told me.'

'Talk about the devil looking after his own,' sniffed Connie, lighting a fag and puffing out a screen of smoke.

'Can we talk about something else?' Ruthie asked. She didn't want to hear about Annie right now. She couldn't take it.

'You know about her and that painter fella?'

'I know.' Ruthie sipped some tea. The cup was cracked. You got used to cups being broken around Connie. She was often so drunk that she dropped things, and they were rarely replaced.

'He's got an exhibition coming up,' said Mum, her mouth twisting in disgust. 'Did you know? Pictures of her in it, I suppose.'

'I don't care,' said Ruthie.

'It's being held at—'

'Mum!'

The sharpness of Ruthie's tone made her pause. 'What?'

'I don't want to know, all right? I've had enough. I don't want to discuss it. Is that plain enough for you?'

Connie looked hurt. 'All right. If you say so.'

'I do.'

'Kath been telling you all about it then has she?'

'Yes. She has. Now, no more. Understood?'

Connie nodded and changed the subject.

But Ruthie should have understood, too – that Kath and her mole Ellie inside the whorehouse were far from discreet and that information could easily pass in two directions, not just one. Because within days, her and Mum had a visitor. One that shocked them.

34

It was Annie.

'She don't want to see you,' Ruthie heard Mum telling her at the door.

And Ruthie recognised her voice – Annie's voice – straight away. Low and husky. Seductive, she supposed. She could easily imagine men being charmed by it. She could imagine Max being charmed by it. Damn him. A sudden spurt of temper sent her out into the hallway, sent her to the door to stand behind Mum.

Annie licked her lips. Stared at her sister. Then she said: 'Hello, Ruthie.'

And somehow Ruthie kept her voice even as she replied.

'Hello, Annie. Well, aren't you coming in?'

'You don't have to see her if you don't want to,' Connie told Ruthie, looking at Annie with open dislike.

But Ruthie said: 'What good would that do? Let her in, for God's sake, Mum.'

'Don't think you're getting a fucking cup of tea,' snapped Connie as they moved into the kitchen, Connie ahead of the pair or them, scattering venom and fag ash and drink fumes. 'What did you think I'd do, roll out the red carpet for a fucking little whore like you?'

'Mum,' Ruthie said warningly.

'Well, she's got a nerve, showing up here. Hasn't she done enough damage?'

Ruthie told her to give them a few minutes and huffily Connie withdrew. Ruthie shut the kitchen door behind her, then sat down at the grubby table and looked at her sister.

'What is it you've come for, Annie?' she asked her.

'I've come to see how you are.'

Ruthie looked her dead in the eye. 'Let me tell you about my life, Annie. I've been spending most of my time sitting alone in that mausoleum in Surrey now that poor little Eddie's gone. If I go out to get my hair done or go shopping I have to take my minder with me. Nobody talks to me down there. The stockbrokers' wives with their little Pony Club kids and their twinsets and pearls don't like my London accent or Max's dodgy connections and they shun me. I don't see my husband very often, he's a busy man. Mum's in bits on her own but Max won't let her come and stay with us in Guildford because she might mess up Queenie's rugs or leave drink stains on the table in the annexe. So here I am, back in the Smoke. If I go out to the shops here, I've got to take my minder with me. The shopkeeper will serve me first, I go straight to the front of the queue, even if I say I don't want to. I have to apologise to the others, but they'll say, oh, don't worry, Mrs Carter, we're not in a rush. But they'll stare at me and they hate me and they envy me. They're afraid of me, too. Or rather, they're afraid of Max. That's my life, Annie. That's my life.'

Suddenly there were tears in Ruthie's eyes; she couldn't seem to stop them. Annie came to the table and sat down quickly, extending a hand. Ruthie snatched hers away.

'Don't you fucking dare pity me,' she told her.

'I don't.'

But of course she did. Ruthie knew it. She knew *her*.

'Did you hear about the two Delaney clubs going up in flames? The Galway and the Liberty?' Annie asked.

'Yes. I heard.'

'A lot of people are saying it's Max. After – you know – after Eddie.'

Ruthie had nothing to say on that. If the Delaneys had been behind sweet little Eddie's death, then good luck to whoever had torched their fucking clubs.

And then – at last – Annie said what she had really come for.

'Are you and Max still together, Ruthie? I mean – as man and wife?'

That was it. There, out at last. In the open.

'I'm probably going back to Guildford at the weekend,' Ruthie told her coolly. 'And Max is joining me there.' She said this without a single idea as to whether Max would be there or not. She just wanted to hurt Annie, the way she had been hurt. 'Don't think you're going to step into my shoes, Annie Bailey. I'm still wearing them. Would you jump into my grave as quickly as you'd jump into my marital bed?'

'I just wanted to see you,' she said, and Ruthie saw Annie's face flush at the lie. 'We were so close, before.'

'Before? You mean, before you fucked my bridegroom?'

'I'm sorry,' she said.

'Yeah,' Ruthie spat back. 'Of course you are. Now – I think you'd better go.'

35

It was like a sickness now with Ruthie; she was like someone who stuffs their face with doughnuts and then complains they have a fat arse. She couldn't stop indulging in this perverted fixation: Annie and Max, together. Annie had betrayed Ruthie, ruined her wedding, destroyed any hope of a happy marriage and yet, Ruthie couldn't seem to force herself to stay clear of her. She was both fascinated and repelled by the tantalising possibility that Annie and Max were still 'at it'.

She went up to town several times and loitered at the end of the street in Limehouse, unable to resist. She watched men going in and out of the whorehouse. Once, she even saw Annie at the door, welcoming in a wealthy-looking type, ushering him inside. There was no sign at all of Aunt Celia, but on one occasion she saw a steel door being carried inside the house by workmen in overalls.

'Can I help you?' someone snapped at her one time when she was standing there, watching.

She turned. A woman in a pinny was there, a scarf around her head, an iron-grey fringe in curlers, a brush in her hand as she stood at her open front door eyeing Ruthie with suspicion. 'What you standing here looking at then?'

'No . . . ' Ruthie started, moving away.

'Don't I know you?' The woman's eyes narrowed. 'Aintcha . . .?'

Ruthie hurried off.

Kath brought reports from Ellie, that the whorehouse was busy, that Annie was happily bossing everyone about, that Aunt Celia was still missing, that security had been tightened up – which explained the metal door and convinced Ruthie that Kath wasn't bullshitting her – and Kath said that Redmond Delaney was still backing Annie financially.

God – Annie and Redmond?

Could that possibly happen? Maybe the thing with Max had been passing, fleeting. Maybe *Redmond* was the one now?

But then – that look at the graveside.

No, Ruthie didn't believe it.

Mum had said that Kieron Delaney was planning an exhibition of his work – work that included a nude of Annie that was apparently going to be the centrepiece of the whole thing – in the renowned art dealer Toby Taylor's Jermyn Street gallery. Ruthie knew she'd have to go. Couldn't resist it, even if what she saw there caused her pain. She wanted to see first-hand the kind of life her sister was leading, the kind of depravity she'd allowed herself to sink into.

Ruthie was nervous on the night, doubtful. Annie was bound to be there. Maybe even Max, and how could Ruthie explain her presence there to him if they came face to face? Would he be annoyed at her being there? Or wouldn't he even care?

As it turned out, she needn't have worried. The gallery was a huge space, easy to get lost in. It was hung with around forty canvases and the first one you saw as you entered the door was – of course – Annie; her portrait was placed at the centre of the landing above the big double open-tread staircase. It was brightly lit and impossible to overlook. Other nudes abounded, and some gorgeous African landscapes, but the centrepiece, the thing that instantly drew the eye, was her.

The gallery was crowded to the rafters. Scores of people mingled and chatted, the roar of their many conversations almost deafening even without the backing soundtrack of Vivaldi's *Four Seasons*, which was playing on what sounded like a very expensive sound system.

Ruthie snatched a glass of champagne from a passing waiter's tray, took a sip to clear her throat, which was dry with nerves, and looked around. There was Redmond and his twin Orla, the pair of them tall and beautiful, looking over a study of warthogs at a watering hole. And there were the Regans and the Foremans of Battersea, and the Nash family and the Kray twins. Good job Charlie and Eddie Richardson had been nicked, because there was needle there, them and the Krays, Max had told Ruthie. And there was a sleek-looking set of people, coated with the unmistakeable gloss of wealth – Ruthie caught the American accents as she passed by – a silver-haired man, a couple of teenage boys with him, one dark, one fair, and a woman, Italian-looking.

She saw Max over by the stairs, talking to . . . oh yes.
There she was.
Of course, he was talking to Annie.
Their heads were close together.
It was as if nothing else existed in the entire room. Only them.

Ruthie felt her stomach tighten, felt a surge of acid rise into her throat.

'So what do you think of it?' asked a voice by her ear.

She jumped, slopping champagne onto the pink marble floor. Then she turned and looked at the man who had come up and was now standing beside her. He was wearing jeans and a Harris tweed jacket over a white T-shirt – very underdressed for such an occasion. It was the man she'd seen talking to Annie in Harrods. One of the Delaneys. Stunningly good-looking, strawberry-blond hair, green eyes.

'Sorry,' he said, laughing. 'I startled you. Oh don't worry about that . . .' He reached out, snagged a passing waitress, took two full glasses from her tray, pointed out the spillage on the floor. The girl wiped it briskly with a napkin and then carried on circulating among the guests.

He gave Ruthie a glass of champagne and held out a hand. 'I'm Kieron. Kieron Delaney. All these – I'm the artist. I was asking what you thought of the painting?'

'Oh.' She shook his hand and drank, felt a little steadier. She *wouldn't* look over there again. She wouldn't see Annie and Max together. She wouldn't. And what was Kieron asking . . .? The painting? She had been standing in front of it but now she looked at it for the first time. A tiger, crouching in long grass. Almost invisible; waiting to pounce. Beautifully, skilfully done. There was a red dot on the bottom right of the canvas.

'It's fabulous.'

'And sold.'

'So I see.'

'And you are . . .?'

'Oh. Sorry! I'm Ruthie Bailey.' Then she shook herself. Stupid, how she kept forgetting her married name. Almost as if the marriage didn't exist. As if it had never happened. 'I mean Carter.'

'Oh! You're . . .?' He indicated Max with a nod of the head.

'Yes. That's me.'

'Right. I see.'

'Really? Do you really?' Ruthie sniffed. Any mention of her sham marriage hurt her, and there was something about the way he'd said it that instantly got her back up. 'I don't think you do.'

'Um, I do. I promise you. Sorry. I'm speaking out of turn.'

Ruthie stared at his face. So handsome! And then she realised. 'Oh,' she said. She drank some more. 'She's told you, has she? During one of your sittings, I suppose? Yeah, that's it. Annie's told you all about how she betrayed me? Slept with Max? Disgraced herself?'

'Um, I—'

'And yet, here she is, the centre of attention still. The star of the night, yeah? And – oh yes.' Ruthie pointed to where Annie and Max stood in such close proximity. 'Always comes out smelling sweetly, that's our Annie. She just can't help herself.'

'I'm sorry. I've upset you. That wasn't my intention.'

Ruthie drained her glass and handed it to him.

'Forget it,' she said, and left.

36

To her surprise, Kieron Delaney followed her outside. He caught her arm. She stopped walking. Her minder Dave, who had been waiting behind the wheel of the car, opened the door and was half out of his seat, coming toward them. Ruthie shook her head at him, irritated at him, at the world, at everything. She wanted to smash something, hit something hard. Inside the gallery she could see all those happy chattering faces and she could also see *her*, Annie, naked and glorious on the wall, the centrepiece of the whole exhibition. The winner. And what was Ruthie? Yeah. The loser. What else would she be?

Ruthie could see her own reflection, and Kieron's, in the gallery's sparkling glass windows: a big handsome red-haired man and a thin woman, expensively dressed, not mousy blonde anymore but ice-blonde, beautifully coiffed and exquisitely made up. Good God – was Kieron Delaney actually coming on to her?

No. Of course he wasn't.

Who the hell was she kidding?

He was probably just curious about her. After all, she was Annie's sister. If he was looking for a way in with Annie – and he probably was, because after all, who wouldn't? – then why not try through Ruthie?

'What the hell do you want?' Ruthie spat out at him. 'And take your bloody hand off me, or you'll be sorry.'

He let his arm fall away. He'd seen Dave, ready to approach. It wasn't an idle threat.

'Jaysus, keep your fur on, will you? Let me buy you dinner,' he said.

'What?'

'I suppose you do eat sometimes? Although look at you, you're so slim. So pretty that I do wonder. Have a salad if you must. But I want dinner with you. I want to sit across a table from you and just look at you. You're *stunning*.'

'What?' She was staring at him with hostile eyes. 'No. Fuck off.'

'Please.'

She wasn't used to this – a man, seducing her with words this way. He thought she was *stunning*? 'No. Go away.'

She was walking away from him, heading for the car, and Dave. Suddenly she wanted to be back at Mum's place, in the room her and Annie had shared all their lives growing up. She wanted to go to sleep and never wake up again. She wanted some of the pills the doctor had given her, the ones he'd promised would 'lift her mood', which they hadn't seemed to do. But most of all, she wanted a drink.

That look, shooting between Annie and Max at Eddie's graveside . . .

Oh God – Eddie! She missed him so much and she'd been so cripplingly lonely since his death, so tormented by all that he'd suffered. He'd been her one true friend, her little brother – and now he was gone.

And then seeing Max and Annie here tonight, standing so close together . . .

Ruthie couldn't take the pain any longer. She wanted to die. Her life was a joke. A fucking joke. She couldn't pretend any longer, to Mum, to Kath, to Miss Arnott, to Dave, to the cleaners, the gardeners, to the whole nosy intrusive world. It was all too much. Only Max knew the truth of what there was between them.

There was *nothing*.

Not a kiss, not a hug, not a single solitary fuck. And she'd offered. She'd *tried* to be a wife to Max, to give him what he wanted. But of course he didn't want her.

It had been over before it had even begun and they both knew it.

And here was Kieron Delaney, standing in front of her, offering – well, what? A dinner. Honeyed words. Flattery. Food that might choke her because all she wanted to do, really, was drink. She'd graduated from sweet sherry to vodka. She'd get out of her skull on it, forget everything else.

'Please,' he said, following her.

Dave was about to get out of the car again, about to read Kieron Delaney the riot act. Damn it! If Dave hit Kieron, there would be more trouble and Max wouldn't want that. Did she care?

She was surprised to find that she did, a bit. After Eddie's horrible death, there had been the fires at the Delaney clubs, and she didn't think Max was finished with the Delaney mob yet, not by a long chalk. But she didn't particularly want this Delaney hurt. Not really. He was an artist, different from the rest of them, surely? He must be softer, more sensitive. And he was doing his best to charm her and she *liked* that, just as any woman would who had been so completely neglected. And here the stupid fucker was, putting himself in harm's way.

'All right,' she said, exasperated, giving up. 'Dinner. Okay? Just dinner. And don't for a minute think you're getting anything else. You got that?'

He was smiling, amused.

'Okay,' he said.

37

Ruthie woke up next morning in Kieron Delaney's bed – proving that drink, despair and a sumptuous hot dinner with a very charming man were no recipe for mental stability.

She woke inch by inch, aware that her mouth was dry and sour from all the champagne she'd drunk the night before. Her head was aching. Coarse beige pillows – not hers. A coco-brown lamp at the side of the bed – again, most definitely not hers. A high ceiling. Maybe a loft apartment?

'Hello,' he said, leaning over her.

Oh Christ.

Ruthie had a feeling she looked like death warmed over. He, however, looked much the same as he had last night. Stunning, a little rumpled, the morning sunlight illuminating his beautiful hair – oh, and he was naked.

'What the hell?' she groaned. Something was making an annoying yapping noise.

'Shh, Bertie! You drank rather a lot last night,' he said, smoothing her hair back off her face. Something like a small hairy missile sprang up on the bed and growled at her.

She drank rather a lot *every* night. But he wasn't to know that. Was she in fact turning into her mother? Rotten, horrible thought.

'I don't remember coming here. Where are we?' She sat up. Her head banged like a gong. Oh God, she was naked too. And sore. They'd done the deed, no doubt about that.

Not that she could actually remember it happening. The dog kept growling. She *hated* dogs.

'My place. Battersea.'

All the Delaneys lived around Battersea. Max had told her so. Max, her husband. It crossed her mind then, shockingly, that she had been unfaithful to her marriage vows, unfaithful to her husband. Her, the Sunday School kid! Then she thought of Max and Annie, in the gallery last night. And at the graveside, when they'd buried poor sweet Eddie. Max was probably being unfaithful to her right this minute, with her sister, the woman he should have married.

Holy hell, what if I'm pregnant? she thought, aghast.

Her headache intensified and her stomach turned over.

What if, nine months from now, a little baby popped out of her, red-haired and green-eyed, a baby that in no way could be passed off as Max's since the kid's colouring would be all wrong, and anyway they hadn't slept together since the wedding night? A baby that looked like every single Irish Delaney there had ever been?

Max would kill her, probably. He wouldn't stand for that. God, the embarrassment. A Delaney pup, sired on his own wife? No way. He would crush her, and who could blame him? She would have humiliated him in the worst possible way.

'I have to go,' Ruthie said, scrambling out of Kieron's awful beige sheets, hunting down her bra and knickers and stockings, her dress, her coat, her bag.

The dog nipped at her heels.

'Get *off*, you little fucker,' she snapped and Kieron laughed and gathered up the dog, out of harm's way.

'Poor Bertie, did the nasty lady shout at voo, did she then?' he cooed, and kissed the mutt.

'Call me a taxi, can you? Hurry up,' she said.

He sauntered bare bollock naked over to the phone, made the call.

Ruthie was dressed; ready to go.

'No one must ever know about this,' she said, terror of Max edging every word. What the *hell* had she been thinking, coming here?

'Breakfast? Some toast?' he offered. Still, the smile was in place. It occurred to her then – too bloody late – that she had unwittingly handed the Delaney clan a club to beat Max over the head with, and if they ever used it, then she would be in the firing line too.

She could barely wait for the taxi to arrive. When it did, she was out of there straight away and on her way back to Mum's place, kicking herself all the way. *How* could she have fallen for all that Irish blarney?

But she knew how. She'd been lonely and desperate and hurt.

If Max found out . . .

God! She shivered at the thought of that.

Or the other Delaneys?

What would they think, Kieron knocking off Max Carter's own wife?

Every way she turned, she saw danger.

And had Kieron *meant* any of what he'd said to her anyway in those sweet flattering tones. I love you, I want you, you're fantastic . . .

Well – had he?

Surely not.

She was glad when she got back to Mum's place. She had to think all this through, get her head straight. If she could.

But it had been nice, the flattery. *So* nice. And . . . maybe he *had* meant it?

38

At Connie's, Ruthie walked straight into another shit storm. Not from Mum – after all, Ruthie was Mrs Max Carter and she could do anything she damned well pleased – but from, of all people, her 'minder'. Dave was waiting for her in the grubby little kitchen, Connie pouring him tea. A thick pall of cigarette smoke hung over the table where they sat.

'You didn't tell me what a nice young bloke you've got driving you around.' Connie sat, tapping ash at a saucer and spilling it onto the pink plastic tablecloth instead.

'Give us a moment, would you please, Mrs Bailey?' asked Dave, very polite.

He's lovely, Mum mouthed at Ruthie as she went out into the hallway. She closed the door behind her. Instantly Dave stood up and the charming smile vanished.

'What the fuck was that?' he asked, looming over Ruthie.

'What are you talking about?' she asked, but she knew he could see guilt and shame all over her. She couldn't stand this, not on top of everything else. Horrible snapshots kept sailing through her brain. Kieron Delaney on her, in her. She hadn't enjoyed it, had barely known it was even going on, so why the hell had she done it? Her head thwacked and banged like fury. Was she going to vomit, the final humiliation, right here in front of this man – her husband's employee – who was looking at her with raw disgust? She knew how she looked. She was disgusted, too.

'You took off with Kieron Delaney. Spent the whole damned *night* with him, didn't you. I waited round the corner and I saw you get into a taxi this morning so don't bother denying anything. I couldn't believe it. Put myself in fucking *danger*, loitering around there I can tell you. Now how am I supposed to square all that with Mr Carter?' His eyes swept over her, up and then down. 'You look like you've been on the nest all night. Christ's sake! You crazy?'

She said nothing. She wanted a bath, some pills for her head, a drink, oh God yes please, a *drink*, not this goon standing in front of her giving her hell.

'I'll have to tell Mr Carter about this,' he said.

The final nail in her coffin. But maybe she could front this out. Find some power from somewhere. Start fighting back.

'Tell him what you like,' said Ruthie. 'I don't care. And I don't think he does, either.'

'What, you got a bloody death wish or something?'

'I told you. I don't care what you say to Max. So you can take the bloody car off down to the Guildford place. I don't want you hanging around me up here, you got that straight? Tell Max anything you like. Meanwhile, I'll be telling him the truth.'

He squinted at her. 'The what? What you talking about? You been out half the night – no, *all* the night – with Kieron fucking Delaney, that's the truth.'

'I mean the truth about you and me, Dave,' said Ruthie flatly. Her heart was pounding hard. She was going to do it, she had to. But did she have the audacity? She swallowed and took a deep breath.

His mouth had actually dropped open. 'Wha—?'

'You've been pestering me to have an affair with you,' said Ruthie. 'And now you're going to try and cover your tracks by spreading vicious lies about me and Kieron Delaney?' She shook her head slowly, tutting with her tongue against the roof of her mouth. 'Dear me, talk about desperation. I was here all night with Mum. She'll swear to that. I'm her favourite daughter. She *worships* me. And she don't want to upset Max, not now, not ever. He's her meal ticket.'

Realisation dawned on his face. 'You bitch,' he said flatly.

'Yeah,' said Ruthie. 'So off you go, Dave. And I really think – don't you? – that you should keep shtum. Okay?'

He went.

Ruthie sagged. She'd done it! Her. Timid little Ruthie.

Mum came back in, looking at her in puzzlement. 'Where were you last night then? Dave's supposed to be your minder, you should keep him in the picture, you know. For your own safety.' She puffed herself up. 'You're important now, Ruthie. Don't forget that. You're Mrs Max Carter.'

'As if any of you will ever let me forget it.' From somewhere, she dredged up a thin smile. 'Listen – I was here, wasn't I. With you. All night. That's right, isn't it?'

Mum stared at her. 'What's going on?'

'That's right, isn't it?' Ruthie repeated firmly.

Connie shrugged, nodded. She looked uneasy. 'Sure. Okay. Yes. That's right.'

'Good,' said Ruthie, and went upstairs to wash the scent of Kieron Delaney off her.

Half an hour later, a bouquet of fifty red roses arrived at the door.

Love you lots said the card.

'Who . . .?' asked Connie.

'Max, of course,' said Ruthie, wondering what Kieron was playing at. He barely *knew* her. But this was a lovely gift. So nice. She thought back to last night, how he'd charmed her over dinner. Well – maybe she *deserved* to be charmed, maybe she was *worth* charming.

She was changing – growing stronger every day. So maybe she *deserved* a little adoration in her life. But . . . how had he known where to send the flowers?

She could see that Connie was also thinking about last night – and the lie that she was with her.

'Ruthie . . .' Connie started uneasily.

'They're from Max,' she insisted. 'Stick them in some water, will you?'

39

Later that day, Kieron called in at Mum's place, the dreaded dog trailing behind him on its lead. Ruthie was appalled but also flattered.

'How'd you find me? How'd you know where to send the roses?' she demanded.

'What, the address of Max Carter's mother-in-law? Every Delaney knows little details like that.'

He told Ruthie that the spectacular nude of Annie had been sold after a bidding war between two punters – an American called Constantine Barolli, a Mafia don, apparently – and Max Carter.

'You shouldn't be here,' Ruthie told him, nervous. She'd fronted Dave out over last night with Kieron, but she didn't want to push her luck any further.

Kieron didn't seem to care.

'Carter won out,' he said, and went on to tell Ruthie the ridiculous eye-watering amount it had been sold for. 'Your husband, spending all that cash on a portrait of your sister? Jaysus.' He blew out his lips. 'That must hurt.'

Was he taunting her?

But she ignored the remark and accepted his invitation to dinner. Why not? She had nothing else to do, no one else to see. A feeling of helplessness, of things moving way beyond her control, was engulfing her. Inevitably, Max would find her out. Probably, he would throttle her with his bare hands, kick Mum out of her home. Just like Mum, Ruthie was living off the bottle now and the irony of that did not escape her. She had watched her mother slowly destroying herself with drink and now she was headed the same way. The thing was, though – she couldn't seem to bring herself to care. She'd cleared out Bond Street until she was bored with the whole process. She had bags and bags of high-end wares stuffed into the bottom of her wardrobes; the truth was, she'd ceased to be interested in any of that.

They dined at Claridge's. All through dinner he was so attentive, speaking to her about his art, asking her what she thought of this and that, actually taking an interest in her opinions. Max never did that. Then Kieron drove her back to his place in Battersea. This time, he shut the dog in the kitchen. Bertie scratched at the door and howled.

Ruthie told herself that this time she wouldn't sleep with him, but when he kissed her and paid her such close attention the way Max never did, told her that Annie was nothing, nothing at all compared to her, it soothed her, reassured her. And of course the drink helped. She seemed to be forever half-cut these days. It dulled the pain of reality.

'I'm not going to sleep with you again,' she told him as they kissed on the sofa. Was her voice slurring? Yes. It was. Just a bit.

But he was opening her blouse, pushing her bra out of the way. Pulling her onto his lap, pushing aside her underwear, guiding her hands to his already naked cock. Groaning when he touched her, saying yes, yes, yes when she guided him in. Tugging off his shirt so that they were skin to skin and she was moving on him and he was muttering endearments and saying her name . . .

Was that her name?
She was a little drunk.
Well, a lot.
But had she heard what she thought she'd heard?
Had he said her name?
Or had he said *Annie*?
No. Of course not.

He was kissing her, biting her neck, his hands on her hips, keeping her there and she wondered, what the hell am I doing? But his hand on her clitoris stilled her, stopped her objections. The overwhelming sensation of satisfaction was spreading over her, blinding her, deafening her, making her nothing but female, crying out for this, for passion, for what this Irish charmer could give her when her husband would not.

It was too late to back out now, far too late. Feeling appreciated, feeling wanted, was like a drug.

They came together, devouring each other, and as orgasm enveloped them both she heard him say a name again, and it wasn't her name, not her name at all.

She'd been right.

She'd heard him whisper not her name but her sister's.

He'd said *Annie*. Hadn't he?

But she was drunk. She wasn't sure.

And the bloody dog was still howling its stupid head off.

40

It happened weeks later, in one of the very ChiChi little boutiques Ruthie often frequented – where the staff were always sickeningly keen to give her glasses of champagne, to flatter her, to say that she was so slender (she was still bony in fact, painfully thin) that clothes looked absolutely dreamy on her, exquisite. They picked up their commission on the sale and were happy; Ruthie took her treasures home and stuffed them somewhere, anywhere, out of the way. Max never queried the amount she spent. Ruthie guessed that being so generous made him feel a little less guilty about the indifferent way he treated her.

She was half in the door of the boutique, a smiling saleswoman already making her way straight toward her like a shark slicing through water. They had a fine eye for a wealthy client, the women who worked in these places. This one had spotted a mark, and that was Ruthie. But then someone stepped between them.

'Ruthie? That you?'

The woman who was just exiting as Ruthie was entering paused, touched her arm. A tall elegant woman, older than her, beautifully dressed, black-haired.

'Lara! Hello,' Ruthie said, and smiled politely and would have passed straight on but Lara stopped there, blocking

Ruthie's way, much to her annoyance – and the saleswoman's too.

Lara leaned in, kissed Ruthie's cheek, her eyes sweeping over her, top to bottom. Weighing her, assessing her – and of course finding her wanting. 'How lovely to see you! Are you well?'

'I'm fine,' Ruthie told her, wanting only to get away. 'In a bit of a hurry, sorry.'

'Time for a coffee though – yes? Oh of course you have!' she said, smiling, pouting, her eyes hungry for gossip.

Well, Ruthie had nothing of much interest to tell. Nothing that she wished to share with Lara – or with anyone else, come to that.

They ended up in Harvey Nicks. The coffee tasted sour to Ruthie, but then she'd been drinking the night before and all she could really taste right now was acid bile.

'Now, listen, darling, I've heard a rumour . . .' she started.

'Really? About what?' Instantly, Ruthie felt nervous.

She laughed. 'About you.'

'Saying . . . ?' She just wanted to be gone. There were drinks, *proper* drinks, waiting for her over in Battersea. But of course she wouldn't drink until later, she wasn't Mum, she wasn't Connie bloody Bailey spark out on the sofa, but Kieron was expecting her and she knew he didn't like to be kept waiting. She wished he'd shoot that damned dog, though. He kissed it on the mouth! Wasn't that *filthy*?

'Saying that you were hanging out with one of the Delaney brothers.'

41

Ruthie stared at Lara and felt her heart stall in her chest. If *Lara* had heard, then so had Max – surely? 'So?' asked Ruthie, dead cool, but Lara's words had shaken her.

'Well – is it true? Darling, that's really not wise.'

'Is it really anyone's business?' Ruthie was aware that she sounded tetchy: defensive.

Lara looked startled by her tone. 'Ruthie,' she said after a beat. 'It's certainly Max's business. Don't you think? Our men are like that, aren't they. We're free to do pretty much as we like so long as we don't break the code.'

'The code?'

What the hell was Lara talking about? Not that she much cared. She was falling in love with Kieron Delaney, who seemed to be in love with her too. She'd forgotten that mistake he'd made, murmuring 'Annie' and not 'Ruthie'. And he'd treated her so well since then anyway, taking her to swish hotels, gifting her more flowers, Godiva chocolates, and he'd stood on Southend beach with her and said how much he loved her, which was a shock but wonderful too. They were *in love* and she was almost happy.

But now – *this*.

Lara nodded, sipped her espresso. 'Our boys don't expect us to be nuns, do they. But they do expect us to be discreet, and in particular they expect us to be selective about the liaisons we have. I mean really, Ruthie. A Delaney boy? You know how much Max hates them. For God's sake, they were implicated in the whole Eddie business, he's never going to forget that. Or forgive it. They're bitter enemies. They've been fighting over territory for years. And here you are, sleeping with the other side? I'm surprised Max hasn't spoken to you about all this already. In very harsh terms.'

'Lara . . . ' Ruthie was going to tell her to fuck off, mind her own damned business, and tell her also that Max wouldn't have spoken to her about this because Max did not give a toss who she slept with, he didn't give a single solitary damn about her at all.

'No! Wait, Ruthie. Really, please listen.' Lara's eyes were earnest as they stared into Ruthie's. 'The Delaneys are seriously bad news. The whole family's crazy, that bloodline's tainted.'

'That's rubbish, that's—'

'There's a sister. Orla. She's downright peculiar.'

Kieron often mentioned his sister Orla. She had a small artistic talent and he liked to tease her over it. Small, insignificant – she was not a showstopper, he said, not like him.

'And Pat, have you met Pat?'

Ruthie shook her head.

'You don't ever want to, either. He's a bastard. And then there's the worst of the lot . . . '

'Who?'

'Redmond. Cold to the bone.'

'I've never met him.' She'd seen him, and Orla, at the gallery though.

'Be glad of that. He's poison.' Lara drained her tiny cup and tilted her head, staring at Ruthie's face. 'I've heard tales, you know. Maybe you haven't heard them too. About Redmond.'

'What about him?'

'About the things he does to his women. Gets them hooked on stuff. You know. Drugs. Then he watches while they fall apart. It seems to amuse him.'

Ruthie didn't know what to say. Redmond sounded like every woman's idea of a nightmare, Lara was right about that.

'I suppose everything is all right, you and Max?' she asked, lighting a cigarette, offering Ruthie one from a monogrammed silver case. Ruthie shook her head.

'What do you mean?' Ruthie just wanted to get away.

'Well, I've heard rumours,' said Lara, blowing out a plume of smoke. 'About him. About Max. And I'm sorry to mention this, but I do think someone should have the decency to tell you – about Max and your sister.'

'Look, I have to go.' Ruthie stood up, knocking the table in her haste, spilling the remains of her coffee.

Lara reached out, grabbed her wrist. Her eyes on Ruthie's were very intent. 'Only it's a dangerous game you're playing – and a dirty one, Ruthie. Are you deliberately goading Max by siding with the Delaneys? Word is it's Kieron Delaney you've taken up with, but any one of them would be equally bad. Look . . .'

'What?'

Lara glanced around them. No one was listening. 'Apparently your sister's moved out of Limehouse and now she's running a high-end establishment on the corner of Park Street and Oxford Street. Buck House is just up the road, and the Ritz is only a step away in Piccadilly.'

'So?' Ruthie didn't want to hear this.

'So she's doing damn well for herself. The Houses of Parliament are close by, she'll do a ton of trade around that area.'

'I'm not interested in my sister's "trade",' Ruthie said sharply. 'I'm going.'

She snatched her wrist free, grabbed her bag and walked away, out of the restaurant, out of the store, out into the street. She stepped to the edge of the pavement, flagged down a cab with its yellow light illuminated – and gave the cabbie Kieron's address.

42

'Hiya, sweetie,' said Kieron when she let herself into the flat with the spare key he'd had cut for her. He was sprawled on the sofa, watching TV. Bertie was laid out on his lap. At the sight of her, the dog lifted its upper lip, showing its teeth in a silent snarl.

Yeah, I hate you too, thought Ruthie.

'Drink?' offered Kieron.

Oh God she needed one. Lara had unsettled her. Made her doubt everything.

Ruthie nodded and he poured the drinks. She went over to the table, picked up the glass, drained it. Her trembling stopped.

She looked at him: her lover.

He was so, so handsome.

And of course he was arrogant and actually maybe it *was* unnecessarily mean of him, saying his sister had a 'small talent'. But then – arrogance could be attractive, couldn't it? Yes. In a man, arrogance was like a sex drug, catnip to women. He refilled her glass and she drank again.

Feeling better, she stripped off her coat. Kieron lounged back on the cushions and watched her.

'I love you, Ruthie,' he said.

'Yes. I love you too.'

'Keep going,' he said.

'What?'

'I want you naked.' His green eyes narrowed. Like a tiger, his eyes. She often thought that. 'Have you ever thought of changing your hair colour?'

What?

Slowly, she started to unbutton her blouse. 'No,' she said flatly.

'Your sister's hair is very dark, isn't it.'

'What . . .?'

'Or what about red, like Orla's? My sister has beautiful hair.'

And Ruthie's wasn't up to scratch? Wasn't that what he meant? It was thin, it was an ashy blonde, it wasn't the dazzling Annie's or the stunning Orla's; it was just hers.

'Come on,' he said when she hesitated. 'Get it off,' he said lazily.

The last time they'd been together – and oh God, why was she remembering this now? – he'd said Annie's name by mistake. It had been a mistake – hadn't it? Or was it like the comments about her hair, her weight, how sallow her skin was, was it all meant to make her feel more needy, more inferior?

'You have such sweet tiny little tits,' he said as she peeled off her bra.

Was that a compliment or an insult?

She couldn't decide.

Again there was the same crushing sensation of being less than what was required, less than Annie, less than Orla, not up to the job. Not beautiful. A washed-out woman, a sorry excuse for a seductress, and too damned nice for her own good.

Fuck it. Maybe she *would* change her hair colour. Polish up her image. She threw off the rest of her clothes and went to Kieron, grabbing Bertie and consigning him to the kitchen, where he started yapping.

Pretty soon, she was able to shove Lara's words of warning about the mad Irish Delaneys to the back of her mind, to drown in sensation again, to forget to think; to just *be*.

When it was over, they went and lay together on the bed and Kieron said: 'How about a holiday?'

'Great,' she said. To get away from reality? Yes, that was *great*. 'To where?'

'Comillas.'

'Where's that?'

'Cantabria,' he said. 'Spain. The family's got property out there. And it's empty.'

'How long?'

'Maybe a week. I have a studio there, I can paint in peace.'

So that was it. He wasn't relishing the idea of a week alone with her, he was wanting to get to his oils, to lose himself in his art. And her? She'd be lying by the pool, she supposed, alone.

But that was okay. Wasn't it? And Max wouldn't query where she was. She never even saw him, these days.

Maybe she'd read a few books, get a suntan.

What was wrong with that?

'Okay,' she said. Bertie was still yapping his head off, out there in the kitchen. 'But who's going to look after the dog?'

'Orla,' he said, grinning, kissing her. 'Love you.'

'Love you too,' she said.

43

The Spanish place was beautiful, but Ruthie was very surprised by it. For one thing, it wasn't set in a Spain that she had ever imagined. Cantabria was so green; there was no parched desert here and few olive trees. And although the house itself was large and beautiful, it was obvious that the place had been left untouched and unloved for a long period of time.

Out on the roadside, the first giveaway of the house's state was immediately visible. There were two tall brick columns supporting an arched metal sign with BOTEGA SIERRA written in rust-covered Gothic script. Both columns were choked at the base with weeds, and the driveway leading a good half a mile down to the house itself was treacherous and bumpy, the hire car pulling and straining all along its considerable length so severely that Ruthie feared for its suspension.

To the right and left as they proceeded there were grapevines, row upon row of them, all untended, hung with rotting fruit that seemed to be picked only by birds, the gaps between each line thickly overgrown with weeds.

Slowly, the house itself was revealed. And it was beautiful, with Arab roof tiles and an impressive façade, huge windows set in a series of grand arches, every window framing the fantastic views of the vineyard all around.

'I always thought of Spain as dry. Dusty,' said Ruthie as Kieron switched off the hire car's engine outside of the main entrance.

'That's southern Spain,' Kieron told her. 'This is different. Cantabria's got a humid ocean climate.'

'What does that mean?'

'It's warm in the summer, mild in the winter. Ideal for grapevines.'

'These look a bit – well – neglected.'

'Yeah, well, nobody tends them now.' Kieron pulled a face. 'With Dad going back to Ireland after his blue-eyed boy Tory died, there's not the will to see to the place. But I use it more than anyone else. It's peaceful, great for working in. Come on, come and see inside.'

But inside was scarcely an improvement. There were pale wooden beams all throughout the interior. Dust sheets cloaked all the furnishings. The air smelled musty, faintly damp.

'Seven bedrooms, three bathrooms,' Kieron told her as they stood in a huge sitting room that was lined with big curving windows to take in the vineyard views. 'In May we get the rhododendrons coming out. Very pretty.'

Within a day they'd settled in. Kieron headed for the studio block that was set up at the back of the finca near the covered-in pool; the studio was a square featureless room, stuffed with oils in progress.

'I don't like to be disturbed when I'm working, so it's good to have this space outside of the actual house,' he told her.

Having told her this, Kieron took the hire car down to the village and brought back bread, meats, cheeses and wine. Then he retreated to his studio to work on pieces for his next exhibition. He worked on into the night and at one in the morning Ruthie heard splashing coming from the pool. She grabbed her sarong and wound it round her, tying it at the throat. He'd finished working, obviously, so at least she wouldn't be accused of 'disturbing' him. She wandered out to see what was going on.

This is a dead place, she thought, and felt a shiver run through her. Above the drooping, neglected vines the moon was full in the velvet-black sky. Kieron was doing lengths, back and forth. When Ruthie walked out onto the lamp-lit terrace he stopped beside the steps down into the pool and swept his hair back out of his eyes.

'Join me?' he said.

'How'd the painting go?' She wondered if she dared ask.

He shrugged. 'Great. You know, it's this place. It's so relaxing. I work better here than I do anywhere else in the world. Come on, it's lovely.'

She dropped her sarong and waded down into the pool. *Blissfully* cool. Exquisite. But dirty, she suspected, trying to ignore that. Everything seemed dirty and uncared for, here. She did a couple of lengths and Kieron did the same. Then they rested at the far end of the pool and gazed up at the moon and the stars while the frantic plunging and fluttering of moths on the terrace kept them company.

'Do you come out here very often?' Ruthie asked him.

'As often as I can.'

'And the rest of the family?'

'Nah, they don't bother anymore. It used to be a great place. Produced thousands of bottles of wine. Good stuff too. No rubbish. It all changed after Tory went. I always thought that if I wanted to be buried anywhere, it would be here, along with something or someone I loved.'

'That's a dark thought,' she said, shuddering a little.

'Why?' His eyes glinted as his head turned toward her. 'I'll take you to the cemetery tomorrow. It's very nice, very civilised, rows and rows of neat little vaults set into this big wall, lovely inscriptions, and the grieving relatives put beautiful flower arrangements there on each one; it's very pretty. Very peaceful. And there's an angel over the top, the Angel de Limone, keeping guard.'

She had to laugh at that. 'Keeping guard against what?'

'Demons. Fiends from hell.'

'Oh! Right.'

'I'll show you. I'd like to be buried there with one of my pets, you know. Like a pharaoh buried with his living wives. Or maybe here, in the vineyard. That would be nice.'

'Okay.' It all sounded creepy.

'Seriously.' He moved closer, water lapping around them. One big hand cupped her breast. 'Tiny little tits,' he whispered, stroking her nipple, teasing it into hardness. His other hand slid between her legs then moved back further, delved inside her. She moaned, losing control, and he kissed her. 'Sorry I've been a bit short lately, Ruthie,' he murmured against her lips. 'It's just the work, you know. Sometimes it gets you down. Trying so hard, you know, and it's all pearls before swine.'

Sometimes, he could be nice. Better than nice. Like now.

'Ah, it's your own fault, so it is,' he murmured, turning her so that she was leaning against the side of the pool. 'Being so gorgeous. That's it, little Ruthie, that's it.'

'What if somebody comes?' she objected. 'What if they see the lights on here and they come to see what's going on?'

'There's no one around for miles. Ah, that's good,' he breathed out, pushing into her.

And it *was* good.

If only he could stay nice, like he was right now. And if only she could forget that he'd called her Annie, by mistake.

44

The 'holiday' was soon soured. Late one night, wondering if he was okay, Ruthie awoke and thought: *The hell with this. Spending all this time alone. I'm supposed to be his girlfriend, aren't I? So why can't I go out to the studio and see him?*

Feeling nervous about the decision, still she sauntered out and into the studio block. Instantly she wished she hadn't; she could see that the work wasn't going well. He was standing in front of a canvas, daubing paint here and there, his expression thunderous.

'Shitting *thing*,' he snapped.

'What?' she asked, wondering whether or not to just retreat, go back to bed.

He flung a brush down onto the floor, splattering the tiles with viridian green. 'You get horsehair brushes that cost a fortune and the hairs come out. What bloody use is that?'

'Well, I—'

'Oh shut up, Ruthie. Just bloody shut it, will you?'

And he turned and *whacked* her alongside the head with his open hand.

Ruthie reeled back, stunned, not believing that this could be happening, not here, not where he was so calm, so relaxed. Her right ear throbbed hotly. She staggered on her feet and suddenly the world was quiet but for a low humming. She shook her head and to her horror felt a trickle of blood squirm out of her ear, run down her neck.

He hadn't seen.

Hadn't even *noticed*.

'Sorry, Ruthie.' He said it absently, as though it didn't even matter.

He was already turning his attention back to the shedding brushes, turning away from her. As if what he'd just done was *normal*.

She heard herself saying *that's okay*.

But it wasn't.

She stumbled back to the house and stood in the bathroom mopping up that thin stream of blood. She felt sick, unsteady.

She tried to sleep that night, but it was difficult.

She was in pain.

45

The next day, as promised, Kieron took Ruthie to the cemetery of Comillas, and it was every bit as pretty as he'd said.

'I definitely want to be buried out here. I want turquoise ribbons and turquoise flowers on a circular wreath on my tomb,' he said as they wandered along the great wall, the protective angel perched high above their heads.

'You've given it a lot of thought then,' said Ruthie. She still felt shaky after the scene in his studio last night. And something odd had happened to her hearing. On the left-hand side she could hear perfectly well. On the right – nothing. And she was dreading the trip home to London because she'd heard that flying with an ear infection was agony.

What about a ruptured eardrum? she wondered, because that was what she suspected she had.

'I have indeed given it a lot of thought. And what about you, Ruthie?'

'What about me?'

'Your grave! What do you want.'

'Actually, I don't want a thing.' Except to understand why he felt she deserved such treatment.

'Meaning?' he stopped walking and stared at her, puzzled.

'I don't even want a funeral. I want . . . nothing. Just to be gone. That's all.'

He looked shocked. 'What a weird idea.'

'Is it though? Or how about a sky burial like they have in Nepal?'

'And what is that exactly?'

'The body's left out to feed the birds and the animals.'

'Christ!' He wrinkled his nose. 'That's gross.'

'It makes the deceased a part of nature,' she said.

'Oh, would you like your mother laid out for the bears to eat?'

'It would be good for the bears. And – let's face it – she wouldn't feel it.'

'What an odd little thing you are,' he said, and laughed.

46

When they got back to London – the flight had been, as she'd expected, excruciating – Kath was keen to talk to Ruthie and tell her the latest.

'None of this is news,' Ruthie cut her off, thinking of other things. She'd taken a suite at the Langham and Kath called on her there. 'I'm not paying for this.'

She wouldn't go to the doctors, they might ask what had happened to damage her ear. She kept quiet. Slowly, the pain receded. The only trouble was, she now had to tilt her left ear anxiously toward whoever was speaking, because she couldn't hear anything on the right-hand side at all.

Kath was deflated. Jimmy might be a good earner but he was horribly tight with his cash; Ruthie's payments were a very welcome addition to the meagre 'housekeeping' he provided.

'What, you knew? About Annie getting in amongst the nobs, satisfying their twisted upper-crust perversions?' asked Kath.

'I knew. Yes.'

'Has Max spoken to you about it?'

'No. He hasn't.'

'Then how . . .?'

'Lara Beaconsfield has.'

'Ah. And what is Max going to do about it?'

'What? Well, why should he do anything? Annie can do what she damned well likes. Maybe Max isn't too bothered anymore.'

Kath's whiny voice was getting on Ruthie's nerves. Since Spain, she'd had a horrible dull buzzy headache and intermittent pain in her right ear; it made her feel miserable.

But the painting – and that bidding war between Max and the American. Ruthie knew for sure now that whatever had been between Max and Annie was still there, bubbling away. And it crushed her, the thought of them together. She had never been a confident girl or a confident woman. She was by nature a homebody, an introvert. She needed approval, someone to reassure her. Once, that had been Annie. Now, Ruthie didn't have her support and she was obviously never going to get it back, either.

She'd been into Vidal Sassoon's frantically busy place in Monmouth Street and had her hair cut and restyled like he'd done Nancy Kwan's, the Hong Kong-born American actress, in a face-framing bob. Then it was dyed a fetching shade of red. But it made no difference. Ruthie looked in the mirror and still she saw an uncertain stranger there. Kieron said the red looked okay, but Ruthie didn't like it. It seemed too sharp, too *loud*, for her.

'You're kidding yourself if you think Max isn't interested in her anymore,' said Kath with a snort of derision. 'Jimmy says—'

'I don't give a fuck what Jimmy says!' Ruthie burst out.

'Jimmy says,' Kath pushed on, 'that Max is obsessed with Annie. He can't leave her alone.'

'Shut up Kath.' *Oh God, please shut up.*

'He says Max has been round to the Limehouse place and laid his cards on the table with her.'

'What does that mean?'

'Ellie says Darren showed Max Carter into the front room and Annie joined him in there and he *heard* them.'

'Heard them what?' demanded Ruthie. But she knew. Of course she did.

'You know. *Doing* it. It was obvious what they were up to. And there's more. Ellie says that a place that cow Annie's rented in Upper Brook Street has been snatched—'

'Kath. Please shut up!'

'Snatched by *him*. By Max of all bloody people. He's bought it out from under her, and he's gifted her with it. Jimmy says it's true. He says Max has fitted her up with a flash car to get driven around in. With a bloody chauffeur of all things. They're at it like knives, the pair of them. A full-blown affair. He says Max and her can't keep their hands off each other.'

'Kath – shut your mouth.'

'All right. I will. But that don't alter a thing. It don't make any difference. It's going on. It's happening. You can ignore it if you want, but there it is. It started before your wedding and *it's still going on.*'

'Shut up, Kath, or by God I swear—'

'Oh all right, all right. I thought you should know the details, that's all.'

'That's kind of you. Now will you shut your ruddy great mouth?'

'I will.' Kath folded her arms over her middle and said: 'But there's just one more thing. Max has heard you've been hanging about with one of the Delaney boys.'

Oh no, oh God help me . . .

Ruthie felt all the blood drain out of her head. She lurched to one side and sat down quickly. She swallowed, tried to speak. Her worst fear was realised.

'So what?' she said, spitting the words out, hoping to sound indifferent when really she was scared to death.

'So what?' Kath let out a bark of laughter. 'Come off it. This is Max Carter we're talking about. The Delaneys did for Eddie, you know they did.'

'That was never proven, was it.'

'Bollocks. And now you're hanging about in Battersea with them?'

'It's none of your bloody business,' Ruthie told her.

'No. That's true. But we're cousins. I don't want you ending up under a fucking bridge somewhere, dead.'

Ruthie felt herself go pale.

'Look, Annie's driver Donny told Jimmy that there was a set-to. With Kieron Delaney. Kieron's jealous as fuck of Max Carter because he's got Annie – and Kieron wants her.'

Ruthie stared at Kath. She couldn't, for a moment, even take it in. But Kieron was her . . . well, what was he? Her 'boyfriend' sounded a little tepid. 'Lover' was more like it. Yes. He was her lover. Hers. And . . . oh Christ . . . Kath was saying he'd been seen, fighting over Annie?

Ruthie thought of Kieron, whispering Annie's name, not hers.

Oh God.

It had happened with Max. Now it was happening with Kieron.

'You're lying,' Ruthie said defensively.

'Think what you want. I'm just telling you not to trust the Delaney bastard, that's all. It's not you he's focused on, you can be very sure of that.'

Ruthie was stunned. It was too bloody awful. First Annie had snatched her husband away and now she had Kieron dancing to her tune.

'I don't believe you,' she told Kath.

'Believe what you want. I'm just telling you, that's all. And what the hell have you done to your hair? Red? Everyone knows you can't trust a redhead.'

'Fancied a restyle,' Ruthie said, thinking that at least if her ear started to bleed again, it wouldn't show, not like it would against the blonde.

'Well – it don't suit you.'

47

That weekend, Ruthie went down to the Surrey place and thought she would have a quiet time of it; so she was dismayed when Max showed up there too. She'd just unpacked her overnight bag and decided to settle in for some drinking time on her own when she walked into the drawing room and found him standing right there, by the fireplace.

'Oh!' she said, surprised.

'How are you, Ruthie?' he asked.

Like she was a stranger and he was politely enquiring about her health. Well, she felt like shit. Her ear ached and her deafness on that side made her feel disconnected from the real world.

Max hadn't been here or anywhere else in her orbit for months. He hadn't phoned, hadn't written. Nothing. Now Ruthie's fuzzy head was full of all that Kath had told her. Max and Annie, having a passionate affair. And what about her? She was nothing, left out in the cold. Abandoned. Useless. And her lover – *her* lover Kieron – was getting involved in fights over her sister.

'I'm fine,' she said. 'You?'

'Yeah. Fine.' He stared at her. 'Red hair?'

She shrugged. 'Just trying it out. But I'm going back to the blonde. Don't like it very much.'

'They reckon it's something to do with the Vikings invading,' said Max. 'A lot of redheads among them and even now some people still don't like red hair. Race memory. Shit like that.'

'Right.' Ruthie went to the sofa. Sat down. She wished he'd just leave. She craved a drink badly, but if he saw her drinking this early in the day there would be questions asked, and she felt far too tired to be bothered with any of that. She suspected he marked the bottles.

He let out a sigh. 'You poor little bitch.' He was staring at her. His eyes were fixed on her face. 'You didn't ask for any of this. You certainly don't deserve it.'

'I don't know what you mean.'

'Yeah, you do. And I'm sorry for it, Ruthie. The way it's all turned out. I really am.'

She thought of all that Kath had told her. The high-end apartment. The car and chauffeur to drive Annie wherever she chose. Annie had snatched away the life Ruthie should have had. And yet still, stupidly, *still* Ruthie found she couldn't really hate her sister; in fact, the truth was that, deep down, she still *missed* her. Missed the cosy chats, the once steady and reassuring companionship, and the way Annie could always, even in the depths of misery, make Ruthie cheer up. How pathetic was that?

She was a useless, unwanted impediment: an obstacle. How long before Max decided she should be removed? He'd done it before with people who'd crossed or frustrated him, she knew that. Not divorce, no. That wouldn't do, that wouldn't reflect well in the circles he moved in, or on the streets he ruled.

Another death in the family?

A chill swept over her despite the warmth of the room.

How long before one of his men said, *I'll see to it, boss. I'll clear this little problem away for you.*

She thought of the story of Thomas à Beckett she'd heard back in Sunday school, the King of the day asking, who will rid me of this troublesome priest? And the knights going to kill the Archbishop at Canterbury. Had the knights been the King's favourites, after that? She didn't remember, she only remembered that the story had appalled and shocked her because it was no fable, no fairy tale; it was true.

'After Eddie went,' Max said, 'I was low. I was on the ground. And she was there.'

He paused. Was he apologising? For fuck's sake! Really? After all this bloody time? 'Look – I'll keep this brief,' he said.

'Keep what?'

'About Kieron Delaney.'

'What about him?' she asked. But Lara had warned her of this, hadn't she. That Max would speak to her about it; that he wouldn't be pleased.

'He's dangerous, Ruthie. That whole family's crazy. You ought not to go near him,' said Max.

'Well,' she said defensively. 'You don't come near me. So I don't see why he shouldn't.'

'I told you why. He's a nasty little creep. He might seem different to the rest of them, but I promise you, he's not.'

'I suppose this is about him fighting with Annie's minder?'

'You heard about that?'

'I did.'

'He's playing with you, Ruthie. It's Annie he's after. He's just muddying the waters with you. Trying to rile me up. Enjoying causing trouble.'

'What, by saying he's fucking Mrs Max Carter? Letting that be known around the town? I can see you wouldn't want that.'

'You're right, I *don't* want it,' he said, and there was a glint of something dangerous in the look he gave her then. She thought of what Kath had said: her, dead under a bridge somewhere, buried under concrete. She shivered.

'I won't bloody have it,' he went on. 'So call it off, Ruthie. I won't put up with this. You think I can have people laughing at me, poking fun? You're wrong. I can't have it. And I won't. Not now, not ever.'

Ruthie stood up and felt the first rebellious pangs of fury. How dare he come here, say this to her after the way she'd been treated? They were running her life as well as ruining it, weren't they – Annie and Max. They were the major players and what was she? The poor patsy who'd somehow fallen, innocent, stupid, unknowing, into the middle of it all. And Kieron? She couldn't believe what Max had just told her. Didn't want to. But Kath had told her it too.

No. Kieron loved her. He always told her so. Deep down, she knew he did. Didn't he?

'Can you just go, Max? I'm sure you're very busy,' she said stiffly.

'Ruthie.' He came toward her. Was he going to hit her? He looked coldly, cruelly furious. 'This can't go on. You know what I overheard in one of my clubs the other day? That Kieron Delaney was giving Max Carter's missus the old pork sword.'

He came closer. Suddenly, Ruthie was afraid.

Now he was so close he could hiss it in her face, very low: 'End it, Ruthie. Right now. All right?'

She didn't know where she got the nerve from. The words just seemed to leap into her throat and out through her mouth: 'And what about you and Annie? Are *you* going to end *that?*'

Max stood there, staring into his wife's eyes from inches away. He was going to *kill* her.

Long moments passed.

Then he drew back and simply repeated: 'End it.'

He brushed past her, went out of the drawing room, across the hall – and then he was gone. She heard the Jag start up and released a breath, realising she'd been holding it. Her heart was hammering in her chest, very loud. She could see now why people were terrified of her husband; he didn't have to shout to get his point across. All he had to do was *whisper*.

Then Miss Arnott tapped on the door and came in, eyes avid.

'Did I hear you call, Mrs Carter?' she asked.

Bitch.

'No,' Ruthie said as calmly as she could. 'But since you're here, get Donny to bring the car round, will you? I'm not staying.'

48

Ruthie didn't go home. Home! Where was that, anyway? Was that Mum's place? Or Max's old town hovel, the one Queenie had lived in, that he kept for – apparently – sentimental reasons, or a convenient place to meet up with his people? Most certainly 'home' was not the Guildford place. Maybe she had no home at all, not anymore. She felt happiest staying in hotels. Or there was always Kieron, over in Battersea. And she was meant to be calling that off, wasn't she? That was what she'd been *told* to do, anyway.

Ruthie went to Battersea. Kieron was there in his apartment, watching TV. The young darling of the Delaney clan. The gifted one. The one who always stood apart. Or did he? Did he have anything to do with the family's scrap metal business? And what about the other parts of the Delaney empire; the illegal parts? Robberies from delivery lorries out on the roads, huge hauls of goods thieved from trucks and from all around docklands. And there was the new thing too. The drugs. Drugs like Lara had told her Redmond Delaney fed to his girlfriends.

And Eddie! They'd done for Eddie. Sometimes she was bewildered by what she was doing here, with him. What was she thinking of? One of his mob had destroyed Eddie's life, left him for dead. How could she square that with her relationship with Kieron? Maybe she ought to end it, as Max said.

But what would she have then?

Nothing.

No one.

And what would Kieron's reaction be if she *did* break it off? He'd already struck her. What would he do to her if she told him it was over? She didn't like to think about that. She only knew that she couldn't muster the courage to do it, so where did that leave her?

Yes – stuck between the threat of Max's anger and the certainty of Kieron's.

Oh God! If only she had Eddie here with her, to talk to, to confide in. She missed him so badly.

Kieron looked up as she entered.

He grinned.

'Mrs Carter! What a very nice surprise.' The dog, which had been peacefully asleep on his lap, woke up and barked.

'Shh, Bertie,' he smiled at it. 'It's only Mrs Carter, you see?'

He liked calling her that. It tickled him, somehow. Now it made her think of what Max had hissed at her in the Guildford drawing room.

End it.

Was she going to do that?

She ought to.

Max's word was law. Wasn't it?

But this was *her* life, not his. All right, their marriage was a wreck. But he had Annie. Ruthie could see it now, how similar her and her sister's paths in life were turning out to be. Both of them were walking a thin dangerous line between two powerful warring gangs of men, the Carters and the Delaneys.

And what happened in wars?

The innocent got hurt.

That was always the way of it. They were both in the firing line, weren't they?

While Max had the comfort of Annie, his reaction back in Guildford told Ruthie that it was serious between them, not a whim, not just sex; there was more to it. But there was some obstinate part of Ruthie, some stronger part, that rebelled against his control. If he had all that, why then should she not have this, with Kieron Delaney, who said he loved her. Yes, he hit her – the artistic temperament accounted for that, she supposed – but he loved her. And more and more, he loved keeping her all to himself. Regularly, he turned down invitations from friends and colleagues in the art world, and from his own family too, just to spend time alone with her.

Which was flattering. Wasn't it?

'You know,' Kieron said, standing up, coming over to her, enfolding her in a hug, squashing the dog between them. It gave a growl. 'I've been thinking.'

'Oh yes? About what?' asked Ruthie. Honestly! He knew how much she detested the silly yappy little thing, yet here it was again, thrust under her nose.

'I didn't like the blonde so much, did I. And the red? Doesn't suit you. Too harsh for your colouring.'

'Right.' Ruthie's shoulders slumped. She was tired; tired of this life, tired of the whole hair-colour thing. She might just let it go back to its natural shade: mouse. It suited her. Maybe it suited her nature.

'You know what I think would suit you best?'

'No. Tell me.'

'Why not brunette? A nice rich dark brown? That would suit you beautifully.'

A nice rich brunette – just like Annie's.

And oh God, Max's words, echoing in her head. 'It's Annie he's after really. Not you.'

Kieron wanted to turn Ruthie into Annie. Not Ruthie the blonde or Ruthie the redhead. He wanted her not as Ruthie at all; he wanted a copy of Annie.

'And you know those elegant shift dresses your sister wears? Those little Chanel suits in warm berry reds and strawberry pinks and plain black with long ropes of pearls? Those would look really, really good on you. I know it. Why don't we make you another appointment and get your hair sorted out, and then we'll go shopping up West, all right?'

What could she say?

'We'll see,' she said. There was no way she was going to do any of it. She felt sick at the thought.

'I love you,' he murmured, and kissed her.

49

Then the dog snarled and snapped again.

'Can you not put that damned thing in the kitchen?' she burst out, and then she got the shock of her life.

This time it wasn't a slap. It was a *punch*.

Ruthie felt the impact from his fist and fell back.

Her left eye throbbed hotly. She blinked at him, open-mouthed. Not believing what had just happened.

Suddenly from being twisted with rage, Kieron's face was now full of apology.

'Sorry! Oh darling, I'm so sorry,' he said quickly, his face crumpling up. Tears sprang into his eyes. 'Oh Ruthie, please forgive me, I'm so sorry.'

The dog barked.

'I didn't mean . . . only I've had him since he was a pup, he hates it in the kitchen, oh please honey, forgive me, I'm so sorry.'

She couldn't believe it.

He'd hit her.

'Oh God, how could I do that?' he wailed.

Ruthie's face throbbed. She stared at him. 'Kieron . . .' She didn't know what to say or do. He'd *hit* her. Again.

'I didn't mean it. It will never happen again. I swear.'

Now he was earnest, pleading with her.

'It's . . .' Ruthie started. This was wrong. This was *horribly* wrong. But he was so distraught. So *sorry*.

'Never again,' he said, over and over. 'Never.'

'I'm going to bed,' she said, and pulled away from him, wondering what the hell had just happened.

'Forgive me, Ruthie.'

'I do. All right? I do,' she said, and went to bed.

50

When Ruthie left Kieron's place next morning, she wondered if she would ever return. She put on her shades to help cover up the bruising. Kieron fawned around her, cooking her breakfast, apologising all over again.

'I don't know what came over me,' he said. 'It will never happen again. It was you, you see. Asking me to shut the dog in the kitchen. I just . . . I swear. I swear on my life. Never again.'

So it was her fault. She went back to Mum's place and found Auntie Mo and Cousin Kath waiting there on the doorstep and was instantly alarmed. She'd been phoning Mum off and on, but Connie hadn't been answering. So she'd finally asked Kath to call round, check Connie was okay. Seeing her there, and Mo too, anxiety seized her.

'What's happened?' Ruthie asked.

'It's your mum. It's Connie,' said Auntie Mo, and burst into tears. Kath hugged her mother and her eyes met Ruthie's over Mo's shoulder. Kath shook her head.

Ruthie was surprised that Annie even came to the hospital. Relations between Annie and Mum had always been sour but they'd been ten times worse since Max and Ruthie's wedding. But Annie turned up and it seemed that hostilities were suspended for a while. The sisters sat by their mum's bedside for hours, and the nurses trotted around and were kind when Ruthie asked if there was any hope.

No, they told her. There wasn't.

Already, Connie Bailey was drifting away, departing the world. They sat by her and Ruthie kept her shades on to cover her bruised left eye. Her hands shook because she hadn't had a drink yet today. She was sitting here by Connie's bedside and the drink was finally killing her mother. Before very long, Ruthie felt, it would kill her, too. She seemed to be sinking into a prearranged pattern of behaviour, aping her mother's failings but unable to stop. Whereas Annie, who was stronger and more sensible by far, never seemed to touch alcohol. She hated the stuff because of what she had seen it do to Mum.

Ruthie's mind churned. Kieron loved her, didn't he? Yes, he'd lost his temper, but after all, hadn't she pushed him to that? It was a mistake, him hitting her. Just like it had been a mistake, calling her by Annie's name that one time. Just a mistake . . .

A male doctor came by and said it was cirrhosis and that they had drained off a lot of fluid from the liver and administered strong painkillers to make Mum more comfortable. Truthfully, Connie Bailey looked pretty much dead already. Her breathing was shallow and she was yellowish, pale, hollow-eyed.

'Is she really not going to recover?' Ruthie asked him.

'I'm afraid you must prepare yourself for the worst,' he said.

So that was it. He left them there. Ruthie looked across the bed at Annie and said: 'Please stay. Don't leave me with her. Not like this.'

Annie looked startled. As well she might. Ruthie was startled too, she couldn't believe she'd just said it.

'Of course I won't,' said Annie.

They were still both sitting there hours later when Connie quietly died.

51

On the day of Mum's funeral, when the ceremony was over, Ruthie noticed that there was some sort of weird kerfuffle going on with Annie and a woman she'd brought with her to the church. The woman who'd accompanied Annie looked blonde and a bit cheap – probably, Ruthie thought, she was one of those common Limehouse tarts.

The droves of black-clad mourners were milling around outside the church and Ruthie took the opportunity to edge into the shelter of the lychgate so that she could see and hear what was going on.

Annie and the Limehouse tart were talking intently to a woman wearing a thick black veil. Ruthie watched Annie grab the veiled woman's shoulders, try to catch hold of her hand. They were standing beside a taxi with its back door open and Ruthie distinctly heard the driver bark out: 'Hey! You gettin' in or you havin' a friggin' dance?'

Then the blonde tarty type and Annie's minder joined in.

'Make your bloody mind up love, in or fuckin' out?' said the taxi driver.

Annie's minder told him to shut his mouth, and the cabbie drove off.

Ruthie watched for a while longer, struck by something really strange: the woman in the veil had a left hand, but her right arm stopped at the wrist in an angry-looking stump.

'Don't tell him you saw he me here today,' the woman in the veil was saying.

The woman's voice trembled, but there was something about it that rang a faint bell in Ruthie's head. Her demeanour too, the way she stood.

Aunt Celia?

But her hand. What the hell had happened to Aunt Celia's hand?

And then Annie spoke, confirming it. 'Celia, what happened?'

Ruthie couldn't hear Aunt Celia's reply. Nearby, Auntie Mo was sobbing over the loss of her sister, Kath was patting her shoulder. Ruthie hustled over and drew Kath to one side.

'What was all that?' she asked.

'All what?'

Ruthie told her about the veiled woman with one hand outside the lychgate, and about Annie and the other woman trying, it seemed – and failing – to stop her leaving.

'I don't know nothing about any of that,' said Kath.

'Well something's obviously going on. Find out. Ask your mole at the knocking shop.' Aunt Celia and no right hand? That couldn't be right, but there was no doubt in Ruthie's mind that that *had* been Aunt Celia. Had she been in some sort of accident? But . . . those words she'd spoken, shaking with fear.

Don't tell him you saw me here . . .

Don't tell *who*?

Max?

Oh God – did she mean *Max*?

'Ellie wants more money,' said Kath.

'She *what*?'

'She says thirty quid.'

Which was far more than a working man's weekly wage.

'Oh for fuck's . . .' Ruthie tutted. 'You wouldn't be screwing me over, would you Kath?'

'No! Of course not. We're family.'

'Yeah, and Jimmy's a tight bastard.'

'Well, I—' Kath was puffing herself up with outrage.

'All right then. Thirty.'

'What happened to your eye? It's all bruised.'

'Nothing.' Ruthie put the shades back on, irritated with herself that she'd forgotten the state of her face and taken them off in a moment of exasperation. 'I tripped – that's all.'

52

By the time she got back to Kieron's Battersea apartment Ruthie was worn out, needing a drink. Max had been perfectly polite to her throughout the day, had played the supportive husband to perfection; but she wasn't fooled by that. He would be with Annie tonight. She knew it.

'How did it go?' Kieron asked her. His face was set in angry lines.

Uh-oh, she thought.

Warily she removed her coat and hat, put her bag aside. Kept her shades on, though: seeing the evidence of that punch in the face might annoy him. More and more these days, she really didn't want to annoy him. She remembered the fights of her childhood. Mum and Dad. She didn't want a repeat of that.

'All right. It was sad. You know.'

He paused for a beat, looking her over.

'Didn't we agree . . .?' he started. Then he shook his head. 'No, it's nothing.'

'What? Agree what?' she asked. She went and poured a gin, swilled it back. Felt the rush, the heat, the sudden relaxing of muscles that had all day been so tight, so painful.

'No, it's nothing,' he said again, his face set, turning back to the TV.

'It's obviously not nothing. What's up?' she asked. Suddenly she just wanted to be alone, to cry, to drink, not to feel a damned thing anymore.

He shrugged.

Oh Christ. 'Just say it, Kieron. Whatever it is.'

'It's just . . . well, we talked about it, didn't we. About you smartening yourself up a bit. Getting some clothes.'

Yes. They had. That was true. Clothes like those that Annie wore.

And had she agreed to that? She didn't think so. She swigged back more gin, then replenished her glass. 'Well, I've been so busy. Mum's funeral. Stuff. You know,' she told him.

'No, actually I think you just didn't like the idea.'

That was true enough. Why would she want to turn into a not-very-convincing copy of her much more beautiful, infinitely more successful, sister?

'When's your next exhibition coming up then?' Ruthie asked, trying to sweeten his mood. Whenever the subject turned to him, she'd noticed, he always cheered up. *Like most men, really.*

But not this time.

'Don't change the bloody subject,' he said, and brought one fist crashing down onto the table in front of him.

Bang!

Ruthie flinched.

'And your hair,' he said, standing up and advancing on her. 'You said and we agreed, didn't we, that you were going to dye it. Dark brown, we said.'

They hadn't agreed that at all.

Then he was smiling that charming, devil-may-care grin all of a sudden, his bad mood forgotten. 'Sorry,' he said. 'Did I scare you? I did, didn't I. I made you jump.'

'You didn't scare me,' she assured him, although he had. Her heart was pounding. 'Where's the dog today?'

'In the kitchen. I know you like him in the kitchen. You see? I'm being considerate. Damn, I did scare you, didn't I. Jaysus, sweetheart, I'm sorry. What a bastard I am.' He came to her, rubbed her arms, smiled into her eyes. 'Put it down to the artistic temperament, hm? And anyway, I've thought of a really good solution, a sort of try-before-you-buy idea.'

She had no clue what he was talking about and she was scared to ask in case that prompted another punch in the face. But he'd sworn he wouldn't do that again. Apologised, over and over. Wept with guilt. And she'd forgiven him – hadn't she? – pushed his misdemeanour to one side. Tried – really hard – to forget it, and to forget that she didn't hear too well any more.

'Look,' he said suddenly, excited as a child at Christmas, going to the sideboard, opening a drawer and coming back with a purple bag. 'Come in front of the mirror, I've something to show you.'

Ruthie went to the mirror over the fireplace and he followed, taking something out of the bag. He touched her head and suddenly there was pressure around her scalp and the brush of something like . . . fur? She nearly flinched, but he didn't like her doing that, he thought it reflected badly on him. So she stood very still, fighting the urge to bolt.

'Look. Take a look.'

Ruthie looked in the mirror. She was wearing a brown wig, fringed and cut in a long shoulder-length bob. She looked not like herself. She looked a bit, just a little bit, like Annie. She was horrified.

'Isn't it great? Doesn't it suit you?' he enthused.

'Yeah,' said Ruthie. 'Great.'

What else would she say, with him standing at her shoulder looking so delighted. If she said she didn't like it, that truly she hated it, his mood would turn. And she really didn't want his mood to turn. She was frightened of his moods.

He leaned into her and she felt the hard leap of his excitement against her buttock. Oh God. The wig was tight and her head was aching with the tension of the day – and now this. Side-stepping around his moods again.

He was turned on because Ruthie looked like *her*. She felt weary, disgusted, beaten. She took a huge swig of the gin, emptied the glass, placed it upon the mantlepiece.

'Let's go to bed,' he said, nuzzling into her neck.

Straight away she lifted a hand to pull the damned thing off her head. She would burn it, destroy it, the first chance she got. Chuck it in the Thames if she had to. Do *something* with it. Cut it to shreds. Make sure it was never, ever seen again.

'No,' he said, stilling her hand with his own. 'Don't. Keep it on.'

And he led Ruthie – her sister's doppelganger – into the bedroom.

53

Kath phoned Ruthie when she was at the Guildford house a few days later. Ruthie was busy packing stuff into tea chests; Max had decided to sell the house. He thought it was an unlucky place, having been witness to the deaths of both his mother and his brother – and he'd lived out his barren mistake of a marriage to Ruthie there too. No matter that Max had only married Ruthie to please his mother on her final days on earth, you could see his point. To the outside world, everything seemed fine; but they both knew the truth. They were living out Queenie's dream, and it was their mutual nightmare.

'Listen, I've got loads to tell you,' said Kath. 'Can I come down?'

Ruthie said that she could and two hours later Kath rolled up and paid off the cab. Ruthie took her through to the drawing room where the furniture was – as yet – untouched, not yet packed ready for the move.

'I love this place,' Kath said, sighing as she gazed around.

She loved it; Ruthie hated it. Ruthie sat down and gestured for her cousin to sit too. She left the sunglasses off. The bruising around her eye had faded, at last.

'So! News?' she asked, leaning with her left ear turned toward Kath. Nobody had seemed to notice her partial deafness yet, and she was keen to carry on that way. To have been forced to answer questions about it would have made her feel ashamed: embarrassed.

'There's been all sorts happening.' Kath's eyes danced with excitement in her chubby face.

'Go on then.'

'You know the woman you saw getting into the cab, talking to Annie at Auntie Connie's funeral?'

'Yes. Who is she?'

'It was Celia Bailey. Your dad's sister.'

Celia had been wearing a thick veil: impossible to see her face. But Kath was only confirming what Ruthie had already concluded: the mystery woman *was* her aunt.

'I don't actually know her much at all these days,' said Ruthie. 'She was only really about when I was young. I heard a lot of comments from Mum about her, though. Talk of "that whore over there in Limehouse".'

'Yeah, well – what would you have anything to do with a person like that for?' laughed Kath.

But Ruthie had always thought that Aunt Celia was all right. 'So what's happened? Why was Celia there at the funeral? There was never any love lost between her and my mum, was there. So why show up?'

Kath took a breath, hardly able to contain her excitement at all she had to impart. 'God Almighty, where do I start?'

'Just take a breath and tell me. Why was Celia there?'

'To pay her respects, that's all.'

'But what about the hand? The missing hand?'

'The hand's a recent thing.'

Ruthie frowned. 'What d'you mean?'

Kath lowered her voice to a harsh whisper. 'One of Max's gang chopped it off,' she said.

Ruthie stared at her cousin. Didn't know what the hell to say. Then she managed to get out: 'What? What are you *saying*?'

'You heard me. In revenge for Eddie being attacked at the Delaney whorehouse, the Carters cut the madam's hand off. Makes you shiver, don't it? But that's what happened.'

Ruthie felt like she couldn't catch her breath. This was . . . *horrifying*.

'But . . . Max wouldn't do that, would he?'

Was Ruthie asking Kath – or herself?

'Max don't have to do his own dirty work, you know that,' said Kath.

'But he wouldn't order it done. Would he? Surely not. Not that.'

'Maybe he was moaning on about it and one of his boys decided to take the matter into their own hands. Who knows?'

Like the knights and the King and the Archbishop of Canterbury! Ruthie shuddered.

'And . . . what about Annie in all this?'

'What do you mean?'

'Well you told me she was – more or less – living with Max. As his mistress. In a flash apartment.'

'That's true. That *was* true, anyway – until Celia turned up at the funeral and Annie found out what had been done to her.'

'And what then?'

'Annie left him. Moved out. On the very day of your mum's funeral, Annie packed up her bags and was gone, back to the Limehouse brothel. Left a note for Max and the keys with the bloke who drives her around – Donny. Who wasn't very happy about any of it, I can tell you. Well, how would you like to deliver a Dear John letter to a man like Max?'

'What did she say? In the note to Max?'

'"I'm sorry, but it's over",' said Kath.

'That's all?'

'Yep.'

'And this is because of Aunt Celia turning up at the funeral? Annie discovering what Max or his boys had done?'

'That's right. But there's more.'

'Go on.'

'The day *after* the funeral, Max called in at the Limehouse place. Demanded to see Annie.'

'And?'

'He said he had nothing to do with what happened to Celia. He was furious. Boiling mad that Annie'd gone, not even talked to him about it. Then he asked if this had something to do with Kieron Delaney.'

'What?' Ruthie stared at her. 'Why . . .?'

'Because she'd done that nude stuff with him. Remember, Max bought that painting? Well Max obviously suspects there's been something more going on between the artist and the sitter, you know what I mean?'

Knowing what she knew about Kieron and his obsession with turning her into a carbon copy of Annie, she knew exactly what Kath meant. She thought of his requests that she buy clothes just like Annie wore. Well, *that* wasn't happening. Ruthie didn't – couldn't – subscribe to the fashion that Quant had spearheaded in London, that Courrèges was using to shock everyone in Paris: the miniskirt. That looked great on young girls, fantastic on bold women like Annie, but Ruthie was a married woman. She was *Mrs Max Carter*. It just wasn't on.

And that creepy dark wig! God, Kieron had been like an animal on the night she'd worn it; so different. No more the gentle considerate lover. He'd been rough, almost feverish. He'd leaned over her, eyes closed, thrusting into her, biting her breasts, groaning, hurting her, and she lay there unresponsive, coldly aware that it was *Annie* he was having, in his mind.

'After she'd moved out from Nob Hill and Max visited her in Limehouse and she'd told him again that they were done, guess what?' asked Kath.

Ruthie shook her head. Couldn't guess.

'The nude painting of Annie by that Kieron Delaney arsehole turns up on the knocking shop doorstep, slashed right through. A message from Max Carter.'

54

There was silence for a moment. Then Kath said: 'It's causing big trouble, all this.'

'In what way?' asked Ruthie.

'Things have moved on. Annie's sidekick Dolly has been running the Limehouse place as madam, so that position's filled and Dolly's made it clear she don't want to go back to the way things were. So where does that leave Annie? She's done with the place she shared with Max, she's done with Limehouse. Where will she go now?'

'Right.'

Ruthie thought it over. If Annie wasn't with Max, what would Kieron make of it? Now he had his chance, didn't he? There was nothing to stop him anymore. The coast was clear. Maybe Annie's next destination would be Kieron's Battersea love nest, previously shared with Ruthie herself. And Ruthie? Well, she didn't think she'd be very sorry if that did happen. Kieron wasn't the man she'd thought he was. Everyone had told her so. Everyone had warned her. But she was starting to appreciate how very right they all were.

She stood up. Picked up her purse, counted out thirty quid and handed it to Kath. 'Well, thanks for coming Kath. Thanks for filling me in.'

Kath stood up too, her expression bewildered. 'What, is that it? Not even a cup of tea or a kiss-my-arse?'

Ruthie smiled at her coldly. Her cousin. Her spy. Or maybe she was a double agent? How did Ruthie know, after all, that Kath wasn't doing exactly the same thing to her, reporting back all of *her* movements to *Annie*? After all, Annie had called to see her at Mum's place. She had known she was there, and how was that?

'Thanks, Kath.' Ruthie crossed to the bell-pull by the fire. 'I'll get Miss Arnott to call a taxi. She'll show you out.'

55

A Christmas party was held at the grand Battersea home of the Delaney clan. Everyone who was anyone was there. Babs Windsor, Sid James and Bernard Bresslaw all turned up to add to the fun. The tree in the hallway was twenty feet high and decorated in lavish gold loops of tinsel and massive red velvet bows.

The old man, Davey Delaney, once king of this vast Delaney castle, was not in evidence; there were murmurs among the guests that he'd totally lost his head after the death of his eldest son, Tory, and returned home to Limerick. But Molly his wife, the silver-haired matriarch, was there, dressed in a festive red chiffon number, dispensing Irish charm that dried up, abruptly, when Kieron stepped forward with his partner for the evening and said: 'This is Ruthie, Ma.'

The warm smile froze to nothing on Molly's face. She cast a long gaze over Ruthie and then spat at Kieron: 'Kier! What the hell are you thinking?' and turned and walked away.

Ruthie was mortified. She'd tried to be amenable, made an effort to look her best, put a brighter blonde rinse on her hair . . .

'Why bloody blonde again?' Kieron had demanded when she'd walked into his Battersea living room. 'I told you the dark suits you better.'

It suited *him* better, certainly.

Their journey to his parents' house had been fraught and on arrival Ruthie had snatched the first drink she could get her hands on, and then another from a waiter who was passing with a tray. The Delaneys dispensed not only the best, the most expensive and most gorgeous edible treats but also – oh thank God – plenty of vintage Bollinger.

And now – this. She'd been cut dead by Molly Delaney. Well, had she really expected a warm welcome? She had not. She was not just Kieron's girlfriend Ruthie. She was also Mrs Max Carter – and everyone, almost without exception, was convinced Max had done for Tory.

'Have you met Redmond?' Kieron ushered her toward a chilly-looking red-haired man, immaculately dressed, eyes as green as Irish grass. 'He's the boss of us since we lost Tory. Although Pat would probably dispute that.'

Redmond shook her hand. No warmth there, but at least he was civil, unlike his mother. 'Have you met my sister? My twin, actually. Orla?' He raised his voice, called her over. 'Orla, this is Ruthie.'

'Ruthie Carter,' Kieron added, smiling; it was as if he was taunting them all with it, enjoying their reactions.

Orla joined them and looked at Ruthie. Then she looked at Kieron.

'For the love of God, Kier,' she said.

'What?' He laughed.

'You know damned well what. What in the name of hell are you playing at, bringing her here?'

'I'm sure I don't know what you mean,' said Kieron.

'Yes you do.' She looked at Ruthie again. 'I'm sorry to say this, but you've no right being here. None at all. He shouldn't have brought you. But,' she sent a chilling glance to Kieron, 'he does it to be clever. Wind everyone up, isn't that the craic? Isn't it, brother?'

'No need to be quite so sharp, my darling,' said Kieron to his sister, patting her on the side of the head like she was one of his pet dogs. Orla flinched away from him. 'I know you're sore because I'm having such a success with my work at the moment.'

He turned his green-eyed gaze to Ruthie. 'You see, she dabbles, my sister. Did you know? She has a small talent for the oils.' He put his thumb and forefinger an inch apart. 'Just a very, very small talent.'

The colour rose high in Orla's cheeks as his words hit home. But she retorted instantly.

'Safer surely to have a small talent than to take such silly risks with a big one,' she snapped.

'Meaning?' he said, still smiling, leaning into her.

'Meaning nothing, Kieron. Well maybe a little something. Something like Max Carter buying a nude painting of Annie Bailey – *your* nude painting of her – which he then slashed and dumped on the doorstep of a brothel.'

The smile froze on Kieron's face.

'That's not true,' he said.

'Yes it is. The thing's destroyed,' interjected Redmond, and Orla nodded.

Ruthie thought that Annie was right. The Delaney bloodline was tainted. They were all mad, all poison.

'Excuse me,' she said, and fled the room.

She went out onto a massive wrought-iron balcony liberally dressed with Christmas lights, where she could be alone and cool down, hoping that Kieron wouldn't follow. Her cheeks felt hot both from too much champagne and from the cut and thrust of the conversation. What was she doing here? She supposed she could be in Guildford, packing more stuff up in preparation for the big move. But that hardly appealed. And she had nowhere else to go, not really. Any friends she made, Kieron always managed to push them away. Yes, there would be Christmas parties soon at the Guildford place – if it didn't sell first – and Max would be annoyed if she didn't attend. But she *hated* Christmas there, all that false jollity. It made her want to heave.

'Ah, all alone are we?'

Ruthie turned. A bulky man with a mean thug's face and a shock of wavy carrot-red hair held out a hand to her. 'I'm Pat. Who are you?'

She wished he'd fuck off. She didn't like the look of him at all. But she shook his hand. His grip was crushing and she was glad when he finally let go. She went to step past him, to escape back into the dancing, chattering crowds and the deafening blare of Irish folk music, but he blocked her way.

'I'm Ruthie,' she said, then swallowed hard, feeling nervous. 'Ruthie Carter.'

'Yeah. Thought so. You know what I'd do, if you were my wife and not Max Carter's?' he asked.

God, this was a nightmare.

She shook her head. Wanted to run, to hide. But he came closer, invading her space. And when he spoke it was a mere whisper.

'I would throttle the bloody life out of you for coming here and making a fool of me with my enemies,' he said softly.

'I—' She was turning, trying to go. He was very threatening. And for a split second, staring at his face she was reminded – forcibly, *horribly* – of Kieron.

He grabbed her arm. 'No, listen. Truthfully. I would kill you and then everyone would know I was never to be fucked with. But Carter? What's he doing? Ignoring the situation? Or just too busy humping that gorgeous sister of yours? Well, who can blame him for that. We all would, given the chance. Oh yes. But you can't let these things slide, you know. He really ought to put out a marker. Make his position clear. Don't you think?'

'Let go of me,' Ruthie said, very low, her voice shaking.

'You know it's all true. You're playing a dangerous, dangerous game, little Ruthie. Cosying up with my daft little brother who thinks he's the finest thing since Renoir? Well I've news for you – he ain't.'

He released her arm at last and, freed, she ran off inside, back to the noise and bustle of the Delaneys' Christmas celebrations.

56

'Annie's got a new place,' Kath told Ruthie when she visited her some time later at the Guildford house. There was a For Sale sign outside its gates now.

'Oh?' Ruthie asked, feigning a nonchalance she didn't feel. 'I thought she was back at Limehouse?'

'I told you. Dolly Farrell's taken over there now. And Annie's not fitting in. So she's been doing deals with Redmond Delaney and now she's taking on another place, a better one, close to Whitehall. Very up-market, according to Ellie.'

'Go on.' Ruthie was fascinated, intrigued.

'It's in Upper Brook Street. It's like one of those posh old-fashioned gentlemen's clubs, she says. Loads of expensive furniture, dark wood panelling – just like *this* place – big comfy leather chairs. There's a radiogram with Sinatra playing on it and there's champagne and twenty-year-old malt whisky on tap. Oysters and smoked salmon and caviar, bloody great Havana cigars on offer to the clients. And the bedrooms! Huge great rooms they are, all decked out, Ellie says, in reds and golds.'

'And whores,' said Ruthie.

'Yeah, but high-class ones. There's talk that Annie's taken up with Redmond. In *more* ways than one.'

'So it's over, her and Max. And now it's Redmond? Is that true?' She didn't know why she even cared. But she did.

'Oh yeah. Since the business with the slashed painting? Yes. It's over with Max and I reckon Redmond Delaney's turking her now. So she's busy acting as madam at this new place. There was one thing, though . . .'

'Oh? What?'

'Kieron Delaney came calling at Limehouse when Annie happened to be there.'

'When was this?'

'Day before yesterday.'

'And what did he want?'

'Her, of course. He was after Annie. She saw him in the front room and Ellie says there were raised voices and Chris the doorman had to go and grab him and kick his arse out onto the street. Chris told Ellie that Kieron was kissing Annie and she was fighting him off.'

Great. Ruthie felt a chill run right through her.

She rang the bell for Miss Arnott.

'I know, I know,' sighed Kath, taking her bulky arse off Ruthie's sofa. 'Miss Arnott will call for a cab and show me out. What a sour-faced old puss she is.'

'Don't forget to phone,' said Ruthie.

'Oh!' Kath paused. 'Kieron Delaney's got another exhibition coming up. If you're interested.'

'I know he has. He's been telling me about it, wondering if he can trust the guy to do his work justice. He reckons the lighting was bad last time, too much. He's giving him another chance, anyway. It's at Toby Taylor's place in Jermyn Street.'

'Are you going?'

'I'll see,' said Ruthie. 'You just keep your eyes and ears open.'

57

One evening Ruthie was up in Eddie's room; it was one of the last rooms to be packed up, ready for the removals men. Miss Arnott was in her bungalow in the grounds and Ruthie was all alone. She didn't expect to see Max. Didn't expect to see anyone – not even Eddie's ghost. She didn't believe in ghosts, anyway. The dead wouldn't hurt you, only the living did that.

Eddie had been such a snappy dresser. So elegant. His clothes were all designer, immaculately clean and well cared for. Ruthie ran her hands lovingly over the finest linen, the fluffiest merino wool, the softest silks. Oh, and the hats! Those lovely hats he'd worn, which she supposed were hers now. He'd wanted her to have them, after all, and Max wouldn't want to keep any of this for himself. The memories would be far too painful.

Halfway through her task, she clutched her drink – undiluted vodka – and went and sat on Eddie's bed, thinking of the lovely chats they'd had here, thinking of Eddie dying here. Thinking of meeting Eddie for the very first time at her and Max's engagement party and getting the warmest of welcomes.

'I love boys,' he'd told her. 'Jonjo is thick, never mind a word he says. And Max is hard. Like rock. So how are you, darling? Ready to settle into the Carter lifestyle?'

But she never had settled in, had she? And now Eddie was gone.

Ruthie took a sip of the neat vodka and placed the glass on the side table. She had to empty the bedside drawers still. She opened the top one and found a stack of brown bottles full of the pills they had given Eddie before he died. Pills to ease the pain. Pills to clear infection. Pills to make him sleep. A fat lot of use any of them had been.

Ah, she was so fed up. So *down*.

Kieron her boyfriend. Who hit her.

Her husband Max, who'd never loved her, not in the least.

Jesus, how she would love to stop thinking, churning her disaster of a life all over and over. How she would love to just sleep!

Maybe spirits did linger. Maybe Eddie was here right now with her, showing her the way. She picked up a bottle of sleeping pills, full to the brim. She unscrewed the cap and shook a few into the palm of her hand. The taste was bitter, as she had expected – but the warm glow of the vodka washed it away.

58

Ruthie wasn't even aware of falling asleep. She drifted off and knew that she would die. Which was okay. Death was by far preferable to reality, anyway. And then she heard – maybe it was hours later, maybe days – someone calling her name.

'Ruthie!'

A woman's voice.

She turned over in the bed, groaning, feeling her stomach roiling around queasily. Oh, go away. Death was good. Death would release her from it all.

Still, that echoing voice.

'Ruthie!'

Everything echoed in this fucking great barn of a place. She hated it.

Footsteps. They echoed too. Someone coming up the stairs?

Ah! Someone was going to burgle the place. Queenie's little annexe had been burgled before, Ruthie knew that. Queenie had died of a heart attack there, during a botched robbery. Oh, so what? Let them take the lot. Who cared? She was aware of the mess in the room where she lay – Eddie's room. There were half-full boxes and clothes and all sorts of stylish accessories scattered around about. She'd drunk too much. Taken some of Eddie's pills. She'd been out of it, gone. It had been *nice*.

Now, reality was stomping its way back into her consciousness, yanking her back to wakefulness, and she was really not feeling very well at all.

'Ruthie! Where the hell are you?'

The woman kept on and on and on, shouting the odds.

Oh you bitch, shut up . . .

If she came any closer, if she actually came into Eddie's room, then she would see the empty voddy bottle, the empty bottles of pills, and she would know that Ruthie was a disgraceful, hopeless drunk just like her mother.

A hurried footstep and then a voice very close to the bed said: 'Oh Jesus – Ruthie!'

Damnation. Suddenly she *knew* the voice. Recognised it. Shrank within herself with loathing, hatred and shame. Oh God. Couldn't she even be allowed to die in peace?

'Oh Ruthie, no,' Annie moaned, clutching at her sister's hand. 'No, don't do this.'

Too late, Ruthie thought.

Far, far too late.

She drifted away.

59

'Come on, Ruthie, don't arse about,' Annie was saying. 'You're scaring me.'

Ruthie snapped awake again.

She didn't *want* to be awake again.

She felt ill. Really ill. And now Annie was patting Ruthie's cheek – *slapping* her cheek, quite hard. Ruthie groaned. Meant to protest but really couldn't.

Cold hands at her neck now. She opened her eyes, saw Annie leaning over her.

'Oh thank fuck for that,' said Annie, hauling Ruthie into a sitting position.

Oh, she was going to be sick . . .

Ruthie closed her eyes, lay back.

'No, Ruthie. Come on.'

Of all the people to see Ruthie like this. Her. Why her? But Ruthie knew. She hadn't been answering Kath's calls or phoning her and so Kath had passed word to Jimmy Bond and he had told Max and Max had told *her*. That was how Annie had got the front door key and let herself into Ruthie's home. She'd got it from Max. Of course Max hadn't come himself. She was nothing to him. Nothing at all. No. Instead, he had contacted *Annie*.

But then, suddenly, Annie was gone. Running down the stairs. *Good. Just fuck off and leave me, will you?*

Peace. Perfect peace. Eddie had lain here on this same bed and felt it too. Just going, leaving all this behind. It was so, so much better than reality.

Fuck!

Movement.

She was back.

'Come on, Ruthie. Drink up,' Annie was saying.

No, she really couldn't drink any more. She was brimming with vodka, awash with pills, please, no more. But she couldn't even get the words out.

Annie hauled Ruthie up again into a sitting position, holding a glass to her lips. Ruthie tasted warm water, thick with salt. She gagged. Tried to turn her head away.

Annie wouldn't stop. Ruthie swallowed a mouthful and gagged again. Oh Christ. She started to heave, salt water spilling down over her dress, over the counterpane. Ruthie protested, pushed against Annie, but she was – as always – much stronger and she made her drink every drop of it.

'Oh you . . . you bitch,' Ruthie gasped, starting to retch.

'That's it,' Annie said. 'Let's get it up.' She was patting Ruthie's back.

'You bitch,' Ruthie groaned, and heaved. Vomit splattered out over the carpet.

'That's it,' said Annie.

'God, I hate you, you bloody whore,' Ruthie whimpered.

Annie laid her hand on Ruthie's forehead. Ruthie was sweating, on the verge of passing out. She blinked, tears of anguish flooding down over her cheeks. She looked at Annie, focused on her for the first time. 'You utter cow,' Ruthie gasped.

But then Annie was going again, back out of the room, down the stairs. Was she leaving? Oh please God, let her be leaving.

No such luck.

She was back within five minutes and handing Ruthie a mug of strong black coffee.

'Drink,' she ordered.

'I bet you're bloody enjoying yourself,' Ruthie told her, wet-eyed and shaking and still feeling horribly sick.

'Drink it or I'll hold your nose and pour it down you,' said Annie.

She would, too.

Ruthie drank the coffee, scalding her lips. Drank it down to the last drop. It tasted vile.

'Come on now, on your feet.'

Ruthie stared at her mulishly. 'Look, just leave, will you?'

'I said on your feet,' said Annie.

Annie grabbed the mug and put it aside. Then she grabbed Ruthie, putting an arm around her waist, and started walking her up and down. 'Call me a whore, call me what you like, but just keep walking.'

Ruthie couldn't walk, couldn't even feel her feet.

'You swore you'd never do this,' Annie was muttering in her ear. 'You swore, Ruthie. On a stack of Bibles. Have you forgotten that?'

What?

'You've got a fucking nerve,' Ruthie told her, struggling to get her legs to work, hating her, hating the whole damned world. 'You jump my husband's bones and now you're lecturing me on what I should and shouldn't do?'

'It's over, me and Max,' she said, dragging Ruthie along, back over the carpet, then round and back again.

On and on and on.

'Like fuck it is. I know Max. It'll only be over when they shovel him into the ground,' Ruthie told her.

'Don't say that.'

'Ah, you don't like the thought of that? And you say it's over? Tell me another.'

Annie let Ruthie go and Ruthie staggered but somehow stayed upright. Annie went to the window and opened it, letting in an icy blast of air that cleared the odour of sickness in an instant. Then she started gathering up all the detritus, the bottles, glasses, empty pill bottles.

'Get yourself washed and changed,' she said. 'I'm going to clear this lot away. I'll see you down in the drawing room. Get a bloody move on.'

60

Later on that same day, Ellie phoned Kath. Kath wasn't pleased. She was short with her informant because Ruthie was getting short with *her*. Ruthie had told her she was getting tired of coughing up money just to hear how well her disreputable sister was doing. Sometimes, Kath had noticed, Ruthie slurred her words, seemed out of it and very snappy. Ruthie had changed. She wasn't the sweet-natured girl Kath remembered from her youth. She was a drunk, Kath thought, and she was going to wind up dead, just like Auntie Connie.

'So what is it this time?' Kath asked Ellie tiredly.

Ellie took in a gasping breath.

Then – nothing.

'Ellie?' said Kath.

Another hitched in-breath, then a shuddering outpouring – almost a sob.

'Ellie? What's up?' asked Kath. 'What's going on?'

'There's been trouble. Terrible trouble.'

'What?'

Silence.

Then the phone was put down. Ellie was gone.

Kath stood there for a while, undecided, listening to dead air. Jimmy was out. Finally she put the phone down, stood there for a while longer, undecided. Ellie had been about to tell her something big. Something *huge*. Hadn't she?

Curiosity ate at Kath and finally she gave in to it. She grabbed her coat and bag, stepped out into the dark rainy street and hailed a cab.

61

The Limehouse whorehouse was very quiet. When Kath knocked on the door it wasn't a mountain of a man who opened it, it wasn't Chris, the usual bouncer on the door, the one Ellie was keen on. It was Ellie herself.

Ellie opened the door wide and let her in. Kath thought she could smell disinfectant wafting out from the place as she did so. Well, at least it was clean, then. No noise of a party going on, no music, no voices. Nothing.

But it wasn't the silence of the place that caught and held her attention. It was Ellie herself. Ellie looked like she'd been hit with a brick. She was yellowish-pale, like she'd been sick. Like she was about to pass out at any moment.

'Ellie? You all right?' Even stone-hearted Kath was moved to concern by the state of the girl.

Kath looked ahead, straight down the hall to the kitchen. People were sitting around the table in there, maybe half a dozen of them. She saw Annie's face there among them. A smear of blood on her cheek. None of the people around the table were speaking. Then she heard movement up the stairs – and to her shock she heard *Jimmy's* voice.

What was Jimmy doing here?

Instantly, suspicion buzzed in Kath's brain. This was a knocking shop. And Jimmy, *her* Jimmy, was all man. Was he upstairs, right now, availing himself of the services of one of the tarts they kept on tap here?

'What the *hell?*' demanded Kath, and she bolted inside, brushing past Ellie, and charged up the stairs to find Jimmy. She was faintly aware of Ellie calling after her, saying *no, no don't*, but she had the wind behind her and a nasty feeling that she was being made a mug of.

At the top of the stairs she turned right on the landing – and there in the far room, the door flung wide open, was Jimmy, and Gary Tooley, and Steve Taylor, and . . .

'What the fuck are you doing here?' Jimmy barked out as he spotted her.

There was blood.

Kath didn't think she had ever seen so much blood in all her life. It was on the bed, on the floor, on the walls, and there were shards of broken glass, broken picture frames, upturned items of furnishing, soiled clothes, tarpaulins spread out and – oh *shit* – Steve Taylor was enfolding some bulky thing in one of the tarps, wrapping it hurriedly when he saw her appear in the doorway.

The sickening metal scent of all that blood filled her nostrils, mingling with pine-scented floor cleaner. Kath felt her throat constrict, felt herself start to heave.

'*Out!*' yelled Jimmy, and he came storming up to the door and slammed it, hard, in her face.

She stood there, shocked, disbelieving.

Ellie came lumbering up the stairs and onto the landing and clutched at her arm. 'Come away. Kath, come away,' she was wailing.

Someone was calling out from the bottom of the stairs, echoing Ellie's words. Numbly, clamping a hand over her mouth for fear she was about to hurl, Kath turned and followed Ellie back downstairs. Followed her into the kitchen. They were all sitting there, their faces blank, shocked, just like Ellie's.

Kath pulled out a chair, sank down into it.

'What the *fuck*?' she demanded, her eyes scanning their faces. A beautiful black woman, her skin tinged almost grey. A blond man in a floral shirt. A bubble-permed blonde woman, her mouth swollen and bloody. And Annie, sitting there shaking, with cuts on her hands and blood on her face.

'What the hell's gone on here?' Kath managed to blurt out.

And the whole story came out then.

All of it.

62

Kath phoned Ruthie next morning.

'There was a set-to last night at the Limehouse place,' she said.

'Oh?' said Ruthie. There had been a pretty big set-to at *this* place, too. She'd nearly damned killed herself. Her head ached. Her stomach was sore. She wished she was dead, but dammit – she wasn't.

'Ellie's in bits and I've seen Annie, she's covered in cuts and bruises. I asked Ellie what happened and at first all anyone would say was Annie and Dolly Farrell had a bit of a ruck. But of course that wasn't the truth. I'd been upstairs and I'd seen . . .' Kath's voice tailed away.

'Wait. What are you talking about? Annie with cuts and bruises? But she was *here* yesterday. And she was fine. And . . . what are you on about? What did you see upstairs?' asked Ruthie.

'This mustn't go any further, Ruthie,' said Kath desperately. 'Or you'll stir up a right old mess. Jimmy's involved.'

'Jimmy? Involved how?'

'All Max's boys too. You know, Steve? Gary? They were there.'

'Was Max there?' asked Ruthie, suddenly suspicious. Surely there was only one reason for her husband to be flouting gangland rules and turning up at the Delaney-run Limehouse place? To see Annie.

'Max? No, he wasn't there. Annie did phone him, though. She asked for his help, because . . .' Again, irritatingly, Kath stopped talking.

'Because of what?' demanded Ruthie.

'Gawd, Ruthie, you won't tell anyone about all this, will you? Because if you do . . .'

'Go on,' said Ruthie.

Kath told her how Pat Delaney had come into the Limehouse brothel, drugged up and looking for trouble.

'Had some bee in his bonnet about Annie. All to do with Max, of course. He was talking about "sampling the goods", saying she was – sorry, Ruthie – saying she was Max Carter's mistress and he wanted to know what was so damned special about her.' Kath lowered her voice. 'And between you and me, it was *more* than that. She's been with that artist one and everyone's saying she's been with Redmond Delaney too – and she deserves a bloody medal for that, he'd scare any normal woman half to death.'

Ruthie put a hand to her throat, picturing that thug Pat, who she'd hated on sight, marauding up the stairs, threatening Annie. 'So . . . she was hurt?'

'Well it looked like a flipping bloodbath when I got there. Ellie phoned me and it sounded like she was in shock or something. I knew something terrible had happened,' Kath said. 'So I went over. They were all sitting around the kitchen table and none of them said a word. Then I heard Jimmy's voice so I went upstairs and it was terrible, Ruthie, I don't think I'll ever forget it as long as I live.'

'What was terrible?'

'Blood everywhere. Shattered mirrors, furniture. Steve Taylor and Gary Tooley were wrapping up something in a tarpaulin and Jimmy damned near exploded when he saw me standing there. He told me to fuck off.'

'What . . .' Ruthie took a breath, swallowed. 'What were they wrapping up in the tarpaulin, then?'

Kath let out a shuddering breath and pressed on. 'It looked like a body, Ruthie. A big man's body. I think I saw red hair but there was so much blood it was hard to say one way or the other. I'll never forget it, not as long as I breathe.'

'Red hair?' queried Ruthie.

'I . . . I thought it was Pat Delaney.'

'Jesus.'

'I went back down the stairs, and there they all were sitting in the kitchen looking like they'd done ten rounds with Cassius Clay. And then they told me what happened. It *was* Pat Delaney. The boys took him away in the back of a van. Jimmy said they were going to dump him in the Channel.' Kath paused. 'And what happened to you? I phoned. No answer.'

'Nothing, I just nipped out,' said Ruthie, wanting to avoid the shameful subject of her drunken pill-taking spree and Annie's part in her rescue. She wouldn't do that again. And she certainly wouldn't tell Kath about it. She really hoped that Annie wouldn't tell her, either. It would be humiliating.

'Anyway . . . apart from all *that*, and what a to-do *that* was, Annie seems to be doing damned well for herself.'

'Oh? Is she?' *Oh shut up.* 'Sounds like she's been in the wars, to me.'

'She's still knocking about off and on with that painter, that Kieron Delaney. Word is she's been servicing both the brothers, him and Redmond too.' Kath shook her head. 'You got to admire that girl's nerve, aintcha?'

'Kath,' said Ruthie.

'Hm?'

'Shut the fuck up.'

63

It was Crook City all over again at Toby Taylor's gallery. The Regans, the Nashes, the Krays, the Delaneys and the Foremans – they were all over the place and Toby the owner was almost at the point of orgasm; he was the original mob whore and being around these people always gave him a dangerously erotic thrill.

Toby was mincing around, smiling and pressing the flesh, his ever-expanding belly straining against his fluorescent green floral shirt, his toupée clinging to his sweat-dampened head. His gold rings and neck chains flashed in the gallery's vivid lighting. Paolo, his young lover, was there too, being swept along in Toby's slipstream.

For this exhibition Kieron had skipped the nudes and African scenes and turned instead to English landscapes: dales and fields, cliffs and thrashing white-topped seas. Some were already sold, but nothing paid like flesh and tonight seemed to be proof of that. The nudes from his first exhibition had sold much better than these landscapes and Kieron was clearly put out about it.

Ruthie watched him circulate, doing the rounds. Making out he was happy, that things were going well. And then, later in the evening, she watched as he approached Annie. Saw how dazzled he was by her.

Then the fight broke out.

She was way across the room, but Ruthie saw what she thought was the start of it. Kieron was talking to Annie and then he put an arm around her shoulders. Ruthie was aware of someone barging through the crowds, parting them like Moses at the Red Sea: her husband. Max.

There were shouts and cries of alarm as Max grabbed Kieron and shook him. Annie was shoved up against a wall. There were raised voices – and then Redmond Delaney coolly stepped forward and broke it up.

Kieron had a fixed defiant grin on his face. If Max had scared him – and Ruthie was sure he had – he was determined not to show it. She stayed back, aware of everyone chattering around her, wondering what had happened, what was the cause of it all; but she knew damned well. Kieron had touched Annie; and Max had exploded with jealousy.

Later on, they left – Annie and Max together. Ruthie's husband and the woman Max truly desired – her sister.

It *wasn't* over.

It was still going on. And Ruthie knew it would, always – unless somebody put a stop to it.

64

Ruthie went back to Kieron's Battersea place by taxi, alone. The dog was in the sitting room and barked when she came in. She'd approached Kieron late in the evening but he'd been snappish, out of sorts. She knew why. Annie again. So Ruthie had left him there and truthfully she wished he'd stay out for the night, because he was exhausting.

Ruthie had decided that she was going to call a halt to all this very soon now. What was the point of continuing this charade, when his interest so clearly lay elsewhere?

But . . . what else did she have?

Somehow, she was going to have to rebuild her life. Maybe talk to Max about divorce. Maybe he might even listen. They both knew this was no good, didn't they. And as for Kieron, well, it was obvious that she was only on a path to self-destruction the longer she stayed with him. She had to break free, to stop settling for second best.

That was it. She would have to start again. Mum was gone, Eddie was gone, and now her only friend in the world was Cousin Kath and really she was no friend at all. The only reason she hung around Ruthie was to get paid. All this was wearing Ruthie down, all this stuff that had begun on the day she married Max and made the biggest mistake of her life. But mistakes could be put right. Couldn't they?

She had to hope so.

She snatched the dog up and put him in the kitchen.

'Shuddup!' she yelled through the closed kitchen door, and went to the bathroom to clean her teeth. She hardly ever bothered anymore and she was dismayed to see blood in the sink when she rinsed. Christ, as if she didn't have problems enough! She was going to have to make an appointment to see that miserable fucker Faulkes the dentist.

Later, she would.

Now all she wanted to do was sleep.

She took off her clothes and fell into bed.

65

Kieron came in at gone one in the morning and Ruthie could tell straight away, starting out of an uneasy sleep to hear him stumbling around, knocking into things, that he was very drunk. Bertie had stopped barking. The exhibition Kieron had had such high hopes for had let him down; sales had, by the end of the evening, not been good.

'Sold half of them! Half!' he bellowed. 'Ruthie? You awake? Sold just half, the tossers don't appreciate fine art do they?'

She was hoping to pretend to be asleep, but he was making so much noise that the dead could be stirring. The dog heard its master's voice and started howling. Ruthie sat up, tired, aching. She switched on the bedside light.

'Well,' said Ruthie, to placate him. 'Half is better than none.'

He came stumbling over to the bed, put a rough hand out to steady himself on the mattress, almost overbalanced and fell on top of her. His breath was like lighter fuel as he stared into her eyes from inches away. His smile was manic, his eyes glittering green jewels of malice.

'Oh you think that, do you?' he said, very quiet.

'It's one exhibition. There'll be others. Better ones.' She was still being sweet, still trying to tone down his anger. Yes, the poor sales were an annoyance – an insult. But that wasn't the real problem, she thought. She knew what was *really* driving this rage of his. Max had left the exhibition with Annie.

'I made a mistake. English pastoral, who the fuck wants all that rural horse shit?' he said moodily. 'Toby said they'd sell on over the next few weeks, and he's probably right, but it's bloody insulting all the same. I'm a great artist. Great. You know I am. We all know I am. Without the work, you see, without the Goddamned work, the sweat, the tears, there's nothing, not a bloody thing. The rest is just shit. I'm a fucking genius, you know I am, everyone knows I am, and they only sold half of my paintings. Half! Mind, they were hung all wrong, so. The lighting was bad. Far too harsh. Did nothing to flatter the work, nothing at all. And there were too many people invited, there was too much of a crush, no one could stand back and get a proper perspective.'

'Right,' said Ruthie faintly.

'I told him, I told Toby, I said, what is this shit? Can't you even display stuff properly in this poxy overcrowded little place? Of course he was all excuses, him and Paolo that fag boyfriend of his, but what they clearly don't know and what they should understand is that these things have to be properly presented. You can have the finest product in the world – and God knows we've got that, everyone says so, all the critics, they love me – but if you don't show it to the public in the proper way, then you may as well forget it. The genius, the product, that's only half the battle. The rest is putting it out there, loud as you can, getting the name known, making the product seen, having it correctly shown, not jammed into an overcrowded hell-hole. That's the last time I waste my time painting fucking landscapes, anyway.

Trees and sheep? Fuck 'em. And it's for damned sure the very last time I grace that poof's fucking gallery with work I've sweated blood over.'

Ruthie didn't know what to say to that. Safer to say nothing.

'I'm going back to life work. That's what pays. That's what gets the accolades. I shouldn't have veered off my true path, should I? I was bound to come unstuck. You'd pose for me, wouldn't you Ruthie? Nudes are where the money is.'

Pose naked? She wouldn't dream of it. She wasn't Annie. 'Maybe,' she said. There was no way she would ever parade her body around for the delectation of other people, for men. They could go to hell.

'No, definitely.' He stumbled off, away, went to the sideboard and poured himself a whisky. She wished she had one. That, and a whole long night alone, in peace. She watched him swig it back, empty the glass.

Then he tottered back to the bed. 'Where's Bertie? You haven't put him in the damned kitchen again?'

'He was barking,' she said. 'He just kept on.'

'The critics are going to have a field day with this,' he rambled on. 'Critics! What the fuck do they know? They're just eunuchs in the harem. They're there on the night, they see it done on the night, and they can't do it themselves.' He glanced around. 'So where's Bertie?'

'I told you. In the kitchen.'

'Right. Look. What I want from you, Ruthie, is a definite yes or no. You going to do it? Pose for me? I know you're a bit scrawny, aren't you, sweetheart? A bit thin. God, I do wish you'd fatten up a bit. But there you go, that's just you, isn't it?'

He gave a low chuckle. She wasn't much, but she would do. A tiny shard of feeble resistance awoke in her then. She wasn't good enough for Max, and she wasn't enough for Kieron. They were both, the pair of them, mad for Annie.

'Look – cards on the table – I'm not posing nude for you or for anyone else, Kieron,' she burst out.

He was stunned by it. There was no other word for it. Stunned. He stood there for a full minute, his eyes staring into hers. There was a questioning smile hovering around his mouth, as if he couldn't quite believe what he had just heard, as if she must surely be joking. Rebellion, from little Goody-Two-Shoes Ruthie? That just couldn't be!

'Oh come on . . .' he said, teasing now, coaxing.

'No,' she said firmly. 'Get to bed, Kieron. I'm tired. I've had enough.'

He drew back. Ruthie was refusing to go along with his plan. This was a turning point for her. At last, she was making her own feelings plain. She started to lay back down and was nearly there when suddenly he grabbed her neck with one large hand and stopped her.

He had her by the throat.

She couldn't breathe.

His eyes had lost their teasing light and now there was clear thwarted rage in them.

'Would you mind telling me, Ruthie,' he said, very low in that soft seductive Southern Irish lilt of his, the tones of which had once seemed so appealing and which now did nothing for her. 'Just tell me, would you.' His voice dropped lower. 'What – exactly – is the feckin' *point* of you?'

'Kieron . . .' she gasped out. Couldn't draw breath. Could feel panic setting in.

'What, Ruthie?' His voice was almost silky now, loverlike. 'Come on, what? You won't wear your hair the way I like it, you won't wear the clothes I love to see you wearing, you keep shutting my damned dog in the kitchen and you know he hates that . . .'

She wouldn't be Annie. That was what he was saying. And he was right. Ruthie might be soft, she might be stupid, but she could be obstinate too. She *would not* pretend to be her sister.

'Kieron, stop—'

'Stop what?' He pouted now, as if surprised. 'Oh – am I hurting you?'

'Yes. Don't—'

'You'll do it then?' he asked and the pressure on her neck increased still further. She felt sweat pop out on her brow. He could snap her like a twig if he chose to. And he was drunk. He didn't know what he was doing. She was in danger here – real danger.

'I'll do it,' she managed to croak out.

He let her go. She fell back onto the pillows, gasping, fighting to get air down into her lungs.

He cocked a hand jokily behind his ear. The bastard. 'Say what?' he asked.

'All right! I'll do it.'

'About fucking *time*,' he said – and then he hit her, *smack!* in the eye.

66

After that, he lay back on the bed beside her, sprawled out. He laughed, very loud. She flinched.

'But what am I thinking? Jaysus! Of course you're as hurt by this as I am. Naturally you are. You must hate them just as much as I do.'

She was trying, wincing with pain, to follow his logic, thinking that he would forget the nude promise by tomorrow because he was so very, very drunk. Yes. He would forget. Like he would forget he'd just hit her in the face. And, after all, he hadn't meant to hurt her or half-throttle her. Had he? Not really.

But . . . hate them? Hate who? Her brains felt scrambled post-panic. What the hell was he talking about, and did she dare ask that question?

No. She dared not.

Her head throbbed. Her eye ached.

But he was going on. Whenever he was drunk, he always had plenty to say. More than plenty.

'Did you see them then? Sneaking off?'

He was talking about Annie and Max. Had to be.

'Yes, I saw them,' she said. 'I saw them leave the gallery, yes.'

If right now he swore the moon was made of blue cheese, she would agree with him. It was safest.

'Sneaking off. And I do appreciate, Ruthie, that you must absolutely hate that fucking sister of yours. God, why wouldn't you? Of all the cheap low dirty tricks, sleeping with your intended like she did.' His words were slurring. Soon – hopefully – he would fall asleep.

'I do. I absolutely do,' she agreed. She wished to God he'd shut up, let it go.

Did Ruthie hate Annie? Her feelings for her sister would always be complex. Yes, Annie had stolen Ruthie's husband out from under her, that was absolutely true and for a long while she had reeled from the hurt of it, felt mortally insulted – but that was tempered by the long shared history they had and the realisation that Annie had – without a shadow of a doubt – saved her life when she had been at her lowest ebb, mourning Mum, mourning Eddie, mourning her failed marriage and – yes – her screwed-up relationship with Kieron Delaney.

'Of course you do,' Kieron agreed, stifling a sleepy yawn. 'Why would you not? We're both injured parties in this, aren't we, little Ruthie? She wouldn't have anything to do with me, and am I not appealing? Jaysus, I've never had the slightest trouble getting women. I'm good to look at – don't you think I'm good to look at, Ruthie?'

'Yes! Of course you are,' she hurried to reassure him. He was. Fabulous to look at. A shame about his personality. And the slaps and punches. Her eye really hurt. Had he damaged the socket? Fractured it?

'Yes! So I am. Handsome as hell, wouldn't you say?'

'I would. Yes.'

'And yet she scorns me and sneaks off with that bloody black-hearted villain Carter. That's just not right, is it?'

'It isn't,' Ruthie agreed.

Annie had apologised to Ruthie for her wrongdoing, had shown extreme – probably fake – remorse over the whole mess of it. And Max? Ruthie had been overwhelmed by Max when they'd first met – overwhelmed by his gypsy-dark looks, by his social position, by his wealth, his power. But had she ever, truly, been in love with him?

Once, maybe. Just a bit, before it had all come crumbling down. But Annie adored him – and her passion for Max had always burned much harder and brighter than Ruthie's ever had.

'See, you agree with me.'

'Yes! I do. Absolutely.'

'So you'll help me then,' he said. He sounded drowsy now, on the edge of sleep.

'Help you?' Help him do what?

Again, she was frightened to ask. Frightened he would call her a fool and turn on her again.

'You're very quiet,' he said.

'I'm just tired, that's all.'

'Poor Ruthie,' he sighed. 'It must be exhausting, being such a nothing, such a nobody.'

He liked being cruel to her. The days of kindness, gifts, sweet surprises, were all over, it seemed. She mourned the loss of that relationship, felt sad at the memory of it. Now, he enjoyed baiting her like this. All she could do was not rise to it, not allow it to wound her.

'But you do agree?' There was a sharp edge to that soft Southern Irish lilt now.

'Of course. Yes.' What else could she say?

'We have to work together on this, Ruthie, on bringing them down,' he said, and yawned again.

'Yes. I can see that.'

'Then we understand one another – yes?'

'Yes,' she said. Go to sleep you bastard. For the love of God, go to sleep. And tomorrow . . .

Well, tomorrow what?

Tomorrow she would get out of here, before he did her real lasting damage.

And Annie and Max? What did he mean, bring them down?

But she knew. He wanted them dead, didn't he – and he wanted her help with that.

Could she?

Oh, they had hurt her, the pair of them. Taken her for a complete fool. And now there was the new knowledge she possessed, the death of Pat at the Limehouse brothel, the fact that Annie had been there, complicit, involved, maybe – *maybe* – even striking the fatal blow. Pat had been coming for Annie, the boys had been packing away his dead body in Annie's room, no one else's – so now Ruthie had a proper chance of revenge. Of *really* settling the score. She turned it over in her mind, hurting, aching, as she lay there and Kieron drifted into sleep, snoring. Both Max and Annie gone, out of the picture? Would she then be free?

Of course she didn't actually *like* the Delaneys. Molly the matriarch had snubbed her in plain view of a hundred others at that wretched Christmas party; Redmond and Orla were cold fish, unrelatable, Redmond with eyes that seemed to freeze you, Orla crazy as a box of frogs, often – it was said – to be found in the graveyard, laying blood-red roses on her dead brother Tory's grave and muttering to herself. Maybe she was mad. They all seemed to be, a bit. Even Kieron, with his art and his temper and his feverish plans for revenge. And there had been Pat, out on the balcony with her on the night of the Delaney party. Horrible. Threatening.

Now he was dead.

Her mind spun in trapped useless circles.

Finally, exhausted, wrung out, aching, she slept.

67

It was one and a half years now into married life for Ruthie. Mostly she was camping out in hotels, drifting rootless with Mum gone and Kieron proving too damned free with his fists. Max had taken the Surrey place back off the market, which was irritating because she had packed most of their belongings up in readiness for the sale, but what the hell. She'd always hated the place anyway. Keep it or sell it, she didn't really care.

He'd laid off Miss Arnott, then taken her back on. If she hadn't known better, she'd have sworn Max Carter, rock steady, untouchable it always seemed, was in the grip of some sort of emotional crisis.

Kath called on Ruthie at the hotel, picked over the posh biscuits, filled her in on the latest gossip.

'So what's been happening with Ellie?' Ruthie asked.

'She's doing a bit of cleaning work over at Annie's new place. But I've got something better to tell you than that.'

'Oh? What?'

'Billy Black. You know him, Billy Black?'

'I know *of* him. Dim-looking chap with a deerstalker, that the one? Works for Max?' I never had much to do with the bloke.'

'Well you'll never believe it.'

'What?'

'Billy Black told me it was certain. He confirmed it. It *was* Pat Delaney who got done at the Limehouse place.'

'Done . . .?'

'Done to death you pineapple. Billy just blurts it out, calm as you like. I'm sitting there in The Grapes, Eric behind the bar chatting to Jimmy who was just getting last orders, and Billy comes right out with it. Says Pat got done and he saw Max's people, Gary Tooley and Steve Taylor, getting the body into the boot of a car, now what do you think about *that*?'

'Why would Billy tell you about it?' Ruthie asked.

'Because he's *weird*,' she laughed, twirling a finger around her forehead. 'And I've got to say, it couldn't have happened to a nicer bloke, could it? Pat bloody Delaney's a monster. Or he was, anyway. Nobody's seen him for ages, and I thought . . . that night I went over there. I dunno. It was a shock. It *could* have been him. I thought it was. But here it is, confirmed.'

Ruthie paused, trying to digest all this. 'So . . . who did it? Max's boys?' Was this finally revenge? For Queenie? For poor little Eddie?

'Yeah, that's the worst bit. The most surprising bit. It was Ellie.'

'You're bloody joking.'

'I tackled her after Billy told me. She went white as a sheet and out came the whole tale. Poor cow was desperate to tell someone, I think. You could see it was eating at her. Pat went upstairs, drugged up, and started trying to get a turn with Annie. Then all the rest of them piled in to defend her, and Ellie went in and finished the job, slit his throat with a kitchen knife. Then Annie phoned Max for help, and his boys came and cleared up.'

'What did they do with the body then?' Ruthie hadn't seen Pat in months – and Kieron had mentioned Pat's absence. Pat frequently went AWOL though, and he was unpopular to say the least, so no one was too concerned about that.

'I told you. They took the bastard out in the Channel.'

'And . . . that's it? It's all over then?'

'Over? You must be joking! Now Ellie's been getting the wobbles, saying it's all too much and she's going to go to the police to fess up. Of course, Annie stamped on *that* idea. And you know you said about that woman turning up at your mum's funeral, the one with the missing hand?'

Ruthie nodded. 'Yes. Aunt Celia.'

'Well Annie told Ellie – and Ellie told me – that it was actually Pat Delaney who did that, lopped off Celia's hand. That it was nothing to do with Max at all. But Pat wanted Max to get the blame for it, to turn Annie against him. The great goon. Another Delaney, obsessed with Annie! He must have thought he was well in for a chance with her. Seriously! Just shows that you never know what's going on in the minds of men. But it worked. Annie couldn't stomach Max after that. She left him, then and there.'

Ruthie felt queasy. 'My God,' she said.

'Yeah, so nobody's going to be missing that bastard Pat much. Except maybe his own family. And they ain't *that* keen.'

'But Annie was blaming Max's mob for what happened to Celia, wasn't she?'

'She was,' said Kath. 'But now she knows he had nothing to do with it.'

68

Kieron was waiting over at Battersea when Ruthie got there. She was barely through the door when she blurted out: 'I've got something to tell you.'

'Oh? What, then?' He was sitting on the sofa, yawning, perfectly relaxed, the dog on his lap. Bertie, true to form, saw Ruthie come in and lifted his upper lip in a snarl.

'Something awful.'

'Go on then. What is it?' He was smiling, as if she was teasing him, just fooling around.

'Pat's dead,' she told him flatly.

'You . . .' Kieron sat up abruptly, stared at her face. '*What* the hell did you just say?'

'You heard me. Pat's dead.'

'Wait, wait.' Kieron let out a shocked bellow of laughter. 'Come on. Where have you heard this? How could you possibly know? Jaysus, are you making this up? Because I warn you—'

'Don't warn me, Kieron. Don't waste your breath. I'm telling you the absolute truth.' Ruthie sat down beside him – another snarl from Bertie – and told him all about the fight at the Limehouse whorehouse; about her cousin Kath walking in on Jimmy Bond, Gary Tooley and Steve Taylor – all Max Carter's men – wrapping what appeared to be Pat's dead body in a tarp, ready for disposal.

Kieron sat there throughout, listening. Making no comment. Finally, Ruthie stopped speaking. Her heart was thundering in her chest and her head ached. But she'd done it. She'd delivered her revenge on her cheating sister, her lying husband, at long last. She felt faintly sick – but also, triumphant.

'Right,' said Kieron, and stood up and went into the other room.

Presently, she heard him talking on the phone.

Bertie eyed her with silent dislike.

Five minutes later, Kieron came back into the room and he said: 'Redmond wants to see you.'

69

Ruthie had never really been in close proximity to Redmond Delaney. The only thing she knew for sure was, he terrified her. With those eyes that stared straight through you, the manner that said you were nothing more than shit on his shoe, meant he was very intimidating. And she was about to tell him this, to break the news of what the girls in Limehouse had done, Annie among them, and what Max's boys had been doing. Disposing of Pat, his brother. Suddenly she lost her nerve. Shook her head. No. *No.*

She couldn't do it.

'Kieron, I can't . . .'

'I'm afraid you must,' he said grimly. 'Redmond's the boss of this family and he wants to know the fine detail and you're the one to tell him, sweetheart.'

'Will you come with me?'

'No. Redmond wants to see you alone. That's what he said, and what he says, goes. You know that.'

God Almighty.

What had she started? *Why* had she started it? Now she was wishing she could take the whole thing back. But she'd gloried in the telling of it, of breaking the news to Kieron, that was the truth. The telling had made her feel important for a change, no longer a humble pawn in the game; for a while, she had actually been calling the shots.

But now she had to tell *Redmond*.

She had to look into those frosty glaring eyes of his and tell it all — and what would be the consequences?

God above, she really didn't want to even *think* about the consequences. Her mind was whirling with images. Annie as a girl, as a woman, Annie *saving her life*. Because she had. Truly, Annie had saved her. And Max? Max had betrayed her, yes, cheated on her, made her marriage to him a sham — but he had never been physically cruel to her. He had never raised a hand to her, not once, which was a thing Kieron seemed to do more and more. Still — and she knew this was pitiful — she kept going back to Kieron because *he was all she had*.

Now she was aware that she was going to put both Annie and Max's lives in danger. Redmond would be out for revenge. And Annie and Max wouldn't have a clue that Redmond was aware of what had happened in the Limehouse brothel. They would go about their business, unknowing, and he would be watching them, picking the moment to strike at his leisure, seeking his blood-lust revenge on behalf of the Delaney family.

'Sweetheart, you can't back out now,' said Kieron, correctly reading the look of horror on her face. 'Redmond's summoned you and you have to go there to the breaker's yard and tell him the truth, the whole truth, just as you've told me. It's too late to think of taking it all back and hoping it'll go away. *Far* too late.'

For emphasis, Bernie yapped at her.

'You see?' said Kieron, cuddling the mutt. 'Bertie agrees.'

70

The yard was alive with activity when Ruthie got there. There was a big metal sign over the closed tall wrought-iron gates saying DELANEY AUTO SCRAP LTD and there was a man behind the gate clutching hold of a snarling Alsatian dog which scrabbled along, fighting against its master's choke-chain. When Ruthie got out of the taxi and told the guard who she was, he let her in and led her quickly across and around the skeletal remains of motor cars, perilously spinning cranes, chugging lorries, whining machinery, a car crusher pounding old and once-loved motors into Oxo cubes, to a Static building which was clearly in service as an office.

The guard knocked, opened the door.

Ruthie went up the steps, feeling like she was ascending to the guillotine.

Why, for the love of God, had she started this?

Well it was too late now. She couldn't backtrack. She stepped inside and the guard with the dog closed the door behind her. She found herself in a bare office. There was a desk at one end and a grey filing cabinet with tea-making facilities on top of it. There was sage-green hard-wearing carpet beneath her feet, and there was a fan heater in one corner making the interior of the Static unbearably hot. And there . . . oh fuck, there was Redmond.

He was sitting in front of the desk, beautifully attired in a charcoal-grey suit, matching tie and white shirt. His red hair was neatly swept back from his forehead and his eyes were just as cold as she remembered them.

And *he wasn't alone.*

Orla his twin was standing by the side of his chair, watching Ruthie as she came in. And there was a girl with long mouse-blonde hair and skinny legs which were clearly displayed by the scarlet mini dress she wore. The girl was sitting, crumpled like a discarded doll, on the floor at Redmond's glossy-leather shod feet.

And . . . Ruthie couldn't believe it.

She was *injecting herself.*

The girl's hands were shaking and she was trying to get the needle into the raised blue vein at the bend of her arm, which was mottled, marked with many past injections – but her hand was shaking too much to do it.

'No, darling, like *this,*' said Orla impatiently, and she bent and dipped the needle into the girl's flesh, pushing the plunger in deep. Clear liquid ran in amid a tiny spurt of blood and the girl's head tipped back against Redmond's thigh, an expression of exquisite pleasure on her face.

Orla smiled like an indulgent nurse and took the empty syringe and dropped it on top of the filing cabinet among the tea-making things. The girl on the floor clutched at Redmond's leg and started to hum a low tune.

'Quiet now darling,' said Redmond, and the girl stopped humming – just like a switch had been flipped. Redmond's attention turned to Ruthie. 'Now. Ruthie, yes? Kieron says you have news and I would like to hear it. Tell me everything. Miss nothing out, from the start to the finish, right?'

Ruthie wouldn't dare miss anything out, not now, not in this horrible little hot-house, not with the pair of them staring at her like curious cats and a drugged-up girl sitting *right there* on the floor at their feet.

But – oh God – Annie. And Max.

Feeling sick to her stomach, Ruthie told them everything, twice over. And when at last Redmond seemed satisfied, she left.

She went out into the road and, shaking, she hailed a cab and climbed into it, grateful to have escaped. But she couldn't stop herself from wondering, worrying, chewing it all over and thinking: *I've done it and it's too late for regrets. But now he knows, what the fuck is going to happen next?*

71

The anxiety over her meeting with Redmond dragged on. As the weeks went past and nothing terrible happened, she even started to fool herself that it might be okay. Every night she fell into a hotel bed exhausted but she couldn't sleep except fitfully and then her dreams were peppered with nightmare images of Annie, dead. Max, being beaten, being killed. Every morning she crawled from her bed as if drugged (and oh that made her think of the mouse-blonde girl again, that poor useless junkie in the Static, and what the hell would become of her, left to the untender care of Redmond and Orla?) and then Ruthie laboured through the days, starting at sudden movements, unable to focus on anything, shaking, unsteady, uninterested in food, taking refuge more and more in drink.

One day she was crossing the road in St James's and she saw a tall dark-haired woman coming toward her, crossing in the other direction. She *knew* this woman. Then she saw a car coming, speeding up, and panicked. She caught hold of the woman's arm and yanked her away, out of its path.

'What the . . . *Ruthie?*' asked Annie in surprise. 'What the hell are you doing?'

Ruthie found she couldn't draw breath to speak. Her heart was galloping in her chest; she felt on the verge of shrieking.

'Ruthie?' asked Annie again.

'The car,' Ruthie gasped out.

'What do you mean, the car? What is it? You all right?' It *was* Annie. Her sister's eyes were staring into Ruthie's face with concern.

'It was coming . . .' Ruthie managed to get out.

Annie half-smiled, frowned. 'Ruthie, the car was nowhere near me. What's the matter with you?'

'Yes it was, it was going to hit you,' Ruthie insisted.

'No it wasn't. Come on. Look, let's go and get you a coffee,' said Annie, and took her arm and led her over to a stylish little café.

Annie got Ruthie seated at a window table. But Ruthie shook her head and stood up again.

'No! Not by the window. It's . . .' Ruthie's words came to a halt. *Too visible to shooters.* But if she said *that*, then . . . 'It's too bright there, in the sun. Back here, all right?'

Ruthie selected a table right at the back of the café and sat down, feeling like her legs were going to collapse beneath her. *Had* the car been coming for Annie? Now, she wasn't sure. She wasn't sure about anything, not anymore.

Annie ordered their coffees and then sat looking at Ruthie. 'Well?' she asked.

'Well . . .?' Ruthie asked, deliberately vague.

'What was all that about?'

'Nothing, nothing. I just thought you were going to get hit. I . . . silly of me. I misread things.'

Annie gave a small smile. 'Well thanks for the rescue. That was good of you, whether the threat was genuine or not. I'm not sure I would be so caring, given the . . . well, you know. But then, I never was as nice as you, Ruthie. We both know that.'

Their coffees arrived.

'How are you?' Annie asked, stirring hers.

'Oh, fine,' said Ruthie.

'You don't look it. You've got thinner. You look a bit . . . strung out,' said Annie. 'Are you feeling okay?'

'I'm fine.' Ruthie eyed her sister. 'Why'd you do it?'

'Hm?'

'What made you do it? Sleep with Max?'

'Oh God, must we . . .?'

'Yeah. Why not?'

Annie heaved a sigh. 'I was in love with him.'

'And you still are?'

Annie nodded.

'And telling me that on my wedding day. Why'd you do that?'

'I shouldn't have,' said Annie. 'I know that. It was cruel. I should have kept quiet.'

'Or not done the bloody deed in the first place,' suggested Ruthie.

Annie was staring at her. 'You ever been in love, Ruthie? *Really* in love?'

'I'm a married woman,' she shrugged.

'That's not what I asked you. Were you ever madly in love? Say – with Arthur from the docks, you remember him?'

'Yes. And no. Absolutely not.'

'And what about Max?'

Ruthie stared back at her sister. 'A little. I suppose. Madly? I dunno.'

'You weren't in love with him,' said Annie.

'What . . .?'

'"*I suppose?*"' Annie snorted. 'What sort of a fucking answer is that? I'll tell you what being in love feels like, shall

I Ruthie? And there's no "suppose" about it. It's torment. You feel it, every time you see him in the street, every time he walks into the room. You feel it in your heart and your head and even in your *cunt*.'

'Annie!' said Ruthie, shocked by the language.

'It's the utter truth,' Annie told her. 'It's deep down and it's devastating. And if it's taken away, what the hell are you left with? Madness, maybe. And the urge to hurt, just like you've been hurt. That's what being in love feels like. You can't take your eyes off him. You can't breathe properly. You can't eat or sleep. When he comes near you, you can't even think straight. *That's* what it feels like.'

Ruthie stirred in sugar and drank. The coffee was good. Bracing. And now she had a dilemma. Carry on keeping the secret? Or blurt it out to Annie now, alert her to the dangers, wouldn't that be the right thing, the *kind* thing, to do? But Annie had just given her a lecture on love. And Ruthie knew that her feelings for Max were nothing, *nothing*, compared to all that Annie had described. But having *felt* all that, could Annie's behaviour be – at all – justified?

Suddenly Ruthie felt very, very tired.

It was all too much. She drained her cup, abandoned any decision and stood up. 'I can't stop,' she said, and gathered up her bags and was gone, leaving Annie staring after her.

72

The minute she got back to the hotel she was currently staying at – she couldn't face Kieron right now, and anyway she knew he was busy, painting at his Shoreditch studio, and he hated interruptions – she phoned Max. Said she had to see him; and he came an hour later, meeting her in the hotel restaurant overlooking Kensington Gardens.

'What's this all about?' he asked when they were seated and the sommelier had sorted out wines for them.

'I have something important to tell you,' said Ruthie, bracing herself as if for an impact. Speaking to Annie, she hadn't been sure what to do; but she was sure now. She *had* to tell Max.

'Something serious?' he asked, his eyes on her face.

Ruthie stared at him, her handsome, cheating husband. He was, without a doubt, stunning. Black hair and dark-blue eyes and tanned skin and the air of a winner about him. An Alpha, wasn't that what they called men like Max? Well, he was. She'd noticed the way the women in the restaurant turned their heads and looked as he entered. And the way they looked at her, so envious.

Nothing to see here, ladies, she thought. *He isn't mine. He never has been.*

Ruthie was feeling very tense. She knew that as soon as she'd told him what she had to, Max was going to explode with rage and then all those admiring ladies who were lunching might have cause to change their minds over his desirability.

'Max,' Ruthie blurted out, unable to keep it to herself a moment longer, 'Redmond Delaney knows what happened to his brother Pat.'

Max sat back, his eyes on her face. 'You what?'

'You heard me. He knows all about it.'

Max's face was blank. 'And what did happen?' he asked.

'You know bloody well what happened. Pat Delaney was murdered at the Limehouse brothel. You know that. And you know who committed the murder. And who cleaned up after it.'

73

'Keep your voice down,' said Max, leaning forward.

'Oh, so now I've got your attention.' Ruthie sat up straighter.

'How do you know about any of this?' he asked.

The sommelier came back, went through the process of Max tasting the wine and nodding his approval. The man poured two glassfuls and departed. The waiter arrived, left menus, told them about the dish of the day.

'Give us a few minutes,' said Max, and the waiter left too.

Max turned his attention back to Ruthie. 'Well?' he asked.

Ruthie shrugged. 'I have my sources.'

'*Do* you. That's interesting. So somebody who was there at the time and they told you?'

Ruthie shrugged; said nothing.

'Ruthie . . .' said Max.

'Look. I just thought you ought to be warned about this.'

'So you've seen Annie?'

'Yes! Did she tell you?'

'Yes she did. She said you seemed very wound up. Said you were pulling her out of the road away from cars. Said she thought you were going a bit mental.'

'Look, she was involved, wasn't she?' Ruthie said in a fierce whisper. 'She was part of it. And your boys were there. *You* were part of it. All right, we may barely have been married at all, but . . . listen, I don't want any harm coming to you. Or to her. Which surprises me, really, because God knows you fucking-well deserve it, the pair of you.'

'It was never our intention—' Max started.

'Oh don't,' said Ruthie in an exasperated sigh. 'I know how it is with you two. I was just stupid enough not to see it beforehand. I wish I had. It would have been less painful all round.'

Max looked into his wife's eyes. 'I'm sorry,' he said.

'What? Oh, are you?' Ruthie took a big mouthful of the wine. 'Well that's all right then.'

'Truly, Ruthie.'

The waiter returned. They ordered.

Now, Max was smiling.

'What?' asked Ruthie through gritted teeth. She'd been pulling her hair out for *weeks* over this. How did he dare sit there now and smile?

'So you think we're in mortal danger, Annie and me?' he asked.

'Yes! Of course I do, because – oh Christ this is awful – I told Kieron Delaney about it, and he relayed that to Redmond, and then Redmond wanted to see me and I went there, over to Battersea, and I saw him and that weird twin of his and there was a girl there, drugged up, it was really, really bloody scary, and I thought, well, they know it all now, about what happened to Pat, and they are going to come after you, and after Annie. Max – listen – you have to take care. I did it for revenge, you know. But I regretted it right away. So I think the two of you should go away somewhere. They'll *kill* you if you don't.'

Max sat back, his eyes intent on her face. 'And you care why?' he asked her.

'I don't bloody know!' Ruthie burst out. 'But I do, all right?'

Max's smile broadened.

'What?' demanded Ruthie.

'Oh bloody hell, Ruthie,' he sighed. 'You're too nice, you know that?'

'What do you mean?'

'Look, let me put you out of your misery,' said Max.

'I don't—'

'We're in no danger.'

'Yes you are.'

'No. We're not. You don't know, do you?'

'Don't know what?'

'The reason why neither Redmond nor Orla nor Kieron will actually give a shit about what's happened to Pat.'

Ruthie frowned, puzzled. 'And that is . . .?'

'It's well known around town.'

'Well I don't know it. What the hell are you talking about?'

'Pat Delaney used to bully the twins when they were small. There was even talk that he was a nonce. That he fiddled with them. Which wouldn't surprise anybody. Pat was a dirty bastard. He had no limits. None at all.'

Ruthie sat back, her expression full of horror. 'That's awful.'

'Isn't it?' Max took a drink. 'Now do you see, Ruthie, why none of the remaining Delaney clan will much care if he's dead as toast?'

'Yes. I do.' Ruthie had a thought. Kieron, being violent toward her. 'Just the twins, then? When they were kids? You don't think . . . not Kieron as well?'

Max shrugged. 'Who knows? All I can think is that, to Redmond and Orla, Pat's disappearance is nothing but a relief. Don't you think so?'

Ruthie nodded, stunned.

'And you do see why they won't be too troubled over whoever did it?'

Ruthie thought of the Static caravan, the drugged girl, Orla with the needle, Redmond and his cold, cold eyes. Tainted, beautiful twins – and Redmond in charge of everything, having free rein, now that his older brothers – first Tory and then Pat – had been struck from the world.

And what about that other one? The previous leader of the Delaney tribe – Tory? What had really happened with him?

'I don't know what happened about Tory,' said Max, as if reading her mind.

'Everyone says you do,' said Ruthie.

'Do they. Well – I don't.'

Was he lying? The word on the streets was that Max had shot Tory dead. A revenge killing for the death of Queenie Carter. Was he seriously saying that wasn't true? Or just trying to make her believe it?

Their starters arrived – pâté for Ruthie, smoked salmon for Max.

'I'm not sure I can eat this. Or anything, really.' Astonishment was receding and now she was becoming aware that Kieron had been playing her. That he had known what Redmond and Orla's reaction would be and that she had nothing to fear from either of them.

But Kieron had let her go to the Battersea breaker's yard full of terror, and he had known – of course he had – that she would be fearful for her sister, and for her long-estranged husband. Because she was just *nice Ruthie*. Always thinking of others, worrying over them, even when they had done her damage. Kieron had known that, had played on it. He'd duped her, secretly laughing at her distress while knowing it had no real basis in fact.

That bastard.

'So Redmond and Orla, they'll be glad Pat's gone,' she said.

'That's right.'

'And Kieron would know that.'

'Damn sure he would.'

That utter *bastard*.

'Now come on, let's eat,' said Max. 'You look too thin.'

74

Ruthie got to Kieron's Shoreditch studio later that afternoon to find him prepping canvases with whitewash, wearing his old painter's shirt and scruffy jeans. She stood in the doorway for a moment or two, just watching him moving under the strong north light cast by the huge windows in the big disorderly room. She was thinking how stunningly handsome he was, and how very much she was growing to hate him.

He looked up, saw her. 'Ruthie, darling! How's it going? Haven't seen you in yonks. So! Good meeting was it? You and my scary brother Redmond?'

Ruthie took off her coat, tossed it aside. Looked at him some more.

'You're very quiet,' he said.

'Am I?'

'Yes you are.' He pouted. 'Was it very bad?'

Ruthie looked at him. 'You really are the most devious, twisted, rotten son of a bitch,' she said.

He actually laughed. 'What are you talking about, darling?'

Ruthie approached him, shaking her head in disbelief.

'You knew,' she said. 'You knew that there was nothing to fear from Redmond over Pat's disappearance, you knew it and yet you let me think the worst. That he was going to do for me. And Annie. And Max. You let me go in there, terrified out of my skin, literally sick with fear, and you *didn't bloody care*. No. More than that. The thought of how upset I was, that amused you, didn't it? It gave you a buzz, didn't it, Kieron?'

He didn't have time to reply.

Ruthie, the mildest of people, lost it. She flew at him, grabbed the brush out of his hand and hit him hard around the head with it.

'Hey!' He staggered back under this unexpected onslaught, the smile dying on his face.

Ruthie kept coming. She hit him, punched him, kicked him while he cowered back as if from a madwoman. Right then, that was what she was. Mad, hurt, furious. She hit and hit and hit until he recovered himself enough to grab her and hold her away from him.

'Now stop that!' he said, and she saw a spasm of actual fear in his eyes. He hadn't expected the worm to turn, had he? She'd startled him, taken him by surprise. If she'd had a gun in her hand, she would, in that instant, have shot him dead and been glad of it.

Still she writhed against him, trying to land more blows.

'Bastard!' she roared out. 'I fucking hate you, you stinking, devious horrible *bastard*!'

'Now Ruthie! Come on!' He was laughing again. Trying to cover his unease. He was stronger than her, he could overpower her easily. He'd proved that, in the past. Hurt her. *Hit* her. And apologised afterwards, been in floods of tears, *I'm so sorry, so sorry, it'll never happen again, I love you.*

She fought like a mad thing. Tried to land more blows. Couldn't. Finally Kieron shoved her back, away from him.

She came straight back at him, grabbed a palette knife from the easel, slashed hard, panting, enraged, at the canvas there, ripped it right down the middle.

'Hey! That cost bloody money you know! Don't.'

'You think I care?' she shouted in his face. She scrabbled in her bag and found her key to his Battersea apartment and flung it on the floor. 'I don't. I am *gone*, Kieron. And you can *fuck right off.*'

75

Ruthie took a cab back down to Guildford. At least there she could be alone, reasonably confident that Max would be elsewhere. She could lick her wounds, have a drink. The newly reinstated Miss Arnott greeted her with the usual chilly politeness and asked how long would she be planning to stay?

'As long as I fucking-well like,' Ruthie snapped, and went into the drawing room.

Miss Arnott followed her in. 'Only your cousin has been phoning. Trying to reach you.'

'I'll call her back,' said Ruthie. 'Get the fire lit in here, will you? It's freezing.'

'Will you be dining . . .?'

'No.'

Miss Arnott withdrew and Ruthie stood alone. She looked around her. Wondered when – if – Max was going to put this place back on the market. She wished he'd make his bloody mind up. There were only bad memories here after all: painful ones. Tiredly she slumped down in a chair, still wearing her coat, and looked around her.

Her home.

She remembered coming here after her wedding to Max, remembering going to bed with him that first time, the one and only time, remembering the dinner parties when she had sat at the foot of the table with him at the head, him in command – as always – and her pretending to be happy, to be chic, to be the smiling supportive wife even though she was dying, inch by painful inch, inside. And Eddie! Oh God, she so missed Eddie. But if his wild gay little spirit was to be found anywhere, it would certainly be here.

'You still here, are you Eddie?' she said aloud into the gaping silence. 'Just you and me now, babe, ain't that the truth? Just you and me.'

She would go upstairs. Have a bath. Get cosy. Why not? Oh yes, and have a drink. Of course that. She left the drawing room and was walking across the cavernous wood-panelled hallway when the phone on the hall table started ringing. Miss Arnott briskly ignored it and proceeded into the drawing room with the coal scuttle, her expression long-suffering.

No change there.

Ruthie snatched up the phone.

'Ruthie?'

Fuck, it was Kath again. She wasn't ready for this, not yet. She wanted – *needed* – to be alone. 'Kath,' she said on a sigh. 'What?'

'What do you mean, "what"? A hello would be nice.'

'Hello, Kath. What do you want?'

'Look, there's no need to be shirty. I'm just phoning to let you know, that's all.'

'Know what?'

'Annie. She's gone and got herself arrested for running a disorderly house at Upper Brook Street. She's in jail.'

'What the hell are you talking about?' asked Ruthie. *And why the fuck are you bothering me with it?*

'Are you listening to me? I always said she'd come to a bad end. Jimmy's right, she's wicked to the bone that one, he's always said so.'

Ruthie thought that she wouldn't trust much that Jimmy Bond had to say. Kath might think the sun shone out of his mean, manipulative arse, but it didn't.

'In jail?' Ruthie was staring at the phone. 'Annie's in jail?'

'She phoned me from the station, said she was in a jam, asked me to get a brief down there pronto.'

'How long are they going to hold her for?' Ruthie asked. *And why do I care about this?*

'One of her "clients" posted bail. She'll be out within a few hours, no bother. Come on Ruthie, surely you don't feel sorry for her? She's brought all this on herself. She *deserves* it.'

'Where will she go?'

'Where do you think? Back to the Limehouse knocking shop I bet. All her old pals are there. I heard from Ellie that Kieron Delaney showed up down the clink, wanting to take her home with him, but she told him to naff off.'

So Kieron was *still* in pursuit of Annie. No surprise there, really.

None at all.

76

Next day, Ruthie had Dave drive her down to the village. She'd run out of vodka so she bought two bottles in the little store there, and picked up the paper and saw the front-page headlines *Jackie Kennedy lookalike Annie Bailey seized by police! The Mayfair Madam under arrest!* There were pictures of her; one in particular showed her walking along a London street, glamorous as a film star, wearing a fur coat and big sunglasses, long dark hair flowing around her shoulders.

Ignoring the knowing smirk from the woman behind the counter, Ruthie took her purchases home and told herself firmly that she was glad. Annie *should* suffer. She *should* be in jail. She *should* get sent down.

Back at the house, Ruthie went upstairs with the papers and the vodka and shut herself in Eddie's room and spoke to Eddie, who was always somehow there these days, hovering close, semi-transparent in his pale floral shirts and trendy jeans, his impish smile embracing her.

'Aren't you the least bit sorry for her?' Eddie whispered in her ear. 'Really?'

'Why should I be? Look how she's hurt me.' Ruthie poured out a glass of neat vodka and sipped it. Lovely. Straight away she felt calmer, better.

'Yeah, but *blood*, Ruthie. She's your blood,' Eddie reminded her.

He lounged at the bottom of her bed, going in and out of focus. Sometimes, he was barely there at all, just the faintest shadow, fading, vanishing until all that remained was that sweet Cheshire-cat smile. But today he was here, he seemed *solid* somehow, he was all she had and she was glad of him.

Ruthie lay back, cupping her glass, savouring the relaxation she felt flooding through her limbs.

'Pat Delaney was no loss,' she said faintly. 'He did for you, didn't he, Eddie?'

'Yes, I'm sure it was him.'

'The evil git.'

'Gone now. Sleeping with the fishes, isn't that what they say?'

'Don't the Mafia say that?'

'Yeah, but this wasn't an American job. Although the Barolli family were over here, weren't they? They could have done it.' Eddie was quiet, fading in, fading out. Then he said: 'You seen that Barolli boss? That Constantine?' Eddie gave a low, lustful chuckle that seemed to reverberate throughout the room. 'Honey, *I* wouldn't kick him out of bed.'

'I saw him. Silver hair and those blue, blue eyes. I don't think there was a woman in the entire gallery who didn't notice him.' Ruthie mulled it all over. 'What about Tory? Who shot him? Max says he didn't.'

'Take your pick,' said Eddie, shrugging. 'I know I buried Max's gun for him around that time.'

'God, really? It's scary,' said Ruthie. 'You want a drink, Eddie?'

But Eddie didn't answer. Ruthie looked at the foot of the bed and he was gone, vanished. Instead, Miss Arnott was standing there, stiff as a board, her face rigid with disapproval.

77

'Yes?' asked Ruthie, irritated by the very sight of her. She swung her legs to the edge of the bed, grabbed a voddy bottle, refilled her glass. Some of the vodka splashed onto the newspapers that were spread out on the counterpane.

'Whoops,' said Ruthie with a laugh, then catching the direction of Miss Arnott's gaze she gathered the papers up and flung them onto the floor.

'I think you should eat something,' said Miss Arnott frostily. 'It's not good to drink on an empty stomach you know. I'll prepare some sandwiches.'

Ruthie shrugged. 'If you want,' she said.

'I'll have them ready in the drawing room in half an hour, yes?'

'Yes, yes,' said Ruthie, tired but giggly. She wished Eddie would come back.

And God, she hoped Annie was all right. Stupid, or what? But she wouldn't lower herself to enquire, not from Annie herself and not from Kath and not even from Max. She was soft, yes – but not *that* soft.

Stupid, soft little Goody-Two-Shoes Ruthie.

'That's me,' she said, but she was speaking to empty air. No Miss Arnott. She'd left the bedroom.

And now – no Eddie, either.

78

The next day, bored and headachy after a long night's drinking, she had Dave drive her back to Mum's place and then she got a cab to Kieron's at Battersea because she had nowhere else she really wanted to go, did she. And what did that say about her, she wondered? She'd been thinking it all over more and more lately. Kieron hit her, abused her, mocked her. Was he *really* the best she could do? The best she could hope for in this crazy, hopeless world she inhabited?

Yes. She realised that he was.

But Kieron was out in the road, just getting into another taxi.

'Oh! It's you. You're back, are you? Listen, I have to pop out. You stay here, yes? Make yourself comfortable.' He gave her the key. The same one she'd flung at his feet yesterday. 'Look after Bertie.'

Ruthie stared at him. *Look after bloody Bertie?*

'Where are you going?' she asked.

'Out, just out. Things to do.'

She went into the flat, shut Bertie in the kitchen, and phoned Kath.

'What's Kieron up to?' she asked.

'What do you mean?' asked Kath.

'He seems jittery. I just wondered . . . is he meeting up with Annie?'

The fact that he might be about to do that still ate at her. She didn't love Kieron – not in the least; in fact, she liked him less and less with every day that passed. He frightened her with his rages. But it niggled her, *annoyed* her, to think that his real quarry was her sister, and he was just making use of her, Ruthie, good old reliable, sweet-natured Ruthie.

'I'll keep an eye out. Have a word with Ellie. How's that?'

'Thanks,' said Ruthie, and gave Kath Kieron's number. She put the phone down and sat there for over an hour, listening in irritation to Bertie whining behind the kitchen door.

Finally she went and opened it.

'What?' she asked Bertie, and his stumpy little tail wagged, just briefly. 'What's this then, truce? You want a walk?'

At the word 'walk' his tail wagged, harder.

Ruthie got his lead and took him out. He did his business and they went back to the flat. She opened a tin of dog food, filled his empty water bowl. Left him to eat and drink in the kitchen while she went on through to the lounge.

To her surprise, not half an hour later Bertie sprang up onto the sofa and sat down beside her.

'Oh! Pals now, are we?' she asked.

Bertie snarled.

Ruthie smiled and gave him a pat on the head. At least the dog was sort of on her side – for a change.

The evening drew in. She turned on the TV, saw Patrick McGoohan playing *Danger Man* and turned it off again. Walked around the apartment. Thought of having a drink but didn't. Then, late in the evening, the phone rang. She jumped off the sofa and ran to pick it up.

'Yes?' she snapped.

'It's me,' said Kath. Her voice sounded off. Shaky.

'What is it?'

'Ruthie, you better sit down. There's been a shooting.'

79

An hour after getting Kath's call, Ruthie sat in the waiting room outside the emergency theatre at the hospital. Kath sat there with her, and Jimmy Bond was there too, pacing restlessly.

'I saw it all happening,' said Jimmy.

'Right,' said Ruthie numbly.

'I *told* him it was a bad do,' said Jimmy. 'I told Max.'

'Right,' said Ruthie.

'She's in shock,' said Kath to Jimmy.

'Aren't we bloody all,' said Jimmy, sitting down with a sigh.

'Do you think it's going to be . . . fatal?' asked Ruthie.

'Could be,' said Jimmy. 'It looked damned bad.'

'Christ,' said Ruthie. She clutched at her head. 'And did they . . . did they catch him? The one that shot—?'

'You mean did they catch Kieron fucking Delaney?' Jimmy shook his head. 'No. He ran. Got away. And he wasn't aiming for Annie, anyway. He came there I reckon with the specific intention of shooting Max dead. *She* got in the way.'

'How the hell—?'

'She threw herself in front of Max. Can you believe that?' Jimmy was shaking his head. Plainly, he couldn't. 'The balls on that girl. She saw that Kieron was going to kill him and she threw herself in the way of a bullet.'

'And now she's in surgery and she might not live,' said Ruthie. This was it – the final outcome of the affair that Max and Annie had been conducting: death and disaster.

'Where's Max?' Kath asked Jimmy, just as Max appeared.

Ruthie was shocked by the sight of him. There was blood all over his shirt and his face was grey, etched with strain. And when Ruthie started to cry, he did something he had rarely done before – he put his arms around her and hugged her and told her that everything was going to be all right. But Ruthie didn't believe anything was going to be all right, ever again.

80

Max and Ruthie sat there together into the small hours of the night. Kath and Jimmy went home since their staying could serve no purpose. The hours dragged and slowly daylight came creeping through the blinds while all around them the hospital woke up and life went on. But did it, Ruthie wondered, go on for Annie?

'The bullet nicked an artery, missed her heart by an inch,' Max told her, not wanting to sugar-coat it because what good would that do? He was convinced he'd lost Annie and he didn't want to get Ruthie's hopes up that the outcome could be any different.

Then all at once the surgeon was there.

'Mr Carter?'

Max and Ruthie looked up. The surgeon's dark-green gown was stained brown at the front. *Annie's blood*, thought Ruthie, feeling sick. He looked young in his cap, his mask pushed down around his neck. Too young to be trusted with her sister's life, surely?

'How is she?' asked Max.

The surgeon took a breath, glanced at Ruthie.

'This is Miss Bailey's sister – my wife,' said Max.

The surgeon nodded. 'We've patched her up, Mr Carter. But she's lost a lot of blood. She's not out of the woods yet.'

'Thank you,' said Max, and Ruthie – to her horror – started to weep. 'When can we see her?'

'Maybe tomorrow. Go home and try to get some rest. Phone tomorrow and we'll see how she's doing.'

81

It was awful, loving someone, Ruthie thought. Doubly awful when you knew damned well that they didn't deserve it. After weeks in hospital, still very frail, visibly ill, Annie had to come out, come home.

But home to *where*?

Max decided that it should be the Guildford house. A private ambulance was arranged and before Ruthie could even get her head around any of it, there Annie was, nurses in close attendance, at the house that Ruthie had grudgingly come to think of as *hers*.

'They postponed the disorderly house trial because she was shot,' Kath told Ruthie later. 'But they're rescheduling now. She'll have her day in court soon. About six weeks' time, they're saying.'

Another worry! Ruthie frowned. 'Do you think she'll get sent down?'

'Oh yeah. Bound to.'

So how the hell could Ruthie complain about Annie being nursed on *her* territory, in *her* house? Annie looked so pitiful, a ghost of herself. Ruthie saw the nurses coming and going, cleaning Annie's alarmingly fragile body. Then one day Ruthie stood at the door to what had now been designated her younger sister's room, watching one of the nurses – a right uppity cow, a proper jobsworth, Ruthie really didn't like her at all – change the dressings on Annie's wound. She saw Annie wincing with pain and had to turn away. But the nurses knew what they were doing, didn't they? Of course they did. She would have to leave them to get on with their job.

Then she heard Annie cry out and something in her went *snap*. She pushed the door open and strode in.

'Don't pull her ruddy skin off,' she said, pushing the woman back, away from her sister. Annie was pale and sweating with pain, Ruthie saw.

That enraged her even more.

'The old dressing had to come off, Mrs Carter,' said the nurse, colouring up with annoyance.

'Why not use a bloody crowbar and have done with it? Go on, get out. I'll do it.'

And so – very much against her better judgement – Ruthie found herself nursing her sister back to health.

'You shouldn't be doing this,' Annie protested time after time while Ruthie brought her bedpans, washed her, disposed of old dressings, put on new, fed her, did *everything* for her.

'I'm your sister,' said Ruthie. 'Who else should do it but me?'

Ruthie had a word with Max and the day nurse was disposed of; they kept the night nurse on, a gentle tubby little woman, so that Ruthie could get some rest.

As the weeks passed, Annie slowly grew stronger. Finally she could get downstairs, sit out in the garden; and Ruthie, watching her sister, watching Max walking out there to sit with her, knew that, at last, it was time.

'I'm going up to London this afternoon,' she told Annie. 'I think I might stay in Queenie's old gaff in Bow. Max won't mind.'

It had been surprisingly nice, having this time with Annie. As she'd grown stronger, the two of them had had long chats together. It had almost been like it *used* to be years ago, the two of them, friends as well as sisters, laughing together, telling each other their woes, commiserating, putting the whole wicked world to rights. But Ruthie knew that Annie understood. This situation was just too difficult to go on with.

'You've been wonderful,' Annie told her.

'That's me. Wonderful Ruthie.'

Annie laughed at that. 'Mum always said you were.'

'Dad always said *you* were.'

So this was goodbye.

On their last day together, Ruthie dropped a quick kiss onto Annie's cheek. Then she hurried off.

It was only when Ruthie had closed the bedroom door behind her that she broke down and cried.

82

Dave brought the car round and suddenly Ruthie was leaving for the last time, leaving the grand Surrey mansion that had been the backdrop to all her misery. She didn't actually know *what* she was going to do now, not really. Yes, she'd mentioned Queenie's old gaff, but she wasn't sure. Maybe she'd travel?

She got into the car and Dave started the engine.

Max didn't come out to see her off.

Of course not.

This was goodbye in many, many ways. She looked at her wedding ring and the super-expensive engagement ring she had once been afraid to wear; the diamond winked mockingly in the pale sunlight. And there was another impressive ring too, a big cabochon-cut emerald. Oh, she had a lot of jewellery. None of it meant a damned thing, not really. She remembered sitting at Max's dining table, dressed up to the nines, the other women eyeing up her clothes, her jewels, coveting them – and coveting Max too. She could have told them right then that they were wasting their time.

Oh God – if only I'd known the truth before it all began, thought Ruthie.

'Queenie's old gaff, yeah?' asked Dave, getting in, starting the engine.

It was then, at that precise moment, that Ruthie saw the figure lurking out by the main gate.

Christ! It couldn't be. Could it?

She half expected Dave to say something, to have seen the figure too. But clearly he hadn't.

'Look, I've forgotten something,' she said quickly. 'Take the car out on the road and wait for me there, will you?'

Dave didn't argue. He was used to her issuing orders, and ever since she had threatened him with Max he had fallen into line very nicely. He did so now; she got out, and he drove off. Ruthie walked out onto the huge lawn beside the gravel driveway, went right to the edge of the border where the shadows of the trees deepened, sheltering the garden from the road.

She waited.

She waited some more.

Had she imagined him there?

Then the figure emerged from the shrubbery.

She hadn't imagined it.

'Oh Christ,' she said faintly.

It was Kieron.

83

He looked dishevelled, like he'd been sleeping rough. He came over to where she stood waiting. He was grinning his usual faintly manic grin. The one that always made her nervous.

'Ruthie!'

She stared at him in stone-cold horror.

'You can't be here,' she said. She wanted to hit him. The stupid bastard! 'What the fuck are you doing? You *can't be here.*'

'What, you going to turn me in? I don't think so.'

'Max is here. I only have to call out and there'll be help here in a second.'

And Tone, Max's minder, he was here too. Where? Round in the garage block? He must be. If Tone got hold of Kieron, there'd be murder committed for sure.

'She's here then,' he said. 'Is she?'

Ruthie closed her eyes. Opened them, praying he'd be gone. He was still there. He'd come here for news of Annie. Not to find *her*, dull boring Ruthie. No! All he was concerned about was hearing how Annie was.

'She's here,' said Ruthie, wondering when this nightmare, this utter bloody *circus*, would come to an end. 'She's here and if you've any thought of getting in to see her you can think again. Max will kill you. I'm just surprised you're not dead already. Where have you been, hiding out somewhere?'

Suddenly she was furious. This bastard, this obsessed *fool*, had nearly killed her sister, who despite all her faults was worth a dozen of him.

'I never meant to hurt Annie,' he said.

'You were aiming for Max, Jimmy said. And Annie stepped in front of him.'

Kieron actually looked distraught. 'When I left the club—'

'When you *ran* from the club,' she corrected him.

'Look, I had to, didn't I? The place was crawling with Carter people. I had to get out, away. I was afraid I'd done her damage but I couldn't wait around to find out for sure.'

'And you were sorry.'

'Of *course* I was sorry.'

Ruthie looked at him in disgust. Whatever his failings, she knew that Max would never have done that, taken the coward's way out. He would have stayed, faced whatever came. He wouldn't have deserted the woman he claimed to love, as Kieron had.

'What will you do now?' asked Ruthie.

Kieron shrugged. 'The Spanish place. I might go there, wait for things to settle down.'

'You think Max is going to simply forget this? God, you don't know him at all, do you? He'll hunt you down until your dying day. I'm not kidding you, Kieron. He would *skin* you if he knew you were hanging about down here.'

Kieron stepped closer. There was something dangerous in his eyes now.

'But you won't tell him, will you?' he said quietly. 'No. Of course you won't. Good gentle Ruthie, aren't you? A fucking fool more like.'

'Kieron . . .'

'You don't know how it's been for me!' he burst out suddenly. 'Half my family dead or dying. And then *her*, that prick tease Annie . . .'

All the chaos he'd caused, and here he was trying to get her to feel sorry for him!

But . . . she *did*, just a bit. She knew the effect Annie could have. She knew that if Annie turned her attention on a man, flirted with him . . . well, many was the man who'd been knocked sideways by a low, sweeping glance from those beautiful dark eyes. Ruthie knew it.

And then there was movement behind her, and Dave was there.

He was holding a gun, and it was pointed straight at Kieron.

84

'Dave!' said Ruthie. The sight of the gun in his hand terrified her. Seemed to choke off her breath.

'Shut up,' said Dave, waving the gun in Kieron's direction. 'You! Delaney! Come on. Walk!'

Dave gestured toward the house, indicating that Kieron should get going.

If he goes in there, he's dead, thought Ruthie.

She could see in Kieron's eyes that he knew it.

'Look, let's work this out,' said Kieron.

'*What?*' asked Dave.

'Come on! We don't have to do this. I can pay you. All you have to do is ignore this. Forget you saw anything. I wasn't here. Okay?'

'But you fucking *are* here, aintcha?' snarled Dave. He waved the gun again. 'Now, no pissing about. Get your arse up to the house, all right, sunshine? Or I'll damned well shoot you right here and *carry* you up there.'

'Kieron's right,' Ruthie managed to say.

'*What?*'

'He is. There's no need for any more bloodshed.'

'I already told you, lady. Shut the fuck up. You don't know what you're dealing with here. Step back, out the way.'

She stepped back. But as she did so, Kieron grabbed her. She felt her feet leave the ground and suddenly he was clutching her against him. She could feel his heart beating thunderously at her back. His grip was crushing.

She looked at Dave, who was holding the gun higher now, pointing the damned thing straight at her. Would he fire? Think of her as collateral damage, gamble on the bullet passing straight through her and hitting its true target?

'Kieron . . .' she managed to get out. Her throat was dry. Her heart was pounding hard, just like Kieron's. Dave was no friend of hers. She had not treated him well in the time he'd been chauffeuring her around. She wished now she had treated him better – and it was too late.

'Move back, out the way,' snapped Kieron. 'We're going. Hand over the car keys.'

'You arsehole, you think you'll get away with this? You won't.'

'The *keys*,' yelled Kieron.

'They're in the car,' said Dave, still holding the gun high.

Was he going to risk taking the shot?

She tensed, awaiting the agony of the bullet hitting her, penetrating her body. She thought of how Annie had suffered and, oh God, she didn't want to go through that. She didn't think she'd have the strength to endure it, not the way Annie had. Or was Dave going for a head shot, hoping to miss her? And what about Max and Annie if she got shot right now, by accident or otherwise? Wouldn't that just be dandy for them? The unwanted wife, out of the way, dead? How neat was that?

'Dave, don't!' she begged.

Don't shoot me. Please don't . . .

Once, she had wanted to die. Now, she found to her amazement that she didn't. She was desperate suddenly to hold on to life, to get a second chance.

Oh so slowly, Dave lowered the gun.

'Go on then. Fuck off out of it, Delaney – and just be glad you'll live to tell the tale. Keys are in the car. But this ain't over. You'll be hearing from us. You can bet on it.'

'Come on,' said Kieron, grabbing Ruthie's arm, still careful to keep her in between himself and the threat of that handgun. Ruthie's feet felt like lead; there was no strength left in her.

They left Dave there, Kieron hustling her along impatiently as they stepped out into the road.

'Where are we going?' Ruthie asked, her voice shaking.

'Shut up,' said Kieron, and threw her into the passenger seat. There was a mad – *insane* – glint in his eyes and she was terrified. He climbed in, glancing quickly back at the drive first – expecting at any moment, she could see, that Dave would come out onto the road after them and start shooting.

Kieron started the engine, slammed the car into first, and they roared away.

85

Ruthie was terrifyingly aware now that she was getting further and further away from help; from Max, from Dave, from Tone. The car roared on and Kieron hunched over the wheel, fully focused on the road ahead, speeding along. She could smell the sour sweat of fear on him, sheer desperation was coming off him in waves.

'You see, you're mine, Ruthie. I *own* you. That's what you seem to keep forgetting,' he said.

He owned her?

Something in the way he said that made her straighten, made her start to think. She had to get away from him. Had to escape. The miles were whipping by and what the hell was she going to do?

She had to do *something*.

But what?

There was only one possible thing.

She grabbed the steering wheel.

86

She could hear Kieron yelling as the car careered off the road.

'You bitch, you silly bitch!'

The car hit the grassy verge at speed as Ruthie threw all her weight onto the steering wheel, ignoring Kieron's punches and shoves as he tried to get her off it. The car bumped and thumped and was suddenly, shockingly, nose-down in a ditch, wheels spinning, engine still roaring momentarily. Then the motor cut out and there was just Kieron, shrieking insults at her. *Thank God for little miracles*, she had time to think, because Kieron's side of the car was in the ditch and her side was up in the air.

She scrabbled for the door handle and shoved the door open with a massive effort, gravity working against her, Kieron battering at her with his fists, the wind snatching at her as she hauled herself out of the door and fell out onto the grass. She could hear birds singing up in the thrashing trees. She was still alive – but for how long? Once she had wanted to end it – but now? She wanted to *live*.

Too far to run back to the house.

Yes. Too far.

Instead she ran away from the house, away from the certainty of help. Her legs trembling, she ran. She could hear him back in the car, shouting obscenities after her, but no matter about that, he was stuck in there for a moment and so it gave her time to get away, if she could.

This was a quiet country road and all she could hear after a while was the wind, the birds, her own laboured breathing. Kieron stopped screaming and shouting and she wished he wouldn't because she could tell where he was if she could hear him, however imperfectly.

She ran.

Focused on it.

Focused on *escape*.

87

When she saw the gravel driveway up ahead, she almost wept with relief. She ran up it but it was very long and she started to panic. At no point had she dared to look back over her shoulder. For all she knew, Kieron could be close behind her, she just didn't know and she was too scared to check.

When she got to the building – a large house, Georgian she thought, a classical piece of architecture – she hammered on a big solid door with a fancy fan light above it, and prayed to God that someone would answer.

Nobody answered.

She thumped at the door harder; the breath was wheezing in and out of her in sheer desperation. Kieron was going to come, he was going to catch her, and he would kill her this time. She knew he would.

The door opened so suddenly that she almost fell inside. A tanned elderly man stood there, bald-headed, reading glasses slipping down his nose. He was dressed in cardigan, slippers, red corduroy trousers.

He looked in astonishment at this bedraggled female standing on his doorstep.

'What . . .?' he started, then Ruthie pushed past him and inside and in a voice heaving with panic she gasped out: '*Shut the door!*'

88

'We should call the police,' the old man told her. 'If you've been involved in an accident—'

'Look, someone's chasing me. I . . . he might have seen me coming in here, I don't know. No police.' She knew that Max wouldn't thank her if she got the police involved. 'I need a taxi, can you please call me a taxi?'

To her relief, he did. And ten minutes later, the taxi arrived, crunching up onto the gravel of the driveway. Ruthie opened the front door, looked nervously outside. She couldn't see Kieron. But then – there was tree cover all around. He could run out at any moment, catch her, hurt her.

'I feel I should do more,' said the man.

But she was bolting out of the front door, running to the taxi, leaving him standing on the steps, watching.

'Waterloo Station,' she told the driver while her rescuer looked on.

This time, she was getting away properly. Getting away for good.

89

Someone was knocking at the front door again.

It was turning into a busy day. First that panicky young woman almost beating the door down, and now this – a thin striking young man with strawberry-blond hair and friendly green eyes stood there. Thaddeus Newman's wife had died five years ago, so living here on his own was a lonely business sometimes, and a knock on the door was usually something he welcomed.

'Hello,' he said, and then to his surprise the young man pushed past him, burst into the hall. Manners cost nothing, after all, and this was simply *rude*.

'Where did she go? My friend?' he asked. 'She came in here. Didn't she?'

The older man stared at this young man suspiciously. The woman had, after all, come here in a state of panic. 'Well, I—'

'You'd better tell me. She's mentally unstable you know. She needs medical help.'

'Well I don't feel that I should,' said the older man.

'Oh come on! I saw her come in here. And I saw a car go out of the drive, did you know where she was going?'

Thaddeus did. He'd heard what she'd said to the taxi driver. But looking at the wild expression in the younger man's eyes, he doubted that he should pass that information on. 'I don't think—'

Suddenly the previously civil young man grabbed the older one by the throat.

'*Listen, you old bastard, tell me where she was going!*'

It was shocking, the transformation. Like Jekyll and Hyde. The older man said: 'I shall call the police.'

'No you bloody won't,' said the younger man, and pushed and shoved the older one back, along the hall, into the kitchen.

90

When she reached Waterloo, Ruthie boarded a train to Portsmouth. She opened the door to the first-class carriage and just before she stepped inside she took off her engagement and wedding rings. The elderly porter helpfully deposited her large handbag – the only luggage she had with her – in the overhead compartment and awaited his tip. She put the two rings into his outstretched hand.

'What the . . .?' He looked at them, then at her face.

'Keep them or sell them, I don't care which,' said Ruthie.

The porter shrugged and slipped them into his pocket, and he shut the door after her.

She sat down, still shaky but feeling at last that she might have a chance at some sort of normal life. Yes, why not?

She was going to have an adventure: she'd never had one before.

The world was opening up to her at last.

There was the toot of the whistle and the train lurched forward and then started to move more smoothly. She sat down, thought of all that she would do with her life, all that was now open to her. She snuggled down into her comfy seat and imagined cool countries. Norway. Denmark. And what about Venice? She'd never been. That would be wonderful.

The door to her little compartment opened.

'Tickets please,' said a voice above her head.

She went to stand up, reach for her bag.

But it wasn't a guard standing there. It was Kieron Delaney.

ANNIE
91

1965

The thing is, she never expected to lose it. Hell, she never expected to lose anything, did she? That was her, Annie Bailey, full of it, stalking, swaggering, *strutting* through life, taking whatever she wanted: businesses, other people's husbands, you name it, she'd scoop it up.

She'd just that day come out of the Limehouse knocking shop and her pals there – Dolly who was running the place, Aretha who was its resident dominatrix and Darren who accommodated the gay gentleman clients – had congratulated her on how well it was all going. Her life with Max Carter. Oh – and especially, the baby. *His* baby, the one which – scandalously – she was expecting.

Everything was perfect, right?

Wrong. For instance, there was this brunette. The one that Kath – Annie's cousin – had not an hour earlier told her that Max had been seen with in town. Kissing. Not that she really believed it. Of course not. But still. She'd won him, hadn't she? Yes she had. First prize in the great raffle of life. He was *hers*.

'She was all over him like a cheap suit,' said Kath.

'Yeah? Says who?'

'Says me. I saw it.'

'Where?'

'Outside Raymond's Revue Bar, in Soho.'

To think of anyone else poaching on her territory? Annie was not pleased, not pleased at all. Talk of a brunette with Max made her feel sick to her stomach. *She* was his brunette, right?

Seriously, Annie was rattled. Because deep down – way deep in her gut – was the loitering feeling that maybe she deserved another catastrophe. The whole business of Max and Ruthie had been squared away, hadn't it? Her sister – Max's wife Ruthie – had left the Guildford house for good and was going abroad she'd said, travelling, and that was for the best. So what was this thing with the brunette? What the hell was that about?

What goes around comes around . . .

Connie, Annie's drunken bum of a mother had said that, time and again. She said it was karma, some shit like that. So maybe Annie deserved to lose the baby, deserved to lose Max to another brunette, deserved to lose her sister Ruthie too, after all she'd done to her. Maybe this was payback time, at last.

The thought frightened Annie; the guilt ate at her.

Nah, it couldn't happen – could it?

That same night, she started to bleed. She should have been nicer to Ruthie. She should never have betrayed her.

Ruthie, I'm sorry, she thought.

Too late though. All too late.

Because sorry or not, Annie still lost Max's baby.

92

Next day, an uncaring private male doctor sat behind his desk and looked at Annie Bailey with clinical detachment. Annie could see herself, just as he was seeing her. An unmarried woman, clearly the mistress of the wealthy man who sat beside her. A high-priced whore who'd sold herself for money.

'The child is no more,' he said.

Annie could see that the doctor was thinking that this must be a relief for Max Carter, actually. Now Max would take more care and he could move on, not be burdened with this – almost certainly unwanted – situation.

'One in four pregnancies ends in miscarriage,' said the doctor, pushing his spectacles further up his long hooked nose.

Annie couldn't believe it. One moment she'd been over the moon, happy, with the man she loved, the next everything was in bits. The baby was simply *gone*.

'My advice? Go home and rest,' said the doctor.

He didn't say try again, thought Annie. *If I'd had a ring on my finger, he'd have said, try again.*

Miss Arnott had a fire waiting in the drawing room when they got back to Guildford. Annie, not even bothering to take off her coat, sat down on the couch and tried to get her head around what had just happened.

What goes around comes around.

She had betrayed her sister's trust, robbed her sister's man, and this was her punishment for all the badness that she'd perpetrated against dear kind Ruthie. She *deserved* to suffer, to have this horrible thing happen to her. She knew it.

Max sat down beside her, pulled her into his arms.

'There'll be other babies,' he said.

Annie shoved him away. 'Yeah – only not *this* one,' she snapped.

Max eyed her steadily. 'Shit happens,' he shrugged. 'You're healthy and you heard what the doctor said, there's no reason at all why you shouldn't conceive again. No reason at all.'

Annie shook her head. No reason, except maybe the fates were against her. Maybe all the badness she'd visited upon Ruthie was now coming back to haunt her. And right now, what she wanted most in the world? To talk to Ruthie, to get reassurance, kindness, a hug from her sweet, kind big sister. Which was out of the question. She needed it – but she'd blown any chance of getting it straight out of the water. Ruthie was gone, back to her own life: travelling, having fun.

'We weren't even trying. It was the last thing on my mind.'

'And mine. But we were smashing the life out of each other, going at it like rabbits. You have to admit that. And not taking precautions.'

'So it's my fault?'

'How the hell would it be your fault? That was down to me, wasn't it. But you never insisted.'

'Oh for fuck's sake,' said Annie, and sprang to her feet.

'What?' asked Max.

'God, you men, you're so bloody practical, aren't you. Lose one baby, have another. Like it doesn't matter, like it's nothing.'

'I didn't say that,' said Max, standing up too.

'No, that's *precisely* what you said,' shouted Annie.

'What the hell are we arguing for?' asked Max. 'We're on the same side here.'

'The way that bastard looked at me,' said Annie, smiling a bitter little smile.

'Like what?'

'Like I was a tart,' said Annie angrily.

'You know what you should do?' asked Max.

'No! What?'

'Go up and have a bath and go to bed. Try to wind down.'

'Meaning I am wound *up*!'

'Yeah! You are! I know it's tough. I know it's hard. But throwing the bloody furniture at each other's not going to make any of it better.'

'Right,' said Annie.

'Time will pass and—'

'Oh, time is a great healer . . .?'

'Well – it is.'

'I deserved this.'

'*What?*'

'You heard. I deserved it. Of course I did. Look what I did to Ruthie. That was a bloody awful thing to do to anyone, but to my own sister?'

'Oh for God's sake . . .'

'I've been waiting for something like this, that's the truth. Just waiting and dreading it, knowing that sooner or later the axe would fall.'

'That's fucking ridiculous,' said Max.

'No it isn't!'

'Yes it bloody well is.' Max approached her again and Annie stepped back, away from him.

'Look, I'm not going on with this because it's pointless and it's stupid, okay? I've got things to do in town; I'll be back late. All right?'

He was walking out on her!

Why did men always do that, not engage, not thrash the thing out? Why did they always just *walk away*?

'Okay,' said Annie coldly. 'You go. I'm okay here, with Cruella de Vil looking after me. Let's hope she don't poison the soup or something.'

Max started to speak, then stopped, shook his head: 'You're not making any sense.'

'I've just lost a baby, that could explain it,' said Annie furiously. 'And that woman's always looked down her nose at me. And what's this Kath's told me about you and a brunette?'

'What are you talking about?'

'You know.'

'I'm going,' said Max.

'Fine! Piss off out of it!'

Max went.

93

Time did pass, but it didn't seem to heal very much. Annie's body recovered. Her periods resumed. But there was a new thing happening and it was horrible – there was an icy sort of gulf between her and Max. He was always out working, she was too often alone at the Guildford house. Once, there had been such passion, such *heat*, between them. Now, there was just this huge yawning void that had formed on the night she lost their baby.

She didn't know how to cross that void. Max was cool, cut off from her. Remote. Whenever she attempted to be warm with him, he was frosty, killing her efforts with a stony look or a brushing-away of a caress.

She hated it.

Was this how he'd been with Ruthie?

She didn't know. But experiencing it now, she felt renewed sympathy for her sister. Max in a foul mood was no easy thing to handle. And his mood, these days, was usually bad.

So it was that the night the call came, Annie was alone in the Guildford place and he was up in town doing something that he didn't discuss with her. Private business. Club business. Gangland stuff. Stuff that, his manner clearly said, had nothing to do with her.

The phone extension in the master bedroom started ringing at about one thirty in the morning. She'd been asleep, alone – of course – and the shrill tone of the telephone made her start violently, like she'd been hit.

Annie sat up in the dark, heart pounding, alarmed. The bloody phone. She hated phones, but just about any damned thing could make her jump out of her skin lately.

She reached over, switched on the bedside light, snatched up the receiver.

'Yeah?' she snapped.

'Annie?' It was a woman's voice.

'Who wants her?'

'Charming as ever.'

Annie squinted at the phone. 'Who is this?'

'You don't even bloody know, do you?'

'That's why I'm asking.' It was some sort of crank call, some bloody nuisance probably drunk and insensible, phoning haphazard numbers and somehow alighting on hers.

'It's me,' said the voice.

'Who the fuck is me?'

'Kath. It's *Kath*, for God's sake.'

'Kath *who*?'

'Fucking hell. Who do you think? Kath your *cousin*.'

Annie scraped a hand through her hair. Kath *never* got in touch with her, if she could avoid it. She braced herself. Kath was Mrs Jimmy Bond these days and busy popping out kids with no discernible trouble at all. Unlike Annie, who just lost them. The pain of it stabbed her again, making her tone sharp. 'What's going on?' she asked.

'The police called me. They found her in a flat near Tower Bridge.' Kath reeled off the block's name, the flat number. 'She still had me in the back of her passport as next of kin. Don't know why, it should have been Max, shouldn't it? But anyway—'

'Who did?'

'God, what's up with you?' Kath asked, her voice suddenly shaky with tears.

Annie took a deep breath. Oh, there was nothing much wrong with her. She'd suffered the trauma of being shot and then the disorderly court case and then she'd lost a baby and had effectively pushed Max away from her. They hadn't made love since the night she'd lost their child. In fact, they'd barely even spoken to each other. She felt frozen, unreachable. Untouchable. Miserable.

'What are you talking about? Couldn't this have waited until morning?' she asked.

'What the . . .' Kath paused, clearly exasperated.

'Who are you talking about?'

'Ruthie. I'm talking about Ruthie. Your bloody sister.'

Annie froze. '*Ruthie?*'

'They found her in some tower block and they got hold of her passport and they called me.'

But Ruthie was away travelling, wasn't she? She'd need her passport, for that.

'What's the matter with her? She's not in any trouble is she?'

Now Annie could feel her heart literally *galloping* in her chest. She was on a very short fuse anyway these days; but what new trouble was this?

'Oh God,' moaned Kath.

'Tell me,' ordered Annie. 'Whatever it is, just for God's sake spit it out, will you?'

'I couldn't believe it, it was so awful. Then they asked me if I would go and identify the . . . the you know, but I couldn't, I couldn't do that, no way.'

Annie felt like icy water had been poured into her veins. *What* was Kath saying?

'I said you'd do it. Gave them your phone number, they should be calling you first thing in the morning.'

Identify it? Identify what?

'Kath, tell me what's happened?' Annie managed to croak out. Her throat felt painfully dry. Her head was spinning. She wondered if she was going to pass out. 'Slow down. Take a breath. Identify what?'

'Her *body*. They want a relative to do it and yes I'm related but I couldn't. I just couldn't, there's no way on God's green earth that I could do that. This needs a man, Annie. This needs *Max* to do it.'

'She's . . .' Annie couldn't even say it.

'Yes! She's dead,' howled Kath, letting the tears come now, not even trying to hold them back. 'Ruthie's gone and killed herself.'

94

Annie tracked Max down to the Palermo. He was cool on the phone, remote: and Annie couldn't help but think again of what Kath had told her, about the brunette and Max. A stab of vicious jealousy hit her then, and it was ridiculous because she had this other and far more dreadful news to concern herself with.

Somehow, she blurted out what Kath had told her. That Ruthie was dead, that the police wanted a positive identification on the body at the city morgue and . . .

Annie ran out of steam. She stopped speaking. Could barely breathe. She could only sit there, wondering what the hell was happening to her world, which had just a little while ago seemed so full of promise but which was now once again lying broken into a million pieces.

'I'll do that,' said Max.

'Thanks,' said Annie.

'I'll be back with you tomorrow morning.'

And he put the phone down.

'Thanks,' she said again, to empty air.

95

It was a pity she didn't drink. Or smoke. Or *something*.
Ruthie . . .
Her dear sweet sister was dead.
Annie still couldn't take it in. Any of it.
Oh God, Max, why aren't you here with me? she wondered uselessly. Well, tomorrow morning, he would be. That was a comfort, at least.

Max was not great at dispensing sympathy. But he was good at solving problems, at seeing the heart of a situation straight away and coming up with solutions. But this was one situation for which there could be no answer.

Ruthie was dead. She'd killed herself. The thought of it wouldn't leave Annie alone, pouring like sour bile into every minute, hitting her again and again and again until she felt punch-drunk, weak, tearful.

But she never cried.

Dig deep and stand alone, that was the creed she lived by. Always had, always would.

And now into Annie's brain came the images. Max and Ruthie's big wedding day. The hurt on Ruthie's face when Annie had told her what had happened on the night before the wedding. Goaded beyond reason by seeing Ruthie about to marry Max, when it should have been *her*, Annie, in Ruthie's place, she'd said the unforgiveable and told Ruthie that she'd had him first. And she remembered back even further, when they were young girls, when Ruthie always had her back whenever Connie was drunk and started flinging blows and insults at her, just because Annie had the misfortune to look like her father.

Connie had never forgiven Annie for being the dead spit of her father.

But Ruthie had protected her younger sister, stood as a barrier between her and their mother's abuse.

Ruthie was eight years old when they'd gone to Sunday School, her and Annie and even sometimes Kath. Annie had no idea why Connie and Mo had suddenly thought it would be a good idea to send their girls off to church. Maybe to get them out of the way while Mo shagged the rent man or Connie got royally pissed out of her brains on the sofa. Maybe that. But they'd gone, and it had been fun. Collecting stickers of Jesus and the angels and the disciples to stick in little booklets. Being given little raffia crucifixes at Easter. Mince pies at Christmas. The vicar's dog had bit Ruthie once, hard, on the knee, which called for a trip to the local hospital and a nasty injection. And then someone burned the church hall down and Sunday School had screeched to a halt.

But those memories.

They were so clear. Ruthie, balancing on a stack of Bibles in the vestry, teetering.

'Get down, Ruthie, you'll kill yourself,' Annie had laughed.

'I would never do that,' said Ruthie, the Bibles toppling over, her laughing and landing, sure as a cat, on her feet.

But Ruthie had tried to. Once. Not too long after her disastrous marriage to Max. And it had been Annie – whose fault it was, anyway – who'd saved her, that time.

This time, there had been no rescue. Ruthie had done it: she'd taken her own life.

Only . . .

After that first serious attempt, they'd talked, her and Annie. And Ruthie had promised her sister, no more.

'I'll never do it again,' she said. 'I swear.'

But Annie, who had been so traumatised by the effort of rescuing Ruthie from death, so exhausted by the ghastly process of making her vomit up the drugs, drink hot strong coffee, keep walking, keep moving, keep breathing, had wanted more. Much more. Nothing less, in fact, than a solemn vow.

'Swear it on my life,' she insisted. 'Ruthie? I'm not kidding around here. I mean it. Swear it on my life.'

And Ruthie had looked into her sister's eyes and solemnly sworn, on Annie's life, that she would never do something so awful again.

But now – she'd done it. She'd given her solemn promise *and she'd broken her word.*

In the middle of the night, Annie went and took a bath. Then wrapped in a towel, she sat down on the bed and rubbed her hair dry, started to comb out the tangles.

Then she paused, looking at the purple scar on her chest where Kieron Delaney's bullet had hit her. Months had passed since the shooting in the club and the wound had healed cleanly. Everything had been improving, slowly coming right. Ruthie was away travelling and they'd made peace with each other before she'd gone. The disorderly house trial had come and gone and Max had worked out okay: Max had rigged the result so that she was free, her sentence suspended. Everything should have been wonderful. But then – losing the baby. And now – *this.*

Ruthie had given her word.

This was the problem with this whole tragic situation. Ruthie had sworn, then gone back on it.

Only . . . Ruthie wouldn't. Ruthie who had cried when the Sunday School was no more. Who had been, somewhere deep in her soul, surprisingly religious and deeply committed to the truth. So . . . would she really do that? Break a vow?

No. She wouldn't.

Annie knew her sister, bone-deep.

Ruthie would *never* break the vow she'd made on Annie's life.

So . . . how the hell could this be suicide?

96

Max arrived at the Guildford place at eight o'clock next morning.

'You okay?' he asked her.

Not even a peck on the cheek. Her lover, the one who in the heat of passion she had betrayed her own sister for. What the hell had it all been about? she wondered. To wind up like this? So remote from each other, like strangers, when their affair had once seemed so overwhelming?

'I'm fine,' she told him. 'Look, I'm coming with you.'

'What?'

'When you identify the body.'

'No,' said Max.

'Yes,' Annie shot back.

'You don't have to do that.'

'I want to. I can't just sit here doing nothing. I'm going mad.'

'Annie. Listen to me.' Now there was a steely edge to his voice. 'You don't want to see that, I promise you.'

Annie felt the colour drain from her face. She didn't want to ask – but she *had* to. 'How . . . ? How did she do it then?'

'Drugs. They said she took drugs,' he said. 'An overdose.'

Oh God.

'Look,' she said at last. 'I won't come in. All right? I'll sit outside while you do it. I just . . . I just want to *be* there, okay?'

Max looked at her. 'All right,' he said at last.

97

They set off, Tone driving, Annie and Max sitting together in the back of the Jaguar Mark X but miles apart, silent.

The city morgue was as bleak and impersonal a building as Annie had ever been inside. The smell of Lysol and the polished, blue-white impersonal look of the place was daunting. For a while she sat with Max in a tiny blue-curtained waiting room. There was a mother and daughter in there already, hugging each other and sobbing. Then, after an excruciating ten minutes, a white-coated male member of staff came in and said: 'Mr Carter?'

Max nodded, stood up. Annie stood too. 'No. I told you. You don't want to see this. You've only just got over the baby. Don't put this on yourself too.'

He was right. And truthfully? She didn't *want* to see what Ruthie had done to herself. It would be awful and it would haunt her.

Max followed the orderly into an adjoining room, and the door closed behind them. End of argument.

Annie sat there and waited. The curtain in front of her moved, just a little. Then again. A fan rotating in the room beyond, maybe? The curtain lifted and . . . oh shit. She could see Ruthie lying there; it was just a tiny, tiny glimpse. She saw the outline of her head, the closed eyes, a slick of combed-back blonde hair on the delicately formed skull. She saw her sister's thin arm, covered in needle tracks. How had she not known that Ruthie was a drug user? She should have known, and she hadn't.

The curtain settled, the gap closed. Then Ruthie was gone.

A minute later, Max emerged from the room.

'Come on,' he said. 'It's her. Let's go home.'

98

Tone drove them back to Guildford; Max came and sat down in the drawing room with Annie. Miss Arnott went to the kitchen to fetch toast and tea. 'Hot and strong,' Max told her. 'Please.'

Annie sat there and stared at the carpet, shocked, seeing that glimpse of the pale porcelain face again and again, unable to wipe it from the mind's eye. *Ruthie was dead.*

The tea and toast arrived. Max poured out two cups, spread some toast with butter and jam.

'I can't eat anything,' said Annie when he offered a slice to her.

'Drink some tea then. You've had a shock. The sugar will settle you.'

Annie sipped at the tea. Hot and strong just as he'd asked for; lovely. But the face, the face. And that thin little arm; the needle tracks. She wished she hadn't seen that. She'd known about Ruthie's drinking and yes, she'd seen evidence of that. But drugs? That was new. And shocking. She *shouldn't* have seen it. Max had been right about that. Now, she couldn't get it out of her head.

And she had to say something. It was important. She had to say it *now*.

She put down her emptied cup and said: 'Ruthie didn't kill herself.'

Max sat back, watching her, silent for a moment.

'It was her,' he said, very gently. 'They said to me, "Mr Carter, is this your wife Ruthie?" And I said yes. Because it was.'

Annie's voice was level; almost cold. 'I don't give a stuff. She wouldn't kill herself.'

'Honey, I know this is hard. But it was suicide. She was very unhappy.'

'No. It wasn't suicide.'

Max heaved a sigh.

'She wouldn't do that. Not ever.'

'It's no good saying that. You wanted the facts? Here they are. She killed herself. She took her own life.'

'No.' Annie was shaking her head.

Max tutted in exasperation. 'Anything that doesn't fit with your preconceived ideas, you just toss them out.'

'I still say no.'

Max stood up. 'Annie – she topped herself. Those are the bare facts. You may not like them, but they are.'

His words were stabs of purest pain to Annie. To think of Ruthie, alone, doing so dreadful a thing and then at the last minute being afraid, maybe realising that she wanted to live after all and badly needing help – but unable to get it. Thinking of her despair, her loneliness, her pain; such a sad ending. *If* that was how it had happened.

'I'm sorry,' he said, more gently this time, seeing how pale she'd become as his words hit home.

'What I don't understand is why she was there at all,' said Annie.

'What?'

'In that place. Kath gave me the address.'

'What do you mean?'

'Can I get a look inside it? Inside the apartment where they found her? Who owns it, do we know?'

He let out a sigh. 'For what purpose?'

'It just doesn't add up, that's all. You know what? I think we were beginning to get back together, her and me.'

No use trying to pretty it up; she'd done a rotten, unforgivable thing. And now there was no chance of making things right. It was all too late. Ruthie was *gone*. The grand reunion, the big hugs-and-kisses coming back together Annie had sometimes hopelessly dreamed of – all that was, now and forever, off the table. Ruthie was *dead*.

Only – how could that be possible?

Annie looked at Max. 'Get me in that apartment, can you?'

'It's a total waste of time. It was suicide, Annie. Nothing's going to change that.'

She stood up. 'Who actually owns the place?'

'Her clothes were in the wardrobe, all her belongings were scattered around. There's no proof that anyone else lived there. No male clothing in evidence. Nothing points to that.'

'She swore to me on a stack of Bibles. When we were kids. That she would never, ever do anything like this.'

'As painful as this must be for you – she has. And anyway she *has* tried this before, with pills and drink. You know that. I sent you here on the night she did it. You pulled her back round, didn't you?'

Annie watched him pacing. He was right. But it still didn't sit well with her. Max, the object of her desire over so many years. From ten years old she'd idolised him, watched him, *craved* him. But now she was full of doubt. Had her and Max, their grand affair, been nothing but animal lust? Maybe that was it. Maybe that was all it had ever been.

Because weren't they both being punished now? He looked washed out. Exhausted. Not himself.

And her?

Things were bad for her too. She'd lost their baby, she'd lost Ruthie, and now – oh God, she didn't even want to think about it – there was the mystery brunette Kath had told her about to puzzle over. Had she now lost Max, too? Lost the very reason all this had even begun?

If so, what was the damned *point* of it all?

She stood up. 'There's the funeral. We have to start thinking about that,' she said.

Max looked at her. 'Yes. We do. And Annie? As for the rest of it? Just let it go, will you? There's nothing to be gained by poking into it all. You'll just upset yourself. And you won't get any answers.'

Let it go?

She stared at him. Yes he wanted her to do that. But maybe there was a reason for that – a sinister one?

'You didn't . . .' she started, then paused.

'What?' he asked.

'Was this anything to do with you? I know you haven't been happy together—'

'What are you saying?'

'I don't know, Max. I really don't. But with Ruthie gone, you're free of an unhappy marriage, aren't you. You don't have to divorce her and lose face on the manor . . .'

'For fuck's sake!'

'You don't have to finish her off under a bridge . . .'

'Shut the fuck up, will you?'

Annie shook her head, thinking, thinking. 'You could get drugs if you wanted to, easily. You could have encouraged her to take them, keep your own hands clean.

'You seriously think—?'

'I don't know *what* to think,' said Annie.

All she knew was that she had to get some answers. She *had* to know the full story of Ruthie's death, or it would haunt her forever.

99

Annie made some calls but nobody was responding. She'd been thinking about Ruthie, thinking about the flat. She'd talked to a mate, who was an estate agent, on the phone, asked him what he knew about that apartment block and he'd laughed and said: 'It's a black hole, that place.'

'What do you mean?' she'd asked, puzzled.

'I mean it's stuffed with monied people who demand a very discreet service and there they can be sure they'll get it. No questions asked, no names, no pack drill.'

So . . . how had Ruthie ended up there? Did she have a wealthy lover who had moved her into an apartment he owned?

At around ten, Annie went upstairs, alone, to the master suite. She hadn't eaten dinner. Couldn't have stomached it. But feeling exhausted, strained almost beyond bearing, she fell into bed and then into sleep.

It wasn't peaceful, though. She was hounded by monsters who slid their way out of red-stained bathtubs. They crawled grinning toward her over floors dyed red with blood, reaching for her with long fingers, with nails curved like scimitars, their mouths grinning, their eyes empty as frosted glass, their bodies puffy as slugs from all the water they'd been submerged in over centuries past.

She awoke suddenly, gasping, mortally afraid that they would touch her. She sat there in the darkness, listening to the thrum of her own heartbeat.

Just a rotten dream, that's all.

She flicked on the bedside light and looked at the clock. Two-fifteen in the morning. She rubbed her hands over her sweating face and shuddered at the memory of monsters crawling toward her, and when they reached her, what then?

'Don't be so bloody daft,' she muttered to herself.

It had been a nightmare. Nothing but that. But now she remembered Ruthie. Ruthie who was dead, lost to her. And . . .

Oh God in heaven!

Had Max killed Ruthie and framed it to look like suicide?

Could he have done that, and got his inconvenient and unwanted wife off his hands for good?

Suddenly she felt tears sting her eyes.

She never cried.

She wasn't going to cry now.

She blinked back the tears, reached over, snapped off the light, lay back down. *Sleep,* she told herself. *Sleep you silly bitch. Stop with the nightmares. None of that's real. You know it isn't.*

And slowly, eventually, she did sleep, telling herself that it was all going to work out, that she was going to find out what had been happening in her sister's life, what fresh disasters could have befallen her to make this awful, unbearable end result come about.

Fresh disasters? said that accusatory voice that was forever lodged in her brain. What about the old ones? What about the ones inflicted by *you*, bitch?

100

Annie contacted Land Registry. Not that it helped much. She discovered that not only the apartment but the actual block itself was owned by a company called Tarrec Holdings, a building firm with offices in the West End.

Skipping breakfast, she got a taxi to drive her into town. She found a glass-fronted door set discreetly beside a bank's main entrance. Tarrec Holdings was embossed on a brass plate there; nothing else. Nobody answered the bell when she rang it and there was a pile of unopened mail on the mat. Annie went into the bank and asked one of the cashiers if she knew anything about the place next door. Had she seen them coming in, going out? Anything?

The cashier just shrugged and said sorry, she couldn't help, she knew nothing about the place.

Annie went back to Guildford. At noon, Miss Arnott let a big dishevelled blond man through the door and showed him into the drawing room.

'Nicholas,' said Annie, standing up and holding out a hand.

'Hello,' said Nicholas.

'Coffee? Tea?'

'Not for me. How can I help?' He set his briefcase aside, peeled off his coat, sat down.

Nicholas was a city contact, an accountant who knew all about more intricate tax affairs and had his ear to the ground in London where some very ritzy clients of his had property.

'Do you know a company called Tarrec Holdings? Building company? Only I've just been over to their offices and the place looks dead. Nobody answering the door, mail on the mat, nothing going on.'

Nicholas smiled. 'You went there and found nothing? Not very surprising.'

'Why not?'

'The company may have a PO address there but it's almost certainly registered abroad.'

'Go on then. Are they clients of yours?'

'No, sadly not. Tarrec is an entirely legitimate business, listed by Companies House, but it's also, I suspect, a front.'

'A front for what?'

'For an SPV.'

'A what?'

'A special purpose vehicle. Which would usually be set up in one of the low-intervention jurisdictions – like Switzerland or the Caymans or Monaco.'

Nicholas made this sound simple. Like any fool could do it.

'Tax avoidance,' said Annie.

'Are you about to make the common mistake, Miss Bailey? The one that ninety-five per cent of the population do? Tax avoidance is not illegal. Tax *evasion* is.' Nicholas sat back, expanding into his chair, warming to this theme. 'So, you get it set up. The SPV lends money through Panama and the Bahamas in a series of dummy transactions that are impossible to trace until the cash finally comes into the owner's account – but of course their name doesn't appear on the shares register or on the list of board of directors.'

'Of course,' said Annie faintly.

'Then when the money's really rolling in, there are other things to do. Important things.'

'Like?' Despite herself, Annie found this fascinating.

Nicholas shrugged his well-padded and expensively suited shoulders.

'Like large donations to charity. D'you remember how the Krays used to donate hugely, back in the day? Such generous fellows. That's the thing to do, you see. Make a huge donation to whatever charity you favour, to as many as you like, donate *massively* with a modest smile on your face, of course, and a protest on your lips. Oh – I wanted to donate *anonymously*, how on earth did that leak out?'

Nicholas paused, smiling.

'Tip-offs to newspapers? Things like that?' guessed Annie.

'Precisely. So, everyone knows what a model citizen you really are. Then you host charity balls, have an auction of priceless objects and luxury trips, invite all your rich pals. A minor royal is good if you can work it, however minor doesn't matter. It adds kudos to the event. Gravitas. And all that makes you look squeaky clean. Many a gong's been awarded through those means.'

'You mean *knighthoods*?'

Nicholas nodded. 'All that goodness pouring out of you and into charitable coffers? It makes people step back in awe. It makes them look the other way. They're impressed and because of that they get nudged off-balance. Polite society starts sending you invitations. They might have heard the odd rumour, but all this smoke and mirrors stuff with the charities prevents them from taking it seriously. They think, "Oh well he can't be all that bad, can he, because

just look what he's doing here . . . look how *generous* he is."
Sleight of hand, you see. Old magician's trick. Don't look over *here*, look over *there*.'

Annie sat back. Well, was all this really so shocking? She'd already come across iffy accountants, super-slick lawyers, questionable fund managers. No big surprise really.

She looked Nicholas dead in the eye.

'So, that leaves only one question,' she said.

'Which is?'

'How do I find out who actually *owns* Tarrec Holdings?'

Nicholas gathered up his coat and briefcase. He shook his head, gave her a look of regret, and said: 'You don't. Not yet, anyway. Leave it with me. I'll try.'

After Nicholas had departed, Annie made a phone call to her cousin Kath, had her repeat the details of the flat where Ruthie had been found. Then she phoned Jackie Tulliver.

'Jackie? That you?'

'Yeah.' He sounded half asleep. 'Who's that?'

'Annie Bailey. Got a job for you. Cash in hand.'

'I dunno—'

'Max has approved it,' she lied.

'Oh! Well, okay then. What is it?'

She spoke.

Jackie listened.

101

Tulliver was an ugly but efficient little gremlin in Max's employ. Annie greased his palm with cash and he did exactly as she asked. Today he was staking out a luxury block of flats. Stake-out duty was pretty bloody boring, but what the hell, he didn't have much else to do right now. He watched a lot of wealthy-looking people going in and out of a building's main entrance. He took photos, made notes.

Several people had gone into the building this morning, a couple of Asian types and a family of what were obviously Russians had come out not half an hour ago, the father shooting him a quick glance, then looking away. Yesterday had panned out much the same; nothing much to report.

Jackie was sitting there peacefully tapping the steering wheel of the appropriately dingy little car he'd loaned off one of Max's other boys. He was vaguely humming along to 'The Girl from Ipanema' and wondering when he could pause and get something to eat when someone tapped sharply on his window.

He swivelled his head round and looked them in the eye. It was a bulky man, middle-aged, thick-browed and with a sweep of dense white hair. The man was mouthing something at him.

Jackie thought about winding down the window and quickly decided no. Then to his surprise the man yanked open the unlocked door, hauled Jackie half out of his seat and said something that sounded straight from the Balkans.

Ah, thought Jackie. The Russian family hadn't liked being watched.

'Hey,' he said, hands up, starting to laugh, to convey his absolute innocence and harmlessness. People were passing on the pavement, carefully not looking in case trouble erupted. Most of Jackie's chest hair was bunched up painfully in the Russian bodyguard's grip. 'Come on, man. What's your trouble?'

The Russian spoke again, his voice seeming to rumble up from somewhere deep in his boots, and Jackie had a sudden feeling that didn't bode well. Something hard was now pressing against his belly and it wasn't the man's dick, he was very sure of that. Concealed beneath his overcoat, the Russian had a gun.

'Hey!' Jackie objected, still half-laughing, trying to prove that he was just an amiable innocent twat, sitting here, behaving himself. What had started out as a simple stakeout was developing into a sticky situation and Jackie wanted to defuse it, soonest.

Then a low voice spoke from behind the Russian. Jackie didn't have a clue what was being said, only that the words sounded Russian too.

The Russian heavy who was gripping hold of Jackie stiffened and grew very still. Then abruptly his vice-like grip relaxed. Jackie felt the hard press of the gun withdraw. He was able for the first time to look past the bulk of the Russian to whoever had stepped in.

The Russian threw a word at Jackie that sounded uncomplimentary, then turned and stalked off, leaving Jackie half-sitting, half-standing there with his heart doing a brisk fandango in his denuded chest.

'You okay?' asked Max, stepping forward, tucking something into his coat pocket.

'Yeah. What did you say to him?' Jackie dropped back into the driving seat, took a gulp of air.

'Just that I was going to slice off his bollocks and post them back to his granny in the Gulag if he didn't back off.'

'That would do it,' said Jackie.

'What are you doing hanging about round here?'

'Annie Bailey asked me to watch this building. See who was coming and going here. She said you okayed it.'

'She did?' Max scowled. 'Well, I didn't. And mate – just a reminder – you don't work for Annie Bailey. You work for *me*. Remember that. Now fuck off home.'

102

'Hey,' said Max to Annie later that day.

'Yes? Something you wanted?'

'Yeah. Don't go getting my people doing jobs for you. Particularly not Jackie Tulliver. He's got more spunk in his balls than brains in his head, the poor cunt.'

'Do you *have* to be so damned crude?'

'Oh! Sorry, Your Majesty, have I offended you?'

Annie brushed that aside. 'I've been thinking.'

'Have you.'

'Yes.'

'What? That I killed her; are you on that again?'

'If not you, then who?'

'Surprise me.'

Maybe it was Redmond Delaney who gave Ruthie the drugs that killed her.'

'What?'

'That's his scene, right? Seduce 'em and get them high?'

'Annie.'

'Hm?'

'Back away from this. Seriously. Leave it alone.'

'The day Ruthie left Guildford. She was going to London, yes? I'd like a word with her minder. He drove her up there, didn't he? Dave, the young git with the blond hair and the attitude? Where's he at the moment?'

'Did you just hear me?'

'No, did you say something? Where's Dave?'

'What?'

'Are you keeping him on? And if so, why? He let Ruthie die, didn't he. He was meant to be minding her. And you just accept that, do you?'

'Annie.'

'Hm?'

'Leave it! Didn't I say leave it?'

'You may have done. That don't mean I will.'

Max squared up to her, eyes narrowed. 'Why does fighting with you always make me horny as hell?' he wondered aloud, shaking his head.

'I don't know. You like the resistance I suppose. I'm not Ruthie, am I.' Annie's mouth curved in a smile. 'By the way, where *is* Dave?'

Max shrugged. 'You want him? You find him,' he said, and left the room.

103

But Dave seemed to have left the scene for now and anyway there was Ruthie's funeral to arrange. Max gave that job to Annie and she knew why – to distract her from digging into Ruthie's death any further. Which made her all the more determined to do that. His resistance struck her as strange. Not quite *right*. Still, she paused and got on with the job in hand.

There were practical, awful things to do. Choose a coffin: an expensive pale peach-coloured limewood. Choose a lining: sky-blue silk. Order flowers: white lilies, for Ruthie. Lots of them. Talk to the vicar, agree the order of service. Annie discussed all that was required with Max, all that needed to be arranged. But apart from the odd skirmish like the whereabouts of Dave and his failed role as Ruthie's minder, they might have been a thousand miles apart, discussing it all over the telephone. And maybe that was just as well. Because maybe – just maybe – he really had killed her.

And then the day of the funeral dawned.

On that day, Annie felt that she was burying the good part of herself. The moral, sweet and reasonable part. Because that had been Ruthie. The light, innocent, tolerant woman who perhaps Annie Bailey might one day aspire to be.

Oh yeah. As if.

Trouble was, Annie didn't, for a minute, believe that she would ever be as good as Ruthie. Just like she didn't believe that Ruthie could have killed herself.

Because hadn't *Annie* always been the dark side, the side not of the angels but of the fiends of hell? She had. She knew she had. She had scrabbled her way through life, bolstered by grit and steel-cored determination, unloved by her mother, abandoned by her father, and really she and her sister should have been united by all those troubles they'd suffered, shouldn't they? But . . .

Goody-Two-Shoes . . .

That was what she had called Ruthie, and really, well, Ruthie had been just that. A sweet child, a forgiving adult, and Christ knew she had enough to forgive, particularly where her two-years-younger sister was concerned.

Annie tried never to look back. But today, standing in the thin drizzle of a miserable London autumn, how could she fail to do that?

She watched Max and five of his boys carry Ruthie's coffin, covered from top to bottom in those sickly sweet-scented white lilies, up the aisle, then they put it down – so carefully – on the dais. To her surprise she saw Dave there, Ruthie's 'minder', spruced up in his Sunday best. Max came to where Annie was sitting and sat down beside her. Not touching. Not even looking. Of course not.

Maybe his conscience pricked him, if he'd been behind Ruthie's death. She didn't *want* to believe he had been involved in it, but she knew she couldn't rule it out and the suspicion of it, the very *hint* of it, made her wary of him, and afraid.

When the service was over and they'd all gone outside, she could still hear the swelling, thunderous roar of the organ playing in the flower-bedecked church and the grim single-note tolling of the funeral bell up in the belfry.

Yes, she was here at her sister's funeral but what she was remembering was a wedding. *The* wedding. The wedding that had changed her own life and ruined her sister's. Confetti falling all around, and her in a hideous bridesmaid's peach gown along with their barrel-fat Cousin Kath. Ruthie had been captivating, almost beautiful for once, in white. Hadn't there been a song? Susan Maughan? The wedding song. Yeah, that had been playing over and over in Annie's head on the day. Like a dirge, the words had echoed around her skull, tormenting her.

That had been the day when it had all gone wrong, when all the wickedness that Connie had always accused Annie of carrying had flowed fast and free, pumping fiercely through her veins, enveloping her, leaving her with no choice but to *let it out*.

I've had years of your cast-offs, Ruthie, but guess what? Today, you're getting one of mine.

Annie's guts curdled with shame, thinking of the words she had so cruelly uttered on that day. Thinking of Ruthie's radiant face growing pale and bewildered as the words sank in, as she groped for and then understood the meaning of them.

Annie Bailey had shown herself up to be what she truly was, what her mother Connie had always accused her of: she was a whore, a sinner, and there was no forgiveness to be had, not from her mother, not from her beloved sister Ruthie, not from *anyone*, after that. Ruthie might now be on her way to heaven, but Annie? She was destined for hell and she knew it.

She couldn't fight it; useless to even try. It was in her, just like it had been in Frank, her waster of a father; that was all you could say. Sometimes, especially today, looking down at that deep muddy hole, and her sister's coffin lying there at the bottom of it while the vicar intoned the final words of the ceremony, Annie really did feel that she was damned: yes, cursed.

'I'm so sorry for your loss,' said the vicar to her, closing his Bible; the funeral was over.

The funeral director was walking away, back to the empty hearse. Back to normal life, to the pub, to the old lady at home, whatever. Tea and cakes were beckoning back at the vicarage. Warmth, a fire, a leisurely evening in front of the TV watching *Green Acres* or *Hogan's Heroes*. Everything neat, everything normal.

Only cold earth for Ruthie though, thought Annie.

Only that.

She *couldn't* have killed herself, could she?

But if she *didn't* – well, what then? *Murder?*

'Thank you,' she said to the vicar, thinking that she couldn't leave Ruthie alone here, in the cold soil. She couldn't. 'Horrible for you,' he said.

'Yes.'

'I can't imagine—'

'No.'

What he meant was, he couldn't imagine how she must be feeling, knowing that her normal, well-adjusted sister had done something abominable: had committed the ultimate sin by taking her own life.

'But she's at peace now,' he said.

'Yeah,' said Annie, and turned and walked away. Max fell into step beside her. He was silent: withdrawn.

I think he's going to leave me, she thought.

And didn't she deserve that?

Didn't she *need* that, if he had been in any way involved in Ruthie's death?

Oh yes. She did.

And then she saw the woman, standing there among the thinning crowds.

104

It was Orla Delaney. Orla was dressed all in black and it suited her pale redhead's colouring; she looked beautiful. Annie walked over, leaving Max behind, and stood in front of her.

'I didn't realise you knew Ruthie that well,' said Annie, glancing around, wondering if Redmond might be here too.

She'd done business with Redmond and she knew there'd been rumours flying about that she'd had a personal relationship with him too; but truthfully? She found him frightening. She and all the Limehouse tarts had hidden the truth of his brother Pat's death from Redmond; she could never forget that, or feel easy about it.

'Hello, Miss Bailey,' said Orla. 'Yes. I knew her. I hope you don't mind me coming . . .? Surrey isn't my usual stomping ground.'

'No. Of course I don't. I'm just surprised, that's all. You're welcome to come back to the house with the rest of the mourners.' Annie paused. A cold wind jostled them. Dry leaves rustled and flew. Orla's hair danced in the breeze, vibrant as a scarlet curtain; she really did look angelic. Or demonic. Annie wasn't quite sure which.

'Thank you,' said Orla.

'No Redmond?' asked Annie, half-expecting him to appear. *Dreading* that, really. The guilty secret of Pat's gruesome death still played on her mind.

'No. He thought it might be awkward.'

'So . . . how come you knew Ruthie?'

'Oh, she was almost a family friend,' said Orla.

'Really?'

'It's hard to believe she's gone.'

'Yes. It is.' *Ruthie? A 'family friend' to the Delaneys?* 'I wasn't aware of a connection between your family and my sister.'

'She was close to one of my brothers.'

Annie's mouth dropped open in shock. 'You . . . *what?*'

'But it's all academic now, isn't it.'

'Which brother?' asked Annie.

'Ah, no. I wouldn't like to say at this juncture.' Orla shook her head. 'It's all in the past, isn't it. Poor Ruthie is with the angels and there's an end to it.'

'Did you hear that she was supposed to have killed herself?' asked Annie, feeling very much inclined to grab Orla and shake her. *Which brother? Not Redmond himself, maybe, who got off on giving his girlfriends drugs?*

Orla seemed to go paler still. 'No,' she said. 'I didn't know that. I'm so sorry.'

Annie was silent, staring into Orla's eyes. 'Orla,' she said.

'What?'

'I need to know what's happened with Ruthie. I need to know which of your brothers she was seeing. Was it Redmond?'

Orla straightened her handbag, looked around. 'Perhaps I shouldn't have spoken,' she said.

'Maybe. But having spoken, why not speak some more? Tell me which brother. It could be important.'

Orla shook her head. Her eyes were panicky.

'Look,' she said. 'I'm sorry to have upset you. I spoke out of turn and I apologise. I really don't see that dragging up the past is going to be of any benefit, do you?'

Annie leaned forward and grabbed Orla's arm. 'Which brother?' she asked.

Alarm leapt into Orla's eyes. 'Ow! You're hurting me.'

'Am I? Sorry. Which brother?'

She thought of Redmond, who had been her financial backer for the Brook Street business, but who had stepped smartly away from all involvement when the law got involved and she'd been facing prosecution. And what about Kieron, who had pestered her endlessly for sex when she had very clearly told him she wasn't interested?

'Where *is* Kieron these days?' she asked Orla.

'Who knows? Probably painting somewhere. Like he does. Look, I have to go.'

Orla wrenched her arm free of Annie's grip and then she was gone, hurrying down toward to the road, to freedom.

Ruthie, a family friend of the Delaneys?

For fuck's sake!

Where the hell had *that* come from?

105

Annie went on down to the lychgate, her eyes searching the crowds for Max. She couldn't see him. He was probably in the car with Tone, waiting for her. Or maybe he'd buggered off without her?

Now she wanted only to be gone and this lousy day forgotten. What she *didn't* want was precisely what now happened. Cousin Kath, who had been standing in the church alongside Jimmy Bond, glowering at her throughout the whole ghastly process, was approaching fast, bristling with ill will as she stormed up to her cousin and planted herself in front of Annie like a solid wall, arms folded, chest heaving with the effort of moving her bulk around at speed.

'You came then,' she snapped out.

'You too,' said Annie.

'Surprised you fucking-well bothered.'

'And yet,' said Annie, 'here I am.'

'Why did you? Now my mum and Auntie Connie are gone, we're all that's left, you and me. Ruthie was all right. A nice person. Which is more than could ever be said for you. Driving her to *that*.'

'Yeah, well.'

Annie wanted to get on. She had things to do. Pretty urgent things. It was all very well for Orla to give her the runaround but that was not going to be good enough. And now here Kath was, blocking her exit.

'If that's all?' she asked.

'All?' Kath's voice rose to a shout. 'No it ain't bloody all, you chilly cow. She would never have said it to you but I'm saying it now. Your behaviour caused her no end of grief. You know that.'

'Then why bother saying it all over again? If I know it?'

'Cold as ice, aintcha,' said Kath.

Oh yeah. That's me. 'So . . . like I said, if that's all?'

'You what? She *killed* herself,' said Kath, and suddenly tears were dripping from her eyes. 'Your sister. My cousin. She was all right, Ruthie. Sound. Better by a mile than you.'

'That's something we can both agree on,' said Annie.

'I ought to knock your teeth straight down your throat,' said Kath, sticking a pudgy finger in Annie's face. 'For all the crap you put her through.'

'Wouldn't advise it,' said Annie. Suddenly she was in just the mood for a ruck, and if she struck hard enough she knew that Kath, pudgy and desperately unfit, would go down like a wrecking ball had struck her.

'Yeah – cold as fucking Christmas, aintcha?' snarled Kath.

'That's me,' said Annie, and shoved past Kath.

She was on her way down to the lychgate and the car when she saw her. Standing a little apart from everyone else, alone. Slim, mousy blonde . . . my God. *Ruthie?*

Annie hurried over there. Was someone playing tricks on her? But Ruthie was dead – wasn't she?

Almost gasping for breath, she approached the woman, grabbed her arm.

The woman turned.

'Ruthie—' Annie started.

It wasn't Ruthie.

The woman stared at her. 'Sorry, do I know you . . .?' she asked.

Annie drew back.

Of all the stupid fucking things to do. Thinking she saw Ruthie, at Ruthie's own funeral . . .

'I'm sorry,' she said, and hurried away.

Max was waiting in the back of the car. Tone was at the wheel.

'All okay?' asked Max when she got in.

'Oh yeah. Fucking fabulous,' said Annie. *Just seeing things. That's all.* And in all the furore, she'd missed the chance to talk to Dave.

The car roared back to Guildford, to where the wake was being set up in the capable hands of Miss Arnott.

Not another word was said.

106

The wake went on. And on. It turned into a party, with someone pissed out of his brains sitting at the grand piano in the hallway and bashing out war tunes, people singing drunkenly along to 'We'll Meet Again' and 'It's A Long Way To Tipperary'. A celebration of Ruthie's life? Maybe, but as Annie later stood in the hall, exhausted, wrung out, ushering the last of the mourners out of the door, she thought that Ruthie's life hadn't been worth the celebrating because *she* had ruined it.

Finally, everyone was gone. Miss Arnott and the catering staff started clearing the plates and glasses and leftover food away, and Max and Annie – at last – retired to the drawing room.

'Give me a drink,' said Annie, thinking of the woman she'd seen right there in the graveyard. Ruthie. Only not Ruthie at all. Not really. She was slowly going *crazy*.

Max looked at her sharply. 'You don't drink.'

'I'm starting.'

Max went to the cabinet and slopped an inch of malt into a couple of tumblers. He came back to where she sat, handed her a glass.

'Thank Christ that's over,' he said, and threw back the whisky in one hit.

'Amen,' said Annie, and attempted to do the same.

She choked.

'Steady,' said Max.

Red-hot liquid was running down her insides, scorching her. '*Jesus*,' she wheezed.

But then the warmth came. The comfort. She took another sip, more cautious this time. Her mother had been a big drinker. So had Ruthie. And now she *almost* began to see the attraction. Alcohol soothed. Calmed. Took away the pain for a while.

'Did you see Orla Delaney at the church?' she asked him.

Max sat down opposite her. Shrugged off his jacket. Loosened his tie. 'No. She was there?'

'She was there because, she said, Ruthie was a family friend.'

'She *what*?'

Annie nodded. 'She said Ruthie had been "close" to one of her brothers. I asked her which one in particular, but she wouldn't say.'

Max put his empty glass aside and let out a breath.

'Ruthie and me might have been married in the eyes of the law, but we lived completely separate lives,' he said. 'You know that.'

'After what we did to her, I'm not surprised,' said Annie.

'You going to beat yourself up about that forever?' he sighed.

'You mean you don't?'

'What's the point? It's done.'

'And we're paying for it, aren't we. *We lost the baby.*'

'That could happen to anyone. It's not bloody divine intervention. It's just random. It happens. That's all.'

'We deserved it.'

'If you want to think that, go ahead.'

'Well what do *you* think?' They had never actually talked about this: their mutual betrayal of Ruthie. The loss of the baby. About *any* of it, really.

Max stood up, went to the drinks cabinet, poured himself another. He held up the decanter to Annie but she shook her head. She'd be on the floor if she drank another sip. She wasn't used to alcohol. Couldn't seem to handle it.

'What do I think?' He came back and sat down beside her, closer this time. 'I'll tell you. The marriage. Me and Ruthie. That was all Mum's idea. Not mine.'

'What?'

'Mum was dying. She knew it. Bad heart trouble. But she couldn't bear to lose control. She wanted me settled before she went. Married. And married to someone – this sounds bad, I know, after all it's my own mother I'm talking about – someone that she could easily dominate in the time remaining to her.'

Annie stared at him. 'Someone like Ruthie.'

'Yeah.'

'And you went along with that.'

'As I said, she was dying. It seemed like no big deal to give her what amounted to her last wish.'

'No big deal,' echoed Annie.

'That's right.'

'But Queenie died way before the wedding.'

'She did, and by that time everything was in place and I was shattered. Felt . . . I dunno. Sort of numb. Shocked. So – yeah, no big deal. It all went ahead. I should have stopped it, I see that now, but I didn't. Truth was, I didn't have the heart to do that. Couldn't seem to care, one way or the other. And it *wasn't* a big deal, not until you and me got together. The marriage was just a convenient thing, a conventional thing. Whereas us . . .' His voice tailed off.

'Oh yes,' said Annie. 'Fireworks.'

She sat there, thinking of that night when they'd come together for the first time, in the club. Such passion. Yes. *Fireworks*. It was still so vivid, in her mind. They'd wanted each other so badly. To hell with convention. To hell with his loveless and fully arranged wedding to Ruthie, which was looming ever closer. They had to be together. There was just no way around it; it *had* to happen.

And now here they were, as if a million miles apart. A chill in the air between them. Their baby, gone. Her sister and his poor unwanted wife – gone.

Of course, Annie's young healthy body had mended. She was well again; she could conceive again. But her mind was full of darkness. Full of dread and guilt. Full of images of Ruthie in the graveyard. Alive, not dead. Full of the fear that Max had been involved in Ruthie's death, and how could she ever forgive him if that was the case?

Max drained his drink. 'I'm tired. Come on. Let's go to bed.'

107

They went upstairs, passing a frowning Miss Arnott in the hallway.

But tonight, there were no fireworks.

There was nothing.

Annie slept in the master bedroom.

Max slept in the dressing room.

As she fell asleep alone – and questioned whether she was glad about that, or sorry, she couldn't decide – Annie thought of Orla standing there at Ruthie's funeral talking about her brothers.

Ruthie – and a liaison with one of that gang of Irish toughs, who were also Max's worst enemies? What would have been her motivation? Revenge against Max for his affair with her sister?

Yes. That was possible.

Which brother, though? Annie listened to the old house settling around her, to the wind whistling ghostly around the eaves. Away in the distance, a door slammed. The caterers, packing up? Miss Arnott, going back outside, to her bungalow in the grounds?

Or Ruthie, walking the corridors, haunting them?

Or maybe Eddie? Oh shit, hadn't Eddie died here?

She was being fanciful. Letting her imagination run riot after a stressful, horrible day.

Now she thought of a cold wind blowing over Ruthie's filled-in grave, stirring the fading lilies that lay there on the mounded earth, sending dead autumn leaves whirling. And Ruthie, lying below the soil, peaceful; as dead as the leaves.

That glimpse through the gap in the curtain. The fine profile. The thin marked arm . . .

No. She had to stop all this. Go to sleep. She turned over, clutched at the pillow. Wished – just briefly – that Max was here with her to chase all these fears away. But she couldn't be sure of Max, could she. Not anymore. And she hadn't a clue which of the Delaney brothers Ruthie had been close to.

But she would find out.

She was determined to do that for Ruthie, at least.

Finally, worn out, she slept.

108

'Do you think this place is haunted?' she asked Max as they finished breakfast next morning.

'You what?' He looked at her in surprise.

'It's very old, isn't it. Maybe it is. I keep hearing things in the night. Doors slamming. People moving about.'

'That'll be Miss Arnott,' he said. 'Making sure everything's locked up for the night.'

'Yeah, probably.' Still, she couldn't forget lying there alone last night and having a severe case of the creeps.

'Old houses,' said Max. 'They settle. They make a noise. Nothing to worry about.' He drained his coffee and stood up. 'Right, I'm off.'

Not even a kiss on the cheek!

Annie watched him go. No explanation. Nothing. She heard the Jag's engine start, heard it crunch away over the gravel drive.

Well, that was Max. He went his own way. Made his own decisions. And had one of those decisions been to get rid of his own wife?

She shivered. First on the agenda? *Which brother?*

She went out into the hall and made a couple of calls. Then she nipped outside and went round to the garage block. The garage doors were half-open and she went inside. There was an old sports car, half-concealed under a sheet. There were tools, and a pit where mechanics could work underneath cars unhindered. She walked in further, watching her step. Old tyres, stacked high. Pieces of panelling. Spraying gear. And right at the back, barely visible, was what looked like another car, completely covered.

Annie untied the laces on the covering and pushed it back to reveal the car; it was a nice unshowy black car, not as grand as the Jag, but nice. She pushed the covering cloth back further, revealing the front of the motor. The driver's side front wheel was buckled, the paintwork scraped, the panelling dented.

'Hello?' said a voice behind her.

She turned. And there he was. Dave, Ruthie's 'minder', in jeans and shirt, looking at her like she had no right to be there.

'Help you?' he asked.

'Yeah. You're Dave, right? You used to drive my sister Ruthie about? I meant to speak to you at the funeral. Didn't get a chance. But you're here now.'

'So . . .?'

'So what happened to the car? This would be the right car, wouldn't it? The one you drove her in?' She indicated the damage to the front offside. 'Only it looks like it's had a pretty nasty smash.'

'You shouldn't be poking about in here. There's machines and things. It's not safe.'

'Yeah, you're right.' Annie walked to the front of the garage, stepped out into the sun. 'So what happened to the car?'

'Just a little scrape,' said Dave.

'Looks like a pretty damned big scrape to me. You know, she looked after me after I got shot, and when it was time for her to leave, when she decided to go, you drove her, right? You drove Ruthie up to London, didn't you? On the day she left here? Was that when the accident happened?'

There was a crunch of car tyres on the gravel and a motor drew up. Annie watched Dave almost sag with relief.

'Taxi's here, is that for you?' he asked.

'It is.' She gave him a bright and entirely false smile.

Ruthie's 'minder'? What sort of minder let the woman in his charge wind up dead? And what sort of husband was Max, when he'd let such a complete dereliction of duty go unpunished?

'We'll talk about this again later,' she told him.

109

Kieron Delaney's Shoreditch studio was a shabby little hole, a plain upstairs flat that was north-facing and very cold but with that crisp, fabulous bluish light that painters loved so much. Annie had been here several times before, while posing for Kieron. She knocked on the door downstairs, tried the handle. The door opened. Looking from side to side along the rain-soaked pavement that was bustling with umbrella-wielding pedestrians, the road that was full of cars swooshing through the deluge, taxis, lorries, everyone minding their own business, all with places to go to in this dire British weather. No one was taking any notice of her. She slipped inside, closed the door behind her. Went up the dirty old wooden stairs and paused in front of the half-glassed door at the top.

She could see into the studio, although the glass hadn't been cleaned in months. It was a square room, littered haphazardly with all the trappings of an artist's work. She could see Kieron's easel, his palette, his prepped canvases. A tired old chaise-longue, she remembered sitting on that for hours on end. There were some finished paintings stacked around the floor of the room. Portraits and animals and some landscapes. Over in the far corner, a few different paintings, clearly not Kieron's work. Huge slashes of bright colour.

Maybe Orla's?

A tatty red silk robe was hung on the back of a closed door across the room. Oh, she *remembered* that robe. Remembered putting it on before posing. There was no movement inside the studio. Still, she knocked at the glass. Then she knocked harder.

No answer.

She waited a beat or two and then gave up.

She went back down the stairs, out into the street. Hailed a taxi.

'Battersea,' she told the driver.

110

In the Static at the Delaney breaker's yard, Redmond was waiting for her. Somehow, they had always got on – business-wise, at least. She didn't doubt for a moment that Redmond was the most dangerous and deadly of all the Delaneys. Indisputably the boss. And beyond a shadow of a doubt, coolly analytical; she couldn't help remembering the way he'd instantly distanced himself from her when her court case had been looming.

But Max had stood by her.

Redmond was alone in the little office and when the guard announced her, he looked up from the paperwork on his desk in some surprise.

'Miss Bailey! Come in. Take a seat.'

Annie walked in, sat down. He smiled. He had a very chilling smile, Redmond. Like he was about to pull your teeth out. Without anaesthetic. 'Something I can do for you?' he asked. 'Only, as I told you, I'm a little busy today, so if we could keep this short . . . ?'

'Yeah, I'll be brief. Where is Kieron?' she asked.

'Kieron? Abroad I think. Probably painting.'

'Abroad where? Ireland? Do you have an address for him?'

The door opened. Orla stepped inside, saw Annie sitting there. 'Oh! You again.'

'Yeah, turned up like a bad penny,' said Annie. She stared at Orla. 'I've just been over to Kieron's studio in Shoreditch but he's not there. Do you have any idea where he is, right now?'

Orla said nothing.

'And can I just ask again – which of your brothers was my sister involved with? Was it him? Was it Kieron?' Annie looked at Redmond. 'Or was it you? Only she's dead and now I'm starting to wonder what the fuck's been going on. Understandably.'

'Your sister's death is, of course, a tragedy,' said Redmond. 'But nothing to do with my family, I do assure you.'

'Were *you* the Delaney she was involved with?'

'No, Miss Bailey. It was not me,' said Redmond.

'It was Kieron,' said Orla. 'If you must keep asking then I'll tell you. Why not?'

Redmond shot her a reproachful look.

'Well it was,' said Orla defensively. 'I don't see why she shouldn't know that. And as for where Kieron is now, well, that's anyone's guess.'

'You do have an address for him?' said Annie, getting tired of this. 'Only if I don't start hearing some sense soon, I'm going to have to refer this matter to a friend of mine, and he's nowhere near as patient as me.'

'Oh – you mean Max Carter?' asked Redmond. He looked amused.

'Him, yes. And others.'

'Frightening though that prospect is,' said Redmond, 'I'm afraid I can't help you.'

He reached and opened a drawer at the top right-hand side of the desk and suddenly there was a gun in his hand. Annie stared with horror down the blue barrel of the thing.

She'd been shot once.

She *couldn't* be shot again.

'Redmond,' said Orla, a warning in her voice.

Redmond's cold eyes were staring into Annie's.

'Do you know just how easily I could make you disappear, Miss Bailey?' he asked.

Annie gulped. Her mouth was dry.

'What – like *you* disappeared when I was facing a court case?'

'You've got a lot of guts saying that to me,' he said, admiration in his voice.

A long moment passed. She stared at the gun. Redmond stared at her.

Slowly, he reached out, put the gun back in the drawer: closed it.

'Look, can we stop this?' said Orla. 'Kieron? He's gone missing, and not for the first time either.'

Redmond gave Annie a catlike smile. 'Missing, presumed dead. Isn't that what they say? Well, who knows? And really – who cares?'

111

There was only one place to go when she felt the world pressing down upon her. Still shaking from her close-up encounter with Redmond and Orla, she took a cab to Limehouse and knocked on the door. Chris let her in. She went along the hallway and into the cosy little kitchen and there they all were: Dolly, Darren and Aretha, attacking the tea and biscuits with gusto.

'All right, girlfriend?' asked Aretha. She frowned. 'We heard your news. Sorry.'

'Talk about the bush telegraph,' said Annie. 'How the hell did you lot find out?' She pulled up a chair and Dolly pushed a cup her way.

'Seems you've not had your troubles to seek recently,' said Dolly on a sigh. 'The court case and the shooting and losing the baby. So much trouble! And your sister. That was horrible. We're sorry as hell. How's Mr Carter taking it?'

Annie paused, pouring her tea. Max wasn't taking it at all. He seemed to be ignoring the situation. Almost ignoring *her*. She thought again of what Kath had said, about the brunette outside the Revue Bar in Soho. *Oh God.*

'You don't see Ellie anymore, do you?' she asked, changing the subject.

'Nah, not much,' said Darren. He darted a look at Dolly, who gave a nod.

'What?' asked Annie.

'We found out something. Actually I was going to get in touch, let you know,' he said.

'About what?'

'About Ellie and your cousin Kath.'

'What about them?'

'Kath was paying Ellie for information about you, finding out what you were getting up to when you lived here and over at Brook Street. And she was passing the info on to your sister Ruthie.'

Annie was silent: stunned. She looked at Aretha, who nodded.

'Ellie told me,' said Aretha. 'I caught her in her room counting out a shedload of money and she looked guilty as fuck. I pressed her, and she admitted it. Told me what was going on. That she was spying on you and telling your cousin all the details.'

'So whatever I was doing, Ruthie knew about it,' said Annie faintly.

They all nodded.

Annie heaved a sigh. 'God, that's spooky. Pity it wasn't a two-way street. Or I would have known what was happening in Ruthie's life too. How she came to do herself in. You know, I still can't believe that.'

'It's awful. You poor duck,' said Darren.

'I mean, I *don't* believe it. I really don't. Ruthie always swore she'd never do that, and Ruthie meant every word she ever said. So it might have *looked* like suicide, but it couldn't have been.'

Now it was their turn to sit silent, not knowing what to say next.

'Did you have to . . .?' asked Dolly presently, reaching across, giving Annie's arm a comforting squeeze.

'Identify the body?' Annie shook her head. 'No. Thank God. Max did it.'

'And he was positive it was her, so . . .' said Aretha, shrugging.

'Yes. He was.'

'Knocks your theory on the head,' said Darren.

'But I still don't understand it,' said Annie, remembering that tiny, tiny glimpse she'd had of her sister at the morgue. There was no doubt. And yet still, somehow – stupidly – she doubted.

'Maybe something changed for your sister,' said Darren. 'Some crisis. Made her alter her way of thinking, I mean. Maybe taking her own life was the only way out of some horrible situation she was in.'

'She was dating one of the Delaney boys,' said Annie, wondering if Darren could be right. 'Kieron, Orla Delaney told me. The artist.'

'If Ruthie had been going out with Kieron, how had that relationship worked? Was it bad? If it *was*, then maybe her thinking really had changed. Maybe she saw suicide as a way out,' suggested Darren.

Annie took a swig of the tea. She was remembering how Kieron had been when he was around her. Obsessive. Fixated to the point of trying to kill Max, to remove the object of her desire so that he could fill that place. Dangerous behaviour. And it could have been fatal. So easily, that bullet she had caught at the club when she jumped in front of Max could have killed her outright.

Had Kieron been like that with Ruthie? she wondered. Ruthie was more docile than her; easier to control. Maybe she was wrong, maybe she was barking up the wrong tree with this. But he *had* been abusive – threatening – to her, so he had it in him to be that way with any woman. Didn't he?

'And you lot? How's tricks these days?' she asked.

'Business is brisk,' said Dolly. 'Plenty of parties going on. We're careful of the neighbours, of course, bearing in mind what happened to you when you opened that place up West. Everything's fine. Profits are up.'

'That's good,' said Annie. 'You got Ellie's address, have you, Doll?'

Dolly rose, went to the drawer of the Welsh dresser and pulled out her address book. She came back to the kitchen table, wrote the details down for Annie on a scrap of paper. 'This time of day? You'll find her at the chip shop in the High Street.'

Annie drained her cup, picked up the piece of paper, pushed back her chair and stood up. 'Doing what?' she asked.

Dolly smirked. 'You'll see.'

'I'll call in,' she said. 'She's not a bad sort, is she, Ellie. Not really.'

Dolly made a rocking motion with one hand. 'Not like you to be so forgiving. She was spying on you, after all.'

'I know. For money. She never had much as a kid, did she. Always crawling about in the gutter wasn't she. Makes a person do daft things, that. You think you'd ever take her back?' asked Annie.

'No bloody way,' said Dolly.

'Fair enough. I'll see myself out.'

112

The large orange-on-purple sign above the door of the chip shop read, not very wittily, FISH PLAICE. Annie alighted from her taxi and stood there on the pavement, looking up at it with something less than admiration. It wasn't funny. Certainly wasn't clever. People shoved past her. Steam was billowing out of the open doorway and a long queue was forming, winding out onto the pavement along the front of the shop. Through the plate-glass window Annie could see three people working behind the deep fat fryers, an older couple and a young woman, all three of them wearing orange pinafores, serving fish and chips and pouring salt and vinegar.

The younger woman was Ellie. Dark-haired and with bright eyes, her face was covered in angry red blotches and she looked like she was busting out of the pinafore. A punter was having sharp words with her and her boss.

Annie edged past the queue and went inside. There was a package of newspaper-wrapped mangled chips on the counter, and the punter was demanding his money back.

'They do look crushed. A bit,' said the man who was probably, Annie surmised, the owner of the chip shop.

'A *bit*?' said the man, who looked, in dungarees and donkey jacket, like he'd come off a building site. 'Look, mate, they're crushed to buggery and I ain't paying for them. She might as well have sat on them with her fat arse, the mess she's made of my bloody dinner.'

'Excuse me,' said Annie, pushing further through the queue, many of whom were taking great delight in this unexpected entertainment. She saw Ellie's eyes dart to her face in one panicky movement. Saw her blotches turn a shade darker.

'What d'you want?' the workman asked Annie. 'I'm not finished.'

'I think you are,' said Annie.

'And who the fuck are you, lady muck?'

Annie's eyes hardened. 'I'm a close friend of Max Carter's. Who are *you*?'

The workman's face fell. His eyes flickered this way and that, aware of the crowd watching, aware of what she'd just said. Back in the queue, someone whispered loudly: 'That's her.'

'*Who?*'

'*Max Carter's fancy piece.*'

'They look like they been stood on,' said the man weakly.

'We'll replace them for you,' said the owner of the chip shop, watching Annie, watching the workman.

The queue was silent now, listening. Annie wasn't bothered. She was used to this sort of reaction.

'Fine,' said the workman.

'Ellie?' said Annie.

Ellie looked at her. 'Hm?'

'Get out here. And take that damned pinny off before you do, all right?'

113

'What the hell happened to your face?' asked Annie when Ellie joined her out on the pavement, minus the orange pinafore.

'It's the grease,' said Ellie despondently, scratching at one inflamed cheek. 'It don't agree with me. And that bloke was right, I *did* crush the ruddy chips when I wrapped them. I'm no good for that job. Too sodding heavy-handed, that's me.'

'Yeah, but you're good at some things, aintcha?'

'Oh yeah? Like *what*?' Ellie sighed.

'Like keeping tabs on people. And reporting back to my cousin Kath, who then reported back to my sister.'

Ellie looked at the pavement. 'I heard about your sister. I'm really sorry. I mean it. I didn't—'

'Come off it, Ellie. This is me you're talking to.'

'It was just—'

'I know what it was "just". The money. Come on. Let's go get a coffee. Or a Wimpy, would you like that? And you know what? There might be some good news coming your way.'

'Like what? I just lost my effing job, in case you hadn't noticed.'

'Screw that. What if I could get Dolly to take you back on, cleaning?'

'I dunno. Things happened at the Limehouse place. *Terrible* things. You know that. Proper shook me up.'

'I know.' Annie thought of Pat Delaney coming at her that night like a wild beast. Ellie had done her a good turn then; now, she wanted to return the favour.

114

Annie got back to Guildford at five and went straight to the garage block and was not terribly surprised to see that the damaged car was no longer there and that Dave seemed to be not on the premises either. However, there was a very pretty little brown-haired teenager coming skipping down from one of the flats over the garage block and she wasted no time in snagging her at the bottom of the steps.

'Hi, aren't you Dave's girlfriend?' said Annie, with no idea whether this was so or not.

'Yeah.' She smiled, brown warm eyes. 'I'm Sarah. You're Mr Carter's . . .' She fumbled to a stop. Her smile faded.

Mr Carter's what? Whore maybe? wondered Annie.

'I'm Annie. Ruthie's sister,' she said, to save the girl's blushes.

'Hello there.' The smile came back.

'Nasty business about the car,' said Annie.

'The what?'

'The car, the one that was covered up in the garage, all smashed up like that.'

'Oh! Yeah.' Sarah lowered her voice. 'Maybe I shouldn't say . . .' she started, looking uncertain.

'Yes you should,' Annie told her. She pulled out her purse and counted out notes. 'Go on,' she prompted.

Sarah eyed the money, hesitated. Then she reached out, took it, tucked it quickly inside her bra.

'Go on,' said Annie.

'It was Kieron Delaney, Dave said. Snatched your sister and drove off with her up there,' she turned, pointed to the left, 'and crashed the damned thing into a ditch. Then she ran off, Dave said, and there was all sorts of trouble.'

God bless pillow talk, thought Annie. 'What sort of trouble?' she asked.

'Dave wouldn't say much about it. Only that Delaney did bad things to some poor old chap up the road so that he'd tell him where she went to.'

'Right. Well, thanks, Sarah. Good talking to you.'

'You know, people say you're a bit of a tart, but they're wrong, aren't they. You're quite nice.'

Sarah raced off around the back of the house – no doubt to go to the kitchens. Miss Arnott let Annie into the front door, took her coat. She went into the drawing room to find Max standing in front of the fire there, wearing black slacks and a white shirt, the sleeves rolled up, his tie pulled loose at the collar. He turned as she entered, stared at her.

'Where have you been?' he asked.

Annie was tired after a long day. The rush hour had been tedious. She had noticed that every time Max went out, he gave no explanation whatsoever as to his whereabouts. But clearly, he thought *she* should.

'Out,' she said, feeling obstinate.

'Yeah. Out *where*?'

'Limehouse. I went to see the girls. And I caught up with Ellie. Couple of other things too.'

Max shook his head. 'For fuck's . . . listen, you ought to keep out of there.'

'Why?' On her way back here, she'd called in on Nicholas to see if he'd made any progress in identifying the owners of the block where Ruthie was found dead. He hadn't. 'But I'm working on it,' Nicholas had told her.

'Don't act dumb,' said Max. 'It's on the Delaney manor. Have you forgotten what happened to Eddie when that thick fucker Deaf Derek led him in there like it was nothing?'

'Redmond wouldn't hurt me,' said Annie, remembering the gun he'd pointed at her and hoping she sounded convincing. What was Max throwing Eddie in her face for? She would never, ever forget the awfulness of what had happened to him. The last thing she needed was to be reminded of it. 'For God's sake, we've been business partners, me and Redmond.'

'And you aren't any more? Or are you? Are you in fact *more* than business partners?'

'What the hell does that mean?'

'You tell me. Do you trust him?'

'Who, Redmond? Of course not, but—'

'Good. You shouldn't do that.' Max heaved a sigh and came to her, pulled her to him. 'Listen,' he said against her hair. 'I don't know how close you are to him. Or how close you've been. But take this seriously. Hurting you would hurt me. So he could turn on you. Never doubt it. He *could*.'

Annie slid her arms around him. So nice, to be held by him. She'd missed this. But – *Ruthie*! She still wasn't sure what part he'd played – if any – in Ruthie's death. He thought she was close to Redmond! And she was too surprised, too *proud*, to start arguing the toss about that right now.

Hurting you would hurt me.

He meant it. She was his Achilles heel, wasn't she? Or at least, she always *had* been. *The brunette*, she thought, and disengaged quickly, drawing back as if stung. It was always brunettes with Max. She knew that. Blondes for Jonjo, brunettes for Max. Boys for poor little Eddie.

'I had a word with Dave's girlfriend just now,' said Annie. 'She told me all about the day Ruthie left here for the last time to go to London. Dave was driving her. Only . . . it didn't turn out that way, did it. Sarah told me that Kieron Delaney snatched Ruthie and drove off with her. Crashed the car. Don't bother to deny that because I have *seen* the car and towing it off somewhere else doesn't make me un-see it. Kieron did a few other things, too, by the sound of it.'

'Ah,' said Max.

'Ah? So come on. What exactly happened on the day Ruthie left here? Are you telling me that what Sarah told me isn't true?'

'I'm saying keep out of it. Let it go.'

'Why?'

'Because I bloody well say so.'

'What's this about some poor old bloke? What happened about him? Who is he?'

Max heaved a sigh. 'Fuck's sake,' he muttered.

'Come on! What?' insisted Annie.

'Let's just say he won't be playing the piano anytime soon,' said Max grimly.

'Is that it?'

'It's all you're getting. Ruthie's gone. Just let it lie.'

'Tell me you didn't do something to Ruthie,' she said.

'Like what?'

'*You know!* Because she was humiliating you, showing you up with Kieron bloody Delaney. And Redmond too, maybe. After all, drugs are his thing. Dammit Max! Please don't say you did something to Ruthie. I couldn't stand it.'

He was staring at her.

'Do you think I would? Do you think I *could*?' he asked.

She thought of all she had ever heard about Max Carter. The violence: the gang warfare.

Yes – he was capable, wasn't he. But . . . against a woman? Against her sister? Against *his wife*?

She suddenly felt unsure: afraid.

'Oh God, if you did it . . .' she started.

Max's face lost all expression. 'Perhaps you ought to go back to London for a while. Give us both some breathing room.'

'Max . . .'

But he didn't answer. He just left the room.

115

Hours later, Annie awoke, opening her eyes to blackness. The master suite was silent. Max was sleeping in the dressing room next door. She thought of their earlier conversation. So . . . he wanted her gone? But would she go? *Could* she, with all that was swirling around her brain?

She lay there, listening. It was so dark, in the country. So *still*. So what had awakened her? She sat up, reached out for the light – and then froze.

A door slammed in the distance. A car? One of the downstairs doors?

Then – silence again. Nothing except the sighing of the wind around the eaves of the old house . . . and was that . . . wait, was that *music*? It was faint, maybe downstairs . . .?

She switched on the bedside light. The tiny clock on her bedside table said that it was just after two. Who would be moving about – playing music – at this time of night? Quickly she put on her robe and went to the door. She paused there, listening. Then she turned the handle, eased the door open. She listened. Cool air rushed in from the landing.

She stepped out there. The music had stopped.

Silence . . .

She felt goosebumps crawl along her arms and she shivered. Then she saw that the window at the far end of the landing was open, the curtains billowing in the breeze. The weights sewn into the bottom of the curtains knocked heavily against the wall. Annie relaxed. That must be what she'd heard. Not music at all, just that hard rhythmic thumping. She flicked on the landing light and walked along there, shuddering, feeling like her skin was literally crawling, glancing nervously behind her.

Nothing.

Nobody.

She pulled the sash down, closed the window. The carpet under her feet was damp from blown-in rainwater. She looked out at the darkness, seeing nothing but her own reflection. Then from behind her, movement.

She turned quickly.

There was nobody there.

Aware of her heart beating very hard in her chest, she walked back to the master suite, went inside. But instead of going back to bed she went over to the adjoining door to Max's dressing room and knocked on it, opened it, entered.

I don't believe in ghosts, she told herself firmly. *Eddie died here, and Ruthie was unhappy here before she died, and didn't Queenie die in the annexe? Yes. She did. But do I believe they're stalking about the hallways in the dead of night, restless spirits unable to settle?*

No. Of course not.

'Max?' she said. Her voice sounded thin, reedy. Had she actually been scared? Of absolutely nothing?

Ghosts don't exist, she told herself. But if anyone deserved to be haunted, wasn't that someone going to be her? After all, she'd been at the Limehouse place when Eddie died there. She had made Ruthie miserable by stealing Max away from her. Yes – it all came back to her, didn't it. She had to admit that.

Payback time.

'What is it?' He was sitting up, yawning. A thin shaft of light from the master suite illuminated him.

'You asleep?'

He yawned again. 'Not now. What's up?'

Hold me, she thought. But she couldn't say it. She still felt so *apart* from him, still unable to bridge the gulf between them, still wondering if Ruthie's death could have been somehow on him. And if it *had* been – oh God, what then? *What then?*

He threw back the covers. 'Come on,' he said. 'Get in. You'll freeze out there.'

Annie hesitated.

What the hell. She stepped inside the room, closed the door, fumbled her way in darkness over to the bed. It was a single, not really big enough for two. She snuggled down, Max at her back; like spoons. She couldn't move, but it felt good, the heat coming off his body, his arm very strong around her, holding her there.

'Couldn't sleep?' he murmured against her ear.

'Thought I heard something.'

'Like . . .?'

'Nothing. Doors, that's all. Music? But it was just the window at the end of the hall. Miss Arnott must have left it open and the rain was coming in. I closed it.'

'Just get to sleep,' he said, yawning again.

She knew she wouldn't sleep at all.

She hardly ever did, these days.

116

As it turned out, she was wrong. She slept deeply and when she finally awoke there was daylight pushing at the blinds on the window – and Max's erect cock was pressing into her back.

'I can't . . .' she breathed, feeling the rush of blood, the sudden need for him. She had been frozen ever since the loss of the baby, unable to reach Max, *unwilling* to reach him. All those hopes and dreams she'd had for their child, she'd lost those too; planning a family life, primary schools to be sorted out, and then raising a teenager, and then the baby would become an adult, getting married and if it had been a girl – she had actually hoped and prayed for a girl – then she would be mother of the bride on a fabulous lavish wedding day and she would have been so proud, so happy.

All gone.

It wrenched her afresh, that devastating loss. *One in four pregnancies ends in miscarriage.*

That smug superior bastard, sitting there telling her that. Like it was nothing. But it had been *something*. It had been her baby. They'd even discussed names. Jason for a boy. Layla if it was a girl. And now it was gone.

And she'd lost her sister too. She'd lost so much, too much, and Max had been seen, clear as day, kissing that brunette . . .

He was turning her, leaning over her, kissing her.

'Who was she?' she asked against his mouth. 'The brunette, who was she?'

'What?' He was kissing her again, easing her legs open, starting to push inside her and she was appalled at her own readiness when his betrayal was so awful, when she suspected him of such terrible things. 'What brunette?'

'Don't deny it,' she said.

'Shut up you mad tart,' he said against her skin.

'Don't you dare come inside me,' she said, but it was a weak defence, her voice husky with need.

'Oops,' he said, breathing hard, entering her fully. 'You know what? You shouldn't be so bloody sexy if you don't want to get fucked.'

'Do you have to be so damned crude?'

'You love it.'

She did. That was the trouble. And she felt bad over it. This mad passion had driven her to betray poor innocent Ruthie. And now he was in her, so hard, so silky, thrusting into her like a fury, over and over and over again, and it was crazy, it was wrong, but she wanted it, she wanted *him*.

'Don't come,' she moaned. 'I don't want another baby, I can't—'

'Get back on the horse, that's the quickest way to get over a fall,' he whispered against her neck, his breath hot on her skin.

Annie was incensed. Furious. She couldn't believe what the insensitive sod was saying. Back on the *horse*? *What was she then, a bloody brood mare?*

'What a fucking despicable thing to say. You callous bastard! That was a baby I lost, not a fucking *race*,' she panted, trying to squirm away from him but unable to. *Unwilling* too, really.

'Will you keep still? Keep your legs open, I'm coming. Oh Christ – *yes*.'

He came.

And then, maddeningly, Max dropped back easily into sleep. For Annie it took longer, but eventually she slept too.

They didn't wake again until after midday.

117

'I want to ask you something,' she said as they ate dinner that night.

Max speared a forkful of steak and looked at her. 'Go on.'

'It's about Ruthie.'

'All right.' He chewed, looked at her.

'It's about when you identified Ruthie's body.'

Max swallowed, swigged down a little red wine. 'Right.'

'Don't they . . . doesn't the Coroner or the pathologist or *somebody* usually check dental records on dead bodies, to confirm their identity?' asked Annie.

Max put down his fork. 'Good Christ, where did *that* come from?' he asked.

'They do though – don't they? I've heard they do that.'

'Yes. They do.'

'So Ruthie—'

'*Annie.*'

'What? I'm not going to apologise for asking. It's been bothering me.'

'Ruthie didn't have any teeth though, did she? So there was nothing for the pathologist to look into.'

'What?'

'She developed pyorrhoea of the gums and had all her teeth taken out not long after we were married. She was starving herself, not taking care of herself at all. The dentist recommended full extraction. Ruthie wore dentures.'

'Oh God.' Annie looked at the food on her plate and put her fork down. The thought of Ruthie, being so miserable that she'd simply let herself go. 'Who was her dentist?'

'Faulkes. In Bow.'

Annie put down her knife, pushed her plate away. 'I never knew any of that.'

'How would you? You had nothing to say to each other at that point, did you. She'd found out about you and me. She hated you then. Hated your guts.'

'Yes, all right.' Annie cringed.

'Well, she did.'

'You don't have to spell it out.'

'What makes you ask about that now?'

'My sister's dead and it bothers me.'

He looked at her half-empty plate. 'Had enough?'

She nodded.

'Come on then.'

They went into the drawing room. Max went to the drinks cabinet and poured himself a whisky, a tonic water for Annie. She sauntered around the room, browsing the half-empty bookshelves, the paintings, the big mirror over the fireplace, the radiogram on the left-hand side of the room. *Had* she heard music last night?

She let down the front of the radiogram – Bang and Olufsen, top of the range, only the best for Max Carter – and looked at the LP that had been left on the turntable there. Mozart's *Requiem*. Max liked classical music. But hadn't she heard something altogether different when she'd stepped out onto the landing last night, some light middle-of-the-road pop?

No you daft cow. You just imagined it.

She had to admit it: she'd been edgy and a bit mad in the head since losing the baby. On top of the shooting at the Palermo, the court case, losing Ruthie, maybe everything was getting just too much for her.

Gingerly she touched her palm to her belly. She had lost one child, but had Max already planted another in her?

Max came up behind her, kissed her neck, wrapped his arms around her waist. 'You all right?' he asked.

'Yeah. A bit freaked out with everything, that's all.'

'You need a good sleep,' he said. 'Let's go up.'

Meaning, he wants sex again, thought Annie. Yes, he could already have made a baby in her. If not already, then tonight, for sure.

But when they got upstairs, Max kissed her cheek, said goodnight and then went into the dressing room again. Leaving her alone.

At around midnight, unable to nod off, Annie went over to his door, opened it, stepped inside.

'You again? What?' asked Max sleepily in the darkness.

'Who's the brunette you were kissing?' she asked.

'Oh Christ – not that again?'

'Who was she?'

'I told you. There's no brunette. Wherever you've heard this from, it's wrong.'

'You're a bastard. Are you lying to me?'

'It's true I am a bastard.' He sounded like he was laughing.

'This isn't funny.' Annie stumbled over to the bed. Stubbed her toe on the edge of it. 'Ow! It's not funny. Not at all.'

'I agree.' There was a hiss of covers and Max was standing right there in front of her, naked, lit by a thin sliver of moonlight. He grabbed her hand. 'Come on, let's continue this conversation in a bigger bed.'

He led her back into the master suite, picked her up, placed her almost gently on the mattress and started kissing her.

'You won't get round me like that,' she said as he shoved the straps of her thin silk nightdress down her arms, baring her breasts. Instantly his mouth got busy there, lapping at her nipples.

'Yes,' he said, 'I will.'

And – of course – he did.

Just as she knew he would.

But still, the questions remained.

And she was going to get answers, if it killed her.

118

'If you're going to piss about around the streets, at least do it with a bit of backup,' said Max next morning.

Big bald-headed and neatly suited Tone with the twinkling gold crucifixes in his cauliflower ears was waiting behind the wheel of the black Jaguar Mark X.

'Don't you need him today?' Annie asked Max.

'Nope. Nothing to do. You take him.'

Tone opened the back passenger door for her with a polite: 'Good morning, Miss Bailey.'

'Call me Annie,' she said, wondering what the hell he must think of her. The mistress; the wife's sister. *Treacherous cow*. He *must* be thinking that.

'I'll stick with Miss Bailey,' he said, and got behind the wheel. 'Where would you like to go?'

That was her told. She gave him the address that Max had given her, tucked off a side street in Bow – M Faulkes BDA. There were six people in the dentist's waiting room, along with a grubby-looking tank of fish and a table stacked with well-thumbed magazines. All the six people – and the fish, come to that – had the look of impending doom that a visit to the dentist can cause to happen.

'Out,' said Tone, in a way that didn't encourage argument.

All six of them filed out.

Tone turned the key in the lock behind them.

'What the hell d'you think you're doing?' the flustered middle-aged receptionist asked Annie when she approached.

The phone was ringing on the desk between them. As the receptionist reached for it, Annie picked up the receiver and slapped it back down, cutting off the call.

'I want to see some records,' said Annie.

Down the hall, a door opened. 'What the . . .?' asked a thin bald-headed man in a neat white dental surgeon's jacket. He caught sight of Tone by the front door of his practice, came closer to reception to look into the waiting room – and saw he had no patients left. He looked at Annie. 'Who are you?'

Annie looked right back at him. 'I need to see some dental records.'

'Get out,' he said.

'You're not going to be difficult about this, are you?' she sighed.

'I'm warning you. I don't know what you think you're doing, but I am going to call the police.'

'Tone,' said Annie.

Tone nodded.

'In here,' he said, and gently took the dentist's arm and escorted him back into his surgery.

Now Annie could hear Tone chatting to the man, almost like he was an old mate.

'This one,' Tone said. 'What does this do then?'

There was the whine of a drill.

'Put that down,' said the dentist.

'Sit in the chair, let's have a look,' said Tone. 'What's this?'

'Those are plaque disclosing tablets.'

'And this?'

'An autoclave.'

'How do I . . .?'

Tone was clearly pressing pedals. A motor hummed.

'Lean back there,' said Tone, and the drill whined again, harder.

'What's he . . .? asked the receptionist, clutching a nervous hand to her chest.

The phone rang again. Annie repeated her trick with the receiver.

'He's not doing a damned thing,' she said.

The dentist's shriek told them otherwise.

'I want to see some records. Mrs Ruthie Carter. Get them. Tone's not hurting your friend. Yet. And he won't if I get the records right now. Okay?'

The receptionist hurried off into the back office.

'What's this stuff?' Tone was asking.

'Don't . . .' the dentist wailed.

'You're fine mate, you're cool. Just lay back there real comfy while we conclude a bit of business. And this, what's this?'

'Amalgam.'

There was the sound of drawers being opened and closed and then the receptionist was back. She was clutching a folder.

'Here,' she said, and nearly threw the thing at Annie. 'I'm going to report this,' she warned.

'Yep, fine,' said Annie, and opened the folder and looked at diagrams of sets of teeth, occlusal, mesial, distal . . .

Full extraction.

There it was. October sixty-four.

'Right. That's fine.' Well, had she really thought Max was lying about it? But here was proof, in black and white. Ruthie had lost all her teeth.

'Thanks for your help,' said Annie to the receptionist.

'Who the hell are you people?' she demanded.

'Tone!' bellowed Annie. 'Quit playing around in there. Let's go.'

119

Tone drove Annie in complete silence to Jimmy Bond's house. She knocked at the door and presently her cousin Kath came and answered it. Kath looked startled to find Annie there on the doorstep.

'Blimey! What brings you here?' she asked.

'Wanted to talk to you,' said Annie.

'About what?'

'Stick the kettle on, eh Kath? We've got things to discuss,' said Annie, receiving no invitation to step in but doing it anyway. 'This is nice,' she lied, glancing around the hallway. It wasn't. The place looked shabby: dirty.

'Well I wasn't expecting visitors,' said Kath grumpily, leading the way into the kitchen, which was a mess. Unwashed cups and saucers all over the place. The top of the stove uncleaned. The worktops crowded with all sorts of shit. The lino under Annie's feet felt sticky.

'You could get a cleaner in here, Kath. Sort things out,' said Annie, thinking of Ellie.

Kath shrugged and blushed. 'Jimmy don't like strangers in the house.'

'How is Jimmy? I don't often see him.'

'He's fine. You know. Busy.' Kath grabbed the kettle and filled it at the grime-encrusted sink. She slapped it onto the hob.

Annie started going through the cupboards, looking for clean cups. She couldn't find any. She gave up.

'No, skip the tea,' she said. 'I just wanted a talk, that's all.'

'About . . .?' Kath turned off the kettle and eyed her cousin nervously.

'About Ruthie. And about Ellie.'

'Ellie who?'

'Never play poker for God's sake, Kath. You haven't the face for it. I mean Ellie who worked at the Limehouse brothel. The same Ellie you had sneaking about after me when I was stopping there.'

'I don't—'

Annie held up a hand. 'Ruthie paid you and then you paid Ellie – to spy on me and report back. Correct?'

'Well I—'

'Correct?'

'Well yes. I suppose so.' Kath's big moon face was crimson with guilt. 'I only did it as a favour to Ruthie,' she rushed on. 'She asked me to do it and I couldn't very well refuse, now could I? Ruthie was always so kind to me and *you* . . .'

'Oh? I wasn't kind? I think you'll find I was. Kinder probably, bearing all this in mind, than you deserved.'

'You can justify it all you like,' said Kath. 'But the fact is, you stole Ruthie's husband right out from under her nose, didn't you. *That's* not kind.'

'You got any idea what would happen if I told Max? About you paying Ellie to spy on me, then running back to Ruthie with all manner of tall tales?'

'Tall tales? My arse,' spat out Kath. 'The things that went on in that place would just about curl your hair, Ellie told me.'

'Yeah, she was probably right,' agreed Annie. 'Supply and demand, Kath. The men wanted servicing, the girls obliged. And Darren too, of course. It's a good business to be in. Exceptional margins.' Annie lowered her voice. 'Max would skin Jimmy – no, the *pair* of you – alive if he found out about you conniving in the background against me. You know it.'

Now Kath looked frightened. But she was still in there fighting, and Annie admired her for it.

'I don't know how you can be so bloody casual about it all,' said Kath. 'You swan around giving yourself airs and graces because Max Carter's got the hots for you, and what are you really? A gangster's moll. A madam. A woman who sells other women to sex maniacs.'

'We didn't encounter many maniacs. Only one that I can think of, really: Pat Delaney.'

'That bastard,' said Kath. She reached out for a chair, heaved her bulk into it. Her flush had diminished; now she was paler and her eyes were vague. She was remembering; seeing the past and not liking what she saw there.

Annie recalled that night vividly: Kath coming bustling into the massage parlour looking for Jimmy on the night Pat Delaney died. Jimmy shouting, ordering Kath out. But Kath had already seen what Jimmy and Max's other boys were doing there: wrapping Pat's bulky red-haired body in a tarp.

'Anyway,' said Annie, drawing a line under that and glad to do it. 'That isn't what I want to know about.'

'Oh? What *do* you want to know about?'

'Well, you're the fount of all bloody knowledge, aintcha? So you can tell me, right now, what's Kieron Delaney's address? I'm guessing like the rest of his lot it's in Battersea?

I've tried his brother and sister but they don't seem to want to cooperate. I've been to his studio – no good. So now I'm trying you instead. So right now, Kath. Tell me because I'm damned sure you'll know this. And spare me any bullshit, please. I'm really not in the mood.'

120

Half an hour later, Annie and Tone stood outside the door of Kieron Delaney's flat in Battersea. It was a nice building: neat, well maintained. Down below, someone was laughing and a radio was playing 'I Like It' by Gerry and the Pacemakers. There was a bike leaning against the wall in the shared communal space between the two flats.

'I'm looking for Kieron Delaney,' Annie told her silent companion. 'My cousin tells me he stays here, most of the time.'

Tone squinted at her. 'Does Max know you're doing this?'

'No. He does not.'

'D'you think he'd be pissed off if he did?'

'Probably.'

'So . . . we might get trouble here.'

'Possibly. What, you want to bail?'

'I didn't say that.'

Annie reached out, rang the doorbell.

They stood there. Waited.

No answer.

Annie rang the bell again.

Silence except for more music. Freddie and the Dreamers now. Someone came out of one of the flats, pushed the bike along, down the stairs to the ground floor and out the front.

'Tone?' said Annie.

'Hm?'

'Think you can get this door open?'

'Piece of piss. Pardon my French.'

'Do it then, yeah?'

Tone stepped back, indicating that she should do the same. Annie did. Tone gave the door a hefty kick. 'Tough one,' he said. Another kick, harder than the first. It held.

'Just getting my eye in,' said Tone.

He stepped back further, lunged at the door. Another kick and this time the lock shattered with a loud *crack*. The door juddered open and Tone moved quickly inside, Annie following.

It was a very presentable flat. Comfy furnishings covered with velvet dark green throws. Big Tiffany lamps. Nice rugs on the floor, big green cheese plants in every corner. 'Seems empty. I'll have a look around,' said Tone, indicating that she should stop by the door. Annie ignored that indication. She walked around the lounge area, opened a couple of cupboards. Walked on into the bedroom. Double bed there. Tone pulled up a chair and opened a loft hatch, flicking on a light switch just inside. Cool air wafted down; nobody was hiding up there.

They went all over the place and ended up at the kitchen. Annie pushed the door open a little but met very slight resistance. She peered through the gap. There was an inert furry little bundle in the way; the weight of the door slid it back, over the tiles. Annie paused, staring down.

'Shit,' she said, seeing empty feeding bowls.

'What's that?'

'It's a dead dog. Poor damned thing must have been forgotten and starved.' She knelt, looked at the tiny circular name tag around the dog's neck. *Bertie.*

She closed the kitchen door. Then she went into the bathroom – there she smelled something deeply familiar and felt every hair on her head stand on end.

Wasn't that Ruthie's favourite perfume – Shalimar, by Guerlain?

It was.

'Ruthie's been in here,' said Annie, going back into the bedroom and opening another wardrobe. A couple of garments were hanging there. Muted colours, soft good-quality materials. The sort of clothes that Ruthie would wear. She lifted a sleeve on a light blue silk blouse and sniffed. There it was again. That sweet vanilla scent.

At the bottom of the wardrobe there was a pile of underwear, a hairdryer, some full bottles of bath oil. Face cream. Shampoo. And something else, right at the bottom underneath all the rest of it. What the fuck? It felt like animal fur. Thinking of the dead dog in the kitchen she recoiled and thought: *not another one?*

She grasped the fibres, pulled the thing out. Stepped back, holding it.

It was a long wig, very thick-textured cheap nylon – not expensive hair, the sort you got from a human head. It was the same colour as her own hair.

She thought of Kieron, obsessed with her.

She thought of Ruthie's perfume, scenting this place, Kieron's flat. She sniffed the wig. Ruthie's perfume, again.

'Looks like nobody's been in here for a while,' said Tone, interrupting her thoughts. 'Hence the dead dog. And did you notice?'

Annie shook her head. She was still standing there, the wig in her hands, trying to piece the whole damned thing together. 'Notice what?'

'There were none in the loft, none down here. I usually keep mine on top of the wardrobe, but there's none. Not even one,' said Tone.

'Don't know what you mean,' said Annie, still thinking, still puzzling. The brunette wig. Ruthie's perfume, wafting around here, coming off her clothes. Unmistakeable. She stuffed the wig into her bag.

'I mean, there's no male clothes here. Not even a pair of Y-fronts.'

'So he's moved out?' she guessed, looking around, half-dazed by all that was going on in her head.

'No suitcases,' said Tone patiently. 'None in the apartment, none in the loft space. He's gone. Vamoosed. Run for the hills.' Tone gave a thin smile.

Yeah, but where? she wondered.

'Damn,' said Annie. 'That's a shame. I reckon Max would have liked a word with that bastard. And so would I.'

121

When they got back to the Guildford house, Tone went into a huddle with Max in the drawing room, telling him what Annie had been up to.

'Grass,' said Annie mildly, listening from the sofa.

'So there's no sign of him. No sign at all,' said Max.

'None,' said Tone.

'I've had word out on all the streets. Every town. Every port, every station. Looks like he's vanished,' said Max.

'I didn't know you'd done that,' said Annie.

'I saw no reason to tell you,' said Max.

'Oh? Cheers.'

Tone glanced between the two of them and assessed the situation quickly. 'I'll go and . . .' he said.

'Yeah. Do that,' said Max.

The instant the door closed behind Tone, Annie launched the attack. 'Why didn't you tell me you were looking for Kieron bloody Delaney?' she demanded. 'I thought I was on my own with this.'

'Well, you're not. If you'd told me what you were doing—'

'If *you'd* told *me* . . . oh dammit. I want him found,' said Annie. She looked at him. Max. Her lover. Ruthie's widower. *Could* he have been involved in her death? How could she bring herself to really believe that?

Maybe she couldn't.

'I know that. So do I.'

'You've tried the farm in Limerick?' she asked.

Max nodded. 'Nobody there but mad old Davey and a few nurses,' he said.

Annie stared at him. Her lover, yes – but also, Ruthie's husband. And now a horrible thought occurred to her. Maybe Max and Ruthie had actually grown *close* over the course of their – seemingly non-functional – marriage? Had she made a terrible mistake, believing Max to be wholly involved with her, thinking he felt nothing whatsoever for Ruthie?

'Oh fuck,' she said faintly.

'What?' asked Max.

'You and her . . . were you?'

'Were we what?'

'You know! Were you involved with her?'

'I was *married* to her.'

Annie felt a surge of jealousy so strong it almost choked her. He'd gone ahead with the marriage that his mother had planned. In honour of Queenie's memory? Or because he'd grown fond of his quiet, sweet-natured fiancée? Because he *liked* Ruthie, maybe even loved her, and so saw no reason to change his plans?

After all, hadn't Ruthie always been perfect wife material – unlike her?

And after all, despite all his protestations to the contrary, hadn't things worked out just fine for him in the end? He'd had a placid, agreeable wife and a mistress who drove him wild in bed. What more could any man ask than that?

'For God's sake Max!'

'What? Are you going to ask me if I killed her again? I didn't.'

'No. Wait. Oh you bastard! Have you been playing me, all this time? Ever since the damned wedding? Or even before that?'

'Don't know what you mean,' he said, going to the drinks cabinet. 'You want something?'

'No. I don't want a bloody thing. What I *would* like is a few answers. Like, what the hell is going on? You think Kieron drove her to suicide? Is that it?'

'I'm having a drink,' said Max, pouring Chivas Regal.

'Is that why you're hunting him down? Revenge? You don't like the idea that he crossed Max Carter and felt he could get away with it? Has he insulted your manhood or something like that? Is that what this is?'

'That and the fact that he tried to kill me.' Max took a sip of the whisky. 'Look, why don't you go on up. Have a bath, relax.'

He was stonewalling her!

And she was making a fool of herself. For fuck's sake, she *loved* him. She always had. She was completely committed to him and she'd been so delighted when she'd known that she was going to have his baby. But now he was so cool, so detached, so secretive. Now he was busy chasing down the man he believed had been instrumental in the death of his wife. Which made a nonsense out of Annie's nagging suspicions that somehow Max himself had been behind her sister's death. Didn't it? Or was Max just being his usual devious self, throwing up smokescreens, directing her attention elsewhere?

And where did all this leave *her*?

Out in the cold.

The mistress. That was what she was. The woman who dealt in the currency of sex. The *bit on the side*.

'I'm going up,' she said, and left the room because she was afraid that she was going to start crying. And she *never* cried.

As she passed by in the hallway, the phone was ringing. She snatched it up. 'Yes?'

It was Nicholas.

'Hey, don't shoot the messenger,' he said.

'I won't if the messenger's pulled his finger out,' she snapped.

'The messenger has.'

'Go on then. Surprise me. Who's on the board of directors of Tarrec Holdings?'

'You've got to be kidding, asking me that. I've no idea.'

'Then what . . .?'

'Tarrec. Think about it.'

'No *you* think about it. That's what I'm paying for.'

'Tarrec,' said Nicholas, 'is an anagram.'

'Of what?'

'Of Carter.'

122

She went back into the drawing room.

'Something else?' asked Max.

'Yes there is. I've just had some information passed to me. Very interesting information, as it happens.'

'Like?'

'Like – and I should have spotted this, shouldn't I really – like Tarrec being an anagram of Carter.'

'Is it? Interesting. What's an anagram?'

'You bloody know. You own the place Ruthie was found dead in – don't you. What, were you sheltering her there? Protecting her from Kieron Delaney? Well you fucked *that* up, didn't you.'

'Annie—'

'You own the flat. You own the bloody building. Don't you?'

'I own it. Yes.'

'I want to get into that flat. I want to see it,' said Annie.

Max's eyes widened. 'For the love of God! Why?'

'I just do. Okay? I don't have to explain myself to you.'

'And I don't have to give you access if I don't want to,' said Max.

'Why wouldn't you want to? Look – indulge me. After all we've been through, I should think that's the least you can do.'

They stood face to face, glaring.

'Well?' said Annie.

'I keep forgetting what a total pain in the arse you can be,' he said.

'It's a request, Max. It's not asking much – is it?'

'It's pointless.'

'Not to me.'

'If I say no?'

'Then I'd have to wonder what the hell you were playing at. Why would you? And why were you so antsy about me getting Jackie to stake the place out, see who was coming and going? Why so bloody secretive?'

'For God's sake,' said Max.

'It's not much to ask.'

'All right! Tomorrow. We'll go. Satisfied?'

123

The place where Ruthie was found dead was, in fact, wonderful. The penthouse flat had huge high ceilings, fabulous tan leather furnishings, big white and tan cow hides on the highly polished wood block floors, massive lamps standing on exquisite side tables – and floor to ceiling windows that looked out onto Tower Bridge.

Annie walked into the flat ahead of Max. He closed the door quietly after them. She went to the couches, looked at the lamps. Went to the windows. Without turning around she said: 'Where was she? When she was found?'

'There,' said Max, indicating the larger of the couches. 'They found her lying there.'

Annie nodded. Went to the door that led out to the balcony. She opened it. It wasn't locked. She stepped outside. A cold gust of wind blasted upward from the river and she went to the edge of the balcony and looked down. The sludgy Thames ebbed and flowed. Merchant barges and pleasure boats sailed by. Traffic roared over Tower Bridge. She thought that she could stand here all day, just watching the scene.

'You have to open the door,' she said as Max joined her out there.

'What?'

'You have to open the door. To let the spirit out. Or it's trapped, inside.' Annie shivered. Thought of Ruthie dying here, alone.

'You're cold,' said Max, and took off his black vicuna coat with the purple silk lining, draped it around her shoulders.

'Thanks,' she said. He stood there behind her, his hands on her shoulders. She could feel the warmth of his body radiating from the coat. Suddenly, she felt on the verge of tears.

'It's going to be okay,' he said.

'How can it be?'

'Well, you've let her spirit out,' he said.

'You don't believe all that codswallop, do you?'

'No. But you do. So I suppose that helps, yes?'

Annie let out a deep sigh. 'Thanks for this,' she said.

'Enough?' he asked.

'Yeah. Let's go.'

124

That night the dreams came again. Dreams of Ruthie, meandering along dark passageways, drifting not like a human woman but like a ghost, the wind catching her filmy white clothes, lifting them so they ebbed and flowed around her like wings. She was smiling.

Hello Annie.

Oh Ruthie, I miss you so much . . .

Annie was reaching out, ready to embrace her sister.

But then the smile became a snarl.

The teeth of the ghost-woman were pointed, ready and eager to tear flesh, and the woman was drifting closer, her eyes blank, the eyes of a demon straight out of hell.

Annie leapt awake, sitting bolt-upright in bed in the master suite. Her hands flew to her mouth to stifle the scream that was building there. She was sweating heavily. Her heart was beating hard and she thought that she was going to die, right now, have a heart attack and be gone, dead.

God, that dream . . .

She reached out with a trembling hand, turned on the bedside light. It was gone midnight. Oh God. That dream. She didn't want another dream like that, not *ever*.

Calm down, she told herself. For fuck's sake, it was just a nightmare.

Max wasn't here with her. He was asleep in the dressing room. She lay back, coming slowly back to reality and then she started thinking of their earlier conversation.

Max was pursuing Kieron because of what happened to Ruthie.

And it stung. Hurt her. It really did.

They'd shared this very bed, hadn't they? Max and Ruthie? How often? Regularly? He'd said just the once, but was that even true? Her pride wouldn't let her ask that question. She just *couldn't*. But her mind kept offering up little snatches of what might have gone on in the Carter marital bed. Tormenting her. Making her cringe.

The two of them, her sister and her lover, having sex right here in this very bed. And what about the apartment in the building Max owned? *Tarrec Holdings*. Had they been meeting there? Had they become lovers?

Oh God.

Noises.

Oh not again . . .

She reached out, snatched up her robe from the end of the bed. A door closed in the distance, the reverberations from it juddering through the big house. Then silence but for the moaning of the wind around the eaves. She got to the edge of the bed and stood up, shuffled into her slippers. She crossed to the door and opened it. Out on the landing, all was still, but there was something – movement – downstairs.

Tarrec was an anagram of Carter.

What the hell was Max playing at? Her brain was spinning.

She didn't think it was Max downstairs. She could hear music playing, light popular music. Not Max's taste at all.

And this time she wasn't going to let it go. She was terrified, but she was going to get to the bottom of this. She *had* to.

The dream, though. The spectre, floating toward her, teeth bared . . .

Annie stepped out onto the landing and went to the stairs. Gently, stealthily, she descended. The music grew steadily louder. The door to the drawing room was slightly ajar, light spilling out into the darkened hallway.

She reached the bottom of the stairs and paused. Moving stealthily, she crossed the hallway and approached the door. Hank Marvin played the intro to 'The Young Ones'. Then another track came on. Chuck Berry singing 'Maybellene'. There came the clink and rattle of a decanter. And there was someone humming along to the tune? Didn't sound like Max.

Sounded like . . . a woman.

No. Couldn't be. Impossible.

For God's sake, she was either going to have to do this or clear off back to bed. *There is no such thing as ghosts*, she told herself sharply.

She raised an unsteady hand and pushed the door open and stepped inside. Chuck's volume increased. There was a woman in a dark robe standing by the drinks tray, sipping amber-coloured liquid from a large tumbler. She was moving, swaying a little to the beat of the music.

The woman was pale blonde and very thin.

She turned as Annie entered – and she smiled.

Annie let out a shriek.

It was *her*, the woman from the nightmare.

It was *Ruthie*.

125

Annie staggered back against the door, so great was the shock. 'No! You're not real. I'm just dreaming . . .'

Ruthie was smiling. No fangs though. Nothing to tear and shred flesh with. But it was Ruthie. And Ruthie was dead. Annie *knew* she was dead.

This couldn't be happening. This was all part of the dream, a continuation of the nightmare. She would wake in a moment and she would be in bed and this would be *nothing*.

'You're dead,' she said faintly. 'I *saw* you dead.'

'Did you?' Ruthie was sipping at her drink, smiling.

'Max identified your body.' Annie was talking fast now, wanting to make this go away before it drove her mad.

'That was kind of him,' said Ruthie.

'What do you mean, kind? He was your husband. Your next of kin.' She couldn't believe this. Ruthie! She was standing here talking to *Ruthie*.

And yet *she couldn't be*.

This *could not* be happening.

'You're not real,' said Annie.

But she could feel the hard wood of the door, solid under her hand. She could hear the music, see the turntable spinning. Could smell that scent again. The scent that Ruthie always wore, the scent she loved, the one that had been all over Kieron Delaney's flat: Shalimar.

'Nah, I'm real enough,' said Ruthie. 'Sorry, did I scare you? Couldn't resist it really. Just little ghostly happenings. Shutting doors. Windows left open. Music. Oh dear, have I driven you mad, Annie? *Have I?*'

'Ruthie . . .?' It was her. It *had* to be. Her voice, her smile. It was *her.*

'But then – maybe not. Because you were always the practical one, weren't you? The steady one. The brave one. Not like me,' said Ruthie.

Annie couldn't even swallow. She felt that the room was lurching around her, that everything was giddy, unreal. She wondered if she was going to pass out cold.

Ruthie was dead.

Max had identified her body.

She had herself glimpsed Ruthie lying there dead on the pathologist's table, through that little gap in the curtains that should have shut her out – and didn't.

She had expected to see Ruthie lying there.

And she *had.*

But had she been so distraught, so shocked by events, that her mind had simply joined the dots – and in totally the wrong way?

But then – what was Max's excuse?

He had identified his dead wife's body as Ruthie Carter.

He *had.*

Now she heard steps on the stairs.

'What's going on . . .?' Max was coming across the hall, pushing the door wide, nudging Annie further into the room. Tucking his shirt into his jeans. 'Oh for fuck's . . .' he said in exasperation. 'I told you about this,' he said to Ruthie.

'So you did. But as I just told Annie, I couldn't resist. Just a small revenge, wouldn't you say? Under the circumstances? And you know my hearing's bad now. Did I have it too loud? Maybe I did. Just a little.' Ruthie swilled back her drink, put the empty glass onto the tray.

Annie stared between the two of them, Max and Ruthie. This was no dream. This was reality. Ruthie was here and she was *alive.*

Max went over to the radiogram and snatched the needle off the record, silencing it instantly. He looked at Ruthie. 'I *told* you about this. I told you to keep to the attic rooms, not come down here. It's not like you to be petty,' he said.

'Yes it is,' retorted Ruthie. 'When a sister snatches a husband away, well, why not? Just a little tiny bit of revenge seems very fair to me.'

'It *is* you. You're bloody alive,' gasped out Annie.

'So I am,' said Ruthie.

Annie looked at Max. 'You identified the body,' she said.

'I had to do that.'

'You *identified the body*,' Annie shouted suddenly. All at once she was furious. Literally *boiling* with rage. 'You did that. You let me think my sister was dead. Why the *fuck* would you do that?'

'Because he had to,' said Ruthie.

'*What?*' Annie's voice rose to a shriek as she stared at Max in confusion. 'But the thing with the teeth, the dental records . . .'

'That was all true,' said Max.

'Oh, was it?' Annie let out a strained hollow laugh. 'You kept this secret from me, all this time. You knew I was in mourning for her—'

'Oh, that's nice,' said Ruthie.

'*Don't*,' snapped Annie. 'Don't you bloody dare. The pair of you, you've deceived me, tricked me. For what reason?'

'Because one of these days that nutter was going to kill her – and I couldn't let that happen,' said Max.

126

'*What?*' Annie stared at them both, not understanding.

'Look,' said Max. 'Kieron Delaney's insane. He'd already beaten her up several times, and each time it was getting worse. She has a little brain damage. Memory lapses. She can't hear on her right side. Because of all he did to her. That last time, that was the worst. He broke her ribs. Fractured her jaw. Split her spleen.'

Annie stared, horrified. 'That . . . when was that?'

'The day she left,' said Max.

Annie looked at Ruthie. She nodded.

'I went to Waterloo, got on a train. But he followed me. He found me.'

'The old man you told me about,' said Annie to Max. 'The one who helped Ruthie that day. What did Kieron do to him? You said something flippant about playing the piano—'

'Did I sound flippant? Delaney took a steak tenderiser to his hands. Broke every bone in them. When I visited Ruthie in hospital, I visited him too. He was a broken man. Literally.'

Annie looked at Ruthie. Ruthie, *alive*.

'I was out of it for a lot of the time,' said Ruthie. 'I was just clinging on to Max's hand, drifting in and out, not having a clue what was going on. All I could see was

Max's hand, and the blue lapis lazuli ring he always wore, and I could hear him saying that everything was going to be all right.'

Max looked at Annie. 'She was desperate,' he said. 'It was her idea to start with, but in the end I saw that it made sense. And we devised a plan. I said, look, if she was dead already, if she were out of it, he'd have no comebacks, would he? Nothing to aim for. I wasn't entirely serious about that, not at first. But the attacks from that bastard were bad and getting worse so soon the idea really took hold.'

'But why not just fight it out with the Delaneys?' asked Annie. 'I don't understand.'

'What – open gang warfare?' Max shook his head. 'Don't think it didn't cross my mind. But no. A lot of people would have died. Maybe even me. Maybe Ruthie. Maybe you. Don't be so bloody reckless.'

'But you could have *told* me,' said Annie. 'For God's sake, why didn't you tell me what was happening?'

'You were estranged from Ruthie anyway,' said Max. 'And I was concerned you wouldn't be able to keep up an act. And – the truth? – I didn't know *where* your loyalties lay. Come to that, I'm still not sure. So I presented you with the fact of Ruthie's death, her funeral, everything. You went into mourning. You didn't have to struggle to be convincing. The fact is, I'd seen how tight you were in with Redmond Delaney. I couldn't take the risk of you passing information onto him and from there to Kieron.'

'You cold-blooded rotten *bastard*,' Annie burst out, striding across the room and hitting him a resounding *whack* across the face. She drew back her arm, ready to hurt him again if she could, but Max caught her wrist.

'Listen – we had to do it,' he said, shaking her. 'He would have killed her. It was heading that way. All we had to do was read the signs. He'd already done her damage. What should I have done? Taken no notice? How many times have we heard things like this? The Old Bill take no action. You hear that don't you? Next thing, the woman's dead and everyone's sorry, of course they are, but the fact is it's too late; it's happened.'

'Max is absolutely right,' said Ruthie. 'Kieron was going to kill me. Without a doubt. So sorry, Sis – turns out I'm alive!'

'Oh shut up, Ruthie. And as for you . . .!' She glared at Max. 'You really are the most devious, twisted, rotten *sod*.'

127

'I'm going back to bed,' snapped Annie. 'You two . . . I don't know what the hell to make of all this.'

But she couldn't rest. Having stormed back upstairs she lay in bed, the light still on, and she could hear them talking downstairs and then she suddenly thought – *The brunette!*

She leapt from the bed and ran across the room, snatched up her handbag from the chair where she'd dumped it the night before. Pulled the brunette wig out. Looked at it. Then she flung open the bedroom door and marched back down there. They both turned in surprise.

Annie threw the wig at Max's feet.

'Where'd you get that?' asked Ruthie.

'Never you bloody mind,' said Annie. She shook her head. 'No, all right, I'll tell you. It was in Kieron Delaney's flat. That's where I found it. What, did he make you wear it? Did it turn him on? Did he pretend you were me?'

'Annie,' said Max warningly.

'The woman kissing Max. That was *you*, I suppose? Wearing this?'

'Not that one,' said Ruthie. 'Another one just like it. That one gave me the idea for a disguise.' Ruthie held up her hands. 'So yes! All right! That was me. I got bored, cooped up here day and night. We had one night out. *One damned night* in town. And I wore a dark wig because I was sure no one would recognise me while I was wearing it.'

'Well you were seen. And I was told.'

'Well, I'm sorry about that. But it wasn't all beer and skittles, I can tell you, confined upstairs in the attic suite like some mad thing. I had to get out *just once*. It was just rotten luck if someone saw us and thought Max was playing around. I do seem to remember – and if this gives you a crumb of comfort, that's fair enough – that I kissed Max, not the other way around. It was just a hug and a peck on the cheek, that's all, out of gratitude. I owed him so much. Although,' Ruthie's eyes sharpened, 'I would have thought you would have known by now – Max don't play around. You're all he wants. All he *ever* wanted, come to that. Which is mostly the trouble, wouldn't you say?'

Annie looked between the pair of them – her lover and her sister who was still – and this hurt – *his wife*. They'd deceived her and that crucified her. They hadn't trusted her enough to let her into their charmed circle. They'd doubted her ability to cope with the situation. And – worse – they'd even suspected her of collusion with Redmond! And she'd been so wrong, so completely misguided about everything, thinking Max could have done for Ruthie. Now, in light of all this, the very idea was a joke.

'I'm—' she started.

'Going back to bed?' suggested Ruthie.

'Oh shut the fuck up,' snarled Annie. Suddenly she grabbed her sister's arm.

'What the hell?' demanded Ruthie.

Annie was staring at Ruthie's arm. It was unmarked. No druggie tracks. Nothing.

'The body Max identified. *That wasn't you.* I saw the marks. The injection marks.'

'Of course not,' said Ruthie. 'I'm alive. And you always were too bloody nosy for your own good. You shouldn't even have been there. I bet Max tried to talk you out of it, but you weren't having it, were you? Good old Annie, going your own way as usual.'

'He did try to talk me out of it,' said Annie.

'Well, you should have listened to him.'

Then Annie had another thought. 'So who's in the coffin? Who's in that bloody graveyard? If not you, Ruthie, then who?'

Ruthie's face grew solemn.

She said: 'It was a girl I'd seen at the Delaney scrapyard, one of Redmond's druggie girlfriends. It struck me that she looked like me, and . . . well, she died. The drugs, you know. She had no family. Max arranged it all. It was quite simple, quite straightforward to set up.'

Annie stared at Ruthie, then her eyes turned to Max.

Max held up his hands. 'Don't look at me. It was your sister's idea to start with, remember. I just saw to the details.'

'Fake doctors,' said Annie. 'For the death certificate.'

Max nodded.

'A fake pathologist?'

He nodded again.

'Morgue attendants?'

'Yeah. My people.'

'An iffy undertaker,' said Annie.

Max shrugged. 'People will do surprising things you know – for a very large amount of money.'

Annie suddenly thought of the night-time call she'd had from Kath, telling her the news of Ruthie's death. Kath, in floods of tears at Ruthie's funeral.

'But . . . Kath wasn't in on it, was she?'

'No,' said Max. 'She had to behave as if the thing had really happened. I couldn't trust her reactions so she had to go in cold.'

'Just like you couldn't trust mine,' said Annie.

'Yeah,' he agreed. 'Just like I couldn't trust yours.'

128

Annie was sure she wouldn't be able to sleep after all that. Much to her surprise she eventually did. By the time she got downstairs again the following morning, Max had already eaten and was in the drawing room. There was an unknown bulky man with a thin scrape of dark hair across his head and big eyebrows standing beside him before the open fire.

No Ruthie this morning. She was upstairs, no doubt, sneaking about in the attic rooms, where once the house servants had slept. Again it washed over Annie, the anger at their deception.

'Annie?' Max stepped forward. 'This is Nico, who works for a friend of mine, Constantine Barolli.'

The big shambling man came to Annie and held out a hand. He was smiling.

'Ah! The lady in the picture,' he said in a thick Bronx accent.

'That's me,' said Annie. Barolli was the silver-haired American who'd been at the exhibition of Kieron Delaney's work. The one who'd bid hard against Max for ownership of the nude of her. 'The picture's gone I'm afraid.'

'Gone where?'

Annie indicated Max with a nod of her head. 'He broke it. When I broke up with him. Left it all slashed through on my doorstep, as a parting gift.'

'That's a real shame,' said Nico.

'What can I say?' said Max. 'I was upset.'

'An act of vandalism,' said Nico mournfully. 'That was a beautiful picture. And that Delaney boy has some real talent.'

'He's a demented little prick,' said Max.

'Well, we think we may have traced his whereabouts so whatever issues you have with the man can soon be resolved.'

'Oh, we've got issues all right. The biggest of which is, he's seriously pissed me off.' Max turned to Annie. 'Constantine has contacts all over the world, so it seemed sensible to ask for help with this.'

'I thought you two were enemies,' said Annie.

'Enemies?' Nico looked surprised. 'No, not at all. Mr Barolli and Mr Carter are competitors, certainly. They like to bid against each other but also, they sometimes work together for their mutual benefit. For instance – Mr Barolli's clubs in the West End. Mr Carter handles door security on those. And very efficiently too.'

'And now your boss is helping him find Kieron Delaney?'

'Exactly.'

'So now what? More shootings? More revenge?' asked Annie.

'Yes to both of those,' said Max grimly.

There was a noise outside in the hall and Ruthie came in. Max made the introductions and she sat down.

'The thing is, what he did to Ruthie, that wouldn't have been the end of it. He wasn't going to stop coming after her. I've seen this sort of thing before. And once he's seen to her? He'll do it all over again, to some other poor cow,' said Max. 'And I can tell you this – I'm not bloody having it.'

129

Nico fished in his jacket pocket and pulled out a photo. 'This is what we've narrowed it down to,' he said, and went to hand the picture over to Max. 'The Delaney family own this place in Cantabria – in Comillas.'

Annie was watching her sister; while Nico spoke, Ruthie was staring hard at him.

'Ruthie?' she asked. 'What's up?'

Ruthie ignored the question. She stood up, went to Nico. 'Show me that,' she said, before Max could take the print from the American's hand.

Nico handed the photo to Ruthie. She stood there, staring at the image, saying nothing.

'Ruthie? Do you know that place?' asked Max.

Ruthie looked up at Max, then at Nico. 'I've been to this place,' she said. 'With Kieron.'

Still holding the print, she stumbled back to the couch and sat down abruptly, her eyes fixed on the photo. 'There's an angel,' she said. 'I remember an angel.'

'My people did mention a cemetery near to Comillas,' said Nico, nodding agreement. 'They talked about a big angel there, perched up on the roof. Wings spread wide.'

'To ward off demons,' said Ruthie. She gave a faint smile. 'Didn't ward off Kieron Delaney though, did it?' She looked again at the picture. 'Yes, I know this place. He took me there once. I'd almost forgotten about it.'

'Is it staffed?' asked Max. 'The place the family own there?'

'No. I don't think so. I'm sorry – my memory . . .'

Annie watched her sister with sympathy. Here was the evidence of Kieron's mistreatment of Ruthie: memory lapses, partial deafness. It was awful, just to think of it.

Nico looked at Max. 'Your guys tried the place in Limerick, right? The farmhouse, the one that's been in the Delaney family for years? Where old Davey and Molly went back to, after Tory got done?'

'We did. Nothing.'

'Kieron has a studio in the Cantabria place. He likes it there. He can work undisturbed,' said Ruthie, her eyes still fixed on the photo.

'He could be there. Or any fucking where, come to that. Can we stake out this Spanish place? See who's coming and going?' said Max.

'It's already done,' said Nico. 'Place looks abandoned. Big grounds, a vineyard, and all of it going to hell.'

130

After lunch next day, Nico took a phone call in the hall. Then he joined Max, Annie and Ruthie in the drawing room and said: 'Well, it's not entirely good news.'

'Go on,' said Max.

'Don't think you're going to get your chance for revenge, Mr Carter.'

'Oh? Why?'

'Because from all I've heard, the bastard could be already dead.'

'What d'you mean, dead? He can't be,' said Annie.

'One of the villagers nearby said he'd died in a car accident,' said Nico.

There was a silence.

'So . . . if that's true, is he buried at the cemetery in Comillas?' asked Ruthie finally, her voice shaking. 'He always said he . . . God, I remember it now. We went there. Kieron said it would be nice to be buried there in one of those little vaults and to have blue flowers on a wreath . . .'

She faltered to a halt. Her eyes filled with tears. Annie sat Ruthie down, patted her shoulder. 'It's all right,' she said. 'All gone now.'

'It's not though – is it?' Ruthie wiped angrily at her eyes and rapped hard at her skull with one small fist. 'He may be dead – I hope he is – but he's still alive *in here*.'

Max was pacing up and down. 'Dead, you say,' he said to Nico.

Nico shrugged. 'That's what a few of my guys tell me. That's the information they've been given. But the villager could be in the pay of the Delaney people. Trying to throw us off the scent. Because the fact is, one of my people said he'd spotted Kieron Delaney out there, alive, in the village.'

'You what?' demanded Max.

'You're being fed a load of baloney Mr Carter.'

Max looked thoughtful. 'We checked all the ports and airports.'

'Yeah, but it's an easy thing to hire a private boat, go out round the Bay of Biscay, pitch up in Cantabria,' said Nico.

'Kieron said he worked better out there in the Spanish place than anywhere else in the entire world,' said Ruthie. 'I think if he's anywhere, he'll be there.'

131

Nico departed soon after that. It had been a long day and Max, Annie and Ruthie were all glad when it was time for sleep.

Max said to Ruthie: 'No need to stay up in the attic any longer. Plenty of bedrooms. Take your pick.'

She shook her head. 'No, I like it up there. It feels . . . safer.'

'Okay. If you want.'

They turned in for the night, Annie alone in the master suite, Max in the dressing room, Ruthie in the attic.

Annie wished that she could sleep with Max, but he didn't ask to join her in the master suite and the narrow bed in the dressing room was uncomfortable; but anyway she would have felt awkward, knowing that Ruthie was so close by. *It would be taking the piss,* she thought. *And hadn't they already done Ruthie enough harm, between them?*

So Annie settled down in the big bed in the master, and composed herself for sleep. It was a long time coming. She was anxious, worried about what that American friend of Max's had told them, wondering if it could be true.

Kieron, dead in a car crash?

They drove on the right in Spain, not on the left like they did in England. Could Kieron have had a lapse of concentration, forgotten? People did. And disaster could strike as a result. Or was it just a blind? Was none of it true at all?

She fell asleep dreaming of open Spanish roads and of a car swerving, spinning out of control, plummeting down a cliff, crashing in flames at the bottom of a deep, deep ravine.

Kieron Delaney, dead?

She thought of Ruthie, hurt, damaged.

And that innocent old man, his hands smashed and useless.

Oh God yes. Make that the truth. Make him dead.

She slept.

132

Annie could smell the flames, wafting up from the mangled remains of the car. She wrinkled her nose, drew breath. She could still smell the fire, the petrol, it all caught at her throat and she started to cough.

Just another dream . . .

Still coughing, she woke up. Felt that the air around her was strangely warm, and that there was a noise somewhere nearby. A sort of roaring sound . . .

Confused, she sat up. Her throat constricted and she coughed again, hard. She *could* smell smoke. Couldn't she? Or was it all part of the dream? She reached out a shaking hand for the bedside light, flicked it on. Blinked and stared, aware that her eyes felt gritty and – it was weird – the room looked *hazy*.

She coughed again and then, feeling increasingly alarmed, she scrambled to the side of the bed, put on her robe.

Oh Jesus – the place was *on fire*!

This wasn't a dream.

It wasn't a car crash.

This was *real*.

133

Stumbling barefoot, she put a hand over her mouth and nose and made her way over to the dressing-room door. Before she could open it, Max was there, flinging it wide, pulling on his jeans.

'Fire,' he said. 'It's down in the hall,' he said, grabbing her hand. 'Come on.' He turned, shouted: 'Ruthie! Wake up! Fire!'

They raced to the door out onto the landing and Max eased it open. They both stopped dead as a blast of vivid light and hot air hit them. To her horror Annie saw that most of the downstairs hallway and even the stairs were well ablaze; the vast mahogany staircase was burning ferociously and on the brink of collapsing into a heap of blackened wood.

'Ruthie!' Max was shouting.

If they couldn't get out down the stairs, then where the hell would they go? Annie wondered in panic.

'Where the fuck is she . . .?' Max said out loud.

Max grabbed the hook and let down the loft hatch, yanked down the steps. Ruthie was already standing there, right by the hatch, peering down at them, seeing the smoke, hearing the roar of the flames. Her eyes were panicky.

'What's happening?' she asked.

'Fire. Come on, get down here,' said Max, and Ruthie hurried down.

He led the way along to the far end of the landing, to the large window that Annie had found standing open some nights ago. He opened it. Tonight there was no rain, but the air was cold, damp – blissful, after breathing in the smoke in the house. Max stepped out over the windowsill and held out a hand to his wife.

His wife, Annie thought. Something in that rankled, badly. In this emergency situation, this *life or death* event, he'd reached for Ruthie first. Not her. He'd thought first of Ruthie's safety. 'Come on Ruthie,' he said.

'I'm not . . .' Ruthie held back.

'Yes you are. You step out here and I'll lower you down onto the next part of the roof and from there it's an easy jump down to the ground. Come on.'

'No, I . . .' Ruthie was stricken with fear.

Annie could only stare at the pair of them. Max, trying to convince his wife that he wouldn't let her fall. Ruthie, frightened, her eyes fixed on him. On the man she had turned to, despite all their troubles, when she had needed help.

And Max had helped her.

He'd helped his wife. Of course he had. Of course he *would*.

Annie stepped forward. 'I'll go first,' she said. She wanted to hit him but this was not the time. 'You watch me, Ruthie. It'll be fine.'

Annie grabbed Max's hand and he pulled her out onto the roof.

But then the nerves hit her.

Because – oh God – it was far from fine.

134

The ground seemed a million miles below and Annie felt herself waver. Her heart was in her mouth. She completely understood Ruthie baulking at this, but she had to go ahead or she had the feeling they would never get Ruthie down to safety. She could feel her feet slipping on the mossy tiles. God, if she fell . . .! Even from this height – what was it, twenty feet? – she could do herself serious damage.

Max caught hold of both her hands and said: 'Step back. I've got you.'

Have you? she wondered. And then it came into her mind, the worst thing possible at that moment. Ruthie had asked Max for help and he had obliged. Again she saw Max reaching for Ruthie, Ruthie first, not her. And . . . was it possible? . . . had Max and Ruthie finally grown close?

Would he guide Annie down to the ground as he said he would?

Or . . . would he let her fall, break her neck, be rid of her, the problematic, difficult, fiery sister, and leave the way clear for the more amenable woman – his wife, after all – to simply step in?

But what else could Annie do but trust him, if only this once? Terrified, she did as she was told. She felt the gutter groan under her feet.

'Christ,' she muttered, but Max lowered her down inch by inch and finally about a hundred years later she felt her feet touch *another* sloping patch of roof.

'Stay there now.' He stepped gingerly down and then he was there, standing right beside her. 'Grab that downpipe and shin down to the ground. It's only a few feet. You can do it.'

Wanting only to stay exactly where she was, Annie nevertheless did what he said. Again she felt the gutter creak beneath her weight and wondered if she was going to fall – onto what? In the faint moonlit darkness she could just see part of the terrace down below, could see the hard concrete slabs. Land on those, and she was going to break something.

But what choice did she have?

She shinned down. Then she felt nothing but air under her feet.

Oh God.

She had to let go, *had* to risk it.

She did. She hated heights. She had *always* hated heights. But she was the brave one, wasn't she?

Yeah, but he reached out for Ruthie first . . .

Somewhere deep in her soul, that hurt. Made her doubt him, doubt everything they'd ever had together.

Was she mad, to trust him?

Oh, to hell with it. Stay in the house and burn – or face her fears?

She let go, dropped down. It felt like she fell forever, but it was just a small drop, it really was just a couple of feet – and then she landed.

She was standing on the terrace and she could hear Max barking out orders above her. To her horror she could, from this new angle, see the flames that were rapidly engulfing the front of the house. She could hear the hard angry crackle of the fire. What if they hadn't woken up? The fire was spreading so fast, the vast amount of wood in the big old building feeding the flames. She shivered, coughed a little more, and soon Ruthie was standing there with her; finally, down came Max.

'You okay?' he asked Ruthie.

What about me? wondered Annie.

Max put a protective arm around his wife's shoulders. 'Come on over to the annexe, I'll phone the fire people from there.'

And – still with his arm around Ruthie – he walked away, leaving Annie to follow on behind.

135

Max had to break a window to get into Queenie's annexe, because he didn't have the key – that was still hanging up behind the kitchen door in the main house. That kitchen was wrecked now, burning fiercely like most of the rest of the building. He couldn't have got within twenty yards of it.

He phoned the fire brigade from the annexe and within ten minutes the fire crew were there, hosing down the crumbling remains of the house. The occupants of the garage block – which was separate from the main building – had woken up. Dave was there, and his girlfriend Sarah, and Tone.

Annie and Ruthie sat in the tiny lounge of Queenie's place, huddled beside a small electric fire. Above it sat the head and shoulders portrait of Queenie, gimlet-eyed and ferocious, staring down at them with evident disapproval.

'What d'you think she'd make of it if she could see us both sitting here now?' asked Annie, wanting to fill the silence with conversation, with anything, because *Max had reached for Ruthie first.*

She couldn't get that out of her head. She doubted she ever would. And she kept thinking about how Max had a route ready-planned to escape from the burning building. She knew Max didn't much like the place. Had he started the fire himself, having first made certain of their route out, to collect on the insurance? After all, when she'd opened the dressing room door he'd already been out of bed, hadn't he? *And* dressed.

Ruthie looked up at Queenie's painting. 'She'd hate the pair of us,' she concluded. 'Nobody was ever quite good enough for her precious boy Max, not even a soft touch like me. You know what? I was scared shitless of that woman. And now? I can't even think why.'

'Can't say I ever met her.'

'You didn't miss a damned thing. She was horrible.' Ruthie stared up at the painting intently. 'It was her that set the whole thing in motion, you know. Of course, had she been going to live, she wouldn't have wanted Max married at all. She'd have kicked up a hell of a fuss. Got rid of all contenders. But she knew she was dying and so the tough old bird did manage to spare a thought for him at the end. She didn't want him to be lonely I suppose. So there she was, looking around for the right bride. And there was I – perfect, yeah? Easy to control.' Ruthie forced a smile. 'Not a bit like you, Annie. She would have hated you.'

'You both okay?' asked Max, coming into the room.

'We're fine,' said Annie. *Yeah, and thank you so much for asking after me. At last.* 'Is the fire out?'

Max slumped down on the sofa beside her. She flinched away, a movement he didn't even appear to notice. 'Yep. But the damage . . . it looks like too much. It looks beyond saving.'

'I'm sorry,' she said, not really caring. She was feeling exhausted, drained in the aftermath of their escape. It was a creepy old place, she'd never liked it and she knew Ruthie hadn't either. And nor had Max. Again it came into her mind – had he torched it himself?

He heaved a sigh. 'You know, I've always sort of hated it. I bought it and for a while I was pleased with it, but soon I saw it as an unlucky place. Things kept going wrong. First week I moved in, the bathroom beside the master suite flooded and all the electrics shorted out. Things like that, they just kept happening, on and on. Then Mum died. And Eddie too. Hard to feel anything for a place where all that's been going on.'

They said nothing to that.

'The fire chief was talking about major use of accelerants in and around the front door,' he said.

Ruthie's expression was full of horror. 'It was started deliberately? It wasn't an accident?'

'Damned sure it wasn't an accident. Whoever started it wanted to make sure that the job was done. That we were asleep and that it would go up quickly so we'd fry.'

Of course Max wouldn't have been so clumsy as to use an accelerant. Whatever Max was, he was no fool. He wouldn't want the finger pointing straight at him, the householder.

'So . . . what do we do now?' asked Ruthie.

'I'll make a call,' said Max.

'Who to?' asked Annie.

'The airport. I'm going to get a flight out to Santander and I'm going to find out whether that fucker Kieron really is dead or not – or if he's just hiding out in the Delaney place in Comillas. Myself? I don't believe he's dead, not for a minute. It's all fucking smoke and mirrors, all this. And it's time it was cleared away.'

'Make that three tickets,' said Annie. 'I think we should stick together.' She looked coolly at Max and then sent a glance toward her sister. 'Don't you?'

136

Now Annie watched them together, her lover and his wife, and although she felt wrenched with pity over everything Ruthie had suffered, she also felt raging jealousy because Max was, all through their trip out to Santander, paying Ruthie very close attention.

He sat with Ruthie on the plane. Helped her with her hand luggage both on boarding and landing. Handed her drinks, food; saw to her every need.

And Annie?

She sat three rows back from the pair of them, alone, raging with insecurity. What was uppermost in her mind was still this: what if Max had decided now that after all he had made the *right* choice, in Ruthie? That Queenie's assessment of the whole marriage situation had been the right one? He'd married Ruthie. They were man and wife. So Ruthie was accorded every respect, but what about *her*?

Oh yeah. She was just *the bit on the side*.

Annie felt wrenched with pity over the rotten deal Ruthie had been dealt. And that was *her* fault, no one else's. As children they had been so close, offering each other mutual support in the wake of their dad's departure and their mum's drinking. They had been sisters and soulmates.

And it was wonderful, of course it was – the most Godawful shock but still wonderful, to find that Ruthie was alive.

She thought of her sister – her sweet, beloved sister – taking up with that abuser Kieron Delaney when her own marriage to Max had seemed to be nothing but a disappointment, a sham. There must have been some comfort in the relationship with Kieron at first; Ruthie must have taken refuge in it, felt happy – before it all turned sour and he became violent.

And really, whose fault was any of it, the whole damned mess?

Once again, Annie had to confront the fact that all Ruthie's trials had come about as a direct result of her chasing Max. She had been shameless, wanting Max so badly. She still did. And she'd felt so crushed to see him with her sister, him *marrying* her for God's sake. When she'd walked up the aisle behind Ruthie and seen Max there at the altar, waiting, she had felt like running from the church and screaming.

Just the night before the wedding, he had been so tender, so passionate with Annie. He'd taken her virginity and she hadn't cared; it was him, the man she wanted, the man she had *always* wanted. If he'd given her his baby right then, she wouldn't have suffered a moment's regret.

But when she followed Ruthie up the aisle, Max had looked right through her. Seemed not to see her at all. All right, she knew none of that was an excuse for her own wanton behaviour when she and Max had resumed their affair later on. But Max had been betrothed to Ruthie and he'd slept with Annie. So really? He was every bit as guilty as her. *Every* bit.

Maybe now this was payback for all the trouble she'd caused.

Maybe – yes – Max had realised that he'd made the right choice and was just waiting now, sorting out this last bit of bother, and then he would say to Annie: 'Fuck off, Annie love. It's been fun but it's all straight in my mind now. It's a hell of a damned thing, but you know what? Mum was right all along. It's a good steady wife I need and it's my wife I want. It's Ruthie.'

She could hear him saying it.

He'd helped Ruthie when she badly needed a friend.

Who else *should* she have turned to – except her own husband?

As they went through passport control in the sudden warmth of Santander airport, she watched the two of them grimly and thought: Yeah, this is it. Once this business with Kieron is over, he's going to do it. He's going to kick me to the kerb.

And the worst thing?

I bloody deserve it.

137

On the ten-minute drive out to Comillas in the hire care, Ruthie sat in the front passenger seat beside Max, who was driving. Annie sat in the back, buffeted by the wind from Max's open window, looking out bleakly at a surprisingly verdant landscape.

At one point Max stopped the car and got out, went to the side of the road, picked up a couple of parcels tucked into long grass. Then he drove on and eventually pulled in through an open pair of ruined metal gates. A huge sprawling house lay ahead, arched walls surrounding the building and covered terraces lending shade in the heat of summer. Rows of neglected vines marched away into the distance on all sides, weeds thick between each row.

Max stopped the car at the front of the house and switched off the engine.

'What the hell are we doing *here*?' asked Ruthie.

'You know this place? You've been here before?' Annie asked her.

'I've . . .' Ruthie seemed unable to get her breath.

Max was gazing at his wife. 'You do remember it? Ruthie?'

'Yes! This is the Delaney place. It's *theirs*. Kieron brought me here.'

'And now we're here again,' said Max. 'We're staying here. If that bastard's alive, we're going to flush him out.

If he's dead we're going to find his body and dance on his fucking grave, okay?'

'No,' Ruthie burst out. 'What? I can't.'

'Yes you can,' said Max. 'Go on. Out you get.'

Ruthie got out of the car, closing the door behind her.

'Go ahead,' said Max, speaking to Annie but not looking round at her. 'I'll bring the luggage.'

In other words, fuck off.

'What the hell are you playing at, Max?' Annie demanded.

'Just get out of the bloody car, will you?'

Annie got out, slamming the door shut. She followed her sister as Ruthie walked to the far corner of the big sprawling building.

'I remember this,' Ruthie said faintly, stepping to the edge of the uncovered circular pool which glimmered, faintly muddy, in the warmth of the day. 'Max has a place, you know. Better than this one. In Mallorca, up near Illetas. Right up on the cliffs, near the monastery.'

'I didn't know that,' said Annie. There was a *lot* she didn't know about Max.

'Hotter there, of course, in the Med. It's chillier up here, in the north. But still beautiful, don't you think?'

'Yeah. It is.'

'We swam here. Me and Kieron.'

'What the hell,' said Annie, suddenly curious, 'possessed you, to get involved with him?'

Ruthie gave a dry smile.

'Well – let me see – it had something to do with you, I think. You and Max. D'you have any idea what that feels like, to be stabbed in the back by your own sister? Cheated on by your own fiancé? No. Of course you don't. Because you were The One, weren't you. Did you see that new Jack Lemmon film?'

Annie shook her head.

'It's called *How To Murder Your Wife*. Virna Lisi's in it. She pops out of a huge cake at an engagement party. Shit, I want to be Virna Lisi. She comes out of that cake in a skimpy white bikini and absolutely floors him, knocks Jack's socks off, with a single look. I don't think I'll ever forget it, the way she looks at him. And I want that. I want to be that powerful. I want to be that blonde, that fabulous. But I never was, of course. Because Virna Lisi, that look she gives him? That's you, not me. And Jack Lemmon? That's Max.'

Annie stared at her. 'I'm sorry, Ruthie. I don't know how many more times I can say it, but I am.'

Ruthie shrugged. 'It doesn't matter anymore. But if Max thinks we're staying here, he's wrong. I can't. I just *can't*.'

She turned back to the pool and was about to speak again when a short, dumpy man in a straw hat, a sweat-stained red shirt and baggy khaki trousers appeared at the other side of it. He was holding a shotgun, and he was pointing it straight at the pair of them.

138

'Oh my God,' said Ruthie, and she did something then that startled Annie, made her feel like the shit heel she truly knew herself to be. Ruthie *stepped in front of her.*

It was a protective gesture, the same one Ruthie had made when Annie had been in trouble at school. Now, with a shotgun aimed at them both, she was doing the same thing all over again. But this time, Annie pushed her aside.

'*Wait,*' she said to the man holding the gun, holding up a hand. *Please wait.*

He said something angry-sounding in Spanish. She didn't speak any damned Spanish, hadn't a clue what he was saying.

'I don't understand you,' she said desperately.

He spoke again. Louder. He sounded *furious.*

Where the hell was Max when you needed him?

He was round the other side of the building, offloading their luggage from the hire car. By the time he got round here, they could both be in very deep shit indeed.

Then Annie saw someone else arrive on the scene; he was coming up from among the vines beyond the pool. A big man, bulky, wearing a sharp black suit. His bald head gleamed brown in the hot sunlight; twin crucifixes twinkled in his ears. He made a winding motion with one hand.

Keep him talking.

'I'm sorry, I don't speak Spanish. I'm English. Do you speak English?' she said quickly.

He answered. Pretty clearly, he didn't speak any English at all.

Tone was advancing from behind, still making winding motions with one hand. She had no idea where the hell he'd come from – he certainly hadn't been with them on the flight out – but she was damned glad to see him, all the same.

Keep him talking.

And say what?

'Are you the caretaker then?' she managed to get out, her mouth dry as dust, her heart thudding away in her chest.

She grabbed hold of Ruthie's hand, praying that her sister wouldn't give the game away, wouldn't look at Tone, wouldn't say something stupid to alert the gunman to the fact that Tone was right behind him. 'Are you looking after the place for the family? Is that it?'

He spoke again. Shouted, this time, and pulled the butt of the gun up onto his shoulder, taking proper aim.

Oh Christ.

Tone raised his right arm. There was a small pistol engulfed in his meaty fist. He pressed the muzzle of it hard against the Spaniard's temple.

'Drop the gun, my friend,' he said sharply. '*Comprende? Si?* Drop the damned gun or I will blow your brains to fuck. Don't be damned silly. You're going to get yourself hurt, carrying on like this.'

The Spaniard froze. Then slowly, inch by inch, he lowered the gun and finally let it drop to the ground.

'*Bueno,*' said Tone, stepping around behind the Spaniard, kicking the shotgun further away.

It should all have been fine then, Annie thought.

But then – at that instant – the dog arrived.

139

It was a huge slavering beast of a dog, tan-coloured, massive and musclebound. It was leaping over the ground, not barking – it would not have been so frightening, had it been barking. Its manner was intent, silent, deadly, and it was heading like a missile for Tone, covering the ground with horrifying speed.

Ruthie let out a shriek.

Tone turned and the dog, jaws agape, teeth bared in a ferocious snarl, was almost on him. He fired the gun once, hitting the dog's chest. The animal gave a yelp and thudded to a halt. Tone fired again. A red rose bloomed on the dog's broad brow and scarlet mist sprayed out. The dog dropped to the ground and was suddenly still.

'Look out!' Annie yelled, seeing the Spaniard lunging for his fallen shotgun. Tone turned, but he was too slow, taken unawares. The Spaniard had the gun back in his hands and he was turning, aiming right at Tone.

Shit!

Then another shot rang out.

Annie cringed, expecting to see Tone fall. But it was the Spaniard who flew backward, who then collapsed and lay still. Annie watched as Max came round the corner of the building, holding a smoking pistol, aiming it at the Spaniard. He glanced at Annie and Ruthie, standing there, frozen to the spot.

'You all right?' he said.

Ruthie nodded. Annie could feel her sister trembling and she put an arm around her, squeezed her shoulder. 'It's okay, it's done,' said Annie. To Max she said: 'We're all right. Now can we just get out of this damned place? Ruthie's in bits, can we . . .?'

Her voice tailed away. He wasn't listening.

Max went over to Tone on the other side of the pool. On one patch of dirt lay the dead Spaniard, half his forehead shot away. On another, the dog, in a similar state.

Max poked the Spaniard with a toe. 'Not too keen on visitors then,' he remarked to Tone.

'Not what you'd call a friendly welcome,' Tone agreed.

'Any more surprises likely to happen?' asked Max.

'I'll take a good look around,' said Tone, and walked off.

'How did Tone get out here?' Annie asked Max. She could feel her heart still pummelling madly at her ribcage. She was sweating with the aftermath of fear.

'Earlier flight,' said Max, tucking the pistol into the waistband of his jeans.

'And the guns! Where did you get them? You couldn't have brought them through Customs.'

'Nico had them planted here.'

She remembered the American; and then she remembered Max stopping on the road, picking up parcels.

'I thought he was going to kill us,' said Annie, staring at the fallen Spaniard.

'Too right he was,' said Max. 'Come on, let's get you inside.'

'What . . .?' Annie stared at him, disbelieving. 'We're not really staying here, are we?'

'I told you – this is the place Kieron brought me to,' added Ruthie, shuddering. 'Max, I don't want to stay here. I *can't*.'

'Yes you can. And you will. We're just borrowing it. For now,' said Max. 'Let's get you in, get you comfortable.'

'*Comfortable?*' Annie echoed. 'How the hell . . .?'

'Tone and I have some clearing up to do. You can rustle up some food.'

'We don't have any.'

'Yes we do.'

The stop on the road. He'd picked up not only guns but food, too.

'Now let's get inside,' said Max.

Annie had a creeping feeling about this. She thought of Max, driving headlong toward all obstacles, laughing in the face of danger. Would he thumb his nose at the Delaney mob, occupy their territory?

Yes. He would.

'How . . .?' she started.

He strolled over to the porch-covered front door and looked at it. It was solid. He looked at the window right beside it. Picked up a rock. Broke the window, casually sucked blood from a cut on his hand.

'That's how,' said Max.

140

Jackie Tulliver turned up at the Spanish house that evening, bringing more food and a lot of beer. During the day, Max had been all over the place, checking that no one was here, concealed.

'What, you think there could be attic rooms like at the Guildford house?' Annie asked. 'You think there could be *occupied* attic rooms?'

'There are attic rooms all right,' he told her. 'But there's nobody up there. There are no cellars either, not in the main house and not in the outbuildings. It's all clear.'

There was much merriment and clinking of beer bottles late into the night as Max, Tone and Jackie discussed matters.

Annie and Ruthie retired to one of the neatly furnished double rooms; they stripped off the dust sheets and found that the accommodation was basic but comfortable, with wardrobes, a dressing table, two single beds.

'Just like old times,' said Annie as they lay there together in the warm darkness.

A roar of laughter came from out in the sitting room.

'Not quite,' said Ruthie. 'God, I hate it here. It doesn't feel safe. What is Max playing at? What's he doing, taking the piss out of the Delaneys like this? And listen to them! They killed that poor bloke, and the dog, and they couldn't give a toss. Sounds like they're having a party.'

Ruthie was right. It did. The sisters lay there, listening.

'We're going sightseeing tomorrow,' she could hear Max saying.

'Oh? Where?' That was Jackie.

'Graveyards and such. Offload a bit of rubbish at the same time,' said Max.

'Who shot the dog then?' asked Jackie.

'Me,' said Tone.

'Damn, I thought you *liked* dogs. Judging by the rough old whores you used to hang around with.'

Laughter. The clink of yet *more* beer bottles.

'Do you think that men are fundamentally different to women?' sighed Ruthie.

'Don't ask me,' said Annie grumpily. 'He's *your* damned husband. And "fundamentally"? Where did *that* come from?'

'Don't be bloody silly,' said Ruthie.

'What did I say?'

'There's nothing between me and Max. I've told you.'

'I just wondered . . .'

'Wondered what?'

'The day you left the Guildford house for London. I was recovered from the shooting, you were wanting to get away from the sight of me and Max together. I do understand that. And I'm sorry. All over again, sorry. I really am. But that day. Tell me about that.'

'I'd rather not.' Ruthie shuddered.

'Go on. Kieron followed you onto the train . . .?'

'Yeah. He did.'

'And?'

'Do I have to . . .?'

'You do.'

Ruthie heaved in a breath. 'He dragged me off the train. Nobody intervened. I'd given my rings to a porter, and he saw, I'm *sure* he saw what was happening, but he didn't step in and really who could blame him. Kieron's *scary*.'

'And what then?'

'He took me outside the station and . . .'

'And?'

'He *beat me up*.' Ruthie started to cry. 'He said . . . he said I had a nerve to think that I could ever leave him.'

Hot rage poured through Annie. She passed Ruthie a hankie. 'And then?'

'He ruptured my spleen. Broke four of my ribs, fractured my jaw, it had to be wired up.'

'How did you get away from him?'

'I didn't.' Ruthie dabbed at her eyes. 'Some kind person found me lying unconscious in an alley by the South Bank Centre. They called an ambulance. I started to come round and could tell them who I was and then the hospital called Max. I just clung on to him for a long time. He was so protective. So *nice*. And I got better. Then he moved me into one of the flats he owns . . .'

'Under the company name of Tarrec Holdings,' said Annie.

'Yes. But I didn't feel safe there on my own. So he suggested I move back into the Guildford place but I couldn't settle, and then he said about the servants' quarters up in the attic, and I felt safe there, I loved it up there, and now that's gone, all burned up in the fire. Max encouraged me to be quiet up there. Swore that horrible old cow Miss Arnott to secrecy. And it all went well, and then *you* . . .'

'Yeah. I arrived on the scene and you just couldn't resist twisting my tail, could you? Not that I blame you. Not after all I'd done to you. For which – again – sorry. You gave me the shock of my life, showing up alive.'

Ruthie smiled slightly.

Then Annie blurted: 'I lost a child, Ruthie. You probably don't know about that, but I did.'

'Oh.'

Silence in the bedroom.

'Unless Max told you?' asked Annie.

Another burst of laughter from the sitting room.

'No. He didn't. It was Max's?' asked Ruthie.

'Of course it bloody was.' Annie paused. 'And you know what? The thing is, I've been wondering. I failed to give him a child. And who's to say I won't miscarry again? But you probably could conceive and deliver a baby, no problem. He probably wants a boy. All men do, don't they? And you're so much *nicer* than me, Ruthie. You just *are*. And the way he's been looking after you, the fact that you felt you could trust him to sort out that nutter Kieron . . .'

'That's not sorted yet.'

'Well, it will be.'

'Redmond Delaney said Kieron could be dead,' said Ruthie. 'That he could have died out here. But Max wants proof. Look, Annie – I'm sorry you lost the baby, I really am . . .'

'That's nice of you. Considering. But I've just been thinking that maybe you and Max have worked something out between you.'

'Worked what out?'

'The fact that you're married. If you had his child, well, there you are. A complete little family.'

'Annie.'

'And I understand that. I do. It would be so neat. No more problems.'

'There's one big problem.'

'What?'

'He's mad about you.'

'Is he?'

'God's sake! Of course he is.'

'You used to spy on me. With Kath and Ellie.'

'What, you think I was jealous?' Ruthie gave a snort of laughter. 'I was hurt, sure. I'd been deceived. But there was never anything sexual between Max and me. There was nothing except the fact that his mother thought I'd be easy to handle and he didn't care enough one way or the other to dump the idea. Hardly the romance of the century, was it.'

Another great shout of laughter from the sitting room.

'They're having fun,' said Ruthie, a faint shiver in her voice. 'God, I hope we can leave here soon. I don't like it.'

'Max thinks he'll find Kieron here. Either alive like Nico says, or dead and buried like one of the villagers claimed.'

'Alive would be worse.'

'Come on, Ruthie,' said Annie, hoping to reassure her. 'You're with Max and a handful of his goons. There's *no way* any harm's coming to you.'

'You believe that?'

It killed Annie to hear the hope in her sister's voice.

'I do,' Annie lied, thinking of the dead Spaniard, the dead dog – and the Kieron Delaney she and her sister had both known to their cost, who was both crazy and dangerous and who loved to play games. Maybe he was playing one with the whole lot of them, right now.

After all – they were on *his* territory, not their own.

141

Next day a car drew up and two men got out. Ruthie was still in bed, her dentures in a glass on the bedside table. The sight of them grinning at Annie shocked her. Made her think again of all that had happened to her sister – and all because of *her*.

Annie washed, dressed and went out onto the front porch. The two men who had arrived were big, squat, dark-haired Steve Taylor and long, skinny, evil-eyed Gary Tooley. Max's most trusted lieutenants. Steve lifted a hand to her and Jackie Tulliver sauntered out from indoors to greet them.

Hearing splashing coming from the pool at the back of the building, Annie went round there. Somehow, overnight, things had been cleared away. The dead man with the shotgun was gone; so was the blood-spattered dog. There were no stains in evidence, not a single mark to show murder had been committed here – and there was Max, swimming lengths of the pool as if he had not a care in the world.

Annie sat down in a chair by the pool steps and called out: 'What, are you assembling an army here or something? How many more's going to show up?'

Max swam to the steps and leaned on the side of the pool, swiping his hair back out of his eyes. He looked up at her.

'Gary Tooley's just got here. And Steve Taylor,' she said.
'Ah, right. Good.'

'*Was* that a caretaker, the bloke you shot?' she asked.

'Who knows? If he'd put the gun aside when he was told, he'd be alive right now. But it's pretty clear he was given instructions that no one was to be allowed near the place except the Delaney mob. And when he saw you and Ruthie – strangers – he was going to shoot on sight, ask questions later. This isn't a holiday home, is it. It isn't lived in or even looked after. It's more like an abandoned fortress. All we have to do is keep an eye out at all times. Which takes more than three people. So I needed Tone and Jackie here, and Gary. And Steve.'

'Do you think anyone could have heard the shots yesterday?'

'It was a local, shooting rabbits. So what? Who's going to take the blindest bit of notice of that? Why don't you come in? The water's warm.'

'It's not that clean.'

'A bit of dirt won't hurt you.'

'No, I'm fine here.'

'Ruthie okay?'

'Peachy.'

'You're looking good.'

Annie gave a sour smile, refusing to be charmed. He looked good too. The legendary Max Carter, king of the East End. Tanned and gorgeous, rippling with muscles. She knew how that lean, toned body felt under her fingers. Knew every inch of it, intimately. Her eyes lowered and then she realised with a start that he wasn't wearing bathing trunks.

'Shouldn't you be wearing something?' she asked, sounding even to her own ears like a ridiculous old maid.

'There's no one here that's very shockable,' he said. 'And let's face it, you've seen the whole thing before, haven't you.' He snatched up a white towel from the side of the pool near her feet and walked up the steps, wrapping it around his waist.

'You feeling all right? After yesterday? Bit of a shock,' he said.

'I'm fine. I think it shook Ruthie up more than me.'

Annie looked around at the vast sprawling expanse of overgrown vines that stretched away into the far distance. Bees buzzed around vast scrubby pots of neglected lavender on the terrace. She brushed her hand over the dried-up flowers beside her chair, inhaled the sweet slightly antiseptic scent.

'So they don't make wine with the grapes, the Delaneys?' she asked.

'I would think a local farmer used to handle production for them, but for now it all looks pretty much forgotten.'

'Yeah? So what if the farmer comes while we're here? Reports back?'

'We're watching. We'll tackle that when – if – it comes. But it don't seem very likely. The place is a wreck.'

'So what happens now?' she asked. 'How long do we stay here? What are you trying to achieve?'

'You know what I'm trying to achieve. What I'm *going* to achieve. Concrete proof that the little scrote is either dead or alive. Today we're going to track down a burial site. A local reckoned Kieron Delaney died out here. So we'll go to the local cemeteries and check the records and we'll see, won't we.'

'Ruthie is freaked out by just being here. I don't know what that arsehole did to her last time she came here – she won't talk about it – but she's losing it. And you were telling the truth about the dentures. She *does* wear them.'

'Of course she does. And look, we're with her. She's safe. Unless you're still in the process of picking a side?'

'She doesn't feel safe. And what the fuck does that mean?'

'I mean you and secret calls to people in the city.'

'What, Nicholas? He's been checking a few things out for me, that's all. Like Tarrec Holdings.'

'Just him? Or someone else too?'

'Like . . .?'

'Like Redmond. Who was until very recently your business partner, yes? Maybe your lover too.'

Annie stared at him, stunned. 'Oh come on. You *what?*'

'Look – if Ruthie's worried, then reassure her. She's safe with me.' He gave her an acid smile. 'I'm not letting either one of you out of my sight.' Max dropped the towel and walked back down the steps and into the water. 'Tell her that. Now I think I'll do a few more lengths. Sure you won't join me?' he said, throwing a challenging look back over his shoulder at her.

'I told you. I'm fine, right here.' She was seething. Couldn't believe he'd said that to her. Redmond, her lover? The fucking *cheek* of him.

'Be ready to go at eleven, yeah? Both of you.'

Max dived back under the water without another word.

142

The cemetery at Comillas was all huge curved arches, steep steps, massive walls and neat lines of tombs – and there was the angel, soaring overhead, wings outspread.

'Kieron brought me here,' said Ruthie. 'He wanted to be in one of these tombs, he said,' she told Annie as they walked. 'Buried with something he loved, like a pet. Buried like a pharaoh, I remember him distinctly saying that. He liked the idea that sometimes their living wives, the poor things, were stuffed into the pyramids alongside them. Just left in there to rot. Isn't that sick?'

It was. There were few tourists here today, but still Annie found that she had to keep glancing around, checking out any strangers. She felt exposed here, despite her and Ruthie being surrounded by a living wall of muscle in the shape of Tone, Max, Jackie and Gary. Steve was back at the house, keeping an eye on things there.

It had been a long day. Max had been thorough, calling on all the churches in the area, checking registers, searching for any sign of Kieron Delaney's burial. And he'd found none. No evidence at all. Now, this was their final port of call and Annie had had enough. Her feet ached and she could see that Ruthie was drooping with tiredness. The sky was a mass of clouds, the air heavy with moisture. Soon, it would rain.

'Can we—?' she started to say.

And that was when it happened.

143

It sounded like a *ping*. Like nothing very dangerous or even serious at all. A puff of brick dust flew off the wall beside Tone's head. Then another, close to Jackie.

Ping, ping, ping.

The noises were almost harmless, a staccato sound like a child's toy would make. Brick dust flew again and again and again.

'*Down!*' shouted Gary.

The few tourists, hearing his warning, scattered like hens in a force ten gale, letting out shrieks and cries of alarm.

Someone was shooting at them.

Annie saw that Max had one hand on Ruthie's head, keeping her down. And what about her? Again, he wasn't protecting *her*, was he. Tone, Gary and Jackie were swivelling, looking all around, trying to get an angle on the shooter, without success.

Ping, ping, ping!

Brick dust flew, half-blinding Jackie.

'Jesus!' he complained, blinking, swiping a hand over his face. 'Where the fuck's the bloke positioned? Anyone see him?'

They couldn't see him. But the gunman's aim was getting better; he was getting closer all the time.

Cars were starting, people were fleeing the scene. Yells and horns, confusion.

Their little group remained crouched on the ground, pinned, unable to move.

Ping, ping, ping!

'I can't, I have to . . .' Ruthie was moaning, trying to stand up, to run, fighting against Max's restraint of her.

'No! Ruthie, keep down,' said Annie loudly, catching her arm, keeping her there more by force of will than anything else.

Ping!

Then . . . nothing.

Dead, total silence.

Gary and Max and Tone exchanged glances. Daringly, Jackie scrabbled to his feet. 'Come on then, you cunt!' he screamed. 'Come and do it, yeah?'

No answer. Nothing.

Annie's eyes met Max's over Ruthie's head. His expression was far from friendly. Ruthie was shivering with shock and Annie could feel her own legs trembling.

Slowly, they all stood up.

Nothing.

'Let's get the fuck out of here,' said Max.

144

'How's she doing?' Max asked, catching Annie outside her and Ruthie's bedroom door back at Botega Sierra as he passed by that evening.

Annie stared at him in amazement. 'How do you think? She's camped out in a Delaney stronghold and people are taking potshots at her.'

Max paused. 'And you?'

She shrugged. 'Tough as old boots, me. You know that.'

'Yeah. I know it.' His eyes were playing with hers. He was standing very close, and now he moved closer still.

There was no sound from Ruthie. Annie guessed she was fast asleep now, worn out by the terrifying events of the day. Chat and laughter came drifting along the hall from Gary and Steve in the sitting room. Outside, she knew that Tone would be taking his turn at patrolling the grounds, and scruffy little Jackie Tulliver would be moving about the place too, keeping watch.

Max's hand reached out, caught hers, caressed it.

'No,' she said. She couldn't forget what he'd said to her by the pool. Did he actually think she and Redmond had been lovers as well as business partners? Really? And if so, where did that leave *them*? There was no trust, none whatsoever, between them, if he could say that.

'Who do you think it was?' she asked him. 'Shooting at us in the cemetery?'

'Well not Kieron Delaney,' said Max. 'He's dead. Apparently.'

'Or is he though? He might have someone else working on his behalf. For the family,' said Annie. 'The Spaniard by the pool when we arrived? Another one like that.'

'Maybe.'

'Maybe Redmond has got wind of us being here. A Carter invasion! Maybe he's sent out the troops.'

'Well you know him better than I do,' said Max.

'You know what? I'm getting sick of your snide remarks. I'm sick of this whole situation. And Ruthie's cracking under the strain. You know she is.'

'And you're playing the concerned sister. Very convincingly too.'

'It's not an act. I *am* concerned. She's been through so much. Don't you think between us we've made her suffer enough?'

He moved closer. The front of his body was touching hers. The hand that had smoothed over hers lifted and deftly unfastened the top button on her cream silk shirt.

I ought to stop him, she thought. But thrilling ripples of sensation were travelling up from her groin to her belly to her breasts.

Another button was loosened. Another.

'Oh God, Max, don't . . .'

'No bra?' His hand slipped inside her shirt and her nipples were hard as rocks. His palm brushed back and forth, back and forth over each one. It was hypnotic; arousing.

'It was too hot today for that,' she said weakly.

'I'm not complaining,' he said, and kissed her, very gently, while his hands cupped her breasts. Then his mouth dipped from hers and went down to one swollen nipple, sucked hard there.

Somehow her arms slid up and her fingers were twined into his hair, holding his mouth exactly where it was. His tongue was flickering over each hard nub, teasing them out into even greater arousal. Now she could feel his cock, pressing hard against her belly.

'Come on.' He drew back.

'What?' she was half-dazed, not even thinking of protesting, even though she knew she should.

Her and *Redmond*? How the hell could he dare say that to her?

'So who do you keep phoning in London?' he asked.

'None of your damned business.'

'Yeah, but I pay the phone bill.'

'Then you know damned well who I'm phoning. And it's *not* Redmond.'

Max took her hand and led her across the hall to his room. One minute she'd been standing there, contemplating a peaceful night, and now, *what the hell was she doing?*

'So this "Nicholas"', he said. 'Gentleman friend, is he?'

145

'Nicholas? He's just a business contact. An adviser,' she said.

Of course she knew what she was doing. What she *always* did. She was succumbing, like she always swore she wouldn't. Then all at once they were in his room and he was closing the door, turning her, flattening her against the wall, kissing her, his tongue teasing hers, moist, sweet, and she was wet for him just like she knew she would be, feeling breathless, hungry for him, weak as a kitten, and he was tugging her pants down, unzipping himself, spreading her legs wide. It was so quick it was almost brutal. Suddenly, he was *in*.

Keep away from Max Carter, everyone had told her when she was growing up. *He's bad*. And that had intrigued her. It certainly hadn't deterred her in any way. Any sensible girl would have run a mile, wouldn't they? But she'd grown up wanting him, even before she was old enough to know what that would mean – this mad craving of female for male. That it would mean this demented sensation of drowning in feeling, of letting him have her, just letting him do whatever he wanted to do.

Madness.

It was all crazy. Her and her sister's husband, and her sister was asleep across the hall, all unknowing. Him pumping into her, and how could she deny she wanted this when she was so desperately turned on? Just like she'd been by the pool yesterday, seeing him naked there, muscular; the same feeling had come over her right then. She'd wanted him. Wanted to abandon all propriety and dive into the water with him, naked, shameless. Had they been alone here, she would have.

'Bitch,' he whispered in her ear, while he thrust into her, again and again.

'Bastard,' she hissed back.

His mouth took hers again, enveloping her, sinking her deep into desire and then his hand was moving between their bodies, finding the place, touching her, driving her crazy, making her arch her back and moan his name.

'Oh that's good,' he groaned against her throat.

'Don't you *dare* come inside me,' she flung back at him, her nails scrabbling at his back, marking him as hers, *yes* – then her orgasm was sweeping over her, washing her away on an overwhelming tide of lust, leaving her limp, almost lifeless.

Too late. He came and he didn't withdraw, almost as if he was punishing her, threatening her with the danger of another child. Another baby that she might miscarry. *His* baby.

Even while she protested, she knew she wanted it. That she would never, ever deny him, under any circumstances – and of course he knew that.

'Don't,' she moaned.

'Hush,' he said, and emptied himself into her, unable to stop, unwilling to.

'I hate you,' she whispered.

'Sure you do,' said Max, and kissed her, more gently this time.

'We could have been killed today – at the cemetery,' she said, shuddering a little, coming back to earth. He let her go and she dropped away from him, gasping, almost insensible. She'd been so determined not to let this happen again, to make some distance between them, to maybe try to let him and Ruthie sort something out. Maybe try to rebuild the very thing she had so brutally torn apart.

But actually? She knew she didn't want that.

Actually, she wanted *him*.

'You're right. We could have been killed,' Max agreed, coolly zipping up his jeans, vanishing inside his clothes.

'I *really* hate you,' said Annie, and meant it.

'Hate away,' said Max, and opened the door. He slapped her arse lightly and pushed her – none too gently – back out into the hall, closing it tight shut after her.

Bastard!

146

Next day, all seemed as normal. After their shake-up at the cemetery, things had tightened right up. Gary Tooley was moving stork-like around the outer limits of Botega Sierra's grounds holding a shotgun and Steve Taylor was patrolling the area closest to the house. Neither of them looked in the mood to greet visitors, should any arrive.

'They know we're here, don't they,' said Annie to Max, over lunch.

'What?' Ruthie's head shot up in alarm.

'The Delaney mob. Of course they do,' said Annie. 'Who else would shoot at us? They know we're in Spain. In Comillas. And probably – Max – don't you think they know we're here, right here, squatting at their place, occupying it?'

'Probably.'

'Probably? *Definitely*. They could take a set of binoculars out to the far corner right over there,' she indicated the furthest reaches of the lines of neglected grapevines, 'and they could see Gary and Steve. They could see you using the pool. What, are you pissing in it? Making like you're marking their territory as your own?'

Max coolly buttered a slice of bread.

'So they know we're here, for sure,' concluded Annie. 'And what about the bloke with the dog? He must have family. Aren't they wondering where he is? Won't they pitch up here trying to find him?'

'She's right. This is crazy. We shouldn't be here,' said Ruthie, going pale.

'Why stay here like sitting ducks?' said Annie.

'To draw them in?' suggested Max.

'Is that it? Is that what you're doing? Using us all as bait?'

'Don't forget they set light to my house,' Max pointed out. 'With me – and the two of you – inside it. They intended us to die. You really think I can let that pass?'

Annie narrowed her eyes at him. 'I thought you might have done that yourself. For the insurance.'

'I didn't do it for the insurance.'

'Only it seemed very slick to me, the way you knew the precise route to take to get out of a burning building.'

'You should *always* have several escape routes planned from a building,' said Max. 'In case of emergency.'

'Yeah? Only it seemed so well rehearsed.'

Max shrugged. Took a bite out of the toast.

'We ought to get out of here,' said Ruthie, shredding a paper napkin anxiously.

'Max doesn't want to get out of here,' said Annie, addressing Ruthie while her eyes remained fixed on Max's face. 'He's enjoying all this, playing cat and mouse with the Delaneys. He wants to entice them in and then he's going to nab them.'

'Is that it? Max?' asked Ruthie.

'Possibly,' said Max, and he sent Annie a thin, taunting smile.

147

After lunch, Annie went in search of Max again, hoping to get him to change his mind about staying here. She expected to find him out in the pool, but he wasn't there. Instead, she saw him moving about in Kieron's studio block; she went in.

He was looking around at the canvases there, and he had his gold cigarette lighter in his hand.

'What are you doing?' she asked.

Max picked up a bottle of white spirit. 'You know about Molotov cocktails?' he asked.

'What?'

He flicked open the lighter; the flame burned, bright and smooth.

'You stuff a rag in the bottle, set light to it and throw it.'

'Is that what you're intending to do?'

'Maybe. I could. What do you think? After all, they did set light to my place with me in it.'

'You think that was them? The Delaneys?'

'Don't you?'

'Had to be. I suppose.'

'Then why not torch Kieron Delaney's studio and all his precious artwork in it? There's a lot here. I bet this is all scheduled for his next exhibition. Don't you think? Turnabout's fair play. If he was still alive, what would his reaction be? You think that little scrote Kieron would get upset?'

'Max . . .'

'But then – how could he get upset, really? Redmond reckons he could be dead. One of the villagers reckons he died in a car crash. But then – Nico says he's been spotted, alive, out here. So what's the truth? What's a lie? Maybe he's watching us right now, wondering when to strike.'

'So what's the plan?' Annie asked him.

'Oh – I'm just thinking out loud.' Max gave her a grin and flicked the lighter shut. 'And as far as this little lot's concerned, I might just decide to strike first. What do you think?'

'I think you're crazy.'

'You didn't say that last night. You were mad for it.'

'Can we draw a line under that?'

'You loved it.'

'You took advantage of me in a weak moment.'

'Yeah, you have a lot of those weak moments around me. What about Redmond Delaney? You get them around him too, do you?'

'Shut up, Max,' said Annie coldly.

Max put the bottle of white spirit back down. Put the lighter back in his jeans pocket. 'He might have this studio bugged, have you thought of *that*?'

'No! And I'm not going to, either. I'm going,' she said, and left him there.

148

Mid-afternoon, Annie went out and sat by the pool, alone. Yes, it did look inviting, even with scum on the bottom and no doubt a load of newts and frogs too, but she wasn't even a little tempted to swim, not with madmen on the loose, taking potshots at them all. And not with Max in this dangerous, reckless mood.

She saw Gary Tooley lighting a cigarette among the weed-infested rows of the vines, the rifle slung over his shoulder. He raised a hand to her and walked on. Tone wandered out, glancing around. Gave her a nod; went back indoors.

She let out a sigh and scanned the horizon. Was someone watching them out there right now? She could understand Ruthie cowering indoors – her sister had declined her invitation to come out, get some fresh air.

'No, I'm not going out there,' Ruthie had said.

To hell with it, Annie thought. She was outside. She didn't give a stuff. Let them come, those mad Delaneys, she wasn't going to hide inside like Ruthie. *Fuck* them.

In front of the lines of vines there were stones, dotted around on the ground. She stood up, walked over, thought she saw some sort of scrawl, like a child's writing, on one of the bigger ones there. Maybe just a scratch. She peered down at the stone, then knelt and looked closer.

Benji

Frowning, she ran a hand over the stone, clearing the dust away. It definitely said *Benji*. She looked around. There were other stones, some smaller, some bigger. And now she was down here, closer, looking, she saw more writing on them.

Lotus. Petra. Bonnie.

'Holy *shit*,' she said under her breath.
    She stood up quickly, backed away, her eyes fixed on one of the bigger stones. Right there, etched across it, was

Kier

Just that.
    And hadn't she once heard Redmond call Kieron 'Kier'?

149

She was so engrossed in looking at the stones that she didn't notice Gary Tooley's approach until he spoke.

'It's pretty damned disgusting, is all I got to say,' he said.

She looked up, squinting against the sun, and saw him there. Her mind was still on Kieron, on the pets he loved, on the dead dog in his flat, on that name slashed into the stone. And the fact that – so far – Max hadn't been able to trace a legitimate, registered grave for Kieron Delaney in this area, which was where, he had told Ruthie, he wanted to be buried.

Kier.

But Ruthie would know more about this than she did. She'd been here, right here, with Kieron, alone. And he had spoken to her about burials.

'You listenin' to me?' Gary asked.

'What?' Annie was standing up, starting to go indoors, find Ruthie, ask her about this.

'It's disgusting. You and him. That's what I think. With his damned wife right across the hall? Yeah – disgusting, I call it.'

Annie snapped back to what he was saying. So he'd heard her and Max making love last night. Bloody Gary Tooley. Sharp-eared, eagle-eyed. She'd never liked him and wondered how Max could stand having the bastard around. And Gary Tooley had little room to talk about anyone's love life – from all she'd heard about him, he kept a vast harem of women, many of them married or on the game on his behalf, so how could he dare pass judgement on anyone else?

'Why don't you mind your own bloody business?' she asked him. 'Or – now here's an idea – why don't you take it up with Max? I'm sure he'd be glad to hear your views.'

'You're a bolshy cow, aintcha?' he asked, looming closer.

'Get out of my face, Gary. I got things to do and losing sleep about offending you *isn't* one of them. So don't push me. You wouldn't like me if I started pushing back.'

Not waiting for another word out of him, she went back inside and found Ruthie in the sitting room.

'I don't know how you've got the nerve to show your face,' said Ruthie.

'What?' Damn! She'd thought Ruthie couldn't hear too well anymore. Since her little chat just now with Gary she had, in fact, *banked* on it.

'You and Max! Last night! Bloody hell, Annie. I mean. *Really?*'

Oh Christ. So Ruthie, despite her damaged hearing, had heard too. The walls of this place might *look* substantial, but they must in fact be paper thin. She wondered who else had been treated to the animal sounds they'd made. Steve? Jackie? Tone? She could feel her innards shrivelling at the thought. They all thought she was a tart; now thanks to Max she'd confirmed it.

'Look. Never mind that,' she said.

'Never *mind*? Gary told me, he said you and Max . . .'

So Ruthie *hadn't* heard.

That *bastard* Gary.

'Kieron,' said Annie, anxious to change the subject. 'He kept dogs, didn't he?'

'What the hell?' Ruthie was looking at her like she'd gone mad.

'And his family called him "Kier" sometimes? Did you ever hear them call him that?'

150

'What is this about?' asked Ruthie irritably. 'You're talking nonsense. Just trying to change the subject, are you? Steer it away from your own shameful behaviour?'

'Just answer the question, will you?' All right, she *was* eager to change the subject. But this was *important*.

Ruthie still looked angry and offended, but she nodded. 'All right. Yes. I went to a family party at the Delaney house in Battersea. His mother – Molly? – she called him Kier. And so did Redmond. Why? So what?'

Annie sat down on the couch with a thump. 'Oh bloody hell,' she said.

Max came in. 'What's up?' he asked, looking at her.

'The stones,' she said.

'What stones?'

'The ones out behind the pool. In front of the first row of vines.'

'I haven't seen any stones.'

'No? Well I have. And I'll show you.'

151

'What's going on?' asked Tone, who was out on the verandah when Max and Annie and Ruthie came out.

Max shrugged and followed Annie over to the stones she'd spotted. Gary was away in the distance, moving among the undergrowth, but no doubt he was watching them. Annie indicated the stone with 'Kier' etched into it. Max squatted down, rubbed a hand over it.

'He kept pets. He loved his pets, isn't that right, Ruthie?' Annie asked her.

'He did. He liked dogs better than he liked people, he did say that. And . . .' Ruthie's eyes clouded.

Annie gazed at her sister. Jackie Tulliver ambled out from indoors and joined in the group. 'What, Ruthie? Go on,' Annie prompted her.

'We went to the Comillas graveyard, looked at the tombs there when we were out here,' said Ruthie after a long pause. 'I told you, we talked about sky burials, funerals and things. And he said he would want to be buried with something he loved, one of his pets maybe.'

'A pet?' said Annie.

'Well – he didn't *say* that, exactly.'

'But that's what he meant?'

'Maybe. I'm not sure.'

Max straightened up. 'This ground don't look like it's been disturbed recently.'

He looked at Annie. Then he called over to Tone: 'They got a shed here? Tools?'

'Round the back,' said Tone.

'Fetch shovels if they've got 'em.'

'You're not going to . . . ', Ruthie gasped out.

'Yes I bloody am,' said Max.

Annie looked around. Something was missing. Something that had been *right there* just a minute ago. What . . .?

'Where's Gary?' she asked.

152

'You seen him out here today?' Max asked her.

'He was here earlier. Came down here after I saw him out the back, long way out, near the brow of the hill up there, checking the perimeter and now he . . .'

Anxiously Annie scanned the horizon. She couldn't see him. They were all here, exposed, and where was the one who was supposed to be watching over them, standing guard?

'I don't like this,' she said.

'Did anyone see him go indoors?' asked Max.

They all shook their heads.

Annie's eyes had locked on to a black *something* on the ground far away in the distance. But it was probably nothing. A dead crow, maybe? There were always crows about, picking at the rotting fruit.

'Tone, go find Gary,' said Max, and Tone nodded and strode away.

'Meanwhile . . .?' said Jackie, shucking off his denim jacket.

'Yeah, fetch the tools. Let's see what we got here.'

153

'Boss, what's that word? Sacred? Something like that?' asked Jackie.

'Sacrilege?' said Max, panting. 'Sacrilegious?'

'That's the one,' said Jackie.

'Forget that. Hold that fucking light steady,' said Max, flinging out another shovelful of dirt. It was nine in the evening now and the daylight was fading to a peach-toned glow in the west, casting the finca and the ruined vineyard all around it into deeper shadows.

'It's going to be dark soon,' Jackie pointed out. Annie and Ruthie were standing to one side, watching.

'What, you scared?' Max asked with a dry grin.

'Just sayin',' said Jackie.

'We're just digging a hole,' said Max, and started work again with the spade, flinging up heavy, muddy dirt. They'd had rain last night and that was making it more difficult.

'Yeah, but it's not a hole, is it. It's a damned grave,' Jackie pointed out.

'Shut up you tart. The sooner I get this dug, and the steadier you hold that damned torch, the quicker all this will be over and done. All right?' Not waiting for an answer, Max thumped the spade back into the soil.

'I don't like this,' said Jackie. 'Is all I'm sayin'.'

Max heaved out another shovelful.

'Noted,' he said. 'Now hold the torch steady and shut up.'

Jackie didn't reply to that. As Max worked on, Jackie fidgeted, nervously glanced around at the dimming outlines of the vines as the light faded and a thickening purple dusk descended.

Jackie had a liking for the church, for all things religious in fact, and deep down he felt that what Max was doing was disrespectful, because if the bastard *was* in there, no matter how big a bastard he truly was, he should be left to lie in peace. Jackie couldn't help remembering a spooky old book he'd once read, about digging up graves, and things crawling out of them not dead but very much alive, vampires and such for Christ's sake, and he definitely didn't like this. Particularly not with the silence of the encroaching night settling all around them, and the warm evening wind now playing with his mind, making shapes and sounds that he really didn't want to even consider.

'We could start again in the morning,' said Annie. She was getting jittery herself, and Ruthie, she knew, would very soon be climbing the walls.

'Yeah, let's do that,' said Ruthie. 'Can't we do that?'

Max didn't answer. He swung the shovel, tossed more dirt aside, then rammed the shovel home again.

The shovel went *clunk*.

'Fuck,' said Jackie.

'Yeah. Something,' said Max, and applied the shovel again.

Clunk.

Max knelt and started sweeping the dirt aside with his hands.

'What?' asked Jackie.

Max had uncovered a dusty sheet of wood. Now he moved up, sweeping more and more dirt aside until finally he revealed the entire shape of the thing.

It was *coffin* shaped.

Jackie froze. God the things he'd seen in a lifetime of working for Max. Shocking things. Now night was coming in fast, sweeping over the land. Stars were winking on up in the heavens. An owl hooted. The breeze wafted again, harder, rustling through the vines, and although it was a warm breeze, Jackie couldn't suppress a shiver as he thought again of things scrambling out of graves. *Vengeful* things.

Max had unearthed a damned coffin.

'No name plate?' asked Jackie, surprising himself by having to swallow hard to get the words out.

'Nope. Hand me that wrench.'

'You're not . . .?'

'I bloody am. Let's get this bastard open.'

And then Annie said urgently: 'Max!'

She pointed.

Max saw.

154

'Tone?' Annie took a step forward. Tone was approaching from among the vines. He was supporting Gary, who looked unsteady on his feet. There was blood on Gary's forehead. '*Max*,' she said again.

Max scrambled out of the hole and approached the two men.

'What's happened?'

'Some bastard,' gasped out Gary. 'There was no one there and I *swear* all at once there was someone right behind me, it was like they'd come out of the bloody *ground*, I turned and *whack*, he hit me and I went down and out.'

'You didn't see their face?' asked Jackie.

'Didn't get the time. Christ, I gotta sit down.'

With Tone's help, Gary lurched onto the terrace and collapsed spreadeagled onto a deckchair. Ruthie said: 'I'll see if there's a first aid box,' and she went off indoors.

'Tone, keep watch out there,' said Max. 'Jackie . . .'

'Got it,' said Jackie, and he started brushing back the last of the dirt from what was – definitely – a coffin.

'They know we're here,' said Annie to nobody in particular. 'Right here. They *know*.'

'Let's get this done,' said Max, taking a wrench from Jackie and starting to lever the lid of the thing up.

Someone had taken a lot of care, hammering the coffin down with four-inch nails. The nails were not easy to get out, but one after another they gave way and then, finally, they were off: the lid was – at last – loose.

Ruthie came back with the first aid box and started tending to Gary's head wound.

Max and Jackie between them hefted the lid off, and put it aside.

Annie couldn't suppress a shudder. If Kieron *was* in there, she was in no rush to see the state of him. But it was hypnotic, almost *compulsive*. She had to look.

She stood up, approached – and peered down, into the grave.

She could feel her skin crawling. She had pictured Kieron's dead body already in her mind. Desiccated bones, bits of dried skin still clinging. Staring green eyes. *Horrible*.

But she looked.

She *had* to look.

And when she did, she got a shock.

155

'What the fuck?' asked Max.

They all peered in.

Stones.

The 'coffin' was full of nothing but stones.

Not human remains. Not animal, either.

Just *stones*.

'Not quite what you expected? Eh?' said a soft Irishman's lilt, close to Annie's ear.

She whirled around, her heart leaping into her mouth.

'Christ! *Kieron?*' she burst out.

'The same,' he said.

Her eyes dropped to the pistol in his hand.

'You,' he said to Tone. 'Put that gun down. Nice and slow.'

Tone had moved, snatching up Gary's shotgun. Now he stood still, holding it across his body.

'Don't be a fool,' said Kieron amiably. 'I will shoot you. And what's to gain by that? Got the grave all ready if you need it. *Thank* you Mr Carter. Neatly done.'

Max was standing there, his eyes locked on the Irishman.

'What, you going to try it again then?' asked Max. 'Like you did in the club? Well this time make sure you get the right bastard in your sights, eh? That's me, in case you're too thick to notice.'

'Max . . . ' started Annie, frozen with fear. What the hell was Max taunting him for? And where the *hell* . . .?

'Where did you come from?' she said, aware that her voice shook. But she had to keep him talking, didn't she? Give Max time to think of something. If he could. He *must*.

Kieron smiled at Max's words. Then his eyes turned, moved – and fastened not on Annie but on *Ruthie*. 'And here's little Ruthie. Alive! When all the word on the street was that you were dead. Which was a lie, of course. Oh, but we had good times together, didn't we Ruthie? Maybe we'll have good times together again, eh? What do you think?'

'You keep the fuck away from her,' snapped Annie, seeing Ruthie shrink back in horror. 'Where the hell have you been hiding anyway, eh Kieron? Under the nearest stone like the worm you really are, I suppose.'

'Ah yeah.' He smiled. 'Diabolically clever, yes? Because what you lot don't realise and what we Delaneys do, is that sometimes we have to take avoiding action. My dad Davey knew this and he excavated tunnels under the house, spreading out in all directions around the plot.'

'But we checked the whole floor,' said Jackie. 'We checked it all. There's no cellar—'

'There isn't a cellar,' said Kieron. 'The first of the underground passages is accessed by a plain panel in the wall, inside the sitting room – they all run off from there.'

'So at any time . . .?' Ruthie gasped out.

'I never told you about it, did I, Ruthie? There are rooms, big spacious rooms under there, you wouldn't believe it. There's storage and food and drink in a dozen different places; everything that's needed for a siege. And don't feel bad that you didn't discover the way in. You wouldn't. It's tucked away, impossible to find. So you see, I could have just picked you off, one by one. *So* easy.'

'That must be how the bastard was able to sneak up on me,' said Gary, wincing, blood still seeping from the cut on his head. 'I told you. Didn't I. One minute I was standing there alone, and then he was just *there*.'

'So all the time we've been here . . .' said Ruthie in horror.

'I've been moving about down below. Listening to you all, sometimes, up above. That's right, Ruthie. And now here we are. Everything set up.'

'So why didn't you just pick us off?' asked Max. 'You had the chance, God knows.'

'What, and spoil the fun?' Kieron grinned. 'Ruin the anticipation? Miss seeing you find the stones and think you were opening my grave? Trust Annie to see it before anyone else. Bright girl. I have to tell you, it's all been very entertaining. And this is a good replica, wouldn't you say, Max Carter?'

'Of what?'

'A replica of that night in the club. When it all went wrong.' Kieron smiled and raised the gun and pointed it at Max. 'When I shot Annie instead of you. But this time? This time it *won't* go wrong.'

156

Everybody was very still. Jackie, beside Max. Gary, beside Tone. Ruthie, beside Kieron who was beside Annie, who was looking around at them all and praying for a miracle.

Oh God please don't let it end like this.

Steve!

Where was Steve?

'Are you looking for the big man, the dark-haired one?' Kieron asked her with a smile.

Annie said nothing.

'Ah, well,' he said, clearly amused. 'Sad to say he's met with an accident and he won't be riding to the rescue, so you can stop looking around for him, because he just *ain't here*.'

'Why don't you walk away Kieron?' asked Annie. 'What the hell do you hope to achieve?'

'Right back at you, so.' Kieron's smile widened. 'You hoped to find me dead out here. That's what my folks told everyone, isn't it? That I got an infection and died here? And someone else talked about a car crash. Well it all took the heat off, didn't it. I saw you all go off to the cemetery and how I laughed! Then back here to my little pet graveyard. I watched you find the stones, Annie, and I laughed at that too. And Max Carter – you spent most of the day digging the damned thing up, and of course I'm not in there. *Nothing* is.'

'Maybe we'll change that,' said Max.

'Max! Don't,' said Annie. *Don't wind him up. Don't. He's dangerous.*

'That's good advice,' said a voice off to their right.

157

Everyone turned and stared. Orla was standing there, her thick fall of straight red hair lifting in the evening breeze, her light cream cotton dress stirring. She looked so pale. Like that angel in the cemetery. But that angel hadn't carried a gun; Orla did. 'Why, my darling Orla!' said Kieron, smiling. 'You didn't even tell me you were here.'

'No. I didn't. Did I. My big talented brother.' Orla sent a smile to her brother and then turned to Max with a grin. 'So sorry about the shooting in the cemetery. Just toying with you. Couldn't resist. Oh – and the fire at your house! Whoops. Me again.'

'Orla, really,' said Kieron, shaking his head, almost laughing out loud.

'Yeah, Kier. Now what was it you always said to me?' Orla looked at him and seemed to ponder. 'Ah yes. I remember. Truthfully, I could never forget, could I? You said I had a "small talent" for art. Nothing like *your* talent of course. Just a small talent. Nothing to write home about. Nothing of any note. That right, Kier?'

'That . . .' he said.

'Oh – and you know what?'

'What?' Kieron was smiling, amused.

Orla smiled too. 'You know you thought I was looking after your dog? Well – I wasn't. Back in Battersea – whoops! I let your damned dog – poor little Bertie – starve,' she said.

The smile dropped from Kieron's face.

'You *what*?' he bellowed, starting toward her.

The shot she fired was loud: deafening. It hit Kieron square in the chest and he staggered forward, clutching at the wound, eyes wide. Then Orla very calmly raised her hand and shot him again.

158

Kieron floundered forward on tiptoe, gasping. It was as if a giant hand had swatted him in the back. He staggered and then fell face-first into the grave, into the open coffin, hitting the stones on its base with a dull reverberating *thud*.

Ruthie was screaming in horror.

Orla rounded on her. 'Stop that,' she snapped.

Ruthie fell silent, her hand over her mouth. She looked like she was going to be sick.

Max stared at Orla. 'Now what?' he asked.

'Now, Mr Carter, you fill it in. Obvious, yes? He always did say he wanted to die here. Now he's got his wish and everyone's happy. All right?'

Max gave her a long cool look. Then he snatched up the shovel and nodded to Jackie, who did the same. Ruthie snatched up the torch to light their way. Together, Max and Jackie started to edge the lid of the coffin back into place. It was a snugger fit than before. They didn't bother to nail it down.

By the time it was full dark, Kieron's fake grave was genuine. Steve had staggered around the side of the building, clutching his bloody head, and joined the rest of them. Annie had taken over torch duty and Ruthie had lit the lamps and was tending to Steve's wound.

'And so,' said Max to Orla. 'I'll ask you again. What now?'

Annie froze. Orla had killed her own brother in cold blood, why would she draw the line at them, the Carters, her family's sworn enemies?

They all held their breath.

Then – at last – Orla shrugged and turned away. 'All bets are off,' she said.

When they all remained standing there, suspecting a trick, a trap, she said: 'Tomorrow morning at nine, you'll all be gone or there'll be trouble. Is that clear? Nine o'clock. It's an amnesty until then. After then – watch out.'

Then she walked away, through the vines, into the night.

Moments later, she was gone.

It was as if she had never been there at all.

159

Nobody slept that night. Next morning they were packed up and ready to go, but Annie looked for Max and couldn't find him. Growing increasingly anxious, she searched high and low and finally found him in the sitting room, pressing the walls, tapping, testing. He turned as she came in.

'So – have you found it? The entrance to this warren of tunnels Kieron was talking about?' she asked.

He shook his head. 'Nope.'

He flicked open his lighter and moved around the walls, watching the flame intently.

'Max . . .?' It was nearly nine. She wanted to be gone. She didn't think Orla was messing with them: not at all.

'A minute,' he said, moving on.

'We need to go.'

Suddenly the flame flickered and almost died. Annie went over to where he stood, put her finger to the source of the breeze. She could feel a tiny gust of air coming from the lower edge of one of the big tapestries that adorned the walls.

'Got it,' said Max.

Then Jackie burst into the room.

'Boss? You better see this,' he said.

160

Annie and Max followed Jackie outside. It was a beautiful morning, bright and cool with a mist clearing, damp sparkling like tiny jewels on the neglected vines.

Tone, Steve and Gary were all there, Ruthie with them. They were all standing in front of Kieron's grave.

'What's going on?' asked Max.

Jackie pointed. The grave, which they had closed up and filled in last night, had been opened, all the dirt displaced. The coffin's lid had been shoved aside. And all that remained inside the coffin was rocks.

Kieron's body was gone.

'Bloody hell,' said Steve.

'I don't like this,' said Ruthie.

'What the fuck?' asked Tone.

Max looked around at them all. 'Let's get out of here,' and then he added to Tone: 'Found it.'

'Okay. Good.'

It was ten to nine, and none of them wanted to outstay Orla's deadline. Still, Tone and Max went back inside the house and emerged five minutes later.

They all piled into the cars and by two minutes to nine they were up at the entrance to the vineyard and turning out onto the main road.

One minute to go and they were free, away.

Max looked at his watch.

Nine o'clock.

Smack on nine o'clock, Botega Sierra exploded.

Boom!

Ruthie let out a shriek. Shockwaves travelled up through the car, rolled over each and every one of them, rattling their teeth, causing them to shudder.

Annie looked back and saw a thick plume of black smoke hanging over the place.

'You blew it up,' Annie said to Max.

He shrugged. 'They torched my place with me in it. And you. And Ruthie. I think they got off lightly.'

Tone put his foot down.

161

As they were approaching the airport, Annie said to Max: 'So was it all a trick, a blind? The shooting at the cemetery? What do you think?'

'Those weren't blanks,' he said.

'And Orla shooting Kieron? Was *that* a fake? A rubber bullet? Something like that?'

'But we saw blood on him,' said Ruthie. 'It was horrible.'

'Yeah, but was it *real*?' asked Annie. 'Don't they do that in films? Little capsules under the clothes, filled with fake blood? They slap a hand to it when the shot's fired, and it breaks and looks like they're bleeding.'

'Who knows,' said Max.

'Who cares?' said Annie.

'The bastard's not dead at all, is he,' sighed Ruthie.

Once back in Heathrow, they went their separate ways. Steve, Tone, Gary and Jackie shared a taxi.

'I'm off to the Langham,' said Ruthie, and departed, leaving Max and Annie standing alone among the rushing holiday crowds.

'Maybe you ought to go with her,' suggested Annie, staring after the retreating back of her sister.

'For what?' asked Max.

Annie gave him an exasperated look. 'Because she's your wife,' she said.

'Ah,' he said.

'And I'm not.'

'You on that again?' asked Max.

'Where will you go then? The Guildford place is wrecked.'

'I'll go round to Mum's old gaff, stop there for a bit. You?'

No invitation to join him. And of course it was better that way.

'I'll go see the girls,' she said. 'In Limehouse.'

And that was that. He didn't even object, this time.

Maybe this was just the way it had always been meant to be.

They'd made a bad mistake, the pair of them – and Ruthie had paid the price for it.

But now it was all over: finished.

162

It was as if she had never been away. Chris let her in with a broad smile, she dumped her case and bags on the floor and strode along the hall. There in the kitchen, seated around the table, were Dolly, Darren and Aretha. No Ellie – Dolly had so far refused to take Ellie back, despite Annie's pleading on her behalf; but Annie would keep working on that.

Dolly was pouring tea and grabbed a spare cup when she saw their old mate and former madam coming in the door.

'How's it goin' then?' asked Aretha, giving Annie a brisk high-five.

'Fine,' said Annie, although of course it wasn't fine at all. Months since she'd last seen them all, and many things had happened. 'No. Not fine. I lost the kid. The baby. I lost it.'

There were murmurs of shocked sympathy.

Then Dolly said: 'You'll have another.' She pushed Annie's cup toward her. 'That is – if you *want* another? Because that one, poor little mite, that was just a happy accident, wasn't it? Not planned?'

A happy accident.

She'd lost her baby – Max's baby – and that hurt so much.

'You know what I'm thinking now?' said Annie, taking a welcome sip. 'I'm thinking maybe – this sounds awful – maybe it was just as well it happened like that. That I lost his baby. Because—'

'You can't say that,' said Aretha.

'I can. I mean it. Because it draws a line under everything, doesn't it. It finishes the whole thing that started on the night before his wedding to Ruthie.'

There was silence around the table.

'What?' asked Annie.

It was Darren who spoke up.

'We heard your sister's still alive,' he said. 'We heard that Mr Carter faked her death to get her out from under that artist nutter. Is that true?'

'She's alive. She's fine.'

'And you and him?' asked Dolly.

'Over,' said Annie. 'That's for the best, isn't it. Fresh start for him. For Ruthie. And for me.'

'What, you think they might give it another go?' asked Aretha.

Annie shook her head. 'She'll divorce him before long, I think, if he'll allow it. I think he will.'

'Well,' said Dolly, 'that's all good then.'

Dolly looked around the table, encouraging agreement from Darren and Aretha. Obligingly, they nodded.

Annie didn't know about 'all good'. There was still Cousin Kath to be confronted and Annie was going to have to tell her that Ruthie had lived to fight another day. She wasn't looking forward to *that* encounter.

'Marvellous then,' said Dolly. 'Where you staying, Annie?'

'I thought . . . if my room's free?' It was ridiculous, but the one place that she would always come to when she was down, the one place that would forever feel like home, was this modest and ever-busy two-up-two-down in Limehouse, her Aunt Celia's old knocking shop where she had really grown up, truly become a woman.

'Damn sure it's free,' said Dolly. 'Girl, you don't even need to ask.'

163

It was all going fine. Business was brisk at the Limehouse knocking shop, the Friday and Monday parties were drawing in loads of punters, everything was just *perfect*. Annie kept to her room mostly, hearing the well-remembered activities going on all around her and finding them – as always – weirdly soothing. Headboards rattled briskly against walls; shrieks and moans seeped out from Aretha's Room of Pain; male MPs in mini dresses, kitten heels and stockings strolled by on the landing.

Time passed. Kath was told the news about Ruthie and – predictably – she hit the roof.

'Why the hell was I kept out of it?' she demanded. 'God, how *could* you?'

'Don't go spare,' Annie told her. 'I was kept out of it too, and you don't see *me* throwing a fit.'

There was no contact between Max and Annie and she felt it was one hundred per cent better that way. Ruthie hadn't been in touch either – although for sure Ruthie would have no trouble tracking her down, she would *know* that Annie would come here. But that was good, really. Annie had accepted now that the close relationship she and Ruthie had shared as kids would never be entirely recaptured. Some hurts cut far too deep for that.

But so be it.

She went out shopping, killed time. Then she came home late one autumn day, in the semi-dark, to see a large black car parked up outside and Tone sitting patiently in the driver's seat. He lifted a finger, acknowledging her.

Oh shit.

She raised a hand. Went up the path, let herself in, said hello very calmly to Chris, who was sitting inside right beside the door, reading the day's paper. Annie saw The Beatles getting their MBEs at Buck House – and a desperate, horrible picture of a Vietnamese woman wading across a river with her four children, trying to escape the American bombers.

'Visitor in there for you,' said Chris, indicating the closed front room door.

Annie dumped her bags by the hatstand. She took off her coat and hung it up. There was an expensive black vicuna number hanging there among the others, very fancy, with a purple silk lining. There were spangles of drying snowflakes on its thick collar.

She looked along the hallway to the open kitchen door. They were all there around the table, gawping at her. Darren. Dolly. Aretha. Darren nodded to the front room door and mouthed: *It's him.*

She already *knew* that. Who but Max Carter would be reckless enough, audacious enough, have the sheer brass *neck* enough, to pitch up here at a Delaney-run whorehouse, on Delaney streets, when he'd just been squatting in the Delaney Spanish stronghold and had almost dared them to displace him – and then flattened the place in a final, ferocious act?

Well, it would be okay, she told herself. If he wanted to talk, they'd talk. No problem. Bracing herself, she went to the front room door, opened it.

Max was standing in the middle of the room.

He looked up as she came in, his navy-blue eyes pinning her, and her heart just seemed to . . . *stop*.

Carefully, she closed the door behind her.

'Hello,' she said, wondering what it must be like, to be him: to have absolutely no fear.

Silence. Then: 'Hello,' said Max.

'I didn't expect you,' said Annie, dry-mouthed, ignoring the stupid pounding pulses of her body.

'Didn't you?'

'No. Something you want?'

'Yeah, there is. Actually.'

'Like . . .?' Annie asked.

'I want to fuck some sense into you,' he said.

'What? Why are you being so damned crude again?'

'You heard. Come here.'

Annie narrowed her eyes at him. 'Why don't *you* come here?' she suggested.

'Bitch,' he said – and did.

'Bastard,' she said, and kissed him.

And who cared now whether it was right or wrong? Annie didn't, not anymore, as she joyously gave in and opened her arms to the only man she had ever truly loved.

Out in the kitchen, they suddenly heard shrieks of laughter coming from inside the front room.

'Think she's all right in there?' asked Darren worriedly.

'She's just *fine*,' said Aretha.

'Yeah, drink your tea, Darren, and keep your neb out. They'll sort it,' said Dolly.

EPILOGUE

A month later, Annie told Max that she was pregnant again. From misery and heartache there might come a new dawn, a new hope. But Annie was scared *shitless*. She wasn't fearless, like Max.

'This one will take,' Max promised her with a kiss. 'It's going to be all right this time.'

Then came the long, long months of waiting, of being so careful, of hoping and then not wanting to hope, thinking of nurseries and then not daring to think of them at all. And baby clothes? No, she didn't dare buy any like she had last time. She was frozen, terrified, feeling her body changing, expanding, feeling awestruck when the baby fluttered like a trapped butterfly inside her – *alive*.

For now, anyway.

And then – it happened. One night after dinner her waters broke and almost before she could even allow herself to think that the baby would be stillborn she was in a private hospital room and had quickly given birth to a healthy seven-pound girl. She discovered a whole new kind of love when she held her tiny new baby daughter in her arms.

'What shall we call her?' asked Max, picking up the baby like she was made of glass and cuddling her close.

'Layla,' said Annie. 'We said that, didn't we.' *The first time, when it had all ended in tears.* 'Jason for a boy, Layla for a girl.'

'Layla. It suits her.' Max rocked his daughter gently against his chest. 'Wonder what's ahead for you, baby girl?' he asked her.

Annie watched him, feeling exhausted but so happy. Their baby would grow up and have a good life. Maybe there would be a handsome man like her daddy in Layla's future? Annie closed her eyes. She was really, really tired and somehow she was thinking of a silver-haired American man and two teenage boys, one dark, one blond, in Toby Taylor's art gallery.

She opened her eyes; she'd almost fallen asleep. 'And what about godparents?' she asked. 'What about a godmother?'

At that instant, Ruthie bustled into her sister's private hospital room clutching a teddy bear and a toy hippo, a wicker basket of fruit and several large bunches of flowers.

'Did I hear someone mention godmothers?' she smiled.

'I thought you were hard of hearing?' said Annie, holding out a hand to her sister, who took it, squeezed it, leaned in for a kiss.

'Got a new hearing aid, it's magic.' Ruthie smiled at Max, dumped all Annie's presents onto the bed and held out her arms. 'Now give me that baby, okay?'

Max handed Layla over.

'*Would* you be her godmother?' asked Annie.

Ruthie beamed at them, delighted. 'I thought you'd never ask.'

ACKNOWLEDGEMENTS

To the team who help me, day after day. Many thanks folks. Couldn't do it without you.